Conte

Cover Credit

Christopher Coyle

darkandstormyknight.com

Thank you for adorning my words so beautifully.

Sandra R Neeley
P.O. Box 127
Franklinton, LA 70438
authorsandrarneeley@gma
il.com

110,739 words

Haven 5: Bonded

Sandra R Neeley

For all those who love 'Haven', and eagerly await each new book.
Thank you for your support and for your acceptance of my people.

About This Book

Kron is an Elite Warrior of the Cruestaci military.

He's temporarily on Earth as support personnel to the Cruestaci Consul to Earth. He's basically happy on Earth, making friends easily, performing his duties in an exemplary manner. There is only one thing he can't do. He can't get Ginger Buchanan out of his brain. And to make matters worse, now her father, Viceroy Buchanan of Earth, has made it clear he expects Kron to marry his daughter. How is he supposed to mate a female who has no idea what that mating would mean? Everything would change for her, including her plans for her future which clearly don't include life with him on an alien warship. He cares too much for her to force her into a situation that she could never escape. Doesn't he?

Ginger Buchanan is a confident, self-sufficient young woman, who has no problem going after anything she wants, or voicing her opinions.

Unless those opinions are voiced to her mother. And that is a big problem, because her mother despises aliens. She considers them invaders from another world, and to the contrary, Ginger has fallen in love with one. Kron is everything she's ever wanted in a male. He's kind, considerate, strong, capable, and handsome. If she could find a way to gain his attention, she would, but he doesn't seem interested. Little does she know, her father has offered her in marriage to the very alien she fancies herself in love with.

Forces are working to push Kron and Ginger toward a mating bond that neither is ready for. On discovering manipulation in play to push them together, Ginger angrily turns her back on Kron. But they're about to find out those manipulations are the least of their worries. A domestic terrorist group known as the Purists have set their sights on driving all aliens from Earth, and are not above using violence and scare tactics to do so. The threat to all aliens and those who associate with them is very real. Kron finds himself thrust into a protective role, watching over the Consul's home and family — which is no great challenge for him — he's an Elite Warrior. But support for the Purists lies in surprising places, leading to the disappearance of his mate, his Ginger. Kron is now more focused, more dangerous than he's ever been. He will stop at nothing to find her and return her to safety, even if she turns her back on him afterward. Will he find her before it's too late? And if he does, will he and the unsanctioned Cruestaci military unit that's sent to help him start a war in the meantime?

Warning: Intended for mature audiences. This book contains abuse both real and implied, betrayal, and sexual situations that may be disturbing for some readers. If you are offended by these subjects, please do not buy this book.

Chapter 1

Ginger sat in the security office of Earth Base 28. She wasn't in trouble, just killing time 'til her father had time for her. Since Consul Diskastes had been removed from his position, and his death, the population of the base had diminished somewhat. Consul Kol Ra Don Tol had assumed the position of Consul upon his exoneration of charges brought against him by Diskastes's family, but those in the government sympathetic to Diskastes's home planet still found ways to complicate things, or so they thought, for Kol and the base he did his best to run.

Those in power had been quietly moving out personnel a few at a time, until the bare minimum required for the base to function was left behind — they'd even reassigned their doctor and replaced him with a medic. The changes created more work for those still at Base 28, but, it was a much more pleasant working atmosphere. Those remaining were loyal to the base and those working there. They admired and respected Kol, Patroon Zhuxi, and Ginger's father — Viceroy Buchanan.

Ginger was particularly happy about the changes. She no longer had to steer clear of the base as a whole. She was now allowed to visit the base at will, and she rather enjoyed the new freedom and welcoming feeling she regularly experienced there. When her father was busy, she'd usually go grab a bite to eat in the cafeteria, or go to his shared offices and visit with whoever was on duty. She was especially fond of those visits when Kron was on duty. Kron was assigned to Base 28 as a support personnel for Kol. They were both part of the Cruestaci military and here with special permission from the Unified Consortium Defense. She didn't believe that Kron was Cruestaci, though. He wasn't the same as Kol in appearance. Kol was a little larger, had huge horns and could be extremely frightening, though he was usually very kind.

Kron, however, didn't have horns. His skin was yellow, which in Ginger's opinion was perfect. Kron always had a bright smile and a sunny disposition. He was friendly to everyone. He had fine, silky, unnaturally white hair that fell about shoulder length. His skin offered different tones of yellow, from a darker yellow to more of a pale color as the mottling and texture moved across his body.

Ginger allowed herself a little shiver thinking of his smile. He had full, inviting lips, and the tips of his fangs were always just barely out of sight, the tips of them pressing just enough into his lower lip to let you know they were there. Ginger had dreamed about those lips pressed against hers. And his eyes, his eyes were so beautiful they were almost indescribable. They were yellow and fringed with lashes of the same color as his hair.

She was absolutely fascinated with Kron. And that was why she was sitting in the security office right this very moment. She'd wandered around the base and looked for him after her father had asked if she could give him a little time to finish up whatever he was doing. He'd apologized for not remembering he'd invited her. He hadn't invited her. Ginger had simply taken it upon herself to make him think he did. She wanted to see Kron. Needed to see Kron, and to do that, she had to go to the base. Only, now that she was here, Kron was nowhere to be seen, so she'd wandered into the security office and was making small talk with the security officers on duty while she glanced at the security monitors and hoped that at some point one of the cameras would catch Kron moving about and she'd know where he was. Then she'd make up an excuse to wander in his direction.

"Ginger! Sorry for making you wait, darlin'. You ready to get something to eat?"

Ginger spun in her chair to find her father smiling at her from the doorway. "Hey, Daddy. Yeah," she said, throwing one last glance at the security monitors that had yet to show her where Kron was. "I'm ready," she said, though not too happily.

Buchanan stood aside and gave his daughter room to move through the doorway and past him. He grinned at the back of her head as she walked by him and began to walk toward the cafeteria. She wasn't fooling anybody, he knew exactly why she was spending so much time here recently. "How was your morning?" he asked.

She shrugged. "Okay. Had a small argument with Momma again."

"She still trying to talk you into dating her friend's son?" Buchanan asked.

"Yes. And I'm just not interested. He's not my type at all," Ginger said.

"Oh, yeah? And what is your type?" Buchanan asked.

Ginger shrugged. "I don't know. But it's not somebody that is so critical of everybody else and thinks animals are a nuisance. I'm planning to work with animals, for Christ's sake. And he does nothing but complain about anything and anybody that doesn't exactly fit into his picture of perfect. I thought he was going to have a stroke when I came home with cat hair on my scrubs to find him there."

"He was there when you got home?" Buchanan asked.

"Yes. And then he wanted to know if I planned to get cleaned up at all. Well, 'I might have planned on it before, you rude ass, but now I think I'll just keep wearing my cat encrusted scrubs'."

Buchanan laughed. "Your mother has some unique ideas of the way things should be. Just don't let her get inside your head and you'll be fine."

"I'm trying," Ginger said, looking up at him.

They got their food and found a table. Ginger ate slowly while she continuously looked around.

"Who you looking for?" Buchanan asked.

"Hmm? Oh, nobody. Just looking around," she answered.

About that time Kron walked into the cafeteria. Ginger lit up like a megawatt light-bulb.

Kron greeted a few people as he moved toward the serving line, then his eyes landed on Ginger. His steps faltered and he came to a complete stop. Then his smile began to curve the corners of his mouth into that smile that made Ginger shiver.

11

Kron changed direction and headed toward Buchanan's and Ginger's table. "Hello!" he called happily.

"Hey, Kron. You done?" Buchanan asked.

"Almost. I'm now waiting for the varnish to dry. Once it's dry, I'll deliver them and see if the boys like them," Kron said.

"What are you varnishing?" Ginger asked.

"Rocking horses. I made them from wood that would just be burned if I hadn't repurposed it. I plan to give them to Kol's two sons. Your father told me of the rocking horse he loved so well as a boy and I thought I'd make some for them."

"He's quite talented," Buchanan said, finishing off his sandwich, and brushing his hands off before wiping his mouth with his napkin. "You should get him to show you."

"I'd love to see them," Ginger said.

"Would you?" Kron asked, not sure if she was just being polite or really wanted to see the toys he'd made.

"I would. I'd love to see what you've made," Ginger said.

"I will be happy to show you. If you have time after your visit with your father, perhaps I'll show you today," Kron said.

"We're done. Show her right now. Or better yet, get you something to eat — I'm sure that's why you came in — then ya'll go look at all Kron's made. He's got a whole workshop out there. The male should be resting when he's not on duty, but instead he's out there in the shed carving all kinds of crap," Buchanan said.

"Daddy! I'm sure whatever he's made is not crap," Ginger objected.

"It's a figure of speech, Ginger. You know I don't mean he makes crap. Anyway, I'm off. Got things to do. You going to see her home, Kron?"

"I brought my own transport, Daddy. I can get home just fine," Ginger said, not wanting to put Kron out. She knew they were all overworked.

"Leave your transport here. Let me get the mechanics to look at it. It needs to be serviced," Buchanan told her. Then he looked at Kron. "You'll get her home?"

"I will. If she is agreeable to the arrangement," Kron answered.

"I don't mind at all. If you don't," Ginger said.

"I would be honored," Kron said. Then he bowed to both of them. "I shall return momentarily."

Kron walked toward the serving line, trying to figure out what he could grab to eat. He wasn't hungry in the least but he wanted it to look as though that was the reason he left his work and came into the cafeteria. In truth, he'd come out of his shed turned workshop to find a tool he needed, and seen Ginger's transport. His heart had leapt at the idea of her being on base and near him and he wasn't able to keep himself from walking through the hallways and offices of the base until he finally located her. He looked over his shoulder toward her table again and smiled when he found her watching him. He took a deep breath and let it out on a contented sigh. She was the most beautiful female he'd ever seen. Her small frame belied the fire in her soul. And the fire in her soul seemed to shine through the top of her head, crowning her with hair so glorious it was a combination of flame colored strands and the paler golden streaks that ran through it. Whatever color it was, it was his new favorite. Tiny little spots sprinkled across her nose and her upper cheeks drew his attention almost as strongly as her hair. He'd been told they were called freckles. He wanted to kiss every single one of them.

Feeling his body reacting to his thoughts about Ginger, he shook his head to clear his mind and focused on the selection of foods offered today. He chose two slices of red cake with a creamy frosting. "I want two of those," he said, pointing to the cake.

"You got it," the server said, taking two plates of cake and placing them on a tray before handing it to Kron.

"Thank you," Kron answered, then walked to the end of the line, paid the cashier and selected two small cartons of milk to go with the slices of cake he'd chosen. As he walked back over to the table, Buchanan stood and patted Kron on the shoulder as he stepped away from the table.

13

"I'm going to get back to it," Buchanan said, pausing only briefly to drop a kiss on Ginger's cheek. "Have a good afternoon, darlin'. Let me know if you need anything, and Kron, let me know if there's a problem getting her home safely."

"There will be no problem," Kron said confidently. "I will never allow Ginger to be harmed in any way."

Ginger grinned and blushed as she watched Kron vow to protect her from harm.

"That's what I thought," Buchanan said. "Oh, and don't forget to show her your wood-working stuff. She don't need to go home right away."

Kron inclined his head and watched as Buchanan walked away.

"Two pieces of cake? Didn't you want a hot meal, or a sandwich or something?" Ginger asked.

"No. I wanted to share my favorite cake with you. One of these is for you," he said, placing one of the slices of cake before her.

"Oh, thank you. How thoughtful," she said, picking up the fork and taking a bite. "I love red velvet cake."

"As do I. I am always surprised that it tastes like chocolate, yet it is red. I expect strawberry flavor, but it is chocolate. It's confounding," he said, taking a second bite.

"It's very rich, and the cream cheese frosting makes it all that much richer," Ginger said, savoring another bite.

"The frosting is made of cheese?" he asked, completely surprised.

"It is, cream cheese," Ginger answered.

Kron lifted another bite onto his fork and looked at it critically. "I just don't understand," he said thoughtfully.

Ginger smiled at him struggling to understand the difference in flavors from those he expected as she finished her cake. "So, Daddy said you have a wood-working shop?"

"I've assembled a small number of tools, and wood that no one seemed to want, and I cleared a space in one of the storage sheds near the back of the building. It is there that I spend most of my free time. I find I enjoy the creative process. It soothes me,

of the base, though they stayed outside the building rather than reentering. "Here," he said, holding out the flower to her.

"What's this?" she asked, reaching out and placing her fingers on the stem, but not quite taking it from him.

"A flower. I don't know which kind, but I've seen it many times as I harvest the wood."

"It's a dogwood flower," Ginger said.

"A dogwood flower," he repeated.

"Yes, it's my favorite flower," she said.

"And this one is a wooden dogwood flower. It is for you," Kron said.

"Really? I can have it?" she asked, obviously very happy that he was giving her the flower he'd made.

"Of course. It was made for you," he said simply, then placed his hand at the small of her back and guided her toward where his transport was docked, not even noticing that her mouth fell open in surprise when he'd said it was made for her.

Chapter 2

Kron and Ginger walked around the outside of the base heading toward the docking bay as they laughed and talked. Neither was prepared for the red-faced, angry, shouting man advancing on them. As he got closer and Ginger stopped what she was saying in the middle of her sentence to focus on the man, Kron literally lifted her off her feet and placed her behind him with a barked, 'stay behind me' then stood to his tallest height and moved to intercept the man.

"You!" the man shouted as he pointed toward Ginger and tried to see around Kron, "are not supposed to be here! I waited for hours for you to return home for our lunch date! And what happens? Your poor mother is left to entertain me, all the while worrying about your welfare while you're gallivanting with creatures like this!" The man was angry, practically spitting with every word he spoke, shoving his fingers and hands in Ginger's direction.

Kron could sense his rage, and actually believed that had he not been here, the man would have laid his hands on Ginger. Kron looked down his nose at the man. "You will not speak to her in such a manner," he said warningly.

"You will not speak to me. You have no right to be here! Don't even think you're worthy enough to look at me! I'll show you what I'm capable of!" the man threatened.

Kron smiled sardonically. "You do not have clearance to be here. Leave. Now. Or I'll have you arrested."

"Ginger?! Do you hear this alien threatening me? He's a danger to the welfare of all humans. Get in the transport. I'm taking you back to your mother."

"Mitchell, I'm not going anywhere. Especially not with you!" Ginger answered, moving just enough from behind Kron to be able to glare at Mitchell.

20

"Oh, yes, you are!" Mitchell snarled, stepping forward and trying to reach around Kron to grab Ginger's arm.

Kron was incensed that any male would attempt to tell Ginger what she could and couldn't do. He'd not claimed her yet, but he'd be damned if anyone else would exert a claim on her, especially, one so heavily laden with anger and threats. His battle armor engaged, spreading hardened, leather like scales over his face and body. Serrated, bladed claws extended from his fingertips, and bladed bone spurs from his elbows. He moved so quickly Mitchell was being held up off the ground with one of Kron's hands around his neck, the other holding firmly to his wrist, which is what Kron suspended him in the air from. "You — will — not — touch my mate," Kron growled. "You will not speak to my mate. You will not approach my mate. If you do, I will kill you, and wear your skin as decoration."

Mitchell's eyes got big, and he ground his teeth as he tried to kick his feet at Kron.

Kron lifted one leg and kicked at Mitchell as Mitchell's foot came near.

Mitchell cried out, gritted his teeth and focused on Kron. "I'll make you pay for this. Do you know who I am? Put me down!"

Kron gripped Mitchell's wrist more tightly, allowing the serrated blades extending from his fingers to press into Mitchell's skin. "Yes, I do. You are the dead man who tried to accost my female."

"She's not yours!" Mitchell screamed angrily. "She's going to do what she's told to do, and that is not to ruin her reputation by cavorting with animals like you! I'll have you brought up on charges! I'll have you removed from this planet. You don't belong here, taking what doesn't belong to you! Better yet, I'll kill you myself! I'll kill you and all the rest like you! And I'll kill your filthy mates, too!"

"I believe you just threatened my life and my mate's life. That means you die," Kron said calmly as the hand he held around Mitchell's throat began to squeeze tighter.

21

"What the hell is going on here?" Buchanan shouted, bursting out of the door that led from the docking area into the base.

"Daddy! He tried to grab me, and he's trying to force me to get in his transport, and he just threatened to kill Kron," Ginger said, clearly upset.

"Kron, put him down," Buchanan said.

"Put me down!" Mitchell shouted, kicking out at Kron again.

Kron let go of Mitchell's throat and used that hand to strike out at Mitchell's leg when he kicked at Kron's body again. The serrated edges of Kron's bladed claws sliced into Mitchell's calf.

Mitchell cried out in pain, reaching for his injured calf, and landing on the cement of the docking area as Kron threw him to the ground. "I'll have you thrown under the jail! Then they'll kill you! You attacked a human!" Mitchell screamed.

"No, he didn't," several of the men working in the docking area said. For the first time Mitchell noticed they'd had an audience the entire time. "You approached them, angrily, trying to order the Viceroy's daughter into your transport. All he did was protect her and keep you away from her."

"He threatened my life! I know you heard that part!" Mitchell snapped.

The soldier looked at his two friends, then shrugged. "I didn't hear any such thing."

"No, me neither," one of the other soldiers said, as the third shook his head.

"If I'd meant to kill you, you'd be dead already," Kron said calmly.

Mitchel made a human version of a growl with his face twisted in anger.

"Kron, please," Buchanan said. Then turned to Mitchell. "Mitchell, it is Mitchell, right?" Buchanan asked.

"You know exactly who I am!" Mitchell shouted insolently at Buchanan.

Buchanan pressed his lips together as he tried to maintain control of his temper. "Yeah, unfortunately I do. You are not allowed on this base. You do not have clearance to be here."

22

"I came at the request of your wife..." Mitchell started to say.

"I don't give a damn if God himself sent you. You don't have permission to be here. Further, you don't have permission to be near my daughter, to speak to my daughter, to even look at my daughter. If I find you at my house again, it won't be Kron you'll be dealing with, it'll be me. And contrary to your little piss-ant 'I hate everybody that's not just like me' organization, I'm a real government official. I will have YOU put under the jail. Now pick your little piddling ass up off my docking floor, and take it away from here. Do not come back, do not speak to my daughter, and do not go to my home ever again in your worthless little life."

Mitchell stared daggers at Buchanan as he tried to get to his feet.

Just when he'd about managed it, Kron lost patience and grabbed him by the neck and the waist band of his pants, marching over toward his transport.

"Put me down! Do you not see him attacking me?!" Mitchell demanded.

It took Kron only a few moments to get to the transport Mitchell had left the door open on. He stuffed the man into the pilot's seat, then leaned forward placing his face, complete with enlarged fangs only a hair's breadth from Mitchell's. Then he roared as loudly as he could. "She. Is. Mine!"

Mitchell was startled with such a loud roar so close to him. As he tried to gather his wits about him again, Kron reached up and placed his hand on the door. "Do not go near her again or I will kill you. If you wish to speak to me, I can be easily found, and am anxiously awaiting our next visit!" Kron slammed the door and waved his arm in the direction opposite the base. "Go!" Kron ordered.

Mitchell flipped them all off, then pointed toward Ginger and left them watching him as his transport lifted into the air and took off.

Kron turned and walked back toward Buchanan and Ginger. He looked into Buchanan's eyes as he approached them.

It was clear he was not happy about having to allow Mitchell to simply fly away after his behavior toward Ginger.

"I'm sorry, Kron. Can't have you killing anybody. It'll get you more trouble than he's worth," Buchanan said.

"He clearly means to make Ginger his. He clearly means to have her bow to his wishes regardless of the means he must use. He should not be allowed near her!" Kron insisted.

"And he's not. You heard me. I made myself perfectly clear. He's not allowed to see her or be near her or my home in any capacity. I will have him arrested," Buchanan said.

Kron wasn't satisfied, but also knew he'd controlled his own reactions because he didn't want his Sire to have to make excuses for the behavior of the Cruestaci again. Everyone expected them to react to every situation violently, and if he did, then it would just be more bureaucracy for Quin to have to wade through and shoulder. He simply shook his head in disbelief at just another example of all they had to endure in an effort to keep everyone happy even when those everyones were the very people making life so difficult for the many who did their best to simply live their lives every day.

Kron turned toward Ginger, surprised to find her watching him with a smile on her face. "Are you well?" he asked.

"I'm fine," she answered, still smiling at him.

"I would not have allowed him to touch you. I am sorry you were subjected to such treatment. Were we on a different planet, his head would be offered to you as an apology," Kron said, his voice slightly growly.

"I'm fine, Kron. And thank you for defending me," Ginger said, stepping closer to Kron and reaching out to try to place her hands on his arm.

Kron pulled his arm back as she reached for him. "Careful," he said, looking down at the bladed claws still extending from his fingers. He lifted his arm just enough to give her a glimpse of the back of his arm, just above the elbow. "They are sharp."

Ginger nodded, then stubbornly, yet carefully, placed her hand on his forearm and looked up at him. "Thank you, for protecting me, for caring about me."

Kron looked down at Ginger, beginning to realize what he'd shouted at Mitchell over and over again. He'd clearly declared that she was his and made it obvious he would tolerate no other male attempting to gain her attentions. Kron swallowed nervously, realizing that his preoccupation with her was not just an attraction — she was his. "Always," he managed to get out.

Ginger beamed as her hand squeezed his forearm just above his wrist, and looked up at him.

"Come on. Let's go inside and make a report so if numb-nuts does the same, we'll have beat him to the punch," Buchanan said.

Kron nodded and fell into step behind Buchanan, indicating that Ginger should walk in front of him.

"You three come along with us. Let's document what you saw, too," Buchanan said to the three soldiers who'd witnessed the situation.

"Ginger, I know exactly who that boy is. I don't want him at the house anymore. If your Momma invites him, remind her he's not allowed on my property, and call me, then the cops if she insists," Buchanan said.

"I will," Ginger replied. "But I'm not dating him. She just keeps having him over and trying to force me to spend time with him."

"Who is he?" Kron asked.

"He's got himself all tied up with the Purists. Thinks it makes him all high and mighty, when all it makes him is an asshole," Buchanan said. "Her Momma thinks he'd be a good catch."

"Only if he was being hunted," Kron mumbled.

Buchanan chuckled and looked back at Kron, and noticed Kron's battle armor was beginning to recede. "Handy little features you got there," he said, waving his own fingers in the air.

"Battle, or the need to defend, causes them to extend," Kron said, looking down at his hands still partially displaying the thick, leathery scales and a glimpse of the serrated claws.

"Handy," Buchanan repeated.

~~~

An hour and a half later after they'd finished giving reports, Kron was seated in his transport, with Ginger at his side.

She smiled at him as he brought the transport to the ground just outside Buchanan's home.

"Well, this is it," she said, twirling the wooden dogwood flower Kron had given her in her hands as she looked down at it.

"It is a very nice home," Kron said. "And I do not see evidence of Mitchell here."

Ginger glanced around then shook her head. "He's probably so nervous about my father threatening him, that it will be some time before he decides to try to come back here."

"He should be more worried about my threat to him," Kron said.

"Did you mean what you said back there?" she asked, finally deciding she needed to know if it was just the heat of the moment or if he really knew that she belonged to him.

Kron looked toward her and took a deep breath to steady himself. "I meant every word."

"So, you think I'm yours?" she asked.

"I know that you are mine. But it is not our way to force a female to accept us if she does not approve of the bond we offer," Kron said.

"And if she does approve?" Ginger asked flirtatiously.

The ghost of a smile turned up one side of Kron's mouth. "There is a lot to consider. This is not my world, yet this is where you are."

"That's just logistics," Ginger said. "Besides, you're here. I'm sure my father could find a position for you even if the one you're in now comes to an end."

Kron didn't want to get into it all at the moment, but he already knew, he didn't plan to stay here permanently. He waited so long to answer that she thought he didn't plan to, so she changed the subject. She looked down at the wooden flower in her hand again and lifted it a bit toward him. "What did you mean when you said it was made for me?" she asked.

Deciding as he looked at her that he would never lie to her, he answered truthfully. "I thought of you when I made it. It is yours."

Ginger's lips slowly curved up into a smile. "You did? You thought of me?" she asked.

"I did. I think of you often," he confessed, looking at her lips instead of into her eyes.

"I think of you, too," she admitted.

Kron's gaze snapped up to meet hers.

"In fact," she said, "I came to the base today hoping to see you. The last few times I was there it was so I could see you."

"You didn't say that before today," he said.

"Neither did you," she teased.

Kron was quiet for a few moments before he lifted one shoulder in a non-committal shrug. "I came into the cafeteria today because when I left my workshop to find a tool I needed, I saw your transport, and I just really needed to look at you."

Ginger grinned, her smile taking up so much of her face that he thought it might never go away. Finally, she spoke again. "So, we think of each other, and you've even said that I'm yours. Now what?" she asked.

Kron opened his door and jumped down out of the transport, not bothering to release the small ramp to assist in reaching the ground. He reached up toward her when she scooted into his seat, placing his hands on her hips to help her down. "Now, we get you safely inside. Then I go back to the base and prepare for my shift."

Her brows pulled down over her eyes with her dissatisfaction at his answer.

Kron sighed. He needed time to think things over. Rushing into anything was not a good choice for either of them. They needed to take the time to know one another, discuss all possibilities and make sure that the plans they each had for their lives would be able to intertwine. "We need to take our time, move slowly to be sure that we and our futures are compatible. We do not bond with our mates lightly. It is forever and you will be irrevocably changed. My kind mate only once. If that mate bond is broken, we remain alone for the rest of our days. It is not something I wish to experience," he admitted.

"But you said I'm yours," she said.

"I did. And you are. But it's not unheard of for males, or females, to avoid a mate because it's obvious that bond would not be fortuitous for them."

"I wouldn't hurt you," Ginger said. "But I understand taking things slowly. So, let's do that."

Kron inclined his head and smiled down at her. "Yes, let's."

"So, when will we see each other again?" she asked impatiently.

Kron chuckled, he loved her fire and her spontaneity. He'd seen it several times when her father had pushed her too far, or she'd been excited about something. "I've not spoken to your father yet, nor your mother. Things must be done a certain way in order to have them recognized and respected. I should have spoken to him before escorting you home, even before showing you my workshop, but these things were his suggestion, so they are allowed, I think."

"I'm right here, Kron. And I make my own decisions. If you want to see me again, speak to me," Ginger said.

Kron looked into her eyes. "It is the way of my people, to make intentions known to a female's parents. If those intentions are welcomed, the male will be given permission to proceed."

"You're not on your planet, Kron. You're on mine. And I want to see you, I want to get to know you, be with you. If you want to talk to my father, by all means, do so. You already know I want to spend time with you. But don't bother speaking to my mother, that will never be a good thing."

"Why should I not speak with your mother? She deserves respect as the mother of my Leerah."

"What is a Leerah?" Ginger asked.

"She gave you life. She deserves to have her opinion known and valued. Why should I not speak with your mother?"

"Oh, her opinions are quite known. My mother is... unique. She doesn't see things the same way most everyone else I know does. If you need to speak to my parents, and I understand that you do because it's your custom, just speak with my father first and then maybe you'll understand."

"Very well. I'll speak with him first, then your mother."

"And I'll see you again when?" Ginger pressed him again.

"When are you next available?" he asked.

"I have school tomorrow, so the next afternoon?"

"I will come to your home, here," he said, turning around to glance at the brick home behind him, "to take you to any place you'd like."

"No! No, I will come to you, and then we'll go somewhere. Maybe a restaurant or something to share a meal," Ginger said.

"Very well. I will wait for you to arrive at the base, then we will share a meal. You will choose where we share our meal."

Ginger nodded. "I'm looking forward to it. I'll see you then."

"Come, let me escort you to your door," Kron said.

"You don't have to! Just stand here and watch and you'll see that I'm in the house just fine."

"As you wish," Kron said.

"I'll see you day after tomorrow, Kron."

"I will be waiting for you to arrive."

Chapter 3

Ginger walked into her house with a non-stop grin on her face. Kron wanted to see her. And she wanted to see him.

"Who was that? Don't you know any better than to get into a transport with a stranger? Anything could happen. You could be convinced to throw away all your life's plans and just give yourself to them!" Susanna Jo Buchanan said, looking intensely at Ginger.

"Momma, that's ridiculous. No one can make me do anything I don't want to do. You of all people should know that. Besides he's not a stranger — his name is Kron, he works with Daddy at the base."

"I know he works with your father! I also know about the horrifying treatment poor Mitchell received when he went after you for me! You should be ashamed of yourself, young lady. You had plans with him today, then when he comes to collect you, you're not even here! Then he's gentlemanly enough to offer to go bring you back home, and you have him assaulted!"

"He was not assaulted. He assaulted Kron, when Kron put himself between us to keep Mitchell from putting his hands on me!" Ginger said.

"He was only going to take you by the elbow to escort you to his transport! You stood by and allowed that alien to assault him. His leg might even need stitches!"

"It's a shame Kron didn't slice both his legs," Ginger muttered as she walked past her mother. "He was protecting me!"

"He's a vicious predator who is here to take over our world! You're just falling into his plans!"

"Plans for what? To impregnate all the human women and have their offspring assist in herding us all like sheep into concentration camps where we'll be forcibly enslaved?! Please,

Momma, you have to open your eyes and stop believing everything you read on the internet," Ginger said. "He's here to keep us safe, to keep other species from coming back and invading us again. He's a good male, kind, strong, intelligent, and he genuinely cares for me."

"You don't know that! His kind are capable of manipulating you into whatever they want you to do!" Susanna Jo said.

"Momma, that's ludicrous."

"It is not! Many a young girl has been led astray by their kind! You must be more selective with the young men you choose to spend time with."

"Momma, that's enough. Just stop. Kron is a good person. No matter what you think of where he's from, or even others like him, it doesn't mean you're right. It doesn't mean he thinks and behaves as you expect him to. He's not the race that invaded us!"

"You will keep those opinions to yourself, Ginger. I've raised you better than that. You know well what our world has lost due to those that invaded our way of life!"

"Yeah, and he wasn't one of them. You know what? I'm done. I'm not talking about it with you anymore. It's never going to end any other way than an argument. And to think he wanted to pay his respects to you..."

"The aliens," she said, whispering the word as though it was unladylike to even voice it aloud, "only respect themselves. They don't care what they do to us or our traditions, or lives. You'll figure that out, I just hope it's not too late for you when you do. That's why I've invited Mitchell to dinner tomorrow evening. He's just the kind of boy you should be associated with, and you will apologize to him for your lack of action today. You should have allowed him to escort you to safety."

"He didn't want my safety. I don't believe I'd have been safe with him, you didn't see him! Besides, he can't be here, and I'm not eating with him regardless. I don't like him — not only as a boyfriend, but as a person. He's not a nice guy," Ginger said, turning and walking away from her mother. "And Daddy warned him, told him if he found out he was here, he'd have him arrested."

"Young lady, your father may make the decisions at that base, but this is my home, too. I plan the social engagements in our home. You will have dinner with all of us, as a family, and you will present your best manners. He is a wonderful young man and you will give him the same chance you have given to those who are completely beneath us! He would be an exceptional husband and assure that you would be in a place of respect, maintained in the manner in which you were raised."

"Go ahead, invite him. I'll just call the police like Daddy said. Bet it's the last time he comes over here after he's arrested," Ginger said, as she walked down the hallway and closed her bedroom door. It was a hopeless conversation. Her mother was so prejudiced against anyone not from Earth, she couldn't see past it to the heart, the conscience inside the body. It used to be a subject of mild contention, but lately, her mother had become even more extreme, and the arguments that always ensued just weren't worth the same ending that always finalized them. Her mother was unreasonable and short-sighted, and Ginger was not. She tried to hold her tongue when dealing with her mother, but more often than not, she ended up sitting angrily across the dinner table from the completely smug, arrogant son of one of her mother's friends, who had no desire to do anything but talk about himself. Then the dinner would end and she'd be just cold enough to send the message she was not interested, and the young man would go away.

But not so with Mitchell. He was by far the worst that her mother had dug up to try to set her up with. He was condescending, narrow minded, conceited, and even more prejudiced than her own mother was. It was a shame her mother was married and of the age she was instead of in her early twenties... she'd be a perfect match for Mitchell. And even more of a shame, Mitchell never stayed away no matter how cold, or even rude Ginger tried to be. He just wouldn't take the hint that she wanted nothing to do with him. But that was okay, if her mother insisted on trying to invite him, she'd call her dad, just like he'd said.

32

~~~

Kron returned to the base and went to his quarters to shower and get some rest before his shift began. He smiled to himself as he thought about Ginger. She sought him out, just as he did her, which meant she felt the mate bond pulling them closer as well. As he showered, his mind wandered to their conversation. She'd told him to speak to her father, then if there was anything he still didn't understand, she'd explain it to him when they saw each other next. That had him curious. Why would she think he wouldn't understand anything Buchanan might have to say? His smile gone, his brow furrowed with over thinking all he and Ginger had spoken of, he rushed through his shower, got dressed and went in search of Buchanan.

He was sitting at his desk in the shared administration offices of Base 28, on his personal communicator with his wife when Kron found him. He'd muted the speaker function most everyone used and had the device pressed to his ear, like an old fashioned telephone as was used on Earth for a very, very long time.

"Because Susanna Jo, you're wrong," Buchanan said. "Go ahead and invite that S.O.B., and I'll have him arrested."

Buchanan listened to her reply, his head resting against the raised back of his chair, his eyes closed, his feet propped up on his desk. "It is not a matter of opinion, Susanna. It's a matter of fact. I'll have him arrested if he so much as stands across the street from my house!"

"Because!" he answered after listening to her for a second more. "I pay for the damned house, it's my house! You want to claim half of it, act like you have a damned brain in your head."

Buchanan listened again.

"Yes, legally half is yours. But I know that he came here, assaulted one of my employees, tried to force our daughter into his transport, and threatened to kill Kron, and anyone who associated with him. I can have him arrested regardless of the fact that you own half the house."

He closed his eyes as he listened to her irate musings once more, then seemed to get enough of it.

"I don't care! You don't know him, I do. You can assume all you choose to, it doesn't make you right. If you don't like it, you're going to have to find a way to deal with it. I like him, she likes him, and that's all there is to it!" Buchanan exclaimed.

Then silence before he shouted. "No!" he exclaimed, obviously cutting off his wife in the middle of her sentence since he didn't pause to listen to her words, "I don't care. I don't care at all that you think it's an outrage, embarrassing, an invasion of your personal space, or any of the other over-the-top exaggerative words you've tried to throw at me. It's my house, too, and I will not forbid her from having guests of any type. Except Mitchell!"

He sighed as she obviously began speaking again. "Oh, my God! What is it now?" he asked exasperatedly.

"Tomorrow? You really plan to do this, even after this afternoon?" he asked.

Buchanan paused to allow his wife to speak again.

"You know what? Yes, please do. I'll have the police there shortly after you serve dinner. Appreciate you helping me finish cleaning up this little mess. I'll let the cops know to be sure to have room for him," He slammed the communicator down on his desk, and lifted his hands to rub his eyes and temples.

"Buchanan," Kron said.

Buchanan startled, unaware that he had company. "Hey, Kron! Ginger get home okay?" he asked, knowing full well that Ginger was already home and she and her mother were arguing.

"Yes. She is home. I watched her walk into your home. She would not allow me to escort her inside, or to pay my respects to her mother. Though her mother does deserve all respect as the female who gave her life."

"Mmhmm," Buchanan said, taking a deep breath and dropping his feet from his desk to the floor.

34

"We have decided to share a meal together," Kron said. "If it meets with your approval," he added. "But first, I must let you know that I plan to see her again. It is our custom to express our interests in a female to her father and mother, gain their acceptance, then approach the female in question. I must apologize for not following tradition. I spoke to your daughter without yours or your wife's permission, however I assure you, I meant no disrespect."

"Kron, you talking about taking my Ginger out?" Buchanan asked.

Kron straightened his spine and linked his hands behind his back in a relaxed, but at attention fashion. "I am. If I may have your permission to do so."

Buchanan smiled slowly. "Kron, why do you think I suggested that you show her the stuff you've made?"

"Because you trust me to protect her and see to her welfare first and foremost."

"Exactly. And because of that, I know that whenever she is with you, she's safe, looked after, and probably very happy. I have no problem with you spending as much time with Ginger as you and she want to spend together. Especially since I heard you claim her, out loud before God and everybody this afternoon."

Kron smiled brightly. He inclined his head. "Thank you, Buchanan, for the trust you place in me, and for your approval of my intentions to take your daughter as my mate."

"You're welcome. Now, where are you taking her?"

"I have left the choice up to her. But I've also made it clear that we should move slowly and address any questions that may arise before we are actually mated. The first obstacle is to receive acceptance from the female's family. It is the reason I came to speak with you. Now that you've given me your acceptance, I'll speak with your wife, then I'll begin to win Ginger's pledge."

"Oh, no. You don't really want to do that," Buchanan said.

"But, I do," Kron said, not understanding Buchanan's objection. "Did you not give me permission to claim Ginger as mine?"

"Yes, I did, I'd be fine with that. More than fine, even," Buchanan said, causing Kron to smile again. "But here on Earth, the young lady pretty much makes up her mind who she does and doesn't want to be with. If we're lucky, as fathers, we get to say if we don't like somebody they've chosen, but it's not always that way. Some daughters don't care what their parents think. In Ginger's case, her mother doesn't care what Ginger thinks."

"She said as much, about how on Earth the female makes her own choice. The rest, I don't understand," Kron said. "How could her mother not care for Ginger's choice of mate. It could mean the difference between a lifetime of happiness, or strife."

Buchanan huffed a sigh. "Look Kron, I like you. Ginger likes you. I'm all for a union between the two of you. But her mother does not like you."

"But, I've never met her mother. Once she meets me and sees the male that I am…"

"She won't care. You're not human. In her eyes, all aliens are responsible for the invasion that shattered, as she calls it, her world, her way of life," Buchanan said.

"But, I am not of the invading race. We are here to assist Earth in rebuilding their structure, their government, their freedom. We keep those races away from your planet," Kron said.

"I'm aware, and I'm thankful, and I hope you can overlook her prejudice, but she simply doesn't care, and if you're not human, to her, you're all the same," Buchanan explained. "She will never give her blessing for her daughter to marry an alien. She will never treat you with respect, she will never stop fighting it. So, if you're going to be with Ginger, you'll have to learn to overlook everything that comes out of her mouth."

"It is important that your female's mother is respected and revered. Without her, your daughter would not have been given life to walk beside me," Kron said, his mind racing.

"I'm going to give it to you straight, Kron. If Ginger's mother was deserving of respect in any way, I'd agree. But she's not, not anymore. She's not the same woman I married all those years ago. Sure, there were signs back then that she was a little less

36

than tolerant, but I figured with time and exposure to people from other worlds, she'd see where you come from doesn't matter — it's your heart that matters. Unfortunately it was only wishful thinking on my part. In the years we've been married, and there's been a lot of them, she's gone from being untrusting of anyone not from Earth, to downright bitter, presumptive, angry, and honestly, she's somewhat of a zealot now. But she's all bark and no bite. She talks a good game, so myself and Ginger tend to just ignore whatever she says to try to sway us to her way of thinking. Her opinions are unreasonable and they're wrong, but nobody can convince her she's wrong. So, it's best if you just steer clear of her. You like Ginger, Ginger likes you, then by all means, spend some time together, see where it takes you. I hope you can't spend a single day out of each other's company. But do it without her mother, because if that's a big deal for you, you've already lost the battle," Buchanan said.

~~~

Kron left Buchanan with mixed emotions. He'd received approval from Buchanan, Ginger's father, to pursue her as his mate, but he'd also been warned away from Ginger's mother. In fact, he'd been told not to even bother speaking to her, that it would only end poorly. He'd struggled with this information for the entirety of his shift that night. It just didn't make sense to him. He'd grown up believing that if you had integrity, if you were trustworthy, quick of wit, honorable, capable, and brave, you could be anything, achieve anything, and your mate would always, always return your gift of heart. But this was different. His female of choice seemed interested in him, her father approved of him, but her mother would always see him as the enemy — an invading force, hated for actions that weren't even his or his people's.

That was something he just didn't know how to overcome. If he claimed Ginger, and Ginger's mother renounced her as a result, he wasn't sure she wouldn't eventually blame him for it. He didn't want to, wasn't sure if he could, claim his mate, then walk away if she denounced him to rectify her relationship with her mother. It was a pain, a burden, he simply didn't want to have to endure. He'd rather be alone than be broken from the rejection of his mate. He needed to proceed slowly and with caution, considering carefully all that could occur before he made any decision at all.

Chapter 4

Ginger arrived at Base 28 late in the afternoon, but early for her date with Kron. She'd been thinking about him almost non-stop since he'd escorted her home two nights earlier. As she docked her small transport, which her father had only had cleaned then returned to her, since it didn't really need any maintenance, she looked around and was disappointed to find that Kron wasn't in sight. She'd hoped he'd be as anxious as she was and she'd find him waiting for her. Hiding her disappointment, she returned the smile of several of the males working in the docking area and started her walk toward the base.

She'd almost made it to the door when it was suddenly pushed open and her father walked toward her. "Ginger! I didn't expect you today. Glad to see you. You just wanted to come for a visit, or do you need something, darlin'?"

"I have a date with Kron — remember?" she asked.

Buchanan's brows came down over his eyes and he thought about it for a moment. "Did you tell me that? I don't remember you telling me that."

Ginger smiled at her father and shook her head. "That's because you never pay attention to anything we say when you're home. If I want you to listen to me, I have to come here. Yes, I told you Kron and I made plans for dinner tonight."

"Hmpf," he said, running through his memories for any trace of that conversation. "Must have just tuned that out. Wasn't intentional, though. Kron's a good male, glad to see you two have an interest in each other."

"Tell that to Momma," Ginger grumbled.

"She still saying she's having that Mitchell character over?"

"No, she dropped that, but she's still trying to get me to go meet him out away from the house."

"Just ignore her where he's concerned," Buchanan said.

"I try. She just won't let it go. You should really talk to her about her attitude. I almost can't talk to her about anything anymore, her hatred filled opinions seep into every subject I try to discuss."

"Wouldn't waste my time. Suggest you don't either, unless you decide Kron's your future, then she'll just have to learn to deal with it. Until then though, why make more trouble for yourself than necessary?"

"You're right," Ginger agreed. "And, I do think Kron's my future."

Buchanan smiled happily. "Glad to hear that."

"So, where can I find him? Is he getting ready, or in his workshop?"

Buchanan shook his head. "Neither. He's not here. He went to Kol's house to take a look at some security issues Kol had a concern about," Buchanan said.

"But, he was expecting me," Ginger said.

"I'm sure he'll be back before much longer, especially if he knew you were coming."

"Yeah, you're right. I'll just hang around until he comes back," she said.

"Come on inside, make yourself comfortable while you wait," Buchanan said, opening the door and escorting his daughter inside the building.

~~~

Kol stood on the hill behind his house, looking out over the back pasture of his and Ada Jane's home.

"It cannot be seen from the house, you have to walk up the next hill to be able to look down on it," Kol said. "Can you see it?"

Kron stood beside him, his eyes trained in the same direction as Kol's. "I see it. How did they get to your field without you knowing it? Do you not have security in place?"

"To some degree. I am guilty of becoming too comfortable. We do have sensors in place, but they are often triggered by the wildlife in the area. But no more. This is clearly an act of intimidation at the least, an open threat at best. Changes will be made immediately."

"Have you walked the property perimeter?" Kron asked as they began walking toward the pasture someone had burned the Purists' logo into the middle of.

"I have. There are some signs of minimal disturbance, but nothing I can trace back to anyone," Kol answered.

"The insignia in the center of the field is the evidence," Kron said.

"Not necessarily. Some wishing us to focus on the Purists could have done it as well," Kol said.

"True," Kron conceded, "but why?"

"I have not thought that far ahead. I checked to be sure there was no immediate threat, then called for you. I'd rather have only my Cruestaci brothers involved in the new security I choose to install. It is sometimes difficult to determine which humans are honorable, and which are simply smiling at you while waiting for you to turn your back," Kol said.

"Some are capable of a complexity of emotions, and manipulations," Kron said. "But, are we not as well?"

"But, we're the aliens on this planet. Some see us as an invading force, not realizing we are simply here to keep their ignorance from resulting in the slavery and ravaging of themselves and their planet."

"It is a new thing to be hated simply because you come from a different place," Kron said.

Kol looked at him as they walked. "Have you encountered prejudice personally?"

Kron gave a sharp nod.

"Tell me," Kol said. "Any obvious prejudice should be considered. It could lead to strong reactions by those who live with it."

"Not in this case," Kron said. "Though I am unsure of how to proceed," he admitted, as he walked slowly between the trees at

41

the perimeter line, looking for evidence that Kol may have missed.

Kol had led him to the area he'd found evidence of someone, or something crossing onto his property, and Kron looked around at the tracks critically. Then he moved to stand beside them and lie down.

"Here, right here," Kron said. "They are aware of your security sensors and crawled on their bellies beneath your fencing."

Kol lay down right beside Kron and looked at the area of leaves and debris Kron pointed at. "I see it. Leaves don't fall in a straight line. They were moved to hide evidence of entry."

"Exactly," Kron said. Lying on the ground had given him a different angle of view, and the unusual mounding of the leaves over the crawl marks left behind were then easily seen.

"Ada Jane found several other marks over the last few days, but thought maybe it was her imagination until she found our field this morning," Kol said.

"She should have told you the first moment she thought she might have found evidence of trespassing on your property," Kron said.

"Agreed. She knows it as well. I think she didn't want to accept that her vision of a peaceful, perfect life was not what she'd thought it was," Kol said.

"Do you know where the other signs of entry are located?"

"I do. I've examined them, but would like your input as well. I'll take you to them, then we can go back to the house to eat. I'm sure Ada Jane is making something you will enjoy," Kol said.

~~~

The sounds of high pitched squeals and giggles, along with barks and growls made Kron grin as he and Kol approached Kol and Ada Jane's home.

42

Kol noticed Kron's reaction and chuckled. "It is never quiet here," he said.

"You are a very lucky male, Kol. Your home is filled with the sounds of your young ones laughing, your creatures barking, and the scent of your female preparing the evening meal for all. It is a happiness I had hoped to surround myself with one day."

"You will," Kol said, just as the front door opened and Ada Jane stood there, waiting to greet Kron and welcome Kol home.

"You two hungry?" she asked, kissing Kol as he paused beside her while entering their home.

"Yes!" Kol answered.

"If you are cooking, I will always have a large appetite," Kron said, stopping in front of her to accept her hug.

"Well, come on in, it's just about ready," she said, closing the door behind them and locking it as she heard her sons erupt in squeals when they saw their Uncle Kron.

"Did you see all the insignias?" she asked, when she walked past Kron who'd stopped to pet Billy and Bob when they came to see who was there, as she went back to a steaming pot and added butter and cream before salting it and stirring it.

Kron followed her and Kol into the kitchen, and was bent over almost immediately, smiling as one boy pulled himself on each hand. "I did," he said without looking up. "I agree with Kol that they've been marking your property for several weeks now, starting at the outer edge and gradually working their way in. Waiting to see how long it would take you to notice. If your vigilance was lax, it meant they had more opportunity for whatever they have planned."

"So you think more is to come, too?" she asked Kron, then glanced toward Kol.

"I do. I agree with Kol. They would not go to all this trouble unless they were prepared to elevate their actions if you did not respond in the way in which they expected."

"Well, we're not running away, if that's what they think," Ada Jane said. "And I think that's probably what they wanted."

"I didn't think you would," Kron said. "But, that means to expect more activity on their part."

"So what do we do?" she asked. "I know Kol asked you to come because he didn't want to react emotionally and miss any detail. So, now that you're here, what do you think we should do," she asked, looking back and forth between Kol and Kron, knowing between the two of them, they surely already had a plan. They were warriors by nature, not the diplomats they were doing their best to be here on Earth.

"I want to bring more personnel on board. Station them throughout our property with the intent of taking into custody whoever comes to leave their mark next," Kol said. "Or, I could just handle it myself and kill them when next they come."

"Why not both?" Kron asked.

Kol looked toward Kron. "What did you have in mind?"

"Are you familiar with Zhuxi's people?" Kron asked.

"Somewhat. They are capable of changing shape," Kol said.

"And appearance in general. They can be standing somewhere and you move within inches of them without ever knowing."

"We could ask for a few of them to assist us here," Kol said.

"I'm sure you'd have no shortage of volunteers. They are a people at one with nature, preferring to live in their jungles and forests. They're on a base in the middle of a dry, hot, humid flat land, wearing uniforms each and every day rather than existing in their natural state. They'd most likely thank you for the opportunity. Not to mention, they're quite lethal," Kron said.

"I'll contact Zhuxi and explain the situation," Kol said with a smile.

"Oww!" Kron shouted, looking down at his ankles, but taking great care not to move his feet. One twin each was now wrapped around an ankle, and they were biting him and grinning up at him alternately.

"I am not food!" Kron said, scowling, but tickling both boys relentlessly as they squealed and snapped at his hands with tiny sharp teeth.

Ada Jane laughed, then put down her mixing spoon to pick up Kolby, while Kol picked up Kreed. "Do not bite Uncle Kron!" Ada Jane scolded while she tickled Kolby's belly. Kolby chuckled, shoving her tickling hand away and screeched a string of unintelligible words at her. Then he grabbed her hand before starting to gnaw on her finger.

"Do not bite me either!" Kol ordered, dodging Kreed's mouth as he reached out an arm for Ada Jane to give him Kolby. "I'll put them in their highchairs," he said.

"Thank you. Can you take Billy and Bob in the dining room with you, too?" Ada said as she stepped over one of them to finish cooking.

Kol whistled and both dogs got lazily up and followed him.

"They are not very good protectors," Kron said, watching the huge, but friendly dogs lazily making their way into the dining room.

"Sure they are. They just like you. If they didn't, you'll get a whole different greeting," Ada Jane said.

They could hear Kol's voice as he spoke into his communicator in the other room, having finished strapping his sons into their chairs for dinner. "Good evening, Zhuxi! How are you?"

Ada Jane stopped plating the meal, and stood quietly listening to her male's end of the conversation. She'd let her guard down just enough while listening for Kron to notice the shake in her hands while they hovered over the dish she was filling before she heard Kol speaking.

Kron stepped forward and placed a hand on her shoulder, rubbing gently. "All will be well. Your male will destroy this entire planet if necessary to keep you and his younglings safe."

Ada Jane looked up at Kron. "I know. I'd just hoped that we could have a long, happy life here. But now I'm not all that sure it's a possibility."

"Where you are, Ada Jane, you will always have Kol, and you will never be alone," Kron said.

Ada smiled up at Kron and nodded.

Kolby started screeching from his highchair in the other room and was soon joined by Kreed and both dogs howling. "Though you may wish to be alone sometimes," Kron added.

Ada Jane started laughing and resumed transferring the mashed potatoes to the large bowl she intended to place on the table. A few minutes later she was placing the bowl of mashed potatoes on the table, and Kron was putting the platter of country fried steaks beside it.

"Let me get the corn," she said, returning to the kitchen and coming back with a platter of very buttery corn on the cob.

"Anything else?" Kron asked Ada, as he glanced toward Kol still speaking to Zhuxi.

"Drinks and bread," she said. "Can you bring the pitcher of tea in while I get the dinner rolls out of the oven?"

"I can," he said.

Moments later dinner was on the table, and Kol had finally ended his call.

"My apologies, I wanted to speak to Zhuxi as soon as possible," Kol said.

"What did he say?" Kron asked, pretty sure he already knew the answer.

"He was confident that many of his security forces will volunteer to be temporarily stationed here and provide added security. He said he'll call a meeting and present the option to them tomorrow," Kol said.

"I knew they'd be very inclined to accepting the assignment. They are tired of being at the base, but Zhuxi is careful where he allows them to take rest and recreation," Kron said.

"Why?" Kol asked.

Kron shrugged. "I just assumed it was their way."

Kreed started gurgling and slapping the tray of his highchair while glaring at Kron.

Kron looked over at the boy who was seated between himself and Kol. Ada Jane was blowing on a small amount of mashed potatoes she'd put on each of their small plastic plates, and Kol was cutting up a piece of meat into small bites.

"It's coming!" Kron told him. Then he spoke to Kol. "I thought he was the nice one!"

"He is. Unless it's food. Then you better give him some, fast," Kol joked.

"He's tired of waiting. He's got mashed potatoes, but he wants corn and meat," Ada said.

"Can I hand him an ear of corn," Kron asked.

"Please. I'm working on cutting up their meat," Kol answered. "But you better give Kolby one, too, or he'll be shouting at you next."

Ada Jane watched as Kron selected two of the best ears of corn and blew on them a couple of times to be sure they were cool enough, then handed one to each boy. Kolby's and Kreed's eyes lit up as they sat back in their chairs and started gnawing on the ears of corn Kron had handed them. "You're very good with them," Ada Jane said.

"It's easy. They like me, and I think they're pretty special," Kron said.

"They love you. You come over and roll around with them for hours, just like their Daddy does. You have a way with children. You need some of your own," Ada said, retaking her seat as Kol slid small pieces of country fried steak on the boys' plates from his own.

Kron's expression sobered, and his smile died. "I'm not so sure that's going to happen anymore."

"Why? What's happened?" Ada Jane asked.

Kron shook his head. "Nothing in particular," he lied.

"You may as well tell her, she's not going to stop until you tell her everything," Kol said.

Chapter 5

"I can not find a way to claim my mate without causing dissension in her family. It may be kinder to simply stay away from her and allow her to find another," Kron said reluctantly.

"That's ridiculous," Ada Jane said.

"I have to agree with my Ada Jane. I knew you were not yourself when you arrived, but I had no clue you were considering walking away from your mate," Kol said.

"We have discussed it, but agreed to move slowly to see where it takes us. I assume she would simply move on if I just stopped showing interest," Kron said, trying to justify the thoughts going through his mind.

"But you'd know, and she'd always wonder what she did wrong," Ada Jane said. "And no matter what you did, or who you ended up with, a part of you would always belong to the mate you left behind. How fair would it be for you to leave her wondering for the rest of her life, or for you to promise yourself to another female, knowing full well that your heart would never love her completely?"

"She would love another eventually. And as long as I am faithful, it doesn't really matter," Kron said resignedly. "It would be better than driving a rift between Ginger and her mother. I don't think I could find peace if we bonded and she decided to honor her mother's wishes in order to repair their family. It's much easier to walk away."

"Why would she have to choose between you?" Kol asked.

"I am alien," he said quietly.

"So?" Ada Jane said. "You're also one of the best males I've ever met. You're kind and considerate, brave and loyal. You are smarter than most people I've ever met, you're handsome and funny. I don't understand what the problem is," Ada said.

"Her mother despises all aliens. It doesn't matter where we came from, why we're here. She believes we all have an agenda to take over Earth and enslave all her people, while ravaging the Earth's natural resources for export to our worlds."

"She's nuts," Ada Jane said.

"She's Ginger's mother. I cannot disrespect her. If she'd not birthed Ginger, I'd not have a female at all," Kron said.

"That's ridiculous. So she's her mother, so what? The woman obviously has a few screws loose," Ada Jane said.

"You don't understand, Ehlealah," Kol said quietly. "Kron's customs are different from the Cruestaci. His people require the blessing of both his mate's parents. Without it, they are not able to pursue their mate."

"Why not?" Ada Jane asked, looking first at Kol, then Kron.

"It is just the way things are done in my world," Kron said. "If I were a Cruestaci by blood, I could simply grab her up and explain that she is mine. But I'm not," Kron said.

"Yes, well, you're not in your world either!" Ada Jane exclaimed. "Besides you pledged your loyalty and became Cruestaci. So, live it."

Kol grinned at his mate. He loved when she got all stirred up over something she believed in.

Kron looked confusedly at her.

"You're in my world, Kron. Your mate's world. Here, if you want to get to know someone, you let them know you're interested. The individual you're interested in will either agree to see you, or not. They'll do it, not their parents. On Earth you do not require the approval of someone's parents in order to establish a relationship with them. In fact, there are many, many families who have learned to just get along with spouses of their children, because their children marry and have children with people they don't necessarily care for. It's just the way it is," Ada Jane said. "And if you want to go all Cruestaci, there's something to be said about being carried off by a big, sexy alien."

"Really?" Kol asked with sarcasm.

"Hush, I'm making a point," Ada said, grinning at Kol.

"Is it not considered disrespectful to bring someone into your family who they despise?" Kron asked.

"I suppose it could be, several hundred years ago, but now, and for quite a while, people marry who they love, not who their parents choose for them."

"So, if her mother decides to no longer be a part of her life..." Kron said.

"That's for her and her mother to decide. And if this girl loves you, it's her right to choose her future. You have no right to make that decision for her. And frankly, that would make me more angry than my mother or father not liking my choice of husband," Ada said.

Kron sat there considering all Ada Jane had told him. But he was still having a hard time overcoming his own customs. "But, the approval of both parents is a very important part of the bonding process of my people. We bond families, not just the mate."

"What does her father think?" Kol asked.

"Buchanan is supportive. He said I should ignore his wife at all costs because there is no hope of winning her over. To simply pursue Ginger with his blessing," Kron said.

"Buchanan?!" Kol exclaimed. "Your mate is Ginger Buchanan?"

"She is," Kron confirmed. "Or, if we can work out all the differences she will be."

"You have her father's support, Kron. Don't allow her mother to stand between you and your happiness. And I don't mean you personally, I mean both of you, your happiness together. If Ginger will accept you, her father's already given his blessing. Don't blow this, or you'll be sorry forever," Ada Jane said.

"Maybe not," Kron said, just for arguments sake.

"Do you remember me lying in bed refusing to get up for weeks when Kol was gone?" Ada asked.

"I do," Kron said.

"Let me know what color sheets you want to wallow in, and whether you want to wallow here at our house, or your quarters back at the base. I'll have the sheets delivered to you, along with a matching comforter. Because that's where you'll be if you don't claim your mate. Wallowing, hiding away from the world as your heart slowly dies," Ada Jane said.

Kron looked alarmed, and turned his attention to Kol who was simply eating his dinner.

"This is why she wins most of our arguments. I don't even try to argue most of the time anymore," Kol said.

A knock on the door brought their conversation to a halt as the dogs began howling and barking on their race to the front door.

Ada Jane glanced nervously toward Kol.

"Whoever it is, they didn't come in on foot. All perimeters are protected with lasers now. If the beams were broken at all by any humanoid form, the system would have alerted us," Kol said.

"You have it set to filter out anything other than humanoid?" Kron asked as he rose to his feet along with Kol.

"I do," Kol answered as he started for the door with Kron beside him. Kol stopped at the door to the kitchen and looked at the security screen there. He visibly relaxed and walked with purpose to the door. He pulled it open with Kron standing right beside him.

"Buchanan! Welcome," Kol said, intentionally swinging the door wide so both Buchanan and Ginger could see Kron standing beside him.

"Kol," Buchanan said. "Sorry to interrupt, but I have a worried daughter here, and I'm a little concerned myself, truth be told. They had plans today, and when he didn't come back to the base, we tried to reach him on his communicator." Buchanan looked at Kron and spoke directly to him. "We've been trying to reach you all afternoon, and into the evening. You weren't answering your com, so once I got off duty, I decided to take a ride out and make sure everything was okay."

"My apologies," Kron said. "It was not my intention to cause worry. We were securing the perimeter of Kol's home and I forgot all else."

"Is your communicator broken?"

"No, it is not. I simply left it in the transport. I knew I'd be with Kol and it wouldn't be necessary to carry them both. I apologize again for causing any distress. Thank you for your concern, but all is well," Kron said. He looked at Ginger. "My apologies for my inattentiveness."

"Do ya'll want to come in for dinner?" Ada Jane called out from the dining room. "We've already started, but we've got plenty."

"Yeah, that'd be real nice," Buchanan said, stepping into Kol's home and pulling Ginger in behind him, then just letting her go inside the house as he walked away with Kol. "Kron, keep your communicator on you at all times! You never know who might be trying to contact you," he called out.

"Of course," Kron said.

"I am happy you're here," Kol said, as he walked beside Buchanan, escorting him through the living room and into the dining room.

"Hey!" Ada Jane said, as Buchanan and Kol reached the dining room. "I would have come to the door to invite you to stay, but I didn't want to leave the boys alone. They're escape artists," she said.

"I understand," Buchanan said. "I hope we're not intruding."

"Not at all," Ada Jane said.

"It is refreshing to know that you care personally for our people," Kol said.

"Sit," Ada Jane said, "let me get you a plate."

Kron still stood in the living room with Ginger. He wasn't sure if she was angry or hurt, or a little of both, but she was not happy. They hadn't spoken yet, but stood there, watching each other.

"Would you like to join us?" Kron asked, gesturing in the general direction of the dining room. "Are you hungry?"

"Yes," she said, her arms folded across her chest defiantly. "I'm very hungry. We were supposed to have dinner tonight. Remember?" she asked.

Kron inclined his head.

"So, you didn't completely forget," she said matter-of-factly.

53

"No, I did not," he admitted.

"If you've changed your mind, or you don't want to see me, that's fine, just let me know that so I'm not left wondering where we stand," Ginger said.

"I truly lost track of time. But I was aware that we'd planned dinner," Kron said.

"I was worried. So worried that I pestered my father until he was worried, too. Not showing up after you'd said you were looking forward to seeing me just didn't seem like something you'd do," she said. "And then not answering your communicator, or even returning his messages…" Her gaze wandered off behind Kron as though she could see through the walls to the dining room. "If he'd not accepted a dinner invitation, I'd be making my exit after seeing that you're okay. I honestly didn't mean to intrude on you or on Kol and his family."

"You're not intruding," Kron said. "In fact, we were just speaking about you."

"Oh yeah, about how you had to figure out how to get out of seeing me?" Ginger asked.

Kron shook his head. He'd really made a mess of things, he realized. "We didn't exactly set a time or a place, and I felt that if I didn't contact you, you'd not make the trip to the base. I didn't think you'd go to the base anyway and wait for me."

Ginger nodded slowly, then shook her head. "All you had to do was tell me you'd changed your mind. But you know what? It's fine. Not everyone you're attracted to ends up reciprocating the feeling."

"You don't understand," Kron said, stepping toward her and taking her hands in his.

"No, I honestly do not," Ginger agreed, not even attempting to pull her hands free of his.

"I had decided not to pursue you," Kron said.

At that Ginger tried to pull her hands free of his, but he wouldn't let her go. "It's fine, Kron. I understand."

"No, you don't. Your mother doesn't approve of me. She never will, as your father explained it to me. It is very important among my people to have the approval of both parents, and to pay great respect to the mother of the female you will claim as your mate. It is unheard of to claim a mate without the approval of both parents. Your father has given me approval, your mother will not. I have little hope of ever receiving her approval after speaking with your father on the subject. And if I am truthful with myself, I am more than a little concerned that you will walk away from me after I've claimed you, and I am not sure I could get over that kind of pain. It is these selfish thoughts that kept me away. I will not make you choose between us. I do not know of a mate bond that could survive such a thing," Kron said. "I do not wish to be alone for the rest of my life because I forced you to choose."

"So, you were going to what? Walk away from me, let me think I must have done something wrong? End up spending your own life alone?" she asked.

"Exactly," he said, relieved she understood.

"Bullshit!" she snapped at him. "You have no right to make that decision for me! If I'm that important to you, then respect me enough to allow me to make choices in my own life. Otherwise, you're not much of a mate!"

Kron's eyebrows shot up toward his hairline as he listened to her lecture him, but he still held both her hands in his, since she'd made no more attempts to pull them free.

"My mother will never approve of anyone I choose, human, alien or otherwise, unless it's someone she's personally handpicked. I can never, and will never live my life with anyone she's ever picked for me. She's got a particular type in mind for me, and that type of male could never satisfy me. I will choose my own life partner, mate, husband, whatever you want to call him. And she will come to terms with that, or she will never know her grandchildren. That's all there is to it. She's my mother and I love her, but she's not me. My life is mine to live in any way that makes me happy. It's not her right to choose what I will or won't do with my future, nor is it yours. It's MY choice," Ginger said firmly.

Ginger stopped speaking and waited for him to say something.

Kron was looking at their joined hands, his thumbs running over the backs of them as he thought over all Ginger had said to him. Finally he looked up at her. "Why are they not your type?" he asked.

"Hmm?" she asked, confused.

"The males your mother chooses for you; why are they not your type?" he clarified.

Ginger smiled up at him. "Because they're not you," she said.

Kron's lips curved up at their corners as he realized she wanted him. No matter what difficulties came their way, she'd already decided she wanted him. He was right, she did feel the pull of the mate bond, too, though she may not realize that was what it was.

"Told you!" Ada Jane called out from the dining room.

Kron grinned even bigger.

"What did she tell you?" Ginger asked.

"That I should give you the right to choose your future, not decide it for you no matter what happened with your mother," Kron said.

"Ya'll coming to eat?" Buchanan called out with his mouth full. "I'm not promising you'll have any left between me and these two little boys in here."

"Kol's babies love to eat," Kron said.

"I know Kol, and I've met Ada Jane, but I haven't met their twins yet," Ginger said.

"I'll introduce you," Kron said. "And get you some food before there's none left," he said, releasing one of her hands and pulling her gently behind himself with the other.

"Don't worry about that! There's plenty. You don't become the mate of a Cruestaci warrior, and not figure out to cook four times the amount you usually would," Ada said as Kron and Ginger finally walked into the dining room, hand in hand.

"Hello, Ada Jane," Ginger said.

"Hi, Ginger. I'm glad you're here. We've been telling Kron that his ideas of tradition are fine, but, he's not on his planet

56

anymore. He's on Earth, and we don't do things the way they do back on his planet," Ada Jane said.

"She's right," Ginger said, looking up at Kron.

"I understand now. But it is a new perspective," Kron said confidently.

"You two have all the time in the world, no reason to rush a thing. You'll get used to it," Buchanan said.

"I'm feeling better already," Kron said, smiling at Ginger.

"Here, I made you a plate already," Ada Jane said, setting a plate full of food next to Kron's place.

"Thank you, very, very much," Ginger said, not only referring to the food.

Ada Jane knew she meant for talking sense into Kron as well. "You're very welcome."

Kolby screeched at the new woman standing next to Kron, but Kreed babbled at her and grinned at her, offering her his corn cob.

"Uh oh! I think they like you, Ginger," Ada Jane said.

"They are just so beautiful," Ginger said, taking Kron's seat when he offered it to her, and went to grab another chair from the desk against the wall. Both boys were obviously Cruestaci, but, they had blonde hair, like Ada Jane's. Their skin tone wasn't as dark as Kol's, but it definitely had a light blue cast to it. There were slightly raised bumps on their temples, and their pouty little mouths were full of tiny sharp teeth, but their features, the shape of their eyes and their noses looked like Ada Jane.

Kreed continued to hold out his corn cob for Ginger. She leaned over and pretended to take a bite, which pleased him greatly. Kreed rewarded her with a perfectly angelic smile.

"Oh, you're going to be a heart breaker," Ginger said.

"I have no doubt," Ada Jane said.

Kolby, not wanting to be left out, picked up a piece of his meat and threw it in Ginger's direction with a scowl at Kreed.

Ginger looked down at the small piece of meat sitting right near the top of her shirt and started laughing even harder than she had at Kreed. "Oh, it's like that is it?" she asked.

"They must each do what the other does. There is a struggle to outdo, or at least keep up with the other at all times," Kol said. "It is good. It will drive them both to excel."

Then Kreed handed her a piece of his country fried steak.

"He must really like you," Ada Jane said.

"Kron, you best mate her quickly. Kreed is already making better progress than you are," Kol teased.

"He's my little lover, Kolby is my little warrior. But don't think Kreed won't stand up for himself. He's a warrior, too, you just have to make him angry first," Ada said.

"And make sure there are no females nearby to distract him," Kol added.

Chapter 6

Buchanan rose from the table, patting his belly. "Ada Jane, you are a very talented cook!" he said.

"Thank you, Mr. Buchanan. I appreciate that," Ada Jane said.

Then he turned to Kol. "I thank you for your hospitality, I thank you for the meal, and I thank you for understanding when we came barging in here looking for Kron. We just expected to hear from him at some point, and when we didn't, especially knowing he had a date with Ginger, we got worried," he finished.

"Thank you for your concern," Kron said.

"I'm going to take my leave. I'm heading home. You coming with me, Ginger?" he asked.

"We haven't had dessert yet. You sure you don't want to stay just a little while longer?" Ada Jane asked.

"Naw, but thank you. I got over an hour ride back," he said. Then he looked at Kron again. "Stay in touch next time you're gone for such a long time. I won't have to come in search of you!"

"Does he always go in search of wayward people assigned to the base?" Ada Jane asked Kol.

Kol shook his head. "I think this is more personal," he answered.

"I can hear you," Buchanan said with a grin as he stepped away from the table and pushed his chair in. "You coming, Ginger?"

"Perhaps I should stay the night," Kron said, looking toward Kol. "Especially since we've identified a threat. Once the day comes, I can return to the base, and bring back the Ceresian volunteers."

"What threat?" Buchanan asked.

Kol and Kron shared a look, wordlessly confirming they both trusted Buchanan.

"Purists. They've burned their insignia into one of our fields. They've carved it into several trees. They've been sure to leave their mark so that we'll find it," Kol said. "I do not believe they mean to engage us, just to encourage us to leave by intimidation."

"But they've gotten bolder with each incident. We have no way of knowing what they actually plan," Kron said.

"Maybe it is better if you stay here, Kron," Buchanan said.

"I agree," Kron said.

"I understand. And Kol can't fight anyone if he's also standing guard over Ada Jane and the kids," Ginger said.

Kron was impressed that Ginger understood as much as she did about protecting one's family. "Do you not mind that I don't drive you home?" he asked.

"Not at all. If I thought I'd be any help at all instead of a distraction, I'd offer to stay as well," Ginger answered.

"I think it's best you stay, Kron. And don't worry, Ginger will get home safely," Buchanan said.

"I'll see you soon?" Ginger asked, standing to join her father.

"You will. We must secure Kol's family, then I will have more free time," Kron said.

"Alright then, that's that. Ya'll enjoy dessert, and I'll see you at the base tomorrow," Buchanan said to Kron. "Kol, I don't expect you until this is over. We'll handle things at the base unless you want to bring your family there temporarily."

"Thank you, Buchanan. But for now, we will stay here," Kol said.

Kol and Kron walked Buchanan and Ginger out, then locked the door again before returning to the dining room where Ada Jane was slicing still warm blueberry pie with mountains of whipped cream on top.

"This is the best part," Kol said, accepting the plate she handed him.

Then he looked at his sons, already hands deep in their dessert. "You like dessert, don't you?" Kol asked Kolby and Kreed. He laughed when he was answered by matching smiles, tinted purple from the blueberries in the pie, and whipped cream smeared on their faces.

A short while later Kron stood in the kitchen rinsing dishes and placing them in the dishwasher while Ada Jane and Kol put the kids in bed. He smiled to himself when he thought of Ginger rousing her father enough to make him come in search of him. They were good people. They cared about those around them. And that made Kron even happier. His female had a good heart, and so did her father. That would make for a happy life. Then he thought about Ginger's mother. He still felt on edge where she was concerned. He just couldn't understand rejecting someone simply because of where he came from. But he knew that Ginger wanted him, and that Buchanan approved of him. It wasn't perfect, but it was enough. It would have to be. Now, if they just took things slowly, and gradually built their relationship, there should be nothing they couldn't overcome.

"Look at you, doing the dishes! I might have to invite you over more often," Ada Jane teased.

"I definitely will," Kol confirmed, walking into the kitchen right behind her.

"It is the least I can do. You've fed me, spent time counseling me, and most importantly, you consider me your friend. Dishes are but a small thing I can do to show my appreciation," Kron said.

They made small talk while Ada Jane buzzed around the kitchen finishing cleaning, then she excused herself. "I'm going to take a bath, ya'll do whatever warriors do when your females leave you alone," she said, stopping beside Kol for him to drop a kiss on her lips before she left them to themselves.

"Will we be taking turns to keep watch tonight?" Kron asked.

"There has not been a firm threat yet," Kol reminded.

"No, but they are getting closer to the house. They were in the back pasture last night," Kron said.

"True," Kol said. "It is smart to err on the side of caution, I think."

"I'll take first watch, you take second," Kron said.

"Agreed," Kol said.

~~~

The next morning Kron left Kol's house just after the sun came up. He wanted to be there when Zhuxi had his meeting with the Ceresian security forces assigned to the base. He arrived only minutes after the meeting started and quietly let himself into the meeting room, taking a seat off to the side until Zhuxi finished explaining what was happening and called on him to add what he knew.

"Have they actually been attacked?" one of the Ceresian males asked.

"No, they have not," Kron said. "It seems to be just a few strategically timed and placed warnings. But the placement of each warning seems to be getting closer to their home."

"And it could escalate at any given time," Zhuxi said.

"Exactly. There is no doubt it is the Purists. And since they've decided to make themselves known, it could well be escalating. Consul Don Tol has dogs and the Consul's mate has said she's noticed them alerting more at different times of the day and night, but just thought it was local wildlife. Now that the Purists have decided to leave their mark, it would seem they're ready to take any action they may have planned to the next level," Kron said, "or at least that's our concern. Consul Don Tol would be here to brief you himself, but he is not comfortable leaving his mate and children alone to do so. Hence my presence here in his place today," Kron explained.

"If it is believed Consul Don Tol has had Purists on his land, I think it's best that we take the base up a level, to Code 2," Zhuxi said.

"I agree," Kron said.

"I will make it official as soon as we leave this meeting. We will monitor the situation and adjust if and as needed," Zhuxi said.

"I think it's best if we do not broadcast our level of alert via our online communications in the event they are being monitored in the event any sympathizers have eyes or ears in the higher up ranks of Earth's government," Zhuxi said. "I'll advise those on base personally, as well as Buchanan when he returns from his day off."

"You think the Purists have eyes and ears that high?" Kron asked.

"It is unlikely, but not impossible. They have sympathizers in most regions of this world," Zhuxi said.

Kron shook his head frustratedly as Zhuxi continued addressing his security force.

"We have been specifically requested because of our unique talents," Zhuxi said. "Though, because this is not a base sanctioned military operation, we will not order anyone to take part. If you'd like to volunteer, we will appreciate you, and it will not be forgotten. We are forty in number here," Zhuxi said, looking around at his security force assigned to Earth along with him. They were the best of the best that he'd fought with back on his home planet of Ceres. And he trusted each and every one of them with his life. "We will need some to stay here on base and some will be assigned to Consul Don Tol's home. If you go to Consul Don Tol's home, you will be stationed outside, and in your natural states, sans uniforms. You will take sustenance in your natural forms. There will be no luxury afforded you there. You are to blend in undetected.

"So, basically, we are being allowed to return to our true selves," Zrakad said, with a grin.

Zhuxi gave a single nod. "You are."

"Finally, a relaxing break," Zrakad said, chortling as his kind did.

Several others joined in, and the room filled with a shrill sound reminiscent of the calls of forest animals.

Zhuxi waited until the laughter died down before proceeding. "Once the aggressors are identified and caught, what happens to them afterward is Consul Don Tol's call. But as always, this operation like all others is to be considered classified."

Kron watched as the group of males making up the Ceres security force all spoke rapidly and quietly among themselves in their native language. The Ceresian males varied in color from light brown, like Zhuxi, to dark brown, and even ebony black skin tones. They all had glossy, straight black hair. Some wore it in hundreds of tiny little braids, caught back in a large braid at the base of their skulls. Others wore it in one single thick braid, while yet others kept it cut short enough that it couldn't be styled any other way. They all had dramatically slanted, feline shaped eyes. Most of them had green eyes, but some were golden tinted, and some were a combination of green and gold. Each had heavily lashed eyelids with dark, black lashes, thick lips, and fine, sharp features with wide cheekbones. They made an impressive picture.

Eventually, eleven males stood proudly, and one of them spoke on their behalf. "We volunteer to protect Consul Don Tol's home and family. The rest will stay behind to continue to protect the base with the other security forces here."

"Excellent," Zhuxi said.

"Will you be present at Consul Don Tol's home?" the male, Zrakad asked.

"No, I will remain here to help Viceroy Buchanan oversee base," Zhuxi answered.

Zrakad stood. "Then I'll be volunteering as well. There will be twelve of us going."

"I am most pleased. Thank you," Zhuxi said. "Consul Kol Ra Don Tol and Elite Warrior Kron Val Kere, will be your temporary commanders. Perform well, and with honor."

"Thank you for your time, and your willingness to join our private defense team. We will be leaving shortly to return to Consul Don Tol's home. Please see to any last minute details that you need to, as it could be a week or more before your return," Kron said.

All twelve Ceresian warriors left the conference room on their way to see to whatever they had to address. The others shook Kron's hand and bowed to Zhuxi before going back to their regular posts.

Once they were alone, Zhuxi turned to Kron. "It may become a violent confrontation, but do not question their capabilities if it does. You may not see them once they arrive and have taken up positions, but they are there. They are ever vigilant. They will not fail."

"I have no doubt of their expertise," Kron said.

"If more are needed, if I am needed, simply call for me. If you cannot get to a communicator, any one of my warriors can reach me in an instant," Zhuxi said.

"How?" Kron asked.

Zhuxi smiled at Kron and tapped his own temple. "We hear each other."

"That is amazing," Kron said.

"It is a gift we have been quite pleased to have. It is also a gift we do not make common knowledge of. Along with a few others you've witnessed," Zhuxi said.

"Anything I've witnessed, or been allowed to learn about, will be held in strictest confidence," Kron said.

"I do not have any doubt of that," Zhuxi said. "You are one of the most loyal males I have ever had the pleasure of meeting. I consider you a brother, Kron Val Kere."

Kron smiled and when Zhuxi extended his hand, he shook it warmly. "And I you, Zhuxi."

"Go, deliver Kol's security force so they may see to protecting our Consul and his family. I know the sooner you get my security force to Kol's home, both you and he will be more at ease. All else will be waiting when you return."

"Thank you, Zhuxi," Kron said.

~~~

Kron landed the large transport from Base 28 a short distance from Kol's home and watched as the Ceresian warriors disembarked before following them. When he finally made it to the ground, Kol was there, greeting each of them by name and rank. Kol had always been like that. He made it a point to memorize each male's name and rank, and if they had family, he'd memorize their names as well. He didn't do it to impress those that served under him on his Elite teams. He did it because he genuinely cared. He couldn't see asking any male to give their all, very possibly risking their lives for any military and superior officer who wasn't interested enough in those that served him to learn who they were and what was important to them. Of course, it was impossible for those who commanded huge battalions, but when commanding an Elite team, it was completely doable, and in Kol's mind, required as a measure of respect to each male serving on his team.

Once the initial greetings were over, Kol and Kron walked the property with the warriors, showing them all the graffiti and markings the Purists had left behind. Then they returned to Kol's home where he introduced them to Ada Jane, Kolby and Kreed, and Billy and Bob. Kreed and Kolby wanted to play with them, and Billy and Bob were somewhat mistrustful, but that was to be expected, they were strangers on their territory.

After a strategy had been agreed upon, the males left Kol's house along with Kol and Kron, and moved quietly through the wooded areas of Kol and Ada Jane's land looking for places to lose themselves until they were needed.

From time to time, one of the males would simply step toward the trees, and fade from view.

"Damnedest thing I've ever seen," Kol said as yet another male blended in with their surroundings and couldn't be seen any longer.

"It's simply a matter of a thought to us," Zrakad said nonchalantly.

"It is the best camouflage I've ever seen," Kron said. "It is a trait I would pay to be gifted with."

"Same," Kol said, looking behind himself to try to see any of the males that had stepped away from them so far. But they had no idea just how impressive the Ceresian warriors were in their camouflage techniques. They didn't need trees to hide in. As the group moved across Kol's land, those who were left turned toward the pastures and planted fields. And even there in plain sight, the warriors concealed themselves, blending in so well with their surroundings, they couldn't be seen.

"Unbelievable," Kol said, watching as another male disappeared before his eyes. Kol stepped forward toward the last place he'd seen the male, his arms held out in front of him, waving them back and forth. His hands contacted the male, and his form shimmered, giving the impression of prisms hanging in the air. The male's eyes were visible for a split second, their amused expression easily read.

"I want to learn to do that!" Kol exclaimed, stepping back from the male and dropping his hands.

"Unfortunately, or fortunately depending on which side you're on, it is not a skill that can be taught," Zrakad said.

"I wonder if it can be duplicated," Kol said.

"Possibly, but we won't attempt it. I've given Zhuxi my word that anything we see will be held in the strictest confidence and never spoken of."

Kol only hesitated for a moment as he turned to look at Kron. "Done."

By the time they'd walked around the property and returned to the house, eleven of the Ceresian warriors had chosen their hiding places and disappeared into the landscape. Less than twenty feet from the house, Zrakad, the last of and highest ranking of the Ceresians that had volunteered, winked at them, and disappeared before their eyes.

"What do you say to something like that?" Kron asked.

"I don't know, but I feel safer already knowing we are not alone," Kol said. "I have no doubt that I could protect my family, but it would be very difficult to fight off any attack as well. I couldn't stay with them and fight off multiple aggressors at the same time. They'd have to be hidden away and I'd prefer to know they are protected rather than just in hiding."

"Agreed. If you decide you want more warriors, Zhuxi said to simply let one of his males know and they'll call to him," Kron said.

"How?" Kol asked.

Kron tapped his temple, then shrugged.

"They are an amazing people," Kol said.

"They are indeed."

Chapter 7

Several days later Kron smiled as he walked into the cafeteria. He'd been at Kol's along with the Ceresian security force, but there had been absolutely no activity. They all believed that the Purists were trying to lull Kol into a sense of security before they struck again, only with more force this time.

Kol had decided that it was best if Kron return to the base to help with duties that Buchanan and Zhuxi now shouldered between them. And he was happy to be back. Being back at the base meant he'd get to spend a little time with Ginger again. He'd thought about it, and decided he wasn't ready to give up on Mrs. Buchanan yet. If he took his time and showed the utmost respect, showed that he loved her daughter, eventually he'd win her over. She was after all, Ginger's mother, and no one as bad as they said she was could have raised such a kind, caring, strong spirited female as Ginger.

"Kron!" Buchanan called out from the opposite side of the commissary.

Kron looked toward Buchanan and lifted a hand in a wave to let Buchanan know he'd seen him before he started toward where he stood at his table waiting for Kron to join him.

Zhuxi hurried into Kron's path and greeted him with a kind of handshake they'd gotten into the habit of doing after watching dozens of movies from the 1980's and 90's. Zhuxi placed his hand into Kron's and they performed a sort of slapping routine to the backs and palms of each other's hands before a brief man hug, and then Kron was on his way to Buchanan again. He turned to Zhuxi and shouted jestfully. "I want a rematch of the last sparring session! I know you cheated!"

"I do not cheat! I'm simply better than you are," Zhuxi called back to him, before dissolving into the chortling laughter characteristic of him. "Welcome back, Kron!" he added as he hurried away.

"You giving Zhuxi a hard time again?" Buchanan asked as Kron approached his table.

Kron laughed. "I am. I find it quite enjoyable. As does he."

"I have to admit I haven't seen him laugh quite as much as he does now that you're here to tease him relentlessly."

"I am anxious to train with him again. I pretend it is easy, our sparring, but he's a fierce warrior. I would not want to face him in a true battle," Kron said.

"Nor I," Buchanan said. "Have a seat. I ordered platters of food this morning when I found out you were on your way, so when you got here we could just get down to business."

"What business is it that we must get down to?" Kron asked, somewhat confused. He looked around. "Did we have a breakfast meeting I forgot about?"

"No, we didn't. And the business at hand is my daughter," Buchanan said.

At the mention of Ginger, Kron broke into a wide grin.

"See? That right there is why I wanted to talk to you."

"What?" Kron asked, trying to look down to see a portion of his own face as Buchanan pointed at him.

"That response. I've known you two were right for each other for a long time. Even before you knew it," Buchanan said. "You two have a special connection. I saw it the first time you met, and I saw it again at Kol's house the other night."

"It is no secret. We have discussed it," Kron said.

"But, you haven't spoken since. Now, don't worry, I told her you were on a security mission, and you'd get in touch soon as you could."

"Is there a problem?" Kron asked. "Is she well?"

"No, no problem. And she's doing alright," Buchanan said.

"Then, what are we discussing about her?" Kron asked.

"I just need to confirm that you are interested in a relationship with her," Buchanan finally confessed. "A long time, forever relationship."

70

"I… You don't… It…" Kron gave up and visibly seemed to deflate. "Things have been decided, Buchanan. As I said, we've spoken about it, but, without her mother's initial approval, there is reason to proceed slowly. I've come up with a plan, and regardless of the outcome, I will claim Ginger as my mate, it's just a matter of the right time to do so. You see, we've decided to move slowly. And I've decided that in addition to giving us the opportunity to know one another, I will have more time to prove myself to Mrs. Buchanan. Surely, once she knows me and sees my regard for her daughter, she will give her approval."

"You're missing the whole point, Kron."

"What point?" Kron answered.

"The point that you don't have time to wait. You need to marry my daughter, mate her, bond her, whatever the hell you want to call it. And you need to do it now."

"What?!" Kron exclaimed. "I cannot possibly just bond with her. There is too much that needs to fall into place first. We do not even truly know one another yet!"

"Do you intend to bond with my daughter? Mate her?" Buchanan asked.

Kron glanced away, then back over to meet Buchanan's gaze. "I do. I just said I do."

"Then what's the damn problem? Do it now! Figure out all the details later!" Buchanan insisted. "I don't give a damn what her mother does and doesn't like. She needs you to claim her now. I need you to claim her now."

"There is so much to consider, Buchanan. We cannot just rush into this. Any one of a number of things could go wrong to keep us apart later. I cannot take that chance."

"Let me relieve some of that anxiety for you, Kron. I like you. My daughter likes you. And I've decided that it would be best if you bonded with her now," Buchanan said.

"And what does she say? Is she remotely interested in rushing into this?" Kron asked. "When last we spoke, it was agreed that slow was best."

"And the added bonus is that once you're mated, you can have babies. Little yellow grand babies," Buchanan said, ignoring

71

Kron's last question and sitting back in his chair and sipping his coffee happily while he watched Kron sputter.

"You can't be serious," Kron finally managed to say.

"'Course I am," Buchanan said.

"Have you said these things to her?" Kron asked.

"Haven't told her yet. Figured I leave that up to you, you know," Buchanan said. "But I'm pretty sure she'd jump at the chance. She was really worried about you when you didn't answer your com, was very happy on the way home, and has asked about you since then, too."

Kron sat there, completely flabbergasted, not knowing what to say next.

"Eat something, Kron. I got all this food just sitting here waiting to be eaten," Buchanan said, shoving a platter with eggs and bacon on it toward Kron.

"I don't understand, Buchanan. Why are you suddenly in a rush to bond your daughter to me, knowing full well that we have not addressed everything?"

"I told you to stop worrying about her mother," Buchanan said.

"And for the most part I have. I will still try to establish a relationship with her, but I will claim Ginger regardless. But there are other things to consider."

"Like what?" Buchanan asked.

"To begin with, I'm not on your planet permanently!" Kron said. "If I leave, and we are bonded, she will be expected to go with me. Do you wish to be rid of her so strongly that you will just marry her to the first male you find agreeable?"

"No! No, not at all! I adore my daughter!" Buchanan sat forward and leaned his forearms on the table. He looked at Kron for a moment as he considered his answer, then finally decided if he trusted the male enough to encourage him to marry his daughter, he needed to trust him with the entire truth. "I've got troubles at home, Kron. And they seem to be growing. It's getting to the point that I can't ignore them anymore because they're not going away like I'd hoped. And now, I'm thinking Ginger's future may be in jeopardy."

"What is the source of your concern?" Kron asked, beginning to get defensive of Ginger and anything that threatened her before he even heard what it was that had Buchanan on edge. "I will destroy anything that threatens her."

"This is a different kind of threat. I'm pretty sure my wife is an active Purist, not just a sympathizer, and that's a problem in itself. But now I think she's trying to indoctrinate Ginger to her way of thinking."

"If that is true, your wife will be taken into custody and interrogated," Kron said softly, looking around to be sure no one overheard him.

"To say the least," Buchanan said. "But my dumb ass spent too much time hoping she'd snap out of it. I loved her once. I promised for better or worse, and that's what I'm trying to do. If I have to deal with it sooner rather than later, I will, but if I can find a way around it, I'll do that instead. That's why I'm coming to you."

"I am alien. Do you not see the problem with rushing this? There is very little I could do to help," Kron said. "I believe that mating me immediately would make things worse for Ginger. But I have a plan! I just need a little time…"

"Ever since she saw you drop Ginger off, my wife's been on a rampage. She's pushing a bunch of judgemental, pansy-ass boys at my daughter pretty hard. She knows she can't have Mitchell over, so she's doubled her efforts on all the rest of them. It's even worse now. Before it was just him, now it's a different boy each night for dinner. And they're assholes. The last thing I want is her getting tied down to one of them and ending up trapped in their goddamn Purist movement.

I mean, it's bad. The other night after we'd had dinner with you and Kol and Ada Jane, Ginger said that she admires the marriage Kol and Ada Jane seem to have, and hopes one day she'll have one just like it. She said the way Kol treats his wife, loves her and their kids so deeply is inspiring and romantic. I think Ginger was working up to bringing you into the conversation, but my wife went freaking nuts on her, yelling and screaming at her. Ginger just stopped trying to talk to her. And

73

every single night since Susanna's had these arrogant little fucks in my house, pushing them at my daughter and my daughter at them. Ginger likes you, Kron. I like you. Hell, everybody likes you, you're a good guy. Help me save my daughter from the fuckers my wife is trying to tie her to."

"Can you not force your wife to stop inviting these males to your home as you did with Mitchell?" Kron asked.

"I have Mitchell's behavior here to use against him if I had to. These little assholes are simply at my house for dinner. And I've tried talking to my wife. Then she goes into fit mode, accusing me of having no regard for the welfare of our daughter and preaching about how it's her house, too. She told me last night the only thing that can guarantee our daughter has a long, suitable life, safe from abuse of any type and exposure to the unnatural males trying to sway our planet from our own hands is to marry one of the men she's been trying to set her up with. She says they're all sons of friends of hers, but I don't remember any of them or the friends she claims mothered them.

I'm afraid one day I'll go home and it'll be too late — Ginger will be gone off with one of these assholes. Then I'll be dead or in prison because if some sonofabitch has taken Ginger off to indoctrinate her, or force her into marriage, even with the support of my wife, I'm killing somebody, possibly lots of somebodies. And I'll be okay with that, because the bastards will need killing. And my wife at that point, I can't even say what would happen to her then, but it wouldn't matter because my daughter would be gone. I need your help. I love my daughter. I want her to be happy. When I see her with you, every time I've seen her with you, she's happy. She was glowing, and couldn't stop smiling."

"We have spoken of the future. I have made my intentions known, and Ginger has said she chooses me as well. I wish to claim her, but it is all so fast. I can't believe she would accept another."

"If you plan to mate her, why not do it now?" Buchanan said.

"I can't just walk up to her and invite her to bond with me," Kron said. "There are things that must be made perfectly clear before that step can be taken," Kron said.

"You said she was yours. I heard it. Is she?" Buchanan asked.

"She is," Kron confirmed. "She knows it as well. But, to mate her before she has a full understanding of all that will happen, to understand the physical bond that will take place, the physical changes that will follow could be disastrous. That is what I'm trying to avoid, because once I claim her, it's forever. There is no going back and as much as I insist on not forcing her, I don't believe I could ever let her go afterward. Which is why I'm so insistent on taking things slowly. When I leave here, and I will leave here — I will not live out my life on this planet — she will be expected to come with me. There is no option for that. I would lose control without my mate nearby," Kron explained.

"But you do plan to mate her at some point? Like marrying mate her?" Buchanan asked hopefully.

Kron sighed. He just wasn't ready yet. "I do. She knows that I think of her always. I look for her every time I enter a room on the base in case she arrived without my knowledge. I smile for hours after she is gone. But I'm not sure she fully understands the meaning of mating to my kind. We do not dissolve our marriages if we encounter difficulties. We do not abandon, nor disrespect each other. We grow more attached to our mates as time goes on. She needs to understand all of this. My kind mate for life," Kron said.

Buchanan nodded thoughtfully. "You could bring her back here from time to time to visit, and I can come visit ya'll, so doesn't really matter that you don't expect to stay on Earth."

"Yes, of course," Kron said. "But there is more to it. You know as well as I do that your wife may refuse to have any contact with her daughter if I am in her life. Ginger may grow to resent me. No matter how I love her, she may be very unhappy if her mother refuses to interact with her. And she will change, there is no way to know how our mating will change her. Which may very well happen if I rush her into mating. That is why I plan to take my time, be sure that Ginger understands all my concerns, address any of her concerns, and in the meantime try to win your wife's approval."

"Naw, Ginger wouldn't resent you. The one thing I know for certain is my little girl's heart. Once she falls, she's all in, no matter what her mother or I think. She's all in already, and you just said you love her!"

Kron glared at Buchanan. "I do. And I plan to claim her eventually. And she is aware. But I'm sure she has plans for her own future as well. What kind of male would I be if I took away her ability to see those plans to fruition? There is a lot to consider, Buchanan. What you propose could drive a wedge between us if she feels I've rushed her into a future she was not allowed to choose for herself. She will be at my side forever once claimed. I will love her forever and she could end up hating me."

Buchanan nodded thoughtfully. "You say these things, thinking it will make me reconsider what I'm asking, but to me, that just confirms my choice of male for her. You have her best interests at heart."

"Any good male would," Kron said.

"You're the male, Kron. You," Buchanan said sincerely. "You should call her. Get her to come have lunch with you. Ya'll talk. It's been a few days, hasn't it?"

"It has, and I plan to contact her, but I will not be rushing her to accept my claim. This will be a slow process, Buchanan," Kron insisted.

Buchanan turned and looked at Kron as he held his communicator to his ear. "Take all the time you want, but if Ginger ends up married to some Purist asshole because you were hung up on moving slowly, how you gonna feel then?"

"She will not choose another. We've discussed things — to a degree," Kron said.

"To a degree... you better do better than that. There are young men at my house every night having dinner across the table from her. Get a move on, Kron," Buchanan said, then turned and walked away.

Zhuxi walked up with his tray and took a seat across from Kron. "What has happened?" he asked.

"What do you mean?" Kron asked.

"You seem on edge," Zhuxi said.

"No, I don't," Kron answered, usually a master at schooling his emotions.

Zhuxi smiled at him. "No, you don't. But, I can feel it anyway," he said, taking a bite of his toast.

"Oh, I suppose you think you're an empath or something," Kron said.

Zhuxi grinned at Kron and nodded. "Something like that. His daughter is a beautiful girl, is she not? And she thinks highly of you as well."

Kron stared at Zhuxi. "Did Buchanan talk to you?"

"No, he did not. But it is apparent he wishes you and his daughter to marry, and equally apparent you do as well."

"How is it transparent?" Kron asked.

Zhuxi glanced toward Buchanan who was ending his call, and walking back toward them. "I have a talent for knowing what those near me are thinking."

"So you know what everyone around you is thinking?" Kron asked.

"More or less. Those I care to read anyway. Most I block," Zhuxi said.

"What other talents are you hiding from me?"

"Nothing you should worry about," Zhuxi said, then simply raised an eyebrow at him, and took another bite of toast.

Chapter 8

Ginger walked into Earth Base 28 at exactly 1:00P.M. just as
her father had asked when he called to ask her for a lunch date.
She was thrilled to be here, and had hurried to be here on time
after she'd heard from her father. She looked around herself as
she walked the corridors, intentionally taking an extra turn here
or there on her way to her father's office. Her gaze fell on
everyone she saw and she smiled at them pleasantly, greeting
any she knew by name, but the one male she was looking for was
nowhere to be found.

Anxious to see the male that dominated most of her late
night fantasies, she came to a stop outside the administrative
offices and schooled her expressions before opening the door. If
she'd not seen Kron as she traversed the base, chances were he
was most probably sitting at one of the desks inside admin, or he
was still at Kol's. Trying to keep the grin from her face just at the
thought of him, she blushed. Who the hell was she kidding? He
starred in all her fantasies, not just the late night ones.

Blowing out a calming breath, she opened the door and
stepped inside, smile brightly plastered on her face, only to have
it drop in immediate disappointment when she realized Kron
wasn't in the office.

"Ginger! There you are hon!" Buchanan called out.

"Hey, Daddy. How are you?" she answered, doing her best
to hide her disappointment.

"Busy! I'm crazy busy today. We might have to cancel
lunch," he said, sitting back down and shuffling papers aimlessly
on his desk.

"Oh, well, that's okay. I know work comes first. I can just
grab something at home. I'm not that hungry anyway," Ginger
said, unable to keep her glance from passing over Kron's empty
desk for the third time in only two minutes.

Buchanan caught her looking toward Kron's area and smiled to himself. "You know... maybe I could get someone to escort you to lunch since I won't be able to make it. Would you mind?"

Ginger shrugged. "That's fine, but you don't have to."

Buchanan took out his communicator and tapped out a message on it, before sliding it back into his pocket. "There we go. All taken care of. In just a minute somebody will be here to take you to lunch."

Ginger nodded and fell into the chair across from her daddy. "Have you heard from Kron? Is everything okay out at Kol's?"

"Yeah, yeah I have. Everything's good for the most part. So, you got any plans coming up this week?" he asked.

"Not really," Ginger answered. "Just the usual."

"Nothing with any of those boys that have been hanging around?" Buchanan asked.

"No!" Ginger insisted. "Momma keeps trying to push me into spending time with them, but I'm just not interested. She's upset, and I'm sorry for that, but I don't want to go out with any of them. We don't have much in common, they're very condescending, and I've already set my sights elsewhere."

"So, Kron's it then?" Buchanan asked.

Ginger's gaze wandered over toward Kron's desk again before she looked down at her hands folded across her lap. "He is. I can't seem to stop thinking about him."

"Then why aren't you happier?" Buchanan asked.

"I thought I'd be going out with Kron, spending more time with him, but he's busy, he's got responsibilities, so I'll most likely just spend my time studying. You sure he's okay?" she asked, bringing the conversation back around to Kron.

"He's fine. Don't worry about him," Buchanan said. "Listen, I want to talk to you about your mother and her plans. Don't let your mother marry you off. It's obvious you're not wanting to marry whoever it is she's picked out. Baby, this is your life, not hers. Don't let her make your choices. You need to remember how you feel when you're with somebody that makes you think

79

about forever. You felt that before. I've seen it on your face. Kron does that for you. And he cares about you, too."

"I'm not marrying anyone she shoves at me. And I'm trying to deal with her, Daddy. She's just so full of hate, and so manipulative. Doesn't matter what I want, it's all about what she sees for me. She's so..."

"High-strung," Buchanan said.

"What?" Ginger asked, wearing a slight smile.

"That's what I call it. High-strung. Ever since we've started building ourselves back from the devastation our planet faced, your mother's family has been of a certain mind. I don't agree with them at all."

"It's hard to make her understand that people aren't bad just because they don't look like us. Sometimes I resent her — a lot," Ginger admitted. "I get so tired of hearing her cut down everyone that's the slightest bit different from us. It's exhausting. Sometimes it's just easier to let her ramble on. She just drives me crazy with her preaching."

"Yeah, me too. But don't get me wrong, I've loved your mother most of my life. Married her even though we have different opinions on some things because I couldn't imagine building a life without her. But as we've gotten older, she's gotten more zealous in the beliefs her family raised her in, instead of more relaxed and accepting. Don't let her influence your decision on who and what you want for your life. It's your life, baby. Choose with your heart, not hers," Buchanan said. "I don't care who it is that makes you happy as long as he's good to you. Luckily, he happens to be someone I think highly of."

Ginger smiled as she thought of Kron. Then that smile faded as she thought about her mother. "I just don't want to hurt her. And honestly, no matter who I choose, she won't be happy unless they're as close minded as she is."

"That's why you have to choose for you, not for her. Kron won't let you be unhappy for long. He'll have you laughing in no time."

Immediately her face lit up. "I think of Kron all the time. And we talked about the future being a possibility eventually.

And I say eventually because I get the impression he's not quite ready yet. Besides, I haven't heard from him since we had dinner with Kol and his wife. I don't want to push the issue. If he wants to see me, he'll make the effort once he has time."

The door behind her opened, and before she could turn to look, she heard a voice that sent shivers down her spine.

"What is so important, Buchanan?" Kron asked, walking into the office.

"Kron!" Buchanan said. "Ginger came by to have lunch, and I'm just too swamped to stop and eat. I thought since ya'll enjoy each other's company so much, and already have that special bond, I'd see if you want to take her to lunch instead of me."

Kron shook his head slightly and smiled at Buchanan's machinations. He knew Buchanan had invited her here and had no intentions of eating lunch with her at all. This was his way of getting Kron and Ginger sitting across from one another again.

"You remember, I told you she might be coming by for lunch today," Buchanan said, grinning ear-to-ear.

"Yes, I remember," Kron said, covering for Buchanan. "Hello, Ginger," he said.

"Hi, Kron," Ginger said, beaming a megawatt smile in his direction. His silky white hair was tied up out of his way, and the jumpsuit he wore was covered in just as much grease as his face and hands. And he might have looked sexier than she'd ever seen him look — it was so hard to tell — he was always sexy to her.

Kron lost himself momentarily as he admired Ginger's beauty. My gods I love this woman, he thought to himself.

"Kron?!" Buchanan called out.

"What?" Kron asked, jarred out his reverie as he turned to Buchanan.

"I said, do you mind taking Ginger to lunch today?" Buchanan asked, his tone one of insistence instead of inquiry.

"Oh, I uh, I was in the middle of reconditioning some machinery. But if you don't mind waiting for a little while, I'll be happy to take you," Kron said, looking from Buchanan to Ginger. He hesitated only because it was already past lunchtime, and he had a couple of hours of work to finish before he'd planned to eat.

Ginger's smile had fallen. She'd seen his hesitation and thought he just had too much to do to carve out a little time for her. She reminded herself that her father's job was the same... work always came first. "It's okay. I know it's an interruption of your day. I'm a big girl. I can feed myself," she said, trying to make light of the situation.

"I would like to feed you," Kron insisted, taking a step closer. "If you have the time to allow me to finish my work, then clean up, I would be honored to share a meal with you."

"Are you sure? I don't want to impose," Ginger said.

"I am sure," Kron answered. "You could never impose on me," he said softly looking down into her eyes.

"I can take her," Zhuxi said, ending a conference call he'd been on and walking around his desk at the other side of the room to go stand nearer to Buchanan. "Or, I can have one of my men take her. They are all quite taken with your Ginger when she visits. Zrakad?" Zhuxi called out to one of the soldiers who was standing just outside the opened door talking to another in the hallway.

"Yes, Patroon?" Zrakad asked, stepping inside the office.

"Escort Viceroy Buchanan's daughter to lunch this day. He has become detained with unavoidable work," Zhuxi said.

"Of course," Zrakad said, smiling as he performed a little bow, his gaze glued to Ginger's body.

"No!" Kron insisted forcefully. "I said I would escort her!"

Zhuxi grinned at Buchanan. Buchanan winked at Zhuxi, then focused on Kron. "It's all good. He'll just keep her company while you get cleaned up."

"No, he will not. Ginger," Kron said, his face not giving away the affront he felt at Zrakad trying to step into his place and escort Ginger anywhere, "will you please accompany me? I have a few things to finish up first, then I'll change quickly and we will share our meal. We have much to discuss."

He held his muscular arm and hand out to her, then looked down at his hand and realized it was covered in black grease. He pulled his arm back in, then gestured toward the door.

"I'd love to," Ginger said, walking toward him.

"I promise I will not be long," Kron said.

"It doesn't matter. I'm happy to just tag along for a while," Ginger said.

"Let me know if you get hung up, Kron. We can send Zrakad to take your place!" Buchanan called out pleasantly.

Kron waited at the door for Ginger to walk past him, then he shot a glare toward Buchanan. "You know she will accept no other!"

"You better hurry, others are interested," Buchanan teased.

"Stop it!" Kron snapped, before he reached out and closed the door behind himself and Ginger just a bit too hard.

Zhuxi, Buchanan, and Zrakad all shared a look, then laughed. They knew exactly what they were doing.

~~~

Ginger walked along beside Kron, a gentle smile on her face.

"My apologies for having to ask you to wait while I complete my task," Kron said.

"I don't mind," she said. "I've thought of you. Wondered if things were going well at Kol's home."

"Things are quiet for now. I was there until this morning, then we decided it was best if I came back to base to support those covering for me here. I was simply waiting while at Kol's. He's got plenty of males there to wait with him."

"Good. I hope it turns out to be a false alarm," she said.

"Unfortunately, I don't think it is. There are many who do not want us here. They think anyone from another planet is a threat to them and their way of life. Even those of us sent here to insure your way of life is maintained," Kron said.

"People like that make me very angry. Instead of looking at the heart and the soul beneath the flesh, they look at the flesh," Ginger said.

"I am pleased to hear you say that," Kron said.

"My mother would be outraged to hear me say that. But, I'm not as structured as you'd think," she said.

"Why would I think you structured?" Kron asked.

"My family. They hold themselves to a certain status. I'm a bit more relaxed."

"That is a good thing, I think," Kron said.

"Me, too. My father doesn't seem to mind. His standards are more about success and happiness in life, both personally and professionally. But my mother's status is unbelievable. She thinks if you have a different opinion than she does, you are disrespecting her. She has trouble with my plans for my life. She just cannot seem to accept that I'm not like her and her side of the family," Ginger said. "That I want different things for myself."

"I'm sure she loves you just the same," Kron said. "While she may have her faults, she is still your mother, she gave you life."

Ginger shrugged.

"Do you not think so?" Kron asked.

"I suppose. She's just not very supportive. She's from another time, or at least her beliefs are. She thinks every woman is only as good as the man she stands behind. She has a hard time understanding that I don't agree. I want to make my own way, then marry for love, not position, not because of what my husband does. I don't plan to stand behind anyone. But standing beside someone who holds my whole heart is definitely in the plans."

"And what is it that you want to do?" Kron asked. "Other than stand beside your male."

Ginger flashed him a smile at his teasing tone. "I'm almost finished with school. In fact, I'm waiting to be assigned to my residency."

"Residency?" Kron asked.

Ginger nodded excitedly. "I've finished all my general studies in veterinary science. And I'm done with all my clinicals. I only have to finish my residency, and I'll be a veterinarian."

Kron thought about it as he pushed open the exterior door and held it as Ginger walked through. "The study of animals, yes?" he asked.

"Yes! I'll be able to take care of all kinds of animals. I could open a private practice and work out of there, but I'll need to get a good residency assignment to be able to do what I truly want."

"And that is?" Kron asked.

"Exotic animals. I'm hoping to work with zoos. Some of my classmates specialized in small animal care, others in large animals, but I wanted to go into exotic animal care. That's why it's taking me a little longer, I specialized in small animal applications, then went back and specialized in large animal applications as well. Then I spent some time studying exotic animals and the unique issues that can arise. Daddy didn't mind, but it drives my mother insane. She thinks I should stay home and keep a perfect house for the perfect human diplomat husband with the perfect children, presenting the perfect picture at all times."

Kron came to a stop before a big piece of machinery that had obviously been taken apart. "Exotic, like tigers, camels, primates, shralers and the like."

"Yes, but, what is a shraler?" she asked, intrigued there was an animal she'd not ever heard of.

Kron grinned. "You would love the shraler. They are like the cats of Earth, but much, much larger, almost two hundred pounds when fully grown. Some of your larger wild cats resemble it more. The cloud leopard for example has a similar pelt, but the shraler dwarfs it. The shraler is taller, and thicker with a larger head. And they carry a unique defense. They have a barb on their tail. It delivers a sting which induces paralysis, and sometimes even death if they are angry enough. Our Sirena has made a pet of one. She treats it like a favored child and it in turn would kill for her if asked to." He paused to think about it.

"Actually, it has and it was not asked to. But it was defending her when she was stolen from our Sire."

"That's fascinating. I'm just in awe of everything you've seen. I would love to learn about animals of other planets. It's unlikely I'll ever get a chance to leave Earth, though. I'm sure my mother would sabotage any effort I made, and I'm not sure my father would be very accepting of the idea either."

"I think that it's your life, and you should live it to the fullest, taking every chance to reach your dreams."

"That's a bit different than the usual honor your parents and customs expect from you."

"I have had much to think about. Some of my views have changed, slightly at least," Kron said.

"Thank you, Kron," Ginger said, smiling at him brightly. "I appreciate that."

"I think that you will be successful in all things you undertake," he said, smiling at her.

"That means a lot to me," Ginger said.

Kron smiled at her as he wiped his hands on a towel, then tucked it into his back pocket. "You said you would likely never leave Earth… what if your male left Earth?"

"I suppose it would depend on how long he was going to be gone, and what he was going to do. I wouldn't want to be dumped somewhere without anyone I knew for an extended period." Then she shrugged. "Just depends on the situation."

Kron nodded. She didn't know anyone aboard Command Warship 1, but there were several human mates there, so maybe she wouldn't feel so alone if he had to be called away for a short time.

"What did you want to speak to me about? You said we have to discuss something."

Kron continued tinkering on the machinery in front of him. "I wanted to speak to you about the conversations we had at Kol's house."

"Okay," she said, her adrenalin beginning to pump. She was pretty sure he was going to tell her that he was just caught up in the moment, and felt they weren't truly suited to one another.

"It is important to me that you understand my intentions," Kron said, removing the tool from the piece he was reattaching, and looking toward her.

"Have your intentions changed?" she asked.

"They have not. I plan to claim you. To make you my bonded mate."

Ginger smiled, unable to even consider not smiling as he finished what he was saying.

"But it is not something that will happen overnight. It will take time. I don't believe it's fair to rush you into a life changing occurrence without making sure you understand all the effects that will follow."

"Are you still worried about my mother's approval of you, of us?" she asked.

"Not as much as you would think. But, as she is your mother, it is always a slight concern. In short, I just want to progress slowly, I don't want to look back and think we should have done things differently."

"You're just not ready," she said.

"To claim you? I was ready the moment I saw you, but there are reasons to enjoy this time as we learn about one another," Kron said.

"If you have reservations about my mother, you can't let that influence you," Ginger said. "I have my own reservations about my mother."

Kron chuckled. "It is not only that."

"Then what is it?" she asked.

"It is our way to be sure that we fully know one another. That we are accepting of each other's likes and dislikes. That we are understanding of their life choices, things that will take their attention from us from time to time."

"You want to make sure we're compatible," Ginger said. "That's smart."

"Yes, and it is. Because there is no dissolution of a bond among my people. Even with the very few who are unhappy, they do not let go of their mates. We do not dissolve bonded matings due to unhappiness. Any bond is forever. I would not wish you to be unhappy, nor myself."

"Not that I would be, but, what do they do if they're unhappy? Do they just stay together?" she asked.

"Not all of them. Some leave their mates, returning to their childhood communities, or their native planet. But, the mate they leave behind often spends the rest of their life alone. They are not together, but they are still bound. If you have claimed your true life mate, and they choose to live apart from you, it is practically unheard of to claim another. Your original bond is never broken."

"That's so sad," she said.

"It can be, but it is glorious if you make the right choices and take your time to ensure that you are both accepting of a life bond with each other," Kron said.

"Are the Cruestaci all warriors?" she asked.

"Yes, for the most part, the Cruestaci are. But, those I originate from are not a materialistically wealthy people. They are simple in their ways. Farmers and tradesmen for the most part. But they are happy. I chose a different path. I joined the Cruestaci military, and achieved the status of Elite Warrior. My life is drastically different from those of my family. But all those who matter to me would welcome you unconditionally because you hold my heart, be they my original family, or the Cruestaci. That is what I hope to gain from not only your father, but from your mother as well."

"My father's given you his approval?" she asked.

"He has. And you have as well. Hopefully, your mother will as well, if not, we cannot allow it to hold our future in check. That is, if you are still agreeable," Kron said.

"I don't want you to be disappointed," Ginger began, "but I don't see any chance of that happening."

"You have changed your mind?" Kron asked, dropping his wrench as his chest began to tighten with the immediate anxiety he felt at thinking she was rejecting him.

"No! No, I have not, I will not! But, my mother will never change her way of thinking. She will forever be an angry, bitter, close-minded, prejudiced woman who will miss out on so much in life because she can't see around her own hateful opinions."

Kron understood what she was saying, and if that was how it turned out, so be it, but he wanted to try at least a little while longer. "I would still like to try to befriend her, win her approval," he said.

Ginger stood there for an uncomfortable few minutes, gazing into Kron's eyes, trying to determine if that was a good idea or not. Finally she shrugged. "If it means that much to you, go ahead. But please, do not take her responses as mine. My heart wants the same thing you do. Don't let her change your mind about us. She will not ever be your friend, and she will not ever accept us as a couple. I, on the other hand, find I'm having a hard time waiting for the day we are officially bound."

Kron grinned. "Us," he said.

Ginger smiled at him. "Us," she repeated.

"There is an us," he said.

"There is," she confirmed.

"When we look back, this time taken before I finalize my claim will seem to have moved past very quickly," Kron said.

Ginger smiled at him and nodded, but she wasn't so sure.

Neither seemed to know what to say next, so Ginger changed the subject.

"So, what are we fixing here?" she asked.

"It is a stump grinder," Kron said.

"It's huge! I thought it was a tractor of some sort," Ginger said.

Kron nodded looking at the big, orange piece of equipment. "It is somewhat obsolete. We could easily point a blaster at the stumps I wish to remove and they'd be gone. But, I enjoy the satisfaction of hard work. I prefer to do things the old fashioned hands-on way in some instances."

"I can understand that," Ginger said, reaching out to place her hand on the dirty, orange stump grinder. "What stumps are you grinding?" she asked.

"There are some out near the perimeter fences. The trees were removed to keep the fence line clear and easily viewable.

89

The wood of the trees was harvested rather than going to waste, and that is what I use in my shop, but some of the larger stumps are still there. I thought if I could get it working, I might use it to remove them."

"Only thing is… if you grind the stumps, you can't use them for anything else," Ginger said.

"What else would I use them for?" Kron asked.

"You could make a table, or a chair, or benches or something. If you grind them up, they're just sawdust," Ginger said.

"I hadn't thought of making anything quite so large," Kron said. "I suppose I could."

"Useful, and beautiful," Ginger said. "I love the look of polished wood."

"Perhaps we could make something together," Kron suggested.

Ginger had been looking at the grinder, but she looked up at him suddenly. "Really? I'd like that!"

"As would I," Kron said. "It is a plan. I'll put this back together, and move it back to the shed. Then, we'll eat, and go look at the remaining stumps. We'll choose the one we wish to work with."

Chapter 9

The next hour and a half was spent getting to know one another even more as they reassembled the stump grinder.

"Put your hand right here," Kron said, looking down into the gear case of the grinder.

"Here?" she asked, reaching in to put pressure against a gear he was holding.

"Yes. Exactly. Give me just a moment and I'll bolt it in place," Kron said.

Ginger leaned into the large piece of machinery to get a better hold on the gear Kron wanted her to hold steady. She'd been helping him for the better part of the afternoon, and was thoroughly enjoying herself.

He approached with a drill in hand and paused for a moment to admire the smile she beamed his way. "A very beautiful gift," he said, returning her smile.

"What is?" Ginger asked.

"That smile. It is spectacular. Even more brilliant than any star I've ever seen," Kron complimented before reaching into the gear case and tightening the bolts that would hold the piece Ginger was holding in place.

"Can't help it. You make me smile," Ginger said, letting go of the piece once she felt it was secured to the housing.

"Do I?" Kron asked.

"You do. Every time I think of you, I smile. Even more so when I'm with you," Ginger admitted.

Kron set the drill on top of the grinder and gently turned her face back toward him. "And you make me smile."

Ginger looked up at Kron, her smile faltering. "So, you feel it, too? As strongly as I do?" she asked.

"I do," he answered. "It is the mate bond, pulling us toward one another."

"Would you want me anyway, if there was no bond?" she asked, not willing to look him in the eye.

"I cannot look away from you. I've never seen a more beautiful female. You have me, heart and soul, mate bond or not. I am yours," Kron whispered.

That did it. She turned her blue eyes up toward his and the brilliant smile she'd gifted him with only moments before was back.

"And there's my gift again," he murmured, stopping just an inch away from pressing his lips to hers.

Ginger blushed as she looked into Kron's eyes, and he into hers. She thought he might kiss her, but instead he simply stroked his thumb across her cheek a time or two before stepping back and pulling the cover on the gear case down. "I think that's it. It should be as good as new," Kron said.

"Want to test it?" Ginger asked.

Kron shook his head, sending his silky, straight, shoulder-length, white hair falling from its tie and shimmering about his shoulders and head. "No, I will test it later. Let us go choose the stumps you think will make the best chairs."

"Okay," Ginger said, smiling excitedly.

"We will take lunch with us, and enjoy it outside," Kron said, "if you are agreeable."

"I'd love that. I haven't had a picnic in ages."

Before setting out to choose a tree stump to work with, they went to the commissary and put together the makings of a lunch and had it bagged for them, then left the base, heading for the perimeter.

As they began their walk toward the perimeter fencing, Kron looked down at Ginger walking at his side and extended his hand to brush against hers. She looked up at him right away, then at their hands, and slipped her hand into his, though he was now facing forward.

Both smiled, excited at the fact that there was no more question, they belonged to each other, and would be together forever. It was just a matter of time before it was made official.

They chose the biggest stump to spread their lunch out on and enjoyed a small, but tasty lunch as they told each other stories of their childhoods. Kron left out the part about the reason he joined the Cruestaci being so that he could search for his sister who'd been kidnapped and send money back to his mother at the same time since their father had died when he was just a boy. He didn't want anything to mar their afternoon and it was not a pleasant story to tell, though she had been found. They spent hours just talking. Afterward, as they picked up the leftovers of their lunch, Ginger brushed her hand across the top of the stump. "You see? The wood grain, the growth circles. This would be a beautiful table. And it would certainly be big enough."

Kron stood back and looked at the stump. "You are right. We could shape it and seal it, and it would be very beautiful."

"And that one... we could make a chair from, kind of barrel shaped, just smoothing it out and cutting a seat into this part," she said, walking over to it and demonstrating with her hands where to make the cuts.

"Yes, and another from that one beyond it," Kron said.

Ginger walked over to a fallen tree that had been harvested but never processed. It had just been left where it fell. "I wonder why they didn't use this one," Ginger said.

"It was not straight," Kron said. "Look, see there where it sways to the left and then the right?"

"I do. It's a shame they cut it down for nothing," Ginger said.

"I have thought the same when I'm looking for smaller pieces of wood to use in my workshop. Let me think about it. Perhaps I'll find a way to use it," Kron said.

"I'd like that," Ginger said. "Maybe a bench or something."

"Maybe," Kron agreed. Having spent most of the day outside, Kron decided it was time to get her back to the base. "Are you ready to return to base?" he asked.

"If we must. It's been such a nice day," Ginger answered.

"It has. But I must return to base to ensure all is well, and prepare to accept duties from Zhuxi. I will be resuming my regular schedule this night."

"Oh, I understand," she said, disappointed to have the day come to an end.

"Perhaps, if you're planning to stay on base for a little longer, if we hurry, I could shower, and you could share an early evening meal with me as well. Lunch wasn't very hearty."

"It was enough, but it's been a couple of hours. I could eat again, if it won't make you late or anything."

"I don't think it will," he assured her. "And I find I don't wish to see you leave."

Ginger smiled. "Let's head in then, so we have a little more time together. Maybe I can find somewhere to clean up a bit, too."

"We have guest facilities that will accommodate you," Kron said.

Half an hour later Ginger and Kron stood outside the door to his quarters. As an upper level officer, he warranted his own quarters, more like a small apartment than anything else. He stood with his back to the door, looking down at Ginger. She had grease smudged on her face, and even a bit of black smeared along a strand of her glorious hair. Her hands were as dirty as his and she smiled up at him happily.

"I should have offered a place to cleanse before our walk to share lunch outside. You have grease all over you," Kron said.

"It's fine. I had fun!" she said.

"But now you are as dirty as I usually am," he said.

"I can clean up. It won't take a minute," Ginger said.

"Come. I will escort you to guest quarters so that you may cleanse."

"Why can't I just clean up here?" she asked.

"I would invite you into my quarters to do so, but it is improper. I don't wish to offend you, your family or your family name," Kron said.

"Improper?" Ginger asked. "For who?"

"An unmated female, in the quarters of an unmated male, is frowned upon. If observed, it could damage your reputation. Certainly, your family would demand retribution," Kron said.

Ginger smirked up at him. "Seriously?"

"Of course. I am very aware that you have been placed in my care for the day. Your father has placed his trust in me," Kron said.

Ginger looked at the door behind him, then back up at him, meeting his gaze. "Kron, did you, or did you not say you plan to claim me as yours?"

"You know that I do. We are moving toward that end. I am concerned about not compromising you. I wouldn't want others to question our actions. Anyone could see you entering my quarters alone with me and assume that we are more intimate than we should be."

Ginger thought about it. Maybe he didn't want to be seen with her alone in his quarters because he wasn't so sure of his wants after all. Or maybe he was even having a fling with someone else and hadn't told them it was over yet. He never had any shortage of attention no matter where he went. "I'm sorry. I thought we both wanted the same thing. Maybe I misunderstood."

"You did not misunderstand," Kron said.

"Then what? Is there someone else who doesn't know about me yet?" she asked.

"Absolutely not. And if there had been, the moment I laid eyes on you, it would have come to an end," he answered right away.

"Then, move," Ginger said, reaching out and pushing him aside.

"But..." Kron said, watching as she tried to open his door.

Ginger turned the doorknob but it wouldn't open. "Open the door," Ginger said, looking toward him.

"Ginger..." Kron said, trying to explain about his concerns once more.

"It's okay. I understand," she said, only willing to push so much for what she wanted. She took a step back. "You just don't want me in your quarters alone. It's not a big deal. I'll go ask my father where I can clean up," she said, turning and walking away from him and trying not to let the fact that he didn't want to let her into his private space hurt her feelings.

"What do you understand?" Kron asked, his voice calling after her.

Ginger turned to look at him, still standing outside his closed door watching her go. "That you don't want to allow me into your private quarters. You're only willing to let me know so much. Maybe if you can ever gain my mother's approval you won't be so hesitant to let me into all areas of your life. Or maybe you'll just decide it's not worth the effort and go back to wherever you came from. Because you obviously refuse to accept that we're not on your world, we're on mine. I respect your customs, I do. But keeping me at arms length only makes me question your commitment. In fact, I think I've changed my mind about dinner. I just want to go home now. Thank you for the afternoon," she said, turning her back and walking away from him.

Suddenly Ginger was gasping as she was caught up in strong arms and carried back to Kron's door.

"You don't understand — not at all," he said, as he used his key to unlock the door with one hand while balancing her against his body with the other.

Ginger turned her head and looked him in the eye, only a couple of inches from his face as he held her up off the floor and against himself. "Then help me understand."

Kron stepped into his quarters with Ginger in his arms, and kicked the door closed behind them. He looked down at her as he set her on her feet. "Any who see us together in private quarters will think we have been intimate."

"And you're ashamed of that," she said.

"No, I am not," he said with a slight growly quality to his voice. "It is simply not our way to be alone privately with the female we've chosen as mate until we are ready to mate."

"And I'm messing that up for you. I'm sorry," she said, trying to step around him.

"You are not messing anything up. I simply cannot guarantee you will leave my rooms in the same condition you arrived in. The mating instinct is strong. I'm trying to resist you, but it is not easy. There is nothing I'm hiding from you. I am not

96

preventing you from having access to any area of my life. I'm just trying not to tear your clothes from your body and spend the rest of the night claiming you. It is not time yet. There are still things to be discerned and discussed before we take that final step."

Ginger's eyebrows rose in surprise. He wanted her, and badly. "Okay," she answered.

He looked down at her, his chest rising and falling as he fought his desire for her. "Wait here," he said, turning away from her and striding toward his bathroom. "I will be but a moment. Then the cleansing chamber is yours for as long as you like," Kron said.

Ginger turned in time to see Kron close the door to the bathroom, going to take his shower after telling her to wait for him. Slowly she began to smile. They'd discussed their future and the fact that a mating instinct pulled them toward one another. He'd told her he planned to claim her and make her his mate, and she sure as hell planned to accept that claim, and make him her mate. She felt the flutter in her belly as she walked over to his bed and sat down on the edge of it, ideas racing through her head about what could happen, right here and now, if she was just a little bolder. He was fighting to hold himself in check, and she was ready now. In fact, she didn't want to wait until he won over her mother. That would never happen. She chewed on her bottom lip while she worried about what his customs would guilt him into doing if her mother never gave her approval. He might decide to not claim her at all. Then the sound of running water caught her attention, and she imagined what he must look like, naked and standing beneath the water as it coursed down his body.

She thought about Kron all the time. His smile, his voice, his hands... she loved his hands, they were so masculine and strong, yet beautiful and graceful. She wondered what he looked like without his clothes on, and had on more than one occasion thought about removing said clothes to just see what he looked like without them. She smirked to herself. Okay, maybe there was more of a reason than just seeing his body unclothed — she wanted to taste him, feel him. And now, here she sat on his bed, after he'd very clearly said she was the one he planned to mate, and that it was difficult to restrain himself around her. And she'd also made it clear she wanted to be his mate.

Her eyes shot up to his bathroom door when she heard a deep, throaty, moan of pleasure as he stepped under the hot water. A shiver ran through her body as she imagined that sound being made for an entirely different reason. Taking a deep breath to bolster her courage, she stood, toed off her shoes, unzipped her pants and dropped them to the floor, then dropped her panties, shirt and bra on top of them. Completely naked she walked to the bathroom door. She thought she'd be more nervous than she was, but, though exhilarated, she was strangely calm.

Reaching out she turned the doorknob and walked into the steamy bathroom. She stepped over the clothes Kron had left near the hamper in the corner and opened the glass shower door.

Kron turned quickly, looking at her briefly before his eyes traveled down her body and back up. Slowly he shook his head.

She reached up and placed a hand on each side of his head to stop him from shaking his head. "Don't tell me no," Ginger said, her voice breathy and obviously aroused.

Chapter 10

"You don't know what you're doing," Kron said.

Ginger's eyes ran down the length of his body and back up again, pausing at his pulsing cock. Her eyes flared as she took in all the unusual details he packed there. It was ridged, but each ridge was wavy and irregular. The crown of his cock was sheathed, but the head peeking out of its sheath was almost an orangey color compared to the pale yellow of the rest of his skin. There was a small fleshy protrusion on the shaft of his cock, on the top, just at the place where it met his body, and his testicles were nowhere to be seen.

She looked back up at him, her mouth parted slightly as she licked her lips. "I know exactly what I'm doing."

"You do not. You have been sheltered and…"

"I'm not as sheltered as you might think, Kron," she said, nibbling on her bottom lip as she admired his body. "I'm not quite as inexperienced as my mother, and father for that matter, would like to believe."

He shook his head again. "It isn't simply sex. It can't be undone. You will be changed and you will be tied to me forever."

"You're telling me you never have sex just because you want it?" she asked.

"Of course I do, did," he said, stepping back as she stepped into the shower with him.

"Then what's the problem?" she asked as she reached out and stroked his cock.

A soft snarl left his throat as she forced back his foreskin exposing the head of his cock, then ran her fingers over it.

"Sex with you won't be just sex. You're my mate. If I take you, it is forever. You will not be able to be free of me. Not ever," Kron rumbled. "We need more time, we discussed the reasons."

Ginger let go of him and ran her hands up his chest. "We did. And I understand everything you said. There is no way to break a bond. We are one, forever, after this. No matter what happens, I am yours, and you are mine."

"I will never let you go, it could become troublesome to you if..." he tried to explain.

"It sounds like a problem I'd like to have. I've wanted you since the first time I ever saw you, Kron. I haven't wanted anyone else since. We've talked about you claiming me, and I'm sure that I want to be claimed by you. You fill my every thought. You are what I want my future to be. I've considered all I need to."

"You know nothing of me, or my people," Kron said, allowing her to pull his head down to her level and press her lips to his. He moaned as the tip of her tongue traced his lips. "It will change you, change me."

"I don't care. I'm tired of waiting. I know what I want, I know who I want. And I know the important things. I know I admire you. I know I think you're the most beautiful male I've ever seen. I know you're honorable. I know you want the things I want for myself so that I'll be happy. I know you're selfless in considering my needs before your own. I know you're afraid I'll allow you to claim me, then leave you alone. But I know something you don't."

"What's that?" he asked, his eyes drifting closed as his own tongue slipped into her mouth and he kissed her deeply. When their mouths finally separated, she leaned toward him again as he spoke. "What do you know?"

"That I won't ever leave you. I choose you, Kron. I want you."

"I want you, too. But we should stop. There is still so much you don't know. We cannot just have sex, we will be bound," Kron said, not even realizing he was backing her up against the shower wall as he lowered his mouth to taste her lips, to steal more of her kisses.

"Then what are you doing?" she asked.

"Tasting," he answered as his mouth covered hers and he closed his eyes.

Ginger kissed him back eagerly, holding him tightly as he pulled her body against his own.

Kron stopped kissing her suddenly and looked down at himself.

"What is it?" she asked, looking down as well.

Kron reached down with one hand, cupping his testicles.

"They weren't there before," Ginger said in awe.

"They were. But they only descend when we prepare to mate our female. MATE our female" he repeated forcefully, "not have sex. This cannot be undone!"

"Where are they until then?" she asked, preoccupied with the changes to his body as she reached down, replacing his hand with her own as she kneaded them gently.

Kron's lips pulled back and his fangs were easily seen as he closed his eyes and a snarl filled the shower. The more she played with his balls, the louder the snarl got. When she stopped rolling them in her hand, he opened his eyes and looked at her.

"Where were they?" she asked.

"Inside, safe from injury during battle. They only descend for cleansing, or mating with our one female."

"So, when you were with anyone else, they stayed hidden," she said.

"Yes. It only confirms what I already knew," Kron answered.

"And that is," Ginger said, squeezing them slightly before moving her hand up the length of his thick shaft again.

"You are mine," he said.

Ginger looked up at Kron and smiled at him before returning her attention to all the fun new distractions she'd found on his body. She ran her thumb over the small protrusion and it became firmer.

"Oh my God, I can just imagine the added stimulation this will give," she said, looking up at him as he rolled his hips in response to all her exploration of his body.

Kron's chest rumbled as he moved his hands to her head, his thumbs under her jaw, his fingers under her ears and along the sides of her head and neck as he held her still while he kissed her.

"Why are you waiting?" she finally asked as he lifted his mouth from hers.

"Giving you time to leave," he said, as his eyes closed again while she began to stroke him.

"I'm not leaving," she said.

"If you don't go now, you will never be allowed to go. I am trying to be honorable. I am trying to consider you and all that matters to you. But if you don't go now, I will never let you go, Ginger. You may beg and plead but I'll never let you go."

Ginger smiled up at him. "I'll never beg and plead for anything but to be at your side."

"Your family..." he said, doing his damnedest to do the right thing.

"Will know I want you, I belong with you."

"You didn't say love," Kron said. "Do you not feel love?"

"If it's not love, I don't know what it is. I've never, ever, been so fascinated by a male in my entire life."

Kron looked down into the eyes of the woman he'd willingly die for. She was all he'd ever hoped for and so much more. But she wasn't ready. He knew she had dreams and plans for her future. And those things couldn't be achieved if she was bound to him, with him as he went about his life instead of here on Earth where she needed to be to reach her goals.

"Your future," he said, one last ditch effort to give her the opportunity to walk away. "I am not staying on Earth."

"There are animals where you come from, too. We'll work it out," she promised, then dropped to her knees and took him into her mouth.

"Fuuck!" he shouted, using his favorite human curse word, and fell back against the shower wall, as she took almost all of him into her mouth and throat, using her head and hands to bring him more pleasure than he'd ever even known existed.

Kron looked down at the female pleasuring him and lost all reasonable thought. His instincts took over. This was the female he'd waited for all his adult life. He rocked his hips as she became intimately familiar with all parts of his anatomy. Then he slid his hands down her arms and to the sides of her face, forcing her mouth to release him and her eyes to look up at him.

When she looked at him with her eyes hooded from arousal, her body primed and ready for him, he didn't think. He simply leaned over, picked her up into his arms, and walked out of the shower, leaving it running as he took them both dripping wet to his bed. He laid her out on the bed and simply admired her while she spread her legs for him.

"I want you, Kron," she said.

Kron gave her a single nod. "I will give you anything," he promised, then crawled on the bed with her, pausing at the juncture of her legs to lap at her most private parts.

"Oh!" she cried out, placing her hands behind his head to hold him there.

Kron smiled to himself and settled between her legs, tasting her, teasing her, getting lost in all that was his and only his. It was only a few minutes before he became painfully aware of his need to be inside her. He lifted his mouth from her and met her questioning gaze. "I need to claim you," he said. "I hurt," he growled.

"Yes!" she answered, rocking her hips and reaching for him.

Kron lifted himself on hands and knees and crawled up her body. He nestled his lower body between Ginger's legs and looked down at her, his female, his mate, as she looked up at him, her hands resting on his biceps, waiting for him to push inside her body and make her his.

"Without end," he whispered, waiting for confirmation.

"Without end," she repeated.

Moving one knee closer to her bottom, he aligned his cock with her swollen opening and pushed inside. With every inch he growled, but kept pushing, not letting up for even a second.

"Oh, my God!" Ginger said, her body feeling every groove, every ridge as he pushed inside her.

103

Kron adjusted his weight, then slipped a hand under her, holding her at just the right angle until the protrusion she'd felt earlier rubbed against her clit, then when he felt her press herself against him firmly, maintaining contact he began to stroke into her.

Ginger's eyes rounded and her mouth fell open as Kron started thrusting into her. It didn't matter how hard, or fast, or deep he thrust, he always brought that protrusion back to torment her so sweetly.

Ginger looked up at Kron. He seemed to be lost, his eyes closed, his hips pounding against her inner thighs as his entire body was focused on nothing but giving her pleasure. Then she felt something else, deep inside her as his cock began to swell, and the head seemed to almost tremble inside her.

"Kron?" she asked, her fingers sinking into the skin of his biceps.

Kron looked down at her. "My body is claiming yours. You are mine, Ginger. Only mine. I will kill any other who thinks to take what is mine." Then he increased his speed and moments later she was doing her best to hold in her screams as her keening filled the room while her body began to shake and tense up. He smiled as her body reached its plateau and began to orgasm while he continued to force his swelling cock into her tightly squeezing channel. Then he felt an unfamiliar sensation at the base of his spine and similar sensation simultaneously at the tip of his cock. He knew what it was. All males of his race were taught what to expect when they finally found their one. His body was going to implant his DNA inside her, the way all the males of his race did, and absorb some of hers into his own body. She would forever be one with him. He leaned over and whispered in her ear. "Don't pull away."

Then he slammed into her as deeply as he could one last time before he felt it. The head of his cock anchored itself deep inside her, tiny spines extending from around the crown of his cock to sink into her still sensitive flesh and prevent her from getting away as his body began to make her one with his. Some of the spines were taking a bit of her DNA to mix with his, some were depositing his DNA inside her flesh. But all stayed anchored in place until Kron and Ginger were bound to each other irrevocably, they would forever be a part of each other, no matter where they were.

Ginger held on to Kron, unable to think clearly, she was nothing but a trembling lump of flesh, anxious to see what this fantastic male had to give her next. His whisper to not pull away was the only warning she got before he slammed into her one last time. She didn't look at him, her eyes were closed as she rode out her orgasm, but she did nod her head to let him know she heard and she understood. Kron held her tight as she felt tiny pleasure-pain pricks deep inside her body.

"What's happening?" she asked, unable to keep her body from squeezing around him. The result was the same sensation as when you itch and finally scratch it, but then keep scratching it too much and you're not sure if it hurts or feels good, but you just can't stop.

"Shhh, Leerah," he said. Then he clenched his teeth as his balls emptied, filling her with his seed, as his mating spines, secured deep inside her, tweaked the very cells of their bodies, making them truly a part of one another.

A moment later he felt the spines retract and he rolled to the side, taking her with him. Kron smoothed a hand over her still wet hair, pushing it back off her face and pressed his lips to her forehead.

Ginger relaxed in his arms and allowed herself to relish all his adoring petting.

"Are you well?" he asked, kissing her forehead again.

"Mmhmm. You?" she asked.

"I am very well," he answered.

"So, this means it's just us, now? We belong to each other," she asked.

"It does," he said, stroking his hand across her back as she lay on her side in his arms, her front to his front.

105

"I've wanted this for so long," she whispered. "I hope you're not disappointed."

"My concerns were only for you," he said, "you made it clear that you had already chosen. If you are not disappointed, then I am not disappointed."

"Not at all. And we'll figure out all the rest as we do," she said. Then she became quiet and still. He thought she was sleeping and let his eyes fall closed, too.

Then she asked about something he'd said. "What is Leerah?"

He smiled to himself. "There is no direct translation. It means... my love, my world. My one. Like the Cruestaci word, Ehlealah, but not quite. We do not know our mates instinctively on sight as the Cruestaci do. We may be drawn to them, but it is up to us to heed the mating call, or leave before it gets too strong to ignore."

"You could have walked away from me, but you stayed?" Ginger asked.

"In my case I could never leave you. Even if I'd tried, I would have returned even more determined to make you mine."

Ginger smiled with her eyes still closed as she rested in Kron's arms. "What are we?" she finally asked.

"Cruestaci after swearing my allegiance, but I was born on a different planet. I am by birth Pelarian.

Ginger raised her face to look at him. "Pelarian?" she asked.

"Yes," he answered simply.

"I'm proud to be Pelarian, and Cruestaci, as you are."

"I am proud of you, Leerah. And I can now claim humanity as part of my blood as well, because my mate is human by birth."

Ginger smiled at the word Leerah, she was becoming quite fond of it. Then she remembered what it meant, and the emotion he used when saying it. She lifted her head and looked at him with a silly grin on her face. "You love me?"

"Without end," he said, smiling at her as he looked into her beautiful bright yellow eyes.

"What are you smiling at?" she asked.

"You. I can see me in you."

"What do you mean?" she asked.

"I claimed you, marked you as my female, you will always be identified as part of me, as I will be part of you."

Ginger looked at him with a confused expression.

"It is all new to you, Leerah. You will see soon enough."

She smiled slightly and decided to wait and figure it all out as it came to her. She pressed her lips to Kron's one more time before lying back down in his arms. "I'm happy, Kron. Truly happy. I don't think I've ever felt the things I'm feeling now."

"Nor have I. I will always make you happy, as much as I can, Ginger."

"And I'll make you happy, too," she said, snuggling into his embrace.

Kron closed his eyes and hoped she meant all she'd said. It wouldn't be that long at all before she began to figure out just exactly what she'd pushed him to, and now that the heady intoxication of the instinct to mate was fading, he was acutely aware that she may not have understood all she'd asked for.

Chapter 11

After a short nap, Ginger began to stir in his arms.

Kron smiled as he continued to stroke her back, her arms, her hair, anywhere he could reach.

"Must have fallen asleep," she murmured, stretching as she still lay against him.

"It is to be expected," he said.

"I'm starving now, want to go get something to eat?" she asked.

"Yes, I'm hungry, too," he said, releasing his hold on her so she could sit up.

"I'll get your clothes," he said, rolling to his other side to get out of bed.

"Mmm," she said, watching him walk into his bathroom.

Kron glanced back over his shoulder, and found her staring at his ass.

"You are very, very sexy," she said, watching her mate walk away.

"You are pleased with my body?" he asked.

"Oh, very much so," she said.

"Good. I am happy I please you. I am even more pleased with you. Your body is everything I thought it would be, and your soul even more beautiful. I am very satisfied with our mating. You are a gift in everything you are, everything you give to me."

Ginger smiled at Kron as he walked into the bathroom, then a few minutes later came back and stopped to pick up her clothes before handing them to her. "Here you are," he said, "I think your clothes are clean. I tried to keep you from becoming too dirty when we were working on the grinder," he said.

"It was mainly just my hands and my face," she agreed as she pulled on her panties and her bra.

Kron watched in awe as her breasts were supported by the lace garment she put on, a rounded cup for each breast, holding them secure and upright. He couldn't help himself, he walked over to her and slipped a hand into the garment, lifting a breast up for his kisses.

"You keep that up and we'll end up staying here, no food," she said, smiling at him.

"We will be back here right after we eat," he promised. "I am not ready to leave here, yet I must feed you." Kron kissed her breast again, then gently placed it back into her bra before walking to his closet to get another of his customary Cruestaci uniforms to put on. "I will ask your father to cover my shift as well this night."

"What do you mean?" she asked.

"Earlier this morning he offered to cover my shift if I wanted to spend some time with you."

"Oh," she said, knowing something about that sounded off, but too tired, and too full of mating hormones to even want to figure it out. Then she realized Kron was getting dressed, and she was missing the show. She sat on the bed after she'd pulled on her clothes, and watched as he donned all the pieces of his uniform. He was very impressive in it, very intimidating, though she'd never felt intimidated by him.

Once he was dressed, he turned around to find Ginger running her fingers through her still damp hair and pulling it back with a hair tie she'd pulled out of the pocket in her pants as she watched him.

"I'm ready," she said, smiling brightly at him.

"So am I," he said, holding out his hand to her.

Ginger walked toward him and held out her hand.

Kron linked their fingers together and led her to the door, opened it, and stepped outside with Ginger at his side.

Ginger waited until he locked his door and then they walked hand in hand toward the commissary.

"Ginger, there is much I fear you still do not understand," he said as they walked together.

"Well, I understand you are mine, and I am yours," she said.

109

"Yes, that is true."

"And it's forever. We're one," she said.

"Yes, but there's more to it," he said.

"Tell me," she encouraged, smiling lovingly up at him as they walked.

"I'd hoped to give you more time to learn of me and my people, our people, now, and to know what it was you were committing to," he said, his tension obvious to her.

"Kron, it doesn't matter. If I'd have waited three months, six months, or even a year, I'd have still chosen you."

"I won't ever let you go, Ginger. I can't," he said.

Ginger smiled and stopped walking, turning to look up at him, and put her hands on his chest. "I won't ever let you go either."

"Ginger, what we just did, we are bound, for all eternity. No matter where I am, or where you are, we are one. We cannot be separated for longer than absolutely necessary. If I'm sent on mission, you cannot be there in battle, so of course you'll be back on the ship, but we cannot be in different worlds."

"I understand that," she said.

"In your culture, it is called marriage. In mine it is called mating. We bind not only our hearts, but our souls, and our bodies."

She looked up at him, surprised but not opposed to what he'd said. "Will we one day get married?" she asked.

"Yes, I would like that very much," Kron said with a smile. "But that wasn't my point."

"Oh," she said, smiling still at the idea of marrying Kron. "What was your point?"

"When we mate, we bond all parts of our existence. I can take on traits of yours, and you can take on traits of mine."

"Like, appearances you mean?" she asked, looking closely at him for the first time since they'd left his quarters.

"For one," he said, looking into the beautiful yellow of her eyes, the same yellow he saw in his each time he looked at his reflection.

Ginger raised a hand and gently touched his cheek as her eyes noticed for the first time he had a small smattering of freckles across his nose and upper cheeks. "I never noticed your freckles before. I love them," she said, smiling brightly.

"I have them because we became one," he said, "and your eyes are…"

"There you two are! I was wondering where you got off to!" Buchanan called out, striding toward them down the hall.

"Daddy!" Ginger said happily, turning and running toward Buchanan.

"Well, aren't you happy?" he said with a chuckle.

Ginger threw herself into her father's arms and hugged him tightly. "I'm so happy, Daddy. I hope you'll be happy for me, too."

"Of course, I will, sugar. But what has you this happy?" he asked, grinning at Kron over her shoulder.

"Kron does. We're mated! Once he knew I was serious, it just seemed to happen, and we're going to get married!" she exclaimed, letting her father go and stepping back so he could see how happy she was.

"You're getting married… that's great news!" he exclaimed, looking happily at his daughter. "In fact, I was hoping you two would get married."

"Me, too!" she admitted, looking back at Kron, then turning to face her father again.

Buchanan's expression changed from a happy one to one of concern. "What the hell happened to your eyes?!" he shouted.

"What?" she asked, her hands flying up to her face and touching her eyelids.

"They're now like mine," Kron said.

"Wait, what?" she asked.

"We are one, we share some traits," he said. "I explained it, was still trying to explain it."

"You turned her eyes yellow?" Buchanan asked incredulously.

"Any trait can be shared. It may have been mine that turned to the same blue she was born with," Kron explained. "It is not within our control."

111

"And what did you get?" Buchanan demanded.

"Freckles," Ginger said softly, blinking her eyes quite rapidly.

"Freckles," Buchanan repeated.

"Yes. He's got freckles now," Ginger said.

Buchanan looked back and forth between Ginger and Kron. Finally he threw his hands up. "Damn it, Kron. I asked you to marry her, not change her!"

"I mated her! Exactly as I was meant to do, and any change that comes upon us is the change that is willed. It makes us one!" Kron answered defensively.

"As you were meant to do?" Ginger whispered.

"But her eyes are yellow!" Buchanan exclaimed.

"As will be the eyes of any children we have! Will you love them any less because they are of my eye color?" Kron asked, offended.

Buchanan slammed his lips together, thinking about what Kron had said. "No. No I won't. I suppose I'll just have to get used to it. But I loved her blue eyes, Kron!" Buchanan insisted.

"As did I," Kron said, "but they are beautiful, still," he said, smiling over at his beloved new mate, who was watching both him and her father with a steadily growing rage evident on her features.

"Ginger?" Kron asked, stepping toward her, realizing all was not good.

"You asked him to marry me?" she asked, her voice deadly calm as she pinned her father with an angry look.

"I did," Buchanan said, standing fearlessly for her to glare at him. "I knew you'd be a good match. I've been pushing for it since I figured out your mother was trying to force you into marrying a damn Purist!"

"And you just went right along with it, hopping in bed with me the first chance I gave you," she said to Kron.

"I tried to wait! But you wanted me as well. I forced nothing on you, Ginger. It is not in my nature to force any female. I tried to take time and remind you of all you needed to consider," Kron hurried to remind her.

"I did. But now I'm wondering what you got out of the deal. My father pushed you to marry his poor, weak, unable to think for herself daughter before she allows herself to be married to a man he despises, but what do you get? Why agree to it?"

"Because you are my mate!" Kron exclaimed.

"I suppose making a political alliance with the daughter of one of the Viceroys of Earth had nothing to do with it," she said.

"It did not!" Kron insisted, his voice becoming growly. "I already told you I am not remaining permanently on Earth, so it would do me no good! I mated you because I've wanted to mate you since the day I first saw you! And the males your mother had chosen would not leave you in peace! Now they have no choice. You are mine!"

Ginger nodded slowly. "Funny how you made no attempt to get to know me until my father asked you to take pity on me and marry his poor helpless daughter."

"Sugar, it's not like that!" Buchanan said.

"It's not?" she asked.

"No, it's not!" both Buchanan and Kron said at the same time.

"So, you two didn't scheme to get me here so that Kron and I could spend time together and hopefully get to know one another? You didn't talk about Kron taking me as his mate?" she asked.

"Sure we did, but it's not like you make it sound. He was concerned about how you'd feel, and the things you want."

Ginger nodded slowly. She felt like a fool. She'd thought what Kron had felt for her was as real as she felt for him, but the whole thing was engineered by him and her own father, of all people.

"Every single time I've been alone with Kron, it was because you arranged it. At that first breakfast you arranged it. You sent him to see me home when you said my transport needed work, which it didn't. At Kol's home, you agreed really quickly to take me to make sure he was alright. And now today, you invited me to lunch then bowed out so Kron could spend the time with me instead."

113

"But he wanted to!" Buchanan insisted. "And my part of it was because I love you. It was for your own good. Your mother kept trying to force those damn Purists on you, and don't bother denying it. I know she did, and I know they're damn Purists, and I wanted you to have a chance at a full life. Every damn time you were alone with one of those bastards, I was afraid you'd give in to please her, and I'd never see you again. Your mother is so blind to all the crap they're feeding her I wouldn't have been surprised to come home and find you gone and her fully okay with it! I wanted you to go places and see things, and choose your mate because you liked him, not because they forced you. And I knew Kron liked you and you liked him. And I think the world of Kron. He's a good male, and you were interested in him, too. Don't deny that either! So I asked him if he'd be interested."

"He asked me to marry you," Kron said, wanting to be absolutely truthful with his new mate. "I agreed, because I felt the pull toward you. And I thought that we'd have time to adjust to all the changes before they took place. There were reservations in the beginning, but as we got to know each other, I knew it was right. And I thought we'd have more time."

Ginger shook her head and her eyes began to fill with tears as she blinked them rapidly away. "How is this any different than Momma? How is you coercing Kron into marrying me any different than her insisting I get to know the men she introduces me to because I would be smart to marry one and she knows it would be best for me?"

"It's different," Buchanan insisted. "Because I knew Kron felt the same way you did. And I knew Kron would only want you to be happy, not to serve some damn warped movement or to try to brainwash you into being something you're not."

Ginger looked at Kron, who watched her nervously, then back at her father. "How can I ever be sure now?" she whispered, then walked hurriedly past her father without looking at him, and planned to walk past Kron, too.

But Kron reached out and gently curved his hand around her arm, bringing her to stop beside him. "Ginger, you are my mate. My Leerah. Surely you can't question all you mean to me."

114

Ginger looked up at Kron. Her face gave away no emotion. "I'm questioning everything. I don't know if I'll ever trust you again. Everything you say to me, every time you touch me, I'll wonder if it's what you have to do, or what you want to do. I wish you'd told me before. You should have just been honest, told me what you planned, what the two of you planned, and let me decide for myself. Instead you let me believe that it was me you wanted to please, it was me you wanted more than anything in this world. Instead, now I find it's an agreement you made with my father. You let me believe that I actually mattered. You let me believe that what I wanted was important to you. That I actually mattered to you as more than a strategic pairing and a favor to Viceroy Buchanan."

"Leerah," Kron started, but she interrupted him.

"Let me go, Kron. I don't even want to look at you right now. I want to be as far away from you as I possibly can be."

Kron's features hardened and he placed a finger beneath her chin, forcing her to look up into his eyes. "I told you, there is no going back. You are my mate, even before your father asked me to consider you as mine, I knew you were mine. I knew one day we would be bound. It is not as I would have had it, I wanted to move slowly and allow you to learn all about our bond before it happened, but nonetheless, you are mine. We cannot be separated."

"And now it's my fault for pushing you too quickly," she said, shaking her head.

"I wanted you as badly as you did me. I was merely trying to consider your feelings," Kron said. "But when you came to me, I couldn't turn away. You know this."

Ginger nodded slowly, her eyes set on a point far past him down the hallway. "I also know you told me that you'd be away from time to time on mission and I'd be left behind on the ship, so I know separation can be survived. I'm leaving. Let. Me. Go," she said slowly and pointedly, tugging her arm from his gentle hold.

Kron released her arm and she walked past him, down the hall and out of sight. "Leerah! You know the truth. It is in your

115

heart!" he shouted after her. He stood there, watching the spot he last saw her, feeling so many different emotions he wasn't sure which to identify or act on first.

Buchanan came to stand beside him. "Give her time, she'll come around."

Kron continued staring down the hall.

"Maybe we should have taken a little more time, and you should have told her I asked you to marry her," Buchanan said.

Kron looked at Buchanan with a shocked expression. "I cannot believe you said that. I told you she needed to know all things about me before we considered marriage. I told you we needed time! You did not agree!"

"Then you should have told her!" Buchanan said, smiling sheepishly.

Kron's chest rumbled as he looked at Buchanan.

"What? I'm just saying," Buchanan said with a shrug of his shoulders.

Kron started walking away.

"Where are you going?" Buchanan called out.

"To get my mate," Kron said.

Chapter 12

Kron walked out of the door into the docking area of Earth Base 28, just as his mate seated herself in her small transport. He strode quickly toward it. She saw him coming and hurriedly locked the doors, glaring at him angrily from behind the windows.

"Open the door, Ginger," Kron said calmly.

"No."

Kron gave half a shake of his head, then reached out and tried the handle. When it remained locked, he pinned her with a commanding look. "Open the door, Leerah. Now."

"Step away from the transport, Kron. If you don't, I'm not responsible for you being injured when I leave," she said.

"You will not leave me. We've discussed this, you know we are bound for all time. Open the door. We need to talk calmly and with reason to one another," Kron said.

Ginger watched him, to her credit not even flinching when he rattled the door handle several more times and his expression began to convey his irritation.

"Ginger!" he said, just a slight note of warning in his tone.

"The time for talking rationally is over. I don't want to talk to you. I don't want to talk to anyone. I just want to be left alone to figure out what I need to do next," she said.

"What you will do next is talk to your mate. Together we will find the best way to work through this misunderstanding."

Ginger looked away from Kron and out into the distance beyond the base. Then she looked back toward him. "You said you'd give me anything," she said.

"And I will. You are my focus, Ginger. Regardless of the circumstances, no matter how you think things came about, you have been my focus for some time now."

Ginger nodded, though she was obviously unconvinced. "Then give me the gift of your absence. I don't trust you anymore. I can't even look at you without feeling betrayed and used as a pawn by the two of you. And what hurts the most is that the two men I believed in more than anyone else have conspired together, against me. Neither of you thought I had the brains to make my own choices, my own way, my own future."

"That's not true, Leerah!" Kron exclaimed passionately.

"Don't call me that. My name is Ginger, not some over-the-top term of endearment meant for the female your heart truly chooses. Not the female you mated as a favor to her father. Move away from the transport, Kron."

"My heart chose you! Just as yours chose me!" Kron insisted. "Get out of the transport. We will make things right!"

"Perhaps you should go speak to my father and the two of you can work it out between yourselves. I'm sure you don't need my input for anything — you haven't so far," Ginger said, powering up the transport.

The heat began rushing out from beneath the transport as it lifted into the air and Kron took several steps back so he'd not be burned. He watched helplessly as his mate turned the transport away from the base, and him, and quickly sped away.

Kron's entire system was off balance without Ginger. His sharp, fanged teeth elongated and seemed to become more pointed, and his facial appearance hardened as the scales of his battle armor slid into place as his emotions surged. Even the serrated blade like appendages that extended from his fingertips while in battle made themselves known. His lips curled back over his teeth and he threw his head back bellowing a single, extended roar, pouring all his frustration into it.

Gradually he became aware of the fact that everything around him had stilled and he was being watched. He looked toward his left and found several of the men assigned to the base watching him with surprised expressions. Throwing a mournful glance in the direction Ginger went once more, he turned toward a base issued transport nearby and started in its direction.

"Don't do it," Buchanan said.

Kron looked in Buchanan's direction, surprised the man had been able to walk out into the docking area without Kron being aware.

"I'm just saying, give her some time to cool off. She's angry, and she's feeling manipulated."

"She was manipulated!" Kron snapped.

"Did you make her accept you?" Buchanan asked, clearly as upset as Kron was.

"Of course not! She was the aggressor. I had every intention of taking as much time as necessary. Explaining all that would change with her acceptance of me. Then she stepped into the shower with me and every instinct bred into me for thousands of generations took over. All it took was her hands on me, her eyes looking into mine, telling me that she chose me! I couldn't think, instinct took over!"

Buchanan was shaking his head comically, holding his hands up. "No, no, no, no, no! I don't need to hear this!"

"Then stop asking!" Kron shouted

"All I need to know is she was onboard with it all!" Buchanan exclaimed.

"Of course she was! When she touched me every logical reason I had for waiting disappeared. I claimed her, as we both wanted." Kron looked off in the direction she'd gone once more.

"She wasn't manipulated. All I did was make you aware of her attraction to you, tell you what was going on at my home thanks to my manipulating wife, and invite Ginger to the base so you could spend some time with her. And I let you know I'd be happy with a relationship between the two of you. I encouraged you, but neither one of us manipulated her."

Kron glared at Buchanan.

"And I pretended to be busy so you'd have to entertain her. And maybe Zhuxi and I had Zrakad pretend to be interested so you'd be a little more open to stepping up."

"We were both manipulated!" Kron yelled.

"Only because you needed help getting out of your own damn way. You're too honorable for your own good!" Buchanan complained.

Kron simply stared at Buchanan.

"If there is such a thing," Buchanan conceded.

"Now she hates me. It is exactly as I feared."

"She doesn't hate you. She was happy! Happier than I've ever seen her when she told me you were mates and you were getting married!" Buchanan said.

Kron looked at Buchanan, then he held his hands out, looking down at his legs, then the space all around him as he waved both hands toward the emptiness beside him that should have been occupied by his mate. "Does she look as though she is beside me, happy to be near me? Or that we have made much progress in planning our wedding?!" Kron exclaimed sarcastically.

Buchanan smirked at Kron. "No, she isn't here. But she was, and she will be again. Give her the day to calm down. I'll talk to her when I get home, and we'll get it all fixed. She's not walking away from you, Kron, she's just angry. She's got my temper. She needs time to cool down and think about things rationally."

Kron turned to look in the direction she'd gone once more.

"Come on," Buchanan said, putting his arm around Kron's back. "Give her the time she needs, and it'll all be fine."

"How can you be so sure?" Kron asked.

"She's my daughter. I know her as well as I know myself. Just let her calm down. Give her a chance to miss you. Let her figure out no matter how it may have come about, that she wants to be with you. It won't take a few days and she'll be here with you again."

"I want to go after her. Tell her I love her," Kron said.

"Right now she won't care. Come on inside. I'll give you her number, you leave her a message telling her you love her and you're going to let her calm down. Tell her to call you when she's ready to talk," Buchanan said.

"On my planet, I would simply go to her home and bring her back with me," Kron said.

"Yeah, that's not going to do a thing but piss her off even worse. Let her figure out what she's feeling before you go all cave man on her," Buchanan said.

~~~

Ginger was so angry she could barely function. But the anger wasn't the worst part. She felt betrayed, and manipulated. But most of all, she was embarrassed. She felt like a fool. She'd practically thrown herself at Kron, insisted he mate her because she wanted him as well. And she did want him. She just never thought her father had arranged for Kron to spend time with her, conspiring with him for her and Kron to end up together. She'd honestly thought Kron wanted her simply because he liked her and wanted to be with her. But there was so much more going on behind the scenes that she'd been completely oblivious to. She'd believed his hesitance about mating because he wanted her to understand it fully. But really he'd just wanted her to push the issue so she'd be the one who initiated it. He'd played her like a fool, and she'd made it all too easy for both Kron and her own father. Kron had even had the nerve to clearly point out that the rushed mating was her choice, not his. And he'd not hesitated to do so.

Her tears started again, and that just pissed her off. When she cried it was usually out of anger and frustration, not humiliation. But this time — it was humiliation. They made a fool of her. Made her think Kron really believed she was his mate. But he'd mated her as a favor to her father. What made it even worse was that she couldn't actually blame Kron. No matter what the situation was, or how he'd played it off, she'd been the one to insist and brush away all his caution. Ginger lifted a hand and wiped away the tears that stained her face with the back of it, then pressed her fingertips to her eyes to dry her lashes. The last thing she needed was her mother noticing her crying. If she did she wouldn't give her a moment's peace. The woman was relentless, and would be worse once she figured out she'd mated an alien male who worked for her father.

121

Ginger pulled the visor down and looked at herself in the mirror she kept clamped behind it. "Holy shit!" she exclaimed, seeing the yellow of her eye color for the first time. She looked at herself in awe, shocked to see herself with any eye color other than blue. Especially a color that was not natural to humans. She leaned forward looking closer at her reflection. "It's beautiful," she whispered. "Just like Kron's." She shook her head and slapped the visor back up into the closed position as the tears started again. There would be no forgetting Kron ever. Even if she wanted to, every time she looked at herself, she'd see his eyes peering back from her face.

Pulling into the small docking station at her family home, she wasn't surprised when the front door opened and her mother stood there.

"Damn," Ginger mumbled. Then she remembered she'd have to hide her eyes from her mother, and snatched her purse off the floorboard beside her seat, emptying it onto the passenger seat, looking for the sunglasses she always kept with her. Her blue eyes had been very sensitive to bright sunlight, so she always had a pair with her. She grabbed her dark glasses and slipped them on quickly as her mother came toward her.

"Are you going to get out?" her mother called out from a few feet away.

Ginger nodded, then scooped all the contents of her purse back inside it before releasing the lock on the doors of her transport and climbing out. "I'm getting out," she said, as she stepped onto the transport ramp and closed the door.

"Your father called. He said you left your phone at the base and you should return for it after you've had a rest. Are you feeling poorly?" her mother asked.

"I'm just really tired. Maybe I'm coming down with something," Ginger lied as she silently kicked herself for not making sure she had her communicator with her. It must have fallen out of her pocket when Kron picked her clothes up off his floor.

"Do you have a fever, or is it another of your headaches?" her mother asked.

"I'm not sure, probably a headache," Ginger answered. She wanted time alone and pretending to be sick would make her mother tuck her in bed and let her rest.

"Come inside, dear. Let Momma take care of you. Mitchell was coming to visit this evening, we were going to sneak him in, but I'll let him know you're not feeling well. Don't be surprised if he insists on coming anyway. He's taken quite a liking to you and he may want to see for himself that you're well."

"Momma, I don't want any visitors. Especially not Mitchell, you know he can't be here. And I don't want to see anyone interested in me particularly. I just want to be left alone."

"Ginger, I've told you. That is no way to land a stable, dependable, respectable husband! And with you feeling under the weather, it's a perfect opportunity to see how attuned they'll be to your needs when you're feeling vulnerable."

"My needs are for them to all go away. I don't like any of them," Ginger insisted.

"What does like have to do with it? We all have to do our part in rebuilding our world, young lady. Presenting a solid, unified front to the rest of the world as an example is a wonderful way to contribute. And having a husband that helps pave the way to the purification of our country and even our world is something you should aspire to."

"Momma..." Ginger started, prepared to tell her once again, as much as she was willing anyway, just how unconcerned with those things she was.

"I don't want to argue with you, young lady. I'm simply thinking of what's best for you in the long run. Now, go slip into your nightgown and get some rest."

"Yes, ma'am," Ginger said, too exhausted, her entire psyche too shattered to even care to oppose her mother at this particular point in time.

"And take those dark glasses off. You'll bump into something in the house and bruise your knee," her mother said.

"My eyes are sensitive to the light!" Ginger objected.

"Alright, then, go on and get in bed and I'll make you some tea. Have you eaten?"

"Yes, ma'am. I'm not really hungry."

"I'll just get you a little something to nibble on," her mother insisted.

Ginger went to her bedroom and took off her clothes, shoving them into the hamper in her bathroom, then got in the shower. She quickly washed her body and her hair, then got out and wrapped her hair in a towel. She was brushing her teeth when her mother tapped on the door.

"Will you be long? I have a snack and some tea out here for you. And some medicine for your headache. It's a new combination of medicines that really helps my headaches. I think it will help yours, too."

"That's fine. I'll be right there," Ginger answered.

Ginger looked at herself in the mirror and reached out to her reflection, touching the yellow of her eyes reflected in the mirror as she leaned closer to get a better look.

"Ginger?" her mother called, opening the door and starting to take a step into the bathroom.

"Momma! I'm coming!" Ginger snapped, shutting her eyes quickly and looking away from the mirror to shield her mother from seeing her eyes even in her reflection.

Susanna Jo stood there, her jaw clamped tightly as she tried to pretend she hadn't seen her daughter's eyes. "I just wanted to see if you needed help," she said.

"No, thank you. I can get it. I'm almost done," Ginger said, still looking away from her mother and keeping her eyes downcast. She pulled her nightgown on, then reached for her sunglasses on the bathroom counter behind her, and slipped them back on before turning to face her mother, then following her out of the bathroom and into her bedroom.

It was then that Ginger noticed her mother was holding a silver tray with her tea on it. "You didn't have to go to all that trouble," Ginger said.

"Nonsense, you're my daughter. Everything I do is for the betterment of your life. You know that, right?" her mother asked.

"I do, Momma. I'm just so exhausted."

"And your head hurts," her mother added.

124

"Yeah," Ginger agreed. It just made things easier to let her mother think she had another headache. She climbed in bed and pulled her covers up, leaning on her pillows piled against the headboard of her bed by her mother.

"Here you go, dear," her mother said, sliding the tray into place on Ginger's lap. "Tea and buttered toast. Something easy for your tummy since you don't feel well."

"Thank you," Ginger said, feeling terrible for being so irritated with her mother, when in truth all the woman was trying to do was take care of her. It didn't matter that they had different opinions about the world and who belonged in it. At the moment she was simply a daughter, grateful for the nurturing of her very loving, albeit, overbearing mother.

After Ginger had eaten her toast and drunk almost all of her tea, her mother handed her a round, chalky, white pill.

Ginger looked at it suspiciously. "I don't remember taking these before."

"No, those are the new ones I told you about. I find they help immensely with my headaches. If they help yours, too, we'll get you your own prescription when we go back to the doctor."

"Hmpf," Ginger said, huffing non-committally.

"I have to be honest though, it will make you very sleepy. But when you wake up your head won't hurt anymore and everything will be right as rain."

"I could certainly use some sleep," Ginger agreed. She popped the pill into her mouth and washed it down with the rest of her tea.

Her mother took the cup from her and the tray, then leaned over and pressed a kiss to Ginger's forehead. "I love you, my girl. Everything I do is for you. Just remember that."

"Mmhmm," Ginger responded.

"Ginger, take those glasses off while you sleep," her mother said as she paused to look back at her daughter settling down to get some rest.

"Later. Right now it hurts to even look through them," Ginger answered.

"Alright. Suit yourself." Her mother turned out the light, pulled the door closed and went to the kitchen to wash the few dishes Ginger had used and put away the tray. She puttered around the house, killing time for about twenty minutes, then went back to check on Ginger. She opened the bedroom door, and quietly made her way to Ginger's bedside. "Ginger?" she whispered, reaching out to place her hand on Ginger's forehead. She wasn't warm, so there was no fever. "Ginger?" her mother said again, shaking her slightly. There was absolutely no response. Ginger was knocked out, deeply asleep.

Chapter 13

Susanna Jo left Ginger's bedroom and went to her own purse. She took out a small communicator no one knew she had and brought up the screen she'd been monitoring since Ginger had left that morning to meet her father for lunch. Scrolling through the texted transcripts of the verbal messages that had been sent to her daughter's communicator and were then automatically forwarded to hers, she shook her head in disgust. She'd read them twice before Ginger even arrived home from the base that day, and her outrage steadily grew with each consecutive read of them. No matter how hard she'd tried to protect Ginger, the girl was unfortunately as gullible as her father, and had succumbed to the very same situation she'd been worried about. The alien that had brought her home several days before was to blame, she had no doubt. The evidence was there for anyone to see. Her anger became more focused. It was clear her own husband had endorsed this completely unnatural relationship between their beloved daughter and this... this alien!

Susanna Jo scrolled back to the first message and took her time reading through them all once more, her lips pressed together in anger and outrage, as she read each message slowly to be sure she completely understood all that had happened before she committed to the unpleasant decision that seemed to be unavoidable.

Ginger, Leerah, please, come back to the base. I know there is much to discuss, but one thing
remains absolutely unchanged. I love you. I have wanted you since the first day we met. I would
have claimed you and bound us forever even if your father had not endorsed our mating. I am not

127

sorry that I belong to you. I am sorry only that you misunderstood the reasons behind my actions.

Take all the time you need, then come back to me.

I remain as ever, your male, your faithful and loving mate.

Kron Val Kere X Buchanan

After scoffing about the first message, Susanna Jo read the next.

Ginger, darlin', I know you're angry with both me and Kron, but let me just say, he's heartbroken. I

know it looks bad, but it's really nothing more than me telling Kron that you were interested in him,

just like he was interested in you and encouraging him to not waste too much time. What you two have

is real. Now, he wanted to come after you, but I explained it's better to just let you calm down, and

then you'd be back to talk to him. I know you'll come back. I've never seen you so happy as you were

before. Oh, and wear your sunglasses until we have a chance to break this to your mom. One look at

your yellow eyes and she'll have a fit.

Love you, darlin', Dad.

Susanna huffed in frustration at that one. She hadn't believed that Ginger's eyes actually changed colors until she'd pretended to just open the bathroom door and walk in on Ginger. It had only been a split second, but she'd still caught enough of a flash of the yellow in Ginger's eyes to know that alien had lured her daughter into the depths of depravity she'd worked so hard to keep her from. Susanna closed her own eyes, counting to ten in her head to calm herself before looking down at her communicator once more and opening the final message.

Darlin', Kron just found your communicator in his bedroom. I'm gonna com your mom and leave a message

for you with her at the house to rest then come back up here. Why the hell am I even leaving this message

if your communicator is here with us? You see? I'm upset, too. You should be here, with the male you told

me this afternoon you planned to marry. You were happy, Ginger. You know you were. The path to getting you

two together doesn't matter. It was going to happen anyway! Come on back so we can work this all out.

Love, Dad

Ginger's mother exited the transcription program of the communicator Mitchell had given her in order to keep an eye on Ginger's social life. She'd told him she was concerned because she spent so much time away from home and seemed very curious about the lives of the aliens living and working at the base with her husband. Mitchell had offered to place tracking software on Ginger's phone, and a reporting program on hers, so she could keep an eye on all communications going through Ginger's device. Susanna had agreed, and the happenings of today were exactly why she felt justified in every decision she'd made, and was about to make.

Susanna Jo Buchanan went to the one contact saved in her secret communicator and pressed the name, then waited while it connected her call.

"Mrs. Buchanan. How nice to hear from you," Mitchell said, picking up on the first ring. "I'm looking forward to dinner with you and your lovely daughter this evening."

"I'm afraid you won't think so once I tell you all that has occurred."

"What's happened? Is Ginger alright?" Mitchell asked.

"She's been claimed by that horrible yellow alien my husband has working at the base!" she cried, her tears beginning to flow.

"She's been claimed?!" Mitchell repeated, his voice rising in alarm. "What exactly do you mean by claimed?"

"I'm afraid it means the worst. But, I've done what you instructed, should this ever happen. I've given her the tablets you left with me. She's sleeping."

"Both tablets?" Mitchell asked.

"I put one in her tea, and simply told her the other was a new medication for my headaches. She's had both."

"You know once we begin this, you won't be able to communicate with her for quite some time," Mitchell said. "She'll need deprogramming. She'll have to be convinced they are here to destroy our civilization."

"I know. But it's a sacrifice I must make to save my baby. I just can't believe my husband endorses such depraved activities."

"He's been taken in by them, Mrs. Buchanan. They can be quite convincing — charming even. But in time, he'll see their true natures when we're all in a battle for control of our world once again. But this time, we'll be successful."

"I only pray you're right," Mrs. Buchanan said.

"I have no doubt that I am. And by then, Ginger will see the truth as well. I'll save your daughter, Mrs. Buchanan. It will not be easy, but I'll do it."

"Thank you, Mitchell. Please, come take her. Get her away from here before my husband or that alien comes for her. I'll transfer the credits for her upkeep and for all you'll do for her mental wellbeing and state of mind while she's with you. I just don't know what I'd do without you and your organization to turn to. I never thought she'd be weak enough to fall into the hands of the enemy."

"It will all work out, Mrs. Buchanan. It is my hope that she'll see me in a different light when we've helped her through the worst of it. Maybe together we can help others like her."

"That would be a wonderful turn of events, Mitchell. I must say that would make me the happiest of mothers."

Mitchell assured Mrs. Buchanan that he was on his way, then ended the com. He sat back in his chair and smiled to himself. Finally, the daughter of Viceroy Buchanan would be under his control. It wasn't exactly as he'd planned, but still, it would work out. He'd have a direct line of communication to the inner workings of Earth Base 28 — once he established it via the Viceroy, and thereby the status of the aliens who worked there. He had no doubt he'd be successful. He'd managed to gain control of almost a dozen upper echelon government employees through their families, and Ginger Buchanan simply strengthened the hold he had on them all and gave him access to even more information than he'd originally hoped for. The coup was coming, and he and his people would be successful no matter what they had to do, or who they had to extort.

He got up from his desk in the middle of his expansive office. He strode toward the door and yanked it open. His assistant looked up at him, then hurriedly stood. "Yes, sir?" his assistant said.

"Ready the transport and two attendants. We're going to collect Buchanan's daughter."

"This evening?" the young man asked.

"Now! Right now!" Mitchell said. "And monitor the bank account. Let me know when Mrs. Buchanan's credit transfer hits. The moment it's confirmed, disperse it to the other accounts so that it can't be traced."

"Yes, sir," his assistant said, reaching for his communicator with one hand while typing on his very large desktop computer. He brought up three screens of accounts and watched them, waiting for the credit transfer to hit while he waited for the attendants to answer his com.

Mitchell strolled around his assistant's office while he waited for his instructions to be carried out. He stopped in front of one of the many screens mounted on the walls. Some of them showed security footage of the perimeter of the buildings and property. Some of them showed inner views of the buildings on the property. This one in particular showed the basement the girls, and boys, were kept in once they were snatched from their homes and their alien mates.

Mitchell stepped closer and watched as one of the girls rocked herself back and forth across the small, single bed she lay in. He watched as she rocked harder and harder until she was finally able to rock herself out of the bed. Then she braced herself against the side of the bed and forced herself to her feet, though her hands were useless and chained behind her.

"Send the guard in there!" Mitchell ordered.

His assistant looked up to see what he was watching, then nodded. He reached for another communicator and pressed a button on it. "You've got a female trying to escape!" he shouted into it.

Mitchell watched on the monitor as two guards rushed in and grabbed the girl, picking her up and body slamming her back onto her mattress. Then he smiled as one guard held her down, while the other injected her with something that almost immediately had her head lolling back against her pillow, her eyes rolling back in her head. "When will they figure out that there is no way out? Their families do as they're told as long as we hold them. They're not going anywhere."

"At some point, they will figure it out. They'll be nice, obedient individuals, or live what's left of their lives drugged out of their minds," his assistant said.

"They actually think their families will save them, or better yet, their alien lovers!" Mitchell said. "It's ludicrous to think they're more than a passing thought for the animals they lowered themselves to bed. And their families... they're as humiliated as these people should be."

"It is a shame," his assistant commented.

"When we've won the war, everyone will see we were right. Then they'll see it was a necessary thing to sacrifice their children in order to coerce their parents into a positive working partnership with us."

"You are right, sir," his assistant said before holding up one finger to indicate he was listening to someone on the other end

132

of the com he'd placed. "Prepare to leave right away," he said into the communicator he still held at his ear. "Mr. Mitchell has a pickup that must take place now."

"Tell them I'm already tired of waiting," Mitchell barked out.

"He's already tired of waiting! Get to the transport immediately!"

~~~

Kron walked into the office he, Buchanan, Zhuxi, and Kol all shared together. He was tired of waiting, on edge from Ginger not yet responding to his messages. "Have you heard from her?" he asked, not bothering with any pleasantries.

Buchanan looked up when Kron entered. "Kron! How are you doing? You get any work done?"

"I must go," Kron announced.

"What?! Go where?" Buchanan asked, thinking Kron meant to leave permanently. "You just mated my daughter. You can't leave!"

"What? No! I will never leave her. But I am going after her," Kron said.

"You know what? Before you do that, let me com home right now," Buchanan said, taking out his personal communicator. "If she's still angry, and it wouldn't be unheard of for her to still be angry, all you going there is going to do is get her all fired up again, and cause a confrontation in front of her mother. Which will just complicate the whole damn thing. Let me see if I can get her on the phone before you go off and make things worse."

Kron stood there, his patience wearing thin, as he waited for Buchanan to hopefully speak with Ginger.

"Hey, it's me!" Buchanan said into his communicator when his wife answered. "Ginger around?"

133

"She's sleeping," Susanna Jo said. "She came home not feeling well and said she had a headache. I gave her a little something to eat and then she showered and is already asleep."

"Oh, okay then. She's good though?" Buchanan asked.

"Seems to be. She did take two tablets for the pain, though. So it must have been a pretty bad headache."

"Well, let her know I called again, and you did tell her I comm'd her before she got there, didn't you?" he asked.

"Now, you know I did. I said I'd tell her, didn't I?" Susanna Jo snapped.

"Yeah, you did say that," Buchanan responded.

"If I said I told her, then I told her. She said she'd be in touch when her headache went away."

"Alright. Just let her know I reached out again. And tell her I have her communicator here with me. It's in my office, and we're waiting on her call," Buchanan said.

"Who's we?" Mrs. Buchanan asked.

"She'll know who I mean. Just give her the message. You sure she's okay, maybe I should come home and check on her, talk to her myself," Buchanan said.

"Now, that's ridiculous. She's home, all tucked into bed safe and sound. Just let her rest. You know how our headaches can be."

"Yeah, I do. Okay, then. I'll just wait to hear from her. Oh, and listen, you need to be extra careful. We believe that Consul Don Tol's property has been trespassed on. Until we're sure what's going on, we're all on alert," Buchanan said.

"You know if somebody has ill will toward those aliens, someone like me has nothing to fear from those people. They're only trying to defend their homes."

"I am not getting into this with you right now. I am a public official. That could put a target on our backs for many reasons. All I'm asking you to do is to stay alert for anything unusual. You stay home, keep the doors locked, and tell Ginger to call me when she wakes up," Buchanan said. "I'll be here on duty while needed. You take care at home."

"Fine, then," his wife snapped.

"Fine," Buchanan answered, then ended the com.

Buchanan huffed out a sigh, then sheepishly met Kron's gaze. "That woman will be the reason I start drinking heavily."

Kron didn't even smile. Since Buchanan had spoken to his wife via the speaker function on his communicator, he'd easily heard every word of it.

"At least you know she's home safe and sound," Buchanan said to Kron.

"She had to take tablets for pain?" Kron asked, obviously very concerned about his mate.

"Don't worry about Ginger. You heard my wife say she's got one of her headaches. She took some pain medication for it. That's why she went to bed."

"And now I have caused her to become ill," Kron said.

"No, you didn't. Both my wife and my daughter get these hellacious headaches. You didn't make her sick. It's best she's sleeping. When she wakes she won't be as upset, and her head will be better. Maybe you could do something useful to distract yourself. Maybe it's best she went home for a while. Ya'll both need to take a step back and relax for a day or so. It'll help you remember what you mean to each other."

"I am well aware of what she means to me," Kron snarled, finding it hard to control his anxiety over already being separated from his mate after he'd claimed her less than five hours earlier, and then to find out that she was in pain and he was not there to soothe her. "I should go to Ginger. She is suffering." He was truly torn over what he should do.

"I told you, you should not go to her. Look, trust me. It'll be fine. She wouldn't know you were there anyway. She took her medicine and this is nothing new for her. She'll sleep through it and wake up better like I already told you. Why don't you go check on things at Kol's, I got it covered here. Everything's quiet. I'll stay here until you get back. Ginger's sleeping. Everything's good," Buchanan said.

"And I'll be here as well," Zhuxi said from the open doorway. "All will be well, Kron. I sensed her heart while she was here. She is yours, Kron," Zhuxi said. "Go, assist Kol, and we will

135

be here when you return. I would be surprised if your mate isn't here with us when you return."

Kron thought about it.

"Are you sure?" Kron asked Zhuxi.

"I am. One can pretend to be many things, but one cannot hide their true heart. At least not from my kind," Zhuxi said.

Kron nodded and took a deep breath before letting it out slowly. He'd seen for himself that Zhuxi had unusual abilities and knew if he said he'd sensed her commitment to him, then he'd sensed it. Zhuxi was a male of honor and did not lie.

"You are sure she will be well?" Kron asked.

"Absolutely. Just needs a few hours sleep," Buchanan said.

"Then I will leave all in your capable hands," he said to both Buchanan and Zhuxi. "But, please, if there is any additional word at all from my Ginger, let me know at once."

"Consider it done," Buchanan said, pleased that the large, yellow alien was so concerned about his daughter.

Kron turned and walked rapidly toward the door of the commissary, anxious to get back to Kol's home and distract himself as soon as he could.

"Don't you worry about a thing," Buchanan called out. "If you and Kol need more backup, let us know!" Buchanan said. "Let us know what you find!" Buchanan called out.

Kron lifted a hand in wave to acknowledge their offers of additional support if he or Kol needed it as he walked out of the office. It was a needless offer though, members of Zhuxi's team were already there.

Chapter 14

Mitchell had the transport land a few feet away from the Buchanan house — as close as he could without actually causing damage to the home. He wanted it as close as possible in the event of having to make a quick getaway.

He left the transport with the ramp down, the door open and he with his two attendants walked up the path to the front door. Before they reached the door, Mrs. Buchanan opened the door and invited them in.

She held a tissue in her hand and dabbed at her eyes as she moved aside to make room for all three men to enter her home. "I'm sorry, Mitchell. I'm just having such a hard time understanding how this could all happen," she said.

"Don't let it upset you too much, Mrs. Buchanan. Yours is not the only family to be taken in by these enemies of our way of life. But all will be well. Before you know it, your daughter will be back home and behaving in just the way you expect."

"Thank you. Thank you so much! I just wish this could have been different. It would have been so much less stressful if she'd have just accepted your advances and agreed to spend some time with you," Mrs. Buchanan said, simpering as she guided the men to Ginger's bedroom. She opened the door and turned on the light. "Ginger? Dear? Are you awake?" she called out.

Ginger didn't move, nor respond.

Mrs. Buchanan looked back at Mitchell who stood behind her with an irritated look on his face. "She's still sound asleep. Do what you must."

"She will likely sleep for at least another twelve hours. Don't worry, though. Once she awakes, we'll explain that we are all concerned about her welfare, and we were called in to ensure her complete recovery from dependence on the enemy. It's not her fault that she's fallen under their influence. We'll help her become strong and able to withstand their desires. And as you said, hopefully, she'll see that I'm a much more viable option."

Mrs. Buchanan stood back and watched as the men in white medical suits entered the room and approached Ginger while she slept. One of them pulled back her covers while the other lifted her from her bed. The towel fell from her hair, landing on her pillow, and the sunglasses that she'd been wearing when she'd fallen asleep fell with it.

"Oh, her towel and…" Mrs. Buchanan said.

"It's fine," Mitchell said. "She won't be needing them. We have towels, and sunglasses aren't needed where we'll be."

"Well, if you're sure," Mrs. Buchanan said.

"We're sure. Now, I hate to be rude, Mrs. Buchanan, but we really need to get her back to our facility as soon as possible. We don't want to be interrupted by your husband, or the alien who's claimed her. It would make for quite the scene," Mitchell said.

"Oh, of course. I understand. But I've just spoken to my husband. He won't be home until at least tomorrow, so there's no worry there. Now, how long before we can visit with her?" Mrs. Buchanan asked.

Mitchell rolled his eyes at his two attendants who made eye contact with him before hurriedly leaving the bedroom, then the house with the sleeping woman. He turned to Mrs. Buchanan. "Mrs. Buchanan. I've told you repeatedly, it will be quite some time before she will be allowed any contact with anyone not in our facility. It would be counterproductive to trying to deprogram her mind from its dependency on the alien who's claimed her."

"I know that. I do know that. I'm just so uncomfortable about her going to a facility I'm not familiar with."

"But you are familiar with me. You're extremely familiar with our organization and our agenda. We share a patriotism and faith in our own kind that not all inhabitants of our beautiful planet share. We'll remind her of those things and she'll return to you the loving, loyal daughter you know and love," Mitchell said.

"Of course," Mrs. Buchanan said, feeling better about any doubts she'd experienced while she waited for Mitchell and his team to arrive. "I'll just wait to hear from you."

"It won't be long until both you and your husband hear from us," Mitchell said.

"I have no doubt he'll be angry," Mrs. Buchanan said.

"Don't you worry. We're accustomed to dealing with spouses that aren't fully familiar with our work. He won't be angry for long," Mitchell said encouragingly.

"Thank you, Mitchell," Mrs. Buchanan said, following him out of her home.

"Thank you, Mrs. Buchanan. It is because of citizens like you that we'll once again be able to call our world ours," Mitchell said. He bowed gracefully to the woman, then turned and hurriedly left her house.

She followed him to the front door and watched as the transport carrying her daughter and those who had thankfully come to her aid lifted into the air and turned north. Then she closed the door, and went inside once more.

She went back to Ginger's room and turned off the light, then pulled the door closed. Then wandered around the house aimlessly before finding herself in the kitchen. She saw her personal communicator from the kitchen counter where she'd left it, and went straight to it. "This has been so stressful! I deserve a bit of pampering," she mumbled to herself as she went through her contacts. Finding the one she wanted, she pressed the button before propping her hip against the counter top to wait for them to answer.

"Illusion Beauty Day Spa," the receptionist answered.

"Marta, this is Mrs. Buchanan," she said.

"Hello, Mrs. Buchanan, how can I help you?" Marta asked.

"I need to make an appointment to come in. I've just had the most stressful few days. It's really wearing on me, and I'm sure a day of pampering at the hands of your staff will just have me right as rain."

"Oh, goodness!" the receptionist exclaimed. "I'm so sorry you've had a hard time. But we can certainly make you feel a thousand percent better!"

"Oh, and don't I know it!" Mrs. Buchanan said. "It's just a travesty how little today's children respect their parents and the decisions we make for them. I tell you, my daughter has just put me through the wringer. It'll be fine though when she gets back. I just need to have faith in that."

"Oh, did she take a trip?" Marta asked.

"Yes, she did. That's exactly it. She took a trip," Mrs. Buchanan said, smiling happily to herself now that she'd decided to view it as Ginger being on holiday. "And she'll come back a whole new person."

"How wonderful for her," Marta said. "Now, when do you want to come in so you can feel like a whole new person, too?"

"Well, it's already late afternoon. Would you have something available for the morning?"

"I sure do! I'll just put your name down, and we'll see you first thing in the morning."

"I'll see you then, dear," Mrs. Buchanan said. She ended the com, then returned her communicator to the same spot on the counter she kept it in. She turned and realized the smaller communicator Mitchell had given her to contact him in private was still sitting next to her purse, so she gathered it up, made sure it was switched to silent mode, and hid it in the bottom of her purse, beneath all her things. She knew that her husband never looked in her purse, but it made her feel better to know she'd hidden it down in the very bottom, just in case. Huffing out a sigh of relief, she went to the refrigerator and poured herself a glass of wine. "The things I do for this family..." she complained aloud. "A day of pampering is just what I need," she said. "Tomorrow cannot get here quickly enough!"

~~~

Ada Jane was in the kitchen getting dinner ready when she heard the telltale beeping of the sensor hidden within the tree line near the perimeter of their property. It was connected to a base in their kitchen that beeped, a sound similar to a smoke detector needing its batteries changed whenever someone broke the invisible beam framing the the perimeter of their property. She glanced toward the image the surveillance cameras flashed on the small screen sitting on the cabinet at the opposite end of the kitchen. She smiled when she saw Kol walk past, surprisingly with Kron. He'd obviously returned to make sure everything was still secure.

As Kol and Kron made their way back across the property, different sensors went off and she easily tracked their progress with a simple glance at the screen. The security cameras had been installed for a while, but they hadn't been stringent about activating them, and keeping them online at all times until finding proof of the Purists trespassing on their land. There was no doubt that the surveillance cameras would be engaged at all times now, though.

The timer went off on Ada Jane's oven causing her to look away from the security screens. She pulled two pans of cornbread out and placed them on a cooling rack before pouring melted butter over them. Then she went back to the chili she was making. She tasted it, decided it was perfect, and lowered the flame beneath it to keep it just simmering. Then she took out cheddar cheese and grated a whole pound of it, and spooned sour cream into a serving bowl.

She threw a glance toward the surveillance screen when it sounded again and walked toward the living room to unlock the front door for Kol and Kron. She watched through the peephole until she saw them walk up to the door, then she unlocked the door and pulled it open.

"Ada Jane!" Kron said, opening his arms for her to walk into them for a hug.

Ada Jane didn't hesitate. She walked right into his embrace and hugged him tightly. "You're back!" she said when he hugged her tightly and hesitated before letting go. Kron would always hold a special place in her heart. He'd been the one to force her to live her life while she waited on Kol to come home. Kron had always been there for her, and she'd always be there for him if he ever needed her.

"Did you miss me already?" he asked, smiling at her, though she noticed right away his smile looked forced.

"I always miss you," she said, giving him another quick hug.

A round of chattering, and squeals, and barks sounded behind her as her boys, and their dogs, realized Uncle Kron was back.

Ada Jane laughed. "And they missed you!"

"Kolby! Kreed!" Kron said, letting Ada Jane go and stepping into the house to the delight of both boys. He patted Billy and Bob and gave them good scratches before he carefully walked around the boys trying to get to him and took a seat in the middle of the floor in the living room. "Have you missed Uncle Kron?" he asked.

Kolby and Kreed squealed their delight and hurried to climb all over Kron, as Billy and Bob joined in, making for a mass of testosterone of all ages and species rolling around on the floor.

"You had better be careful! They bite!" Kol warned as he watched his sons stumble-run across the floor and fall against Kron.

"Bite?!" Kron exclaimed. "Who bites? You don't bite, do you? He means Billy and Bob, doesn't he?" Kron asked the grinning, drooling babies with mouths full of sharp teeth. "Owww!" Kron exclaimed as Kreed bit his arm. "I am not food!" Kron said, grabbing Kreed and tickling him.

Kolby climbed across his brother and right into Kron's lap, grinning up at him.

"Hello there, little warrior!" Kron said, smiling happily at Kolby. Kron hugged the boy to his chest and kissed his forehead. Then Kreed forced his way between Kolby and Kron, insisting he get a hug as well. "And you, too. Both such strong little warriors!" Kron said, hugging Kreed and kissing his forehead, too.

"Are you hungry, Kron? I made chili," Ada Jane said.

142

"I would eat it even if I wasn't hungry. You know I much enjoy your meals," Kron answered, just before he screeched for help and went over backward with the weight of both twins and dogs shoving against his chest and shoulders.

"Thank you, Kron," Ada Jane said.

"You are welcome," Kron's muffled voice answered from beneath the twins and the dogs.

"My Ehlealah is a wonderful cook," Kol said proudly. "Billy, Bob! Leave Kron alone! Come!" he ordered. Both dogs immediately stopped rolling around on the floor with Kron and the twins and followed Kol into the kitchen where he fed them and gave them fresh water.

"Yes, she is," Kron agreed, trying to sit up again.

"You both flatter me," Ada Jane said. "And it's time for dinner. Kolby, Kreed!" Ada Jane said. "Are you hungry?"

Both boys stopped and looked at their mother.

"Do you want to eat?" Ada Jane asked.

Kreed was the first to desert Uncle Kron and rush toward his mother, then Kolby followed suit.

"I still cannot believe how much they eat!" Ada Jane said, picking up Kreed and walking into the dining room with him before strapping him into one of the highchairs. Then she turned to take Kolby from Kron who'd swept him up and followed Ada Jane into the dining room.

Having taken care of the dogs, Kol joined them, and before long, everyone was seated with a bowl of chili and all the fixings in front of them.

Ada Jane smiled as she fed Kreed between bites of her own, and Kol did the same with Kolby.

"Our boys are growing big and strong! That is why they eat so much!" Kol said proudly.

"Babies that are nine months old should not be running — albeit it clumsily — and eating as much as I do," Ada Jane said with a chuckle as Kreed grabbed her hand with one of his to guide the spoon she was holding into his mouth.

"On Crustace, they would already be eating rarkashtka."

143

"Ohhh!" Kron said, his eyes widening. "I miss rarkashtka! Though I didn't grow up with it, I became quite fond of it."

"What is that?" Ada Jane asked.

"It's a beast which tastes like your beef, yet swims in the waters and feels like your fish when eaten. We pierce it on long pointed sticks we called fire sticks, then cook it over open flames. It is one of the first things our children eat. It is very spicy, very smoky."

"And very dangerous on a sharp stick!" Ada Jane said.

"Only if you get it too close to your friend's face," Kol laughed. "Have you ever noticed a small, round scar near Ba Re's chin?"

"I didn't. But I will be sure to look next time I see him," Ada Jane said.

"He said it was a battle injury!" Kron exclaimed.

"It was a battle. He wanted the last bite and I wasn't willing to share," Kol said with a grin. Then he turned to Ada Jane to explain. "You share the rarkashtka with your friends by passing the sticks to them to share the meat. You must be careful when passing, and receiving your share."

"You were toddlers eating from pointed sticks?" Ada Jane asked.

"Oh, no! We were almost nine of your earth years of age," Kol said. "We'd been eating from the fire sticks for years by then."

"Still much too young to be eating from pointed sticks," Ada Jane said.

"No! It was fun!" Kol said, grinning. "A coming of age tradition. When we are very young, our fathers take us on excursions. They catch and prepare the rarkashtka, and we all share the rarkashtka. As we get older we learn to hunt and prepare it ourselves."

"If we are ever on Crustace, they can eat it if you think they'll like it. I mean, they love chili and have never, ever eaten what human babies eat, so I doubt seriously that it would be hard for them to digest. But, let's not give it to them on pointed sticks, okay?" Ada Jane asked.

144

"It would be at least three or four years before they were old enough to first eat from the fire sticks."

"You want to give four year old boys a sharpened stick and let them hold it in a fire. Ya'll are going to give me a heart attack," Ada Jane said, shaking her head. Raising Cruestaci babies was so different from raising human babies. Sure they still went through their newborn phase, and their crawling phase, and their learning to walk phase, but they did everything sooner than they should have. And their diets were enough to give a grown human indigestion. They required a lot of meat, and a lot of spice. They did not like bland foods, or soft foods. They wanted substance, protein, and taste.

She took a moment to look at her children objectively and her heart swelled with warmth and love. They were perfect. They were identical twins. Pale blue tinted skin, blue eyes, just like hers, sharp pointed teeth like Kol, and tiny nubs at their temples where their horns would be when they grew up. You could almost see how their jaws would square when they matured, and the sharp outline of their high cheekbones. Her sons were beautiful, and adventurous, and smart, and so amazingly advanced for their ages. At nine months old, they were as big as eighteen month old human babies, and getting around by walking and running rather than crawling, unless of course they were wrestling with their father or Uncle Kron. And while full of mischief and a never-ending desire to play, they were also very loving and loved to cuddle with both parents.

She felt bad sometimes that there were no other babies like them for them to grow up with, and was especially thankful there were two of them for just that reason. But she also knew they were missing out on a lot of their father's culture as well. "You know?" Ada Jane said thoughtfully. "We have a fish here on Earth that has a meaty texture. And when cooked right, it can have a beefy taste. Maybe we can get some and see if it can be cooked the same way you do the rarkashtka."

"I would like this very much, my Ada Jane. What is it called?" Kol asked.

"Tuna," Ada Jane answered.

Kol's face scrunched up as he made a face. "The oily fish in the can? No, that is not rarkashtka."

"Same fish, but different," Ada Jane said with a chuckle. "When you buy it fresh, not canned, it's a completely different thing. Trust me."

"If it does not taste like the canned fish, I will try it," Kol said.

"As will I," Kron said. "Can it be skewered on a stick?"

"I'm sure it can. If not, we'll put it on the grill. I think you'll like it. It's not spicy on its own, but we could add whatever spices you want," Ada said.

"We will cook it soon. Perhaps this weekend," Kol said happily.

"I would like to participate," Kron said sadly.

"Of course," Kol said, looking at Kron strangely, before looking at Ada Jane to see if she noticed anything off about Kron.

Ada met his gaze with a knowing look. Something was wrong with Kron and they both knew it.

Chapter 15

After dinner, Ada Jane put Kreed and Kolby to bed, then came back into the living room to visit with Kol and Kron. She gave each of them a large slice of apple pie, then got one for herself and sat down beside Kol to listen to them talking about security.

"How are Zhuxi's men adjusting to being here?" Kron asked.

"They are never seen or heard unless I make the effort to seek them out. I tried to feed them, offer them water the first days, but they made it clear it was not needed. So now I simply inspect the property, and make myself available in the event they may need anything. Zrakad has allowed me to see him at least once a day, and always finds it amusing that I still offer them food, drink, shelter if they'd like it. He has said they are more at home now than they've been since they arrived."

"Must make them feel more relaxed, closer to their natural habitat," Kron said.

"I think so," Kol said. "I am much more at ease with them here. They are an amazing people."

Kron nodded.

"What is wrong, Kron? Is there an issue you've not told me of?" Kol asked.

Kron shook his head. "I am well." He didn't want to complain to Kol. He had enough on his mind already with the trespassing on his property, coordinating the Ceresian warriors, and keeping his mate and children safe without having to listen to himself venting about how wrong things with Ginger had gone.

"You aren't being honest," Ada Jane said quietly.

"I am well. It is of no concern," Kron said. "Buchanan and Zhuxi are handling all things at the base. I am not needed there, and I thought I could be of assistance here."

"You can. And you're always welcome here, officially or as family," Kol said.

"You are family, you know?" Ada Jane said, watching Kron closely.

Kron smiled sadly and nodded. "I do. And it means more than you know. I am feeling soothed simply by being here with you, playing with Kolby and Kreed, and listening to stories of Cruestace."

"What is wrong, Kron? What happened? I can see the sadness. You normally have no expression other than happiness," Ada Jane said.

"Or fierceness. You can be very fierce," Kol said. "But not sadness. Speak. Tell us what troubles you," Kol said.

Kron sat quietly for several moments before confiding in them. "I claimed Ginger. I wanted to wait until she was more familiar with all it entails, but she was anxious to have it done. I am not sorry," he said. "But, she was unaware that her father had asked me to mate with her. When she learned of our discussions, she felt we manipulated her. She accused me of betraying her trust in order to better my position with her father because of his official position."

"Oh, Kron," Ada said.

"She is very angry. She left and returned to her mother's home. The last I was aware of, she had to take medication because her head was causing her pain, and she was expected to sleep for hours."

"Why does she think you manipulated her? Why wouldn't she just think that her father wanted you two to get together?" Ada Jane asked.

"Because her mother has been manipulating her, doing all in her power to coerce her into marriage with males of her choosing. She now thinks that her father did the same and I agreed, rather than being drawn to her as a mate should be. She will not speak with me."

"She will, Kron. She just needs some time to miss you," Ada Jane said. She looked affectionately at Kol, then reached out and placed her hand in Kol's when he lifted it toward her. "Trust me,

148

I know all about thinking you're being manipulated, then realizing how much you really miss your mate."

Kron nodded, remembering how Ada Jane had run from Kol before they were even mated. She'd run all the way back to Earth.

"How are you, Kron?" Kol asked.

"I am numb. I am worried. I am not sure what to do next. I want to go to her home, pull her from her bed and rush back to Command Warship 1 with her. I want to force her to see what she means to me."

"If you do, keep her away from Rokai," Kol said sarcastically.

"Rokai did not steal me! I ran," Ada said. Then she looked at Kron again. "Don't do that. She'll just think you're trying to force her to your will again. Make it clear that you love her, miss her, and give her a little time. Then you go and ask her if she'll talk to you. If she refuses, tell her you understand, but she at least needs to listen. Then tell her what you feel, tell her you will wait for her to change her mind. Let her see how much you hurt, how much you miss her. Then be outside her home each time she walks outside to go anywhere. Escort her there, make sure she's safe. If she won't let you ride with her, follow, be her bodyguard. Be her friend. Win her over all over again."

"Her mother may have me apprehended. She hates all aliens, no matter the species," Kron said.

"Well, that's helpful," Kol snarked.

Kron nodded. "I feel such pain," he confessed.

"She will come around," Ada Jane said. "If she doesn't, I'll call her and talk to her. I'll tell her my story. Explain that you would never have claimed her for political reasons. This is eternity to you and not worth a political decision over a decision of the heart."

"Thank you, Ada Jane," Kron said sincerely.

"You're welcome," Ada said.

"You will stay here with us. Though there has been no activity, you will stay here. The boys will distract you, and we will spar to reduce your frustration. It will allow the boys to learn of sparring firsthand. They have never been exposed to it," Kol said.

"Wonderful. They already bite. Now you want to teach them to fight?" Ada Jane asked.

"It is our way. Our young warriors learn by watching their fathers and uncles," Kol said.

Ada wanted to object, but she was reminded again that they were missing so much of their Cruestaci culture. "They will love seeing it, I'm sure."

"They will!" Kol said excitedly.

"Now, I have a question that I'm hoping Kron can answer," Ada said.

"What is it?" Kron asked.

"How do Zhuxi's men stay so well hidden?" Ada Jane asked.

Kron grinned at her. "Do you know the lizard that changes colors?" he said.

"The chameleon?" Ada asked.

"Yes, that is it. They share similar tendencies. They can become one with their surroundings. And they are quite lethal," Kol said.

"Oh my gosh! I'd have never guessed!" Ada Jane exclaimed.

"I was surprised as well. In addition, Zhuxi has let me know he is capable of a few other things," Kron said. "I assume it is a gift all of his people have. If so, they will know of the intentions of anyone they are near. They would have no doubt as to the intentions of anyone they encounter here."

"Is that how they get along with the dogs, too? At first I wasn't sure they would, but now they seem to have accepted each other," Ada said.

"I am not sure, but I would not be surprised if they are able to communicate with Billy and Bob on some level," Kron said.

"Agreed," Kol said.

"Why are we being targeted by the Purists?" Ada asked. "We've been here peacefully all this time. Why now?"

"We think it is personal. Not simply because I am not of this planet, or even Consul of Base 28," Kol said.

"So I'm not just being paranoid. They are targeting us," Ada said.

"It is what we believe," Kol said.

"But why?" Ada Jane asked.

"Your Dr. Cavanaugh is rumored to be a founding member of the Purist movement," Kron said.

"I had no doubt he was a Purist, but a founder?" Ada Jane asked.

"We believe so. Perhaps their highest ranking member. They are very secretive about their organization so it's difficult to know for sure. But we believe that he is still feeling slighted that you chose me over him," Kol said.

"He is also angry, I have no doubt. And now that he is sufficiently healed, I fear he is more focused on revenge than I had expected," Kron said.

"Sufficiently healed?" Ada Jane asked, looking back and forth between Kol and Kron.

Kron stumbled over his words for a few moments, then he came clean. "You told me he would not stop visiting your home. Kol was still being held by the Unified Consortium Defense, and it needed to be addressed. So, I went to visit him. I demanded he leave you alone, stay away from you altogether, and threatened his safety if he did not. When I turned to leave, he attacked me. In the scuffle I might have broken his wrist, or both of them, and maybe the bones in a hand, or two," Kron said, looking off toward the opposite wall innocently.

"Both wrists! And his hands?" Ada Jane said, her voice rising.

"Maybe," Kron said, shrugging. "I did not stay to learn of his injuries."

"But he left you alone afterward!" Kol said with a growl.

"Well, yeah. He was probably afraid you'd break something else," Ada Jane said.

"Had it been me, I'd have handed him his heart — literally," Kol snarled.

"It is all finished, now," Kron said. "I made sure he would leave you alone."

151

"Only now, he's determined to get revenge," Ada Jane said.

"It will be fine, my Ehlealah. As I said, I will hand him his heart," Kol said with a sinister smile.

Ada Jane nodded and placed her plate on the coffee table before leaning back against Kol who put his arms around her and hugged her to him before kissing her head. "Do not fear, my Ada Jane," Kol said assuredly. "No one will harm our family. Not a single one of us. I will not allow it."

Ada Jane sighed. "I know. I just hate that they can't just leave us alone."

"They will leave us alone," Kol insisted. "And Kron, and Zhuxi's people are here to help me ensure that it will be so."

~~~

Mrs. Buchanan lay back on the cushioned reclining chair before her favorite clinician at the day spa. Her eyes were closed and cool, thin cucumber slices covered the lids. Her face was slathered with what the spa claimed was an organic blend of nutritious herbs and extracts mixed with honey. Her purse began to ping and vibrate, disrupting the level of calm she'd achieved.

"Mrs. Buchanan, would you like me to get your purse for you?" the clinician asked.

"No. No, that's quite all right. It will only nullify the whole point of being here," Mrs. Buchanan said.

Only a few moments went by before the incessant pings and vibrations began again.

"Mrs. Buchanan..."

"I do not want to answer it!" she insisted.

"But, Mrs. Buchanan, it's ruining the experience for everyone else. Please answer it, or turn it off," the clinician asked.

Mrs. Buchanan reached up and snatched the cucumber slices off her eyes, then sat up. "Very well. Hand it to me!" she snapped.

The clinician handed Mrs. Buchanan her purse. She reached inside and dug around for a moment, finally finding her communicator and taking it out before looking at the screen on it. "Hmpf! After this I may as well just go home! I'm sure it will ruin whatever level of calm I've managed to achieve." She accepted the com and instead of pressing it to her ear, let it go to a visual com, which let the caller see that she was obviously busy. "What?!" she snapped.

"What?" Mr. Buchanan asked, shocked at her attitude.

"I am in the middle of something. What is it?" Mrs. Buchanan asked.

"I'm concerned about Ginger. How is she? Have you checked on her this morning?" he asked.

"No, I have not. She's not even..." Mrs. Buchanan stopped herself from saying she wasn't even there, and changed her attitude at once. "Now, I'm sure she's fine. You know I would never allow anything to happen to her. She's resting well and becoming herself all over again."

Mr. Buchanan's face took on a suspicious expression. "What does that mean?" he asked.

"It means she's fine. Don't worry about her."

Mr. Buchanan looked at his wife and the background of the vid-com. "Where are you?" he asked.

"If you must know, I'm at the spa!"

"The spa? Your daughter is home sick. I told you to remain on alert and at home, and you're having a damn facial!" he barked out.

"I have been under a lot of stress! I need to relax!" Mrs. Buchanan exclaimed defensively.

"You need to use your damn common sense!" he exclaimed.

"I will not speak to you if you are being disrespectful!"

"Did you even check on Ginger before you left this morning? Is the house secure?" Buchanan pressed.

"She's safer than she's been since she started frequenting your place of employment! At least there are no aliens trying to woo her there!" Mrs. Buchanan exclaimed.

Buchanan meant to control himself, he really did. But he was so on edge from all that had happened lately. He was tired of having to bite his tongue because of his wife and her self-imagined delicate nature. She was a bigot. And a meddling one at that. "Let me be perfectly clear, Susanna Jo Buchanan! Every alien I've ever met, with the exception of Diskastes, is a much better person than you'll ever be! You will not speak of my friends that way, you will not insult them or anyone else I respect. In fact, if you continue to do so, I will have no problem packing your butt back to your daddy! I'm done with you!"

"I will not stand for your insults! What about the respect you owe me?!" she screeched into the vid-com.

"Respect is not owed, Susanna Jo. It's earned. And so far, I've seen you do little to earn anyone's!" Buchanan snapped. Then he ended the vid-com, leaving her no way to reply.

Susanna Jo Buchanan was flustered to say the least. She was near hysterical as she jumped to her feet and started to rush off in one direction then the next. She wasn't sure where to go or what to do.

"Mrs. Buchanan. How can I help?" her clinician asked, concerned about the always seemingly frail woman.

"I have to get home," she said, her voice trembling. "I have to get home right away." She looked down at the robe she was wearing. "My clothes. Where are my clothes?"

"They're in the changing room, I'm sure. Come with me. Let's get you dressed and then we'll call a transport to take you home."

Chapter 16

Buchanan slammed his communicator irritatedly to his desktop and got up. He walked around the office, his hands shoved in his pockets as he paced. He'd tried time and again to contact his daughter through the main communicator in his home since he'd hung up on his wife after their argument. But no one was answering. Obviously Susanna Jo wasn't home yet, and Ginger was still sleeping, or she was angrier than he'd thought she was.

"This is bullshit," he grumbled. He walked out of the office all the governing members of Base 28 shared, and set out to find Zhuxi. He'd made a decision, and couldn't wait any longer to implement it.

Locating Zhuxi in the security offices of the base, he waited until Zhuxi was finished speaking with the captain in charge of this shift.

"Is there anything else?" Zhuxi asked.

"No, sir. We fully understand. All is under control. We'll remain on high alert," the captain said confidently.

"Excellent," Zhuxi answered. Then he turned to Buchanan. "You are worried," he said, as he began to leave the security command center.

Buchanan fell into step with him. "Yeah. I am. We're all good here. Kron is assisting Kol. All we're doing is holding down the fort. If you're okay with it, I'm thinking I need to run home and see what's happening there. I spoke to my wife this morning, and she's off at the damn spa despite me telling her to stay at home. Ginger's not answering the main com at home, and I'm not sure if she's still asleep, angrier than I thought, or not even there."

"I do not mind at all. Go. It is best you speak with your daughter. When you return you will have all the answers you need, and we will be able to put Kron's mind at ease as well."

"I won't be long. I'm thinking I'll most likely bring Ginger back here with me. Her mother is just simply off the deep end. I'm done trying to even reason with her. Com me if you need me before I get back," Buchanan said.

"I will," Zhuxi said, patting Buchanan on the back.

~~~

Buchanan brought his government issued transport to a stop just outside his home. He secured it, and opened the door which automatically extended the small ladder-like stairs he'd need to descend to ground level. He hurried down them and into his house.

"Ginger!" Buchanan called out. He paused where he stood, listening for any response. He knew his wife wasn't there yet, but tried to call out to her anyway. "Susanna Jo?!" When there was still no answer, he went directly to Ginger's bedroom and tapped on the door. "Ginger? Baby? You awake?" he called out.

There was no answer. He tapped on the door again, then reached for the doorknob, opening it slowly and peeking inside. "Ginger?" he asked again, flipping on the light.

Then he realized her bed was empty. She wasn't in her room. Buchanan's gaze traveled to her bathroom and he walked toward it, knowing before he got there Ginger wasn't in her bathroom either. The light was off and the door was open. Buchanan poked his head inside and seeing that it was empty, too, he walked over to her bed. A towel lay on top of her pillow. He picked it up and realized it was completely dry.

The sensor on his front door pinged letting him know someone was at his front door. His lips pressed together in thought, he kept his grip on the towel and left Ginger's room on his way to the living room.

As he walked into the living room, Susanna Jo was just closing the door behind herself.

"Where's Ginger?" he asked from a few feet away.

Susanna Jo turned to look at him, holding her purse against her chest almost like a shield.

"You're supposed to be at work," she answered, doing her best to look startled at him being there.

"Do not try to pretend you're surprised to see me. My transport is right outside, Susanna Jo. Where's my daughter?" he insisted.

"You mean our daughter?!" she said defiantly.

"Where?!" Buchanan shouted.

Susanna Jo realized Buchanan was holding the towel that had fallen from Ginger's head when Mitchell's men lifted her from the bed.

"Well, obviously, she took a shower and left," Susanna Jo said, indicating the towel that her husband was holding.

Buchanan looked down at the towel he held, then at Susanna Jo. "This towel is completely dry. If she took a shower and left, it was long enough ago that this towel had enough time to dry. While it was bunched up on her pillow."

"So?" Susanna Jo asked.

"So, it was not recently. You know where she is, or at least when she left. Where is she?" Buchanan asked, advancing on her slowly.

"I have no idea! And if I did, I wouldn't tell you!"

"You will tell me. She's my daughter and I have every right to know where she is! Is she even safe, Susanna Jo?" Buchanan demanded.

"Of course, she's safe!"

"How do you know that?" Buchanan asked. "Especially if you don't know where she is, how do you know she's safe?"

"Because I know!"

"How?" Buchanan bellowed.

"Because I know!" Susanna Jo shrieked. "I know she's safer than she ever was with all those alien creatures you associate with! How dare you expose our Ginger to those creatures?

157

How?!" she accused, her voice high pitched and hysterical. "You did nothing to keep her safe. It fell to me, and I did what I had to to protect my daughter! And did you care? Did you even once have a civil conversation with me about the steps necessary to keep her pure? Did you? No, you just kept brushing my concerns away. So I protected her! She's safe now, because of me!"

"What have you done?" Buchanan asked, a growing dread in the pit of his stomach.

"I did what you should have! I made sure she's in a place that is free from all aliens. She's in a place that will give her time to relax and learn about the mistakes she was making in a nurturing atmosphere. A place where that animal you allowed to have access to her, can't ever find her."

"Where is she?" Buchanan shouted, his expression frightening, his face red and the veins standing out in his neck and forehead as he backed her against the door.

Susanna Jo still held her purse against her chest as she looked defiantly up at her husband. "I am so disappointed in you! How? How could you think cavorting with those planning to control our world would be an acceptable behavior? I just don't even know you anymore," Susanna Jo said, as big, huge tears fell from her eyes. Then the communicator in her purse began to buzz. Buzz, not ping, as their communicators were set up to do.

Susanna Jo's eyes widened and her fake tears dried up immediately when she realized that her husband was focused on the sound coming from the communicator buzzing in her purse. She yanked her purse down and shoved it behind her back.

"Give me your purse," Buchanan said. His voice was no longer shouting. He was calm, deadly calm. And he was tired of her crap.

"No! It's my private property!" she snapped.

Buchanan clenched his teeth to force himself to maintain control, then he grabbed her upper arm and swung her around, causing her to drop her purse when he'd surprised her by grabbing her. Susanna Jo scrambled to pick up her purse, but Buchanan leaned over and swept it up, then turned and walked over to their kitchen table.

Before Susanna Jo was able even to try to snatch it from him, he upended it, pouring the contents of her purse out onto the tabletop.

"How dare you?!" she screeched, lunging for the communicator he'd already grabbed.

"What's this, Susanna Jo?" he asked.

"A communicator. My communicator. Give it back to me right this instant!"

"No, this is your communicator," Buchanan said, showing her the communicator he'd bought for her. He slipped it into his pocket. "Whose is this one? Where did you get it?"

"Give me that back!" she insisted.

"No, I'm not giving either back," he said, digging through the rest of the items that had fallen out of her purse. His fingers moved things this way and that, through the things normally found in a typically over crowded purse any woman might have. But then, he came across something he didn't expect.

"What's this?" he asked, picking up an empty plastic bag. There was a chalky residue inside one of the corners of the bag.

"It's a plastic bag!" she snapped.

"Susanna Jo, you have a choice to make. You can tell me what's happening here, or I can arrest you on suspicion of foul play."

"Foul play? That's not a real offense. And you cannot arrest me, I'm your wife! What would everyone think?" she asked, beginning to get nervous.

"Here's the thing. My daughter is missing. You've tried repeatedly to interest her in the Purist movement. In fact, you've arranged dates for her, invited them to our home against my wishes. And now she's missing. It just happens to be after she became bound to one of my coworkers who is an alien to this planet."

"You should be ashamed for allowing our daughter to lower herself this way!"

"No, you should be ashamed," he said. He shoved the other communicator into his pocket with the first, then he tucked the

159

plastic bag into his opposite pocket. "Turn around," he said, reaching for his handcuffs.

"You can't be serious!" she exclaimed.

"Turn around!" he bellowed, grabbing her again and turning her to lean against the table. He snapped the handcuffs on her, then walked her over to sit on the sofa. Standing in front of her, he took out the unfamiliar communicator and swiped his finger over the screen. He realized the communicator was programmed to her fingerprint and reached out, taking her by the shoulder and forcing her to her side, then her stomach so he could gain access to her hands cuffed behind her back. He took hold of her thumb and pressed it against the security screen, opening the communicator at once.

The entire time he was working toward unlocking the communicator, she hurled insults at him. He simply ignored her.

He released her and straightened up to watch the vidcom message she'd received. Buchanan watched a man he'd met at his own home by invitation of his wife smile at him from the recorded message on the screen. "Hello, Mrs. Buchanan. I thought I'd touch base and update you on the situation. Ginger has awoken, and was somewhat combative. Unfortunately we had to sedate her again, but, it's not all that unusual. It may take us a little longer than we anticipated, but fear not, your daughter will be returned to you as soon as we can. Again, just a reminder to keep our existence to yourself for the time being. We'll let you know when the time is right for family interaction. Rest easy, Mrs. Buchanan, and know that your daughter is in good hands. Human hands."

"You gave her to the Purists? Are you out of your fucking mind?" he turned and shouted at Susanna Jo.

Susanna Jo had been crying and screaming the entire time she sat on the sofa with her hands cuffed behind her, and the level of his shout now startled her into silence.

"What the hell is wrong with you? Don't you realize what they are? What they'll do to her?" Buchanan demanded.

160

"Yes! They'll teach her that the aliens are enemies. They'll teach her that she should not associate with any other than her own kind! They'll save her!" Mrs. Buchanan yelled back.

"You're under arrest for suspected conspiracy against our government and the United Consortium Defense," Buchanan said, yanking his wife up by the upper arm, and forcing her toward the front door.

"You cannot be serious! Release me!" Susanna Jo shrieked. "I am your wife!"

"Unfortunately, you are, for the moment anyway. And I am serious. This is just a start. I'm sure I'll add terrorist acts, kidnapping and any other number of charges I can find to it."

"I am not a terrorist! I'm your wife!" she screamed.

"You stopped being my wife years ago. I only tried for Ginger to keep this house together, and for the way I used to feel about you. But you've shot that all to hell over the last several years. Now your sick ideas have placed my daughter in danger. I can't pretend any more. You will be prosecuted to the fullest extent of the law. And you'd better hope I find her before they hurt her. If I don't, I'll happily go to jail after I shoot you myself."

"I cannot believe you said such a thing! How dare you? Release me!" Susanna Jo screamed at him, kicking at his shins.

"I will. As soon as I get you back to the base and into a cell. You're under arrest, Susanna Jo. I suggest you don't add assault of a government official to your growing list of crimes."

Buchanan ignored the neighbors that came outside their homes to watch the scene being played out as he loaded his wife, still handcuffed, into the back seat of his transport. Then he retracted the stairs, and closed the door as the transport lifted into the air and he turned it back toward the base.

Susanna Jo was screaming and crying hysterically, but instead of trying to calm her, he simply pressed a button that caused a panel of stainless steel to rise between the front and back seats of the transport, silencing her screams on his side. She was rocking herself from side to side so hard in an attempt to get free that he decided to lock the door of the rear cabin which was located behind the rear seats, just in case she managed to get loose, so she wouldn't be able to take refuge in the cabin and try to attack him when he went in after her.

Then he placed a call to the one person he knew would be as interested in finding his daughter as he was.

He waited nervously as the computer on the transport attempted to make contact with Kron. Finally, the com was successful.

"Buchanan, do you have news?" Kron asked, looking into his handheld communicator.

"Unfortunately, I do, Kron," Buchanan said.

Kron's expression became hardened. "She does not want to see me," Kron said.

"No, that's not it. She's gone, Kron. Her mother turned her over to the Purists."

"Tell me where she is," Kron growled.

"I don't know yet. But Susanna Jo somehow got her to the Purists. I don't know if they lied to her, or came to get her, or forced her. But I know she's missing. I've got Susanna Jo with me, under arrest. I'm pressing all charges possible. Hopefully she'll be so afraid, she'll tell me where the hell Ginger is to save her own skin. Only that won't work, I'm not releasing her."

"And if she doesn't?" Kron demanded.

"I have a communicator that belongs to them. Maybe we can figure something out from there," Buchanan said. "Get into it, and see if there's anything on it that will tell us where they are."

"I'm on my way," Kron said.

Kron ended the com and turned to Kol who was standing behind him in the living room.

"I heard," Kol said.

"I have to go," Kron said.

"Go! We will be well. Keep me updated, Kron. I will stand with you when you find her," Kol said.

"No, your family needs you here," Kron said, walking toward the door.

"Keep me updated!" Kol insisted. "I will come!"

162

Kron nodded but left quickly, his heart thundering in his chest, every nerve in his body on alert, terrified for Ginger and whatever she may be facing.

Chapter 17

The room was dark and musty. Humid from the lack of circulation. Ginger's brows pressed down over her eyes as she slowly came awake, irritated to be hot and sticky while she tried to sleep. She tried to roll over but found she couldn't move. She forced her heavy eyelids to open, slowly focusing on the hazy room. "The hell?" she muttered, licking her dry, sticky lips. "Mom! Mom?!"

"Shhh," someone hissed from nearby.

Ginger tried to turn her head toward the sound. "What's going on? Where am I?" Ginger rasped, her throat dry and her voice harsh from sleeping for so long.

"If they hear you, they'll drug you again. Stay quiet," a woman's voice warned.

Ginger listened to the noises around her. The quiet crying. The squeak of the springs beneath the bare mattress she was strapped to. The muffled movements of others in the darkness.

"Where am I?" Ginger asked.

"In hell," a male's voice answered defeatedly.

"I don't understand!" Ginger exclaimed, beginning to become really frightened. "Who are you? Why am I here?"

"You have an alien mate?" the same male asked.

Ginger hesitated, thinking of Kron. He was her mate, technically, but she'd run from him when she felt manipulated by him and her father.

"You don't have to answer. If you're taking this long to think about it, you're obviously trying to figure out how to frame your answer. We're here because we are guilty of associating with aliens. We've all got alien mates."

"Guilty of... it's not illegal to associate with aliens. What is going on? Let me up!" Ginger ordered, beginning to try to thrash

164

her body back and forth as best she could with her hands bound behind her, and her legs and body bound to the bed.

"You really don't want to cause too much trouble here. Just do what they say," the man said.

"Where is here?" Ginger asked, her voice shaky as her body stopped straining against the ties that held her.

"I don't know. But if you cause trouble, if you refuse to cooperate, they'll drug you again. Just do what they say and at least you'll not be zonked out of your head."

Ginger's mind raced with the possibilities of how she got here, but only one phrase kept running through her mind. She couldn't help but voice it. "Kron will come for me," she rushed out, doing her best to control the fear in her heart. "He'll come, I won't be here long. Nobody will be here long. He'll free everybody."

The woman who'd first warned her to be quiet answered with no hope at all. "That's what we all said."

"My mate will come," Ginger said confidently.

A door at the end of the dark room opened and heavy footsteps could be heard. Then a blinding light filled the room as the bare bulbs hanging from the ceiling were flicked on.

Ginger's eyes slammed shut against the lights on her still sensitive eyes.

"Well, well, well. What do we have here?" a man asked, coming to a standstill right beside the bed she lay on.

Ginger turned her head back and forth, unable to lift a hand to shield her eyes.

"Not going to talk today?" the man asked.

Ginger realized that the voice was familiar. She blinked, trying to focus again. "Mitchell?" she asked.

"You should have taken me up on my offer. You'd have been treated with respect, and trained to become an integral part of our organization. A daddy's girl like you would have been infinitely valuable in the intel you could have provided simply from spending time with your father at the base. But no, you think you're too good for me. Stood there and chose a fucking alien over me. Allowed him to disrespect me. Even afterward, acting like you're not interested in anybody at all. You rejected every man that attempted to reach out to you. Instead you chose a filthy alien. A fucking interloper. An invader. That makes you no better than them, now. So, welcome to your new realty."

"I can't just disappear. People will look for me. My mate will look for me! My parents will look for me!" Ginger warned.

Mitchell didn't laugh, he didn't argue. He simply stood there, looking at her for an uncomfortable amount of time. Then he shook his head. "You still don't get it, do you, you dumb bitch? Your mother is the one who drugged you. She drugged you, and called me to come get your ass out of her house. She's done. You humiliated her with your disgusting behavior. You belong to us now. You'll stay here. You'll give us any information we ask for. You'll keep your damn mouth shut otherwise, and we might feed you. You give us any shit and your meals will consist of sedatives — anytime you open your damn eyes, you'll be sedated. You'll sleep the rest of your life away while your father dances at our direction on the opposite end of the strings we pull."

"He'll never compromise his integrity," Ginger said, obviously angry now.

"If the life of his precious baby girl is involved, he'll do whatever the hell we say to do. Including giving us details of the inner workings of Base 28, any fucking alien he knows about, and anything else he has access to," Mitchell spat. "As I said, welcome to the rest of your life. Do your part, and maybe it won't be quite as bad you expect it to be. But then again, I make no promises. It all really depends on how well your father cooperates."

"What makes you think you can get away with this? You'll never get away with this! My mate will find me! He'll destroy you and all you even gave a second thought to. My father will find me! You'll pay for this! You took the wrong girl this time, asswipe!"

"The fact that our world is being quietly invaded and all are made to believe it's a good thing, is what makes me know this is the only way! I'll get away with it because not a single one of them is more intelligent than I am! This is a battle to liberate our

166

planet! And you spread your legs for the enemy. You deserve so much worse than this. Your only saving grace is the attachment Viceroy Buchanan has to your pathetic ass. It won't be long and we'll have the upper hand in the silent invasion that is occurring all over our great land. You, are merely a small, necessary means to an end. In the grand scheme of things, no one will miss you. No one will even remember your name."

"And what about all these people?" Ginger screamed at Mitchell. "You really think this many people can disappear and no one is going to figure out that we all have one thing in common?"

Mitchell's sneer fell from his face and he looked confusedly at Ginger.

"You, you damned idiot! We've all got some type of involvement with you, or people who are associated with you. It won't be long. You'll be at the mercy of those that won't give up on us. We'll be found, and when we are, I'll be the first one to put my boot in your ass!"

"You worthless bitch!" Mitchell snarled, stepping forward and slapping Ginger so hard her ears rang.

The sting of a needle in her arm let her know that she'd pushed Mitchell just about as far as she could. Her head began to swim, and she struggled to maintain consciousness, as she screamed in rage at him drugging her again.

"I have no problem keeping you sedated. You will learn manners, or you will stay this way. Daddy dearest can just as easily be sent photos of you unconscious and drooling as he can you sitting upright and staring into the camera.

"Fuck you," Ginger mumbled, struggling to hold her head up.

"No, fuck you!" Mitchell shouted into her face before backhanding her.

Ginger didn't know he'd hit her, though. She was already out cold.

"Any of the rest of you think to give us any resistance, I can make you more miserable than you already are. I suggest you don't try us," Mitchell said. He turned and walked away, pausing

167

to speak to one man who stood at the end of the room waiting for him. "Keep her tied down. And anyone else that makes any effort to defy you. There will be no leniency! But especially with that one. Stupid fucking bitch!"

"Yes, sir," the man answered.

~~~

Buchanan docked at the base and pulled his screaming, kicking wife from the transport. Her hands were still cuffed behind her back, but her fingers curled and reached as though trying to scratch at him regardless. She was insane with outrage and insult.

Several of the men on duty in the docking area rushed to help him. As they approached, they realized the screaming, fighting woman was familiar — she was Buchanan's own wife. "Sir?" the first to reach him asked, standing back to wait for instruction.

"Mrs. Buchanan is under arrest on suspicion of collusion with the Purist movement. Prepare the cell closest to the interrogation room. I'll be right behind you," he said, a growl in his voice, and his face twisted with the effort to control the squirming, pissed-off woman he struggled to keep under control while he moved forward.

"Right away, sir," the man responded. "It should be ready, but I'll double-check."

"Remove all traces of comfort. Only the bedsprings, and the toilet should remain. She's a risk," Buchanan shouted.

"How dare you?" Susanna Jo screeched! "I'm your wife!"

"Yeah, and that's on me," he mumbled as he both carried and dragged her down the hallways of Base 28 until he reached the security wing. Once there, he did not hesitate. He walked into the cell he'd indicated, looked around and saw that the mattress, the blanket, the pillow, even a paper cup for water from the

168

faucet mounted beside the toilet had been removed. "Perfect," he said, holding her by both shoulders in front of him. He forced her over to the bare springs of the cot and shoved her on to it, leaving her handcuffed. Buchanan leaned over her, right up close to her face and he spoke quietly to her. "You will tell me where my daughter is, or you will die here. If you do not cooperate, the death you suffer will make your worst nightmares seem like happy daydreams."

He turned and strode out of the cell, slamming the heavy barred door closed behind himself. The clanging of the door echoed and Susanna Jo's voice could be heard over it. "You won't kill me! I'm your wife! We have a history!"

Buchanan stood outside the bars of her cell and looked dispassionately at her. He stared at her coldly for a few moments before speaking. "I was just trying to feel anything. Anything at all that a husband should feel for his wife, or that any human should feel for another. There's nothing there. No matter what it began as, no matter what has happened along the way, you putting my daughter in jeopardy because of your fucked up belief system shatters that all to hell. There's no excuse. You will help me find my daughter, or you just might beg me to kill you. Which I'll be pleased to do. Then if I must, I'll go happily to jail."

Susanna Jo's mouth fell open, and he turned and walked swiftly away.

~~~

"You are sure his name is Mitchell?" Zhuxi asked.

"Yes. I had to sit across from the bastard twice in the last couple weeks. I should have shot him then," Buchanan answered.

Buchanan and Zhuxi were both typing hurriedly on their tablets as they searched for males with the first name Mitchell.

Buchanan was searching every listing within a hundred miles for males with the first name Mitchell.

169

Zhuxi was signed into the government mainframe they handled all employee records through, and was searching for anyone named Mitchell.

"Are you sure it is this male who has taken Ginger?" Zhuxi asked.

"Not a hundred percent. But it was his damn face leaving the message about having to sedate my daughter!" Buchanan snapped.

"I'm finding nothing," Zhuxi said.

"Me, neither," Buchanan answered.

"Perhaps Mitchell is his surname," Zhuxi said.

"Could be. I'm going to widen my search area, too," Buchanan said. "With a larger transport, he could make a same day trip without too much inconvenience."

Zhuxi nodded in agreement, then exited out of the program he was in. "I'm going to try to get into the system that secures the sector you live in. Perhaps the transport was captured on surveillance. There are several private as well as public security systems that could have picked it up."

Buchanan stopped typing and looked at Zhuxi. "That is why I want you on my team no matter what the hell we're doing. I didn't think of it!"

"You are not thinking, my friend. Your concern for your child and anger with your mate has clouded your mind. It is of no shame to have friends assist you," Zhuxi said as he focused on his tablet again.

The sound of heavy boots running up the hall toward them caught both Zhuxi's and Buchanan's attention.

"Kron?" Buchanan asked.

"Kron," Zhuxi confirmed.

The door was thrown open at the same time Kron demanded to know where his mate was. "Where is she?" he growled.

Zhuxi's brows rose as he took in Kron's appearance. His hair was a wild mass swirling about his shoulders, normally sharp teeth, were even more so, and his nose seemed to have lifted and flattened itself against his face. His cheekbones were more angular than usual, and his usually elegant, manicured hands were tipped in razor sharp claws, with yet more razor tipped blades protruding from his elbows when he bent them. His skin was covered in a natural armor reminiscent of hard, reptilian scales. He was a frightening thing to behold.

"We don't know yet," Zhuxi answered. "But we're working on it."

"We're trying to work on it. I have only what I think to go on. Susanna won't tell me anything except she'd never harm our daughter and she'll be right as rain when she comes home," Buchanan said.

"I want my mate!" Kron shouted.

"Me, too!" Buchanan yelled. "I already told Susanna Jo all charges will be pressed against her. Told her unless Ginger is found safe and healthy, I'll go to jail happy after I end her myself."

Kron stared at Buchanan. "I could possibly make her tell us all she knows."

"How?" Buchanan asked.

"You do not wish to know," Kron said.

"I'm not ready to go there yet. Maybe you could just intimidate her. Out of fear, she might tell you more than she did me," Buchanan said.

"I will try, but it will be hard not to take her in hand and..." Kron said, his hands out before him miming strangling someone with a scowl on his already altered face.

"I will go with you," Zhuxi said.

Buchanan nodded resignedly and stepped back. "Find my daughter, Kron. I'll do and say anything to explain away any action necessary to find her. Just find her."

"I will find my female, and I will bring her home. That is the only thing I can promise you," Kron said.

"It's all that matters," Buchanan said. "I'm trying to remember she's Ginger's momma. Ginger wouldn't want her hurt, you know?"

"Her being Ginger's mother is why Ginger is missing now," Kron growled as he turned on his heel and walked swiftly out of their offices with Zhuxi falling in right behind him.

Chapter 18

Ginger opened her eyes as the sensation of cool, soothing liquid fell across her forehead and face. Remembering where she was, she tried to sit up hurriedly as she struggled to focus on the room around her. But she couldn't move. She was still tied down. She blinked rapidly, doing her best to figure out what was going on through her still drug induced haze.

"Hello, Ginger Buchanan," a very soothing male voice said, as he used a towel to dip into a pail of cool water and bathe her face and neck with.

Ginger forced her eyes to center on the man's face, but there was no recognition there.

"Trying to figure out if you know me?" he asked, with a gentle smile. "You don't, not yet."

"Why are you being nice to me?" she asked.

He smiled. "Smart girl. Right to the point... not who am I, but what are my reasons. I like that."

"I'm sorry for the way you've been treated so far. My counterparts have a more... shall we say... brutal way about them than I do. But, their methods are sometimes more effective than mine, I must admit."

Ginger didn't say anything, she simply watched the man. His demeanor seemed very different from those she'd already dealt with, but she was not a fool. This man was making every effort to gain her trust, and she had no doubt this man's counterparts as he called them, knew he was here and exactly what he was doing.

"No comment? Hmm, well, I suppose you're still feeling the influences of the sedative you were given."

"I was drugged," Ginger accused angrily.

"Yes, you were. You were becoming quite a handful, I'm told. But, if you'll promise to control yourself, I give you my word

173

that you will not be treated that way again. Unless of course, you become hard to handle. Then it's mainly for your safety, not ours. We don't want you to hurt yourself. You see, any attempt to escape or inflict damage on any of us would be in vain and only your own safety would be at risk. To avoid that, you'd have to be sedated until you were reasonable again."

Ginger's brows pulled down over her bright yellow eyes as she regarded him in the darkness and hot humid air permeating the building they were in. She considered all he'd said, and that coupled with the way she'd been treated, and remembering that it was Mitchell who she'd originally awakened to, decided that this was a group effort to lure her into trusting them, making her comply with their way of thinking and whatever plans they may have had. There was no way she'd ever join their plans, no matter what they were, but she was not above making them think she would if it got her better treatment and maybe even access to communications of some sort to call for her father or Kron.

"Do you understand what I'm saying, Ginger? Or are you having trouble focusing?" he asked.

Ginger took a deep breath and let it out slowly, grimacing. "I understand," she said.

"Are you in pain?" he asked, showing concern for the grimace he saw on her face.

"My shoulders hurt. My arms are asleep. I can't move them," she said softly.

His gaze fell from her face to her shoulders, then to where he could see them no longer as she lay on them. "It is a bit of overkill, I think. If you're strapped to the bed, there is no reason for you to have your hands tied as well. Let me see what I can do about that."

"Thank you," she said.

"You're welcome. You see? Just a little kindness is all it takes to communicate with people. It's not necessary to inflict pain."

Ginger watched him as he stood from the bed she lay on. "I'll be but a moment. Let me call to have the ties around your

174

wrists removed. You'll be a good girl, won't you? I don't wish to have you sedated again. I have no doubt of your impeccable manners and upbringing. I know you know the proper way to behave. Do not disappoint me, Ginger."

"I won't," she replied, still wondering who the hell this man was. Ginger listened to his footsteps echo as he walked across the cement floor and out of the building. A few minutes later he was back with another man.

"Here we are," he said.

"You sure about this?" the man asked.

"Is it your job to question me?" the first man asked.

"No, sir, it's not," he said, leaning over and loosening the buckles on the leather straps that held her to the bed. He grabbed Ginger by the shoulders and yanked her to her side, then extracted a knife from the sheath on his belt.

Ginger's sharp intake of breath let the first man know she was afraid of the blade.

"Don't fear, Ginger. He won't harm you. He's removing the ties on your wrists."

Ginger glanced toward the man who'd been kind to her and waited as she felt the tugging on her wrists.

Then the man with the knife stood up and backed away from her. "There you go, Doc. It's on you if she tries to get away."

"She will not. She's a lady, raised as a lady with proper upbringing," the man answered, then he looked at Ginger. "Aren't you my dear?"

Ginger nodded.

The second man turned and walked away, as the first man turned his attention back to her as she whimpered when she started to try to move her shoulders and arms.

"It's going to hurt," he said. "After being stiff for so long and unused, the blood flow rushing back into your extremities will be painful. And if they've sprained your wrists while restraining you, it'll hurt even more. I have quite a bit of experience with the pain of healing wrist injuries," he said, using one hand to rub his opposite wrist.

"Were you tied up, too?" she asked.

"No. My wrists were broken, by a vicious, uncontrolled creature that has no right to be on our world!" he snarled, his smooth facade falling for a split second before he caught himself. He visibly took control of his emotions once more and then approached her. "If you'll trust me, I'll try to gently work the circulation back into your limbs."

Ginger's first impulse was to not allow him or anyone else near her, but if she played along, it might get her further than refusing. "Yes, please," she said quietly.

Doc, as the guard had called him, walked around the single bed she lay on and took a seat on the edge behind her. "Now, my hands aren't as strong as they used to be, but I can still do a thing or two to ease my patients," he said.

Ginger felt his hands on her shoulders, then whimpered as his fingers began to knead her muscles and joints. She gritted her teeth as he moved down her arm to her elbow, gently bending it, then moving to her wrist before moving around to the front of the bed and helping her to roll over before starting on the other shoulder and arm. By the time he was done, she was actually able to move much more easily than before. She looked up at him as she lay on her back and he stood looking down at her with a gentle smile on his face.

"There, you see? I told you I'd help."

Ginger nodded slightly. "You did," she agreed. "Thank you."

"You are most welcome. Would you like to sit up?" he asked.

"Yes, please," she said, beginning to lift herself from the mattress beneath her body.

He smiled brightly. "I knew you'd had proper training. Was it finishing school?" he asked as he held his hands out for her to hold onto as she raised her body to a sitting position.

"My mother insisted," Ginger said.

"An excellent mother. So many of the finer points of our former culture have fallen by the wayside as the world and its beliefs have been invaded. I hold precious those who still insist the old ways are indoctrinated into our children."

176

Ginger didn't say anything. She was busy trying to make her head stop spinning from sitting up after so long on her back. Then she realized she didn't exactly know how long she'd been here. She looked around at the other beds and found most of them empty. "Where are the others?" she asked.

"They've gone outside for a bit. If you are well behaved, you are given privileges. If not, you must earn our trust before we can allow you out," he said.

"Otherwise they may cause themselves to be harmed," Ginger said, watching him for reaction.

"Exactly!" he said, nodding enthusiastically. "You understand."

"I do," Ginger said, rolling her eyes in her mind at the self-importance this man obviously felt. But, it was a good thing. It made him believe her trust in him without much more effort than a few well placed comments and actions.

"Are you hungry, Ginger?" he asked.

"I'm... I'm not sure," she answered.

"The medication will sometimes throw off your system. But, if you can, you should try to eat a bite."

"We're fed here?" she asked, looking up at him.

"Of course, dear. We're not animals. We're simply trying to help each of you see the traps you've fallen into. Unfortunately it is sometimes necessary to bring the individual to the very bottom of their hopes, their false hopes, to make them realize their believed reality was a farce. Then we help them fight their way back up to become strong, prominent individuals who will stand beside us and fight for our country, and our world."

Ginger just looked at him with her mouth hanging open. These people were nuts, even more nuts than she thought.

"Oh, don't be alarmed," he said, rushing to reassure her. "That won't happen to you. You've got attributes most of the others don't have. You've got breeding and upbringing that most others do not have benefit of. When I heard that you were here, I came at once knowing the extreme measures required for some, would not be required for you."

"Thank you for that," Ginger said.

177

"Not at all. Now, may I escort you to have a bite to eat?" he asked, holding out his hand for her to take hold of and stand.

"I can try, I'm still feeling a little lightheaded," Ginger said, taking hold of his hand and trying to stand. She managed to get to her feet and used both hands to hold onto his forearms. "Am I hurting your wrists?" she asked, remembering that he'd said his wrists had been broken.

"They always hurt a little, dear. But I'm fine. Let me know when you feel steady enough and we'll be on our way. A little food will help you feel better."

"Thank you," she said. Then she looked up at him. He was an attractive man. Well spoken, well mannered and intelligent, with the ability to be kind. It was a shame he was bat-shit crazy, narcissistic and a megalomaniac to boot. "I heard the guard call you Doc. That just seems disrespectful. What is your name? I'd like to address you properly."

The man looked at her thoughtfully.

"If I may," Ginger added quickly.

He smiled at her indulgently. "I am Dr. Jason Cavanaugh. Former director of the Repatriation Medical Center in Washington D.C. And might I add it is quite refreshing to come across a young lady such as yourself in this day and age. One must have the utmost respect for Southern mothers and their insistence at raising their daughters right."

Ginger smiled at him and tried to take her first step despite the dizziness and nausea she was feeling.

"Oh... careful now... slowly," Dr. Cavanaugh said.

"Thank you, Dr. Cavanaugh."

"You're quite welcome, dear."

~~~

A door opened at the opposite end of the room that housed the cells in the detention area of Base 28. She could hear two sets of footfalls. Susanna Jo hurriedly got to her feet and pressed her

178

face to the bars, trying to see if it was her husband coming back for her. She knew he was angry, but he always forgave her, and he would this time, too. It might not be until Ginger came home, but at some point he would — she just knew it.

But her husband wasn't the individual she saw walking toward her. Nor was he right behind that inividual. Her eyes grew wide as she slowly backed away from the steel bars of the door she'd had her hands wrapped around. Her eyes were wide and her fear was clearly seen in her features.

"You go away!" she shrieked at Kron and Zhuxi as she pressed her back against the far wall of the cell. "I'll call for my husband!"

"Call for him," Kron said, making no effort to hide or soften the growl in his voice.

"He'll make you leave me alone! He won't be happy with you!" she threatened.

Kron smirked. "It is you he is not happy with. He knows we are here, in fact, he sent us."

She started shaking her head back and forth quickly. "No, no he wouldn't do that. He knows how I feel about..." she stopped short of saying aliens, "well, those like you."

"Aliens?" Kron asked. "Horrific creatures from another galaxy, or universe even, come here to steal your daughters and enslave the Earth?" he asked.

"Exactly! But, I didn't say that! It's just what other people say!" she lied.

"Why would we?" Zhuxi asked. "It is far too much trouble. We could very easily just blast the damned rock you live on out of orbit."

"Indeed," Kron agreed, still staring at the woman he'd like to tear the heart out of. But he knew if he did that, and Ginger was unhappy with him because of it, there would be no overcoming it. If however, when she was found, not if — but when, if she didn't mind so much, he had every intention of making this female pay for what she'd done to her own daughter.

"You... no, you couldn't do that," she said, looking from Zhuxi, to Kron, and back again.

"You make the same mistake most worlds do. You assume our technology is equal to or less than yours. You are a fool. If we wanted to destroy the Earth, it would already be gone, and you'd have never received a warning or message of any type. Just there one moment, gone the next," Zhuxi said, ending with a chortling sound Kron had learned was his people's way of laughing.

"But why? We have families and we care for each other. Why would you just kill an entire people?" she begged.

"We wouldn't without provocation, you foolish woman," Zhuxi said, shaking his head in disgust.

"Look at me, female," Kron ordered.

Susanna Jo Buchanan looked toward Kron, then quickly looked away. "Go away," she pleaded.

"Look at me!" Kron shouted.

Susanna Jo's gaze shot up and focused on Kron.

"Do you see me? Do you see the familiarity in my eyes? The sprinkling of little flecks of color across my nose and cheeks? Does any of it look familiar to you?"

Susanna Jo looked at Kron, then slowly she began to grasp what he was trying to say. "Oh my God! It's you! You changed my baby! She's got eyes like yours now! How could you?" she screamed, walking halfway back to the bars separating them from her cell.

"How could I?" Kron asked. "Because she is my female. She is my world. We are bound forever, an eternity longer than any you could ever imagine. My heart beats for her! Nothing in this world will stop me from finding her and bringing her home!"

"You forced her!" Susanna accused in a high-pitched voice.

Kron shook his head. "My kind do not force any female to become ours. It is only when a female is willing — the right female is willing — that we are able to bond with them. She chose me, as I chose her. And you sold her to the Purists as punishment for following her heart, as punishment for loving her choice of male. You betrayed your own child."

"I didn't sell my daughter! I would never sell my own child!"

"Then what would you call it?" Kron asked.

"I sent her to be refocused! They'll help her see what a ridiculous path she was on and return her to us happy and obedient once more!"

"They'll kill her and send you her body — maybe," Zhuxi said.

"They will not! They're human just like we are! They have regard for human life, unlike those trying to overtake our planet!" Susanna Jo screeched.

"Purists are interested only in their own agendas. They will not return her, and if they do, she won't be the female she was before you sold her to them," Kron said.

"I didn't sell her! All I had to do was pay for her upkeep and housing while she's away. They'll bring her back, you'll see! Only then she won't want you! She'll choose a nice boy, like Mitchell. Like she should have chosen to begin with. Like she would have chosen had you not clouded her mind!"

"You sold your own child for your political agendas," Kron accused calmly, noticing that the accusation of selling Ginger was what seemed to be upsetting her the worst.

"I did not sell her!" Susanna Jo yelled.

"You did," Kron taunted.

"I did not! Did not, did not, did not! All I had to do was give her the sedative and call them when she was asleep! I watched as they very carefully lifted her from her bed and carried her out to the transport! I didn't sell her! I sent her to a treatment facility to help her become the young lady she was supposed to be!" Susanna shrieked, until she was out of breath and red in the face.

Kron stood watching the woman that had given birth to his Ginger. He was stunned that such a loving, kind individual could have been born of such a narrow minded, angry, little woman. "You don't want her to be who she is. You don't care about her wants, or desires, or even her happiness. You simply want her to become your perfect little puppet to march when you say to march, and sit quietly in the meantime. How could any mother want their own happiness over their child's?" he asked.

"You don't know anything about us! You have no right to pass judgment!" she snapped at Kron.

181

"Consider yourself lucky that I do not have the privilege of passing judgment on you. I would not sentence you to death. I would instead sentence you to a lifetime of labor under the most virulent task master I could locate in the multi-verse. And I'd visit regularly to taunt you with images of the happy life my mate and I will share. Our children, our children's children, and Viceroy Buchanan right along beside us, loving his grandchildren, thankful for the removal of the sick individual who sought to have his daughter's very essence removed from her soul and replaced with a shell of a being with no opinions or thoughts of her own. You are the worst kind of evil I've ever witnessed."

"You don't know me! You have no idea how hard it is to watch your daughter choose…"

"What? A male that makes her happy? A male that worships her? A male that will die for her without pause? That's who I am, Susanna Jo Buchanan. I will save my female that she might live happily on her own terms. If I must give my life in order to achieve it, then so be it, but she will be free to live. The difference between us is that I want her happiness and joy, you want her happy only if she agrees to live the way you choose for her to live. You are not a mother. You are a disgrace." Kron turned from the woman watching him with her mouth hanging open in stunned silence as he accused of her of horrid things. He met Zhuxi's eyes, and Zhuxi gave him a subtle nod.

"You leave my daughter alone! You have no right to sway her mind!" Susanna Jo screamed after him.

"And you have no right to destroy her," Kron bellowed, rushing back to the bars as he snarled at her.

Susanna Jo backed up against the far wall again and watched him fearfully.

"She will never forgive you. You will live the rest of your life alone, be it days or months until your death, they will be alone, knowing you alienated your own child, betrayed her heart, and paid to have her soul ripped from her body to be replaced with your own ideologies. I actually wish you a long, miserable, lonely existence," Kron said, before walking away.

"No. You don't know that. She'll understand!" Susanna Jo objected, her lips beginning to tremble as she started to consider that she might have made a mistake.

Zhuxi followed Kron away from the cell. "Had we met her first, we might have simply disintegrated the planet."

"Agreed," Kron answered before the door at the end of the hallway clanged shut behind them.

Chapter 19

Kron and Zhuxi walked out of the detention holding cells just as Buchanan was coming down the hallway toward them.

"Were you able to get any information from her?" Kron asked Zhuxi.

"No, her mind is filled with visions of Ginger seated at a table sipping tea with dozens of other young women. I believe she's convinced herself her daughter is thankful to have been sent away and is enjoying her stay as though she were on holiday," Zhuxi said.

"I want to kill her," Kron snarled.

"It is an added reason for Ginger to resent you. If she must die, I will do it," Zhuxi said.

"I heard," Buchanan said, finally getting close enough to speak without yelling. "I feel like I should apologize," Buchanan said. "I had no idea she'd become so deranged."

"You are not responsible for her actions," Kron said.

"I should have stepped in long ago," Buchanan said resignedly.

"At least we now know a little more. She has indirectly confirmed that Ginger is in a deprogramming facility somewhere near enough to have been reached by transport."

"And we know for sure now that Mitchell is the male who has her, or at least left our home with her," Buchanan said.

"I will finish my security sweep of your home sector. Perhaps the transport was caught on security footage and we can track it," Zhuxi said.

"Thank you," Buchanan said. His voice and demeanor were quiet and subdued.

"All will be well," Kron said, walking toward the offices Zhuxi and Buchanan had been in when he arrived. "I will make it so." He went over to the work area in the center of the room and began to examine the two communicators Buchanan had taken from his wife.

"Maybe if I'd have acted sooner, I could have prevented whatever is happening to Ginger now."

"Perhaps," Kron answered. "But it did not happen that way."

"I cannot believe I underestimated her greatly," Buchanan said, rubbing his temples.

"Buchanan, I need you to focus. I will need your assistance in finding Ginger. If you are focused on things you cannot change, you will be of no use. Let what you cannot change go. We have much to do."

"I'm trying," Buchanan said, watching Kron as he examined the communicators. He took a deep breath and blew it out slowly, then walked over to where Kron stood. "This one is Susanna's, this one is not. She received a message on it when I was questioning her at home, and I forced her to press her finger against it so it would open. I viewed the vidcom, and I've tried to open it several times since, using her finger to unlock it, but it's not working. I think they shut it down. As far as her personal communicator, we've checked it, there are no unknown numbers incoming or outgoing," Buchanan explained.

"Then she must have exclusively used this one to communicate with those who have Ginger," Kron said.

"I would think so, but I don't know anything about the damn thing. I'm not technologically gifted."

"What did the vidcom say?" Kron asked.

"They wanted to let Susanna know that Ginger was resting comfortably, and assure her that Ginger would return to her the well behaved daughter she was raised to be," Buchanan said. "They said she's combative, and they had to sedate her," Buchanan said. "And they said it might take a little longer than they expected before she came home."

Kron shook his head, as a rumble sounded in his chest and he clenched his jaws.

"What that tells me is that she's fighting. She's not making it easy on them," Buchanan said proudly.

185

"That can be a good thing, or a bad thing. Hopefully, they do no more than sedate her. If they decide to try to reprogram her through torture or forced chemical means," Kron said, shaking his head, "I cannot guarantee that anyone will survive my wrath."

"And I'll be standing beside you when you dole out retribution," Buchanan said. Then he dug in his pants pocket and extended his hand toward Kron.

"What is this?" Kron said, taking the empty bag from him.

"I found it in Susanna's purse. It's got some white residue in it. I think it held the pills she drugged Ginger with."

"We may need to know exactly what drug it is. It should be analyzed," Kron said, looking thoughtfully at the white residue in the bottom of the clear plastic bag, before looking up at Buchanan.

Buchanan met his gaze. "I'll take care of it," he finally said.

Kron handed him back the bag, then looked down at the communicator in his hand and nodded slowly to himself. "If I can manage to open this thing without it becoming inoperable, I could perhaps reverse its programming, I might be able to use it to locate the network it runs on," Kron said. "I believe the network would be within their stronghold. And even if Ginger isn't there, someone there will know where she is."

He turned and started off down the hallway at almost a run.

"Where you going?" Buchanan called.

Kron didn't answer, he just kept going.

Buchanan hurried to catch up with Kron, and Zhuxi followed. Buchanan looked down at Zhuxi who was walking along beside him. "Where's he going?"

Zhuxi shrugged.

Kron turned down a hallway, then another before they figured out he was going to the IT office.

"What are you planning?" Buchanan asked.

"We're going to get into this communicator, and triangulate a location," Kron said.

~~~

Dr. Cavanaugh got Ginger situated across the desk from him in the surprisingly neat and organized office he'd taken her to. She looked around the office, blinking and squinting as he went to a drawer in a wall of wooden cabinets on the opposite side of the room.

"Here, my dear. Perhaps these will help with your eye sensitivity," he said, handing her a very dark lensed pair of sunglasses.

"Oh, yes! Thank you! I don't know why they hurt so much," she said.

Dr. Cavanaugh took a seat at his desk and picked up the classic looking telephone sitting on it. "Have lunch for two sent to my office," he said into the handset before simply putting it back in its cradle. Then he looked at Ginger sitting across the desk from him. He'd adopted the doctor's persona that he'd used for years with his patients when dealing with her on the hunch that she was not like the others that had fallen willingly into the arms of the filthy aliens that now inhabited this world. When he heard she was Viceroy Buchanan's daughter, he'd known two things: One, her mother was a Southern Belle from the best of families that could trace their lineage hundreds and hundreds of years into the path and even birth of this nation, and who no doubt raised her right. And two, that Ginger's father held power that he himself could very easily manipulate if Ginger were to become sympathetic to their cause and join them. Tying her to a bed and beating her false emotions out of her for whatever alien had preyed on her weaknesses was not the way to achieve that.

Now sitting across from the young woman, he had no doubt that he'd made the right decision. She responded to kindness and guidance, not violence. He laid his hands on his desk and linked his fingers. "If I may ask, Ginger, what color are your eyes, dear?"

She wore dark glasses, so he couldn't see her eyes, but her face was turned toward him and she appeared to be focused on him. Ginger thought about his question. He apparently thought

187

she wasn't aware of her eye color. It obviously wasn't a color any human ever possessed, so it came from her mating Kron. Watching him, watching her, she was aware it was again to her benefit to play the victim. "They're green. Well, greenish. If I wear certain colors they'll take on a blue hue. And they've always been light sensitive, but this is just so unusual. I can barely keep from tearing up they're so sensitive to the light. Even inside."

Dr. Cavanaugh smiled at her patiently. "I'm afraid I've got some bad news for you, Ginger."

"What is it?" she asked.

"Have you been intimate with an alien? I hate to put it so bluntly but there really is no other way to say it."

"I... well, it just..." she stuttered, trying to decide just how much to say. Finally she folded her hands in her lap. "Yes. Yes, I have. He said he loved me and wanted only my happiness. I believed him." Ginger didn't say anything more. Letting him read into it whatever he liked.

"Yes, well, they are very good at leading our young women astray. Do not reprimand yourself too much. You are not the only woman to fall for their lies and machinations. You have something they do not. Your mother loves you and was willing to make the sacrifice to call us in, to help you find the woman she knows you to be. We're here to help you dig out from beneath the mountains of lies and fallacies that keep you from seeing the truth about these creatures."

Ginger's jaw clenched as any doubts she'd had concerning her mother putting her here were dashed to bits. She closed her eyes and took a moment to compose herself before opening her eyes and looking at Dr. Cavanaugh again. She remembered almost immediately that he couldn't see her eyes through the sunglasses she wore. Good. He didn't need to see the hate that suddenly flared to life at receiving confirmation that her own mother was responsible for putting her here.

"Are you well, Ginger?" he asked concernedly.

"I am. Just taking a moment to realize my mother is to thank for me being here, away from all that I'd thought was the right choice," she said. She spoke the truth, only twisted it just slightly so he'd get the meaning he wanted from it. She had realized her mother was the reason she was snatched away from all she held dear. Mitchell had shouted as much at her, telling her her mother was ashamed of her. But now she knew it wasn't just an angry Mitchell screaming at her. Her mother had actually betrayed her. Without talking to her, without asking for her to explain her choices, without even a consideration, the woman who'd given her life — the same woman she'd respected because she was her mother — even when she didn't agree with her opinions, had just driven a wedge through every bond she'd ever felt to her.

"She is. And you're lucky, not every mother is strong enough to commit to their child's future as yours is."

"Of course," Ginger said.

There was a knock at the door and Dr. Cavanaugh called out. "Come!"

The door opened and a man walked in carrying a tray. "Lunch, Doc."

"Thank you. Just put it here on my desk," Dr. Cavanaugh responded.

The man delivering lunch seemed surprised when he glanced toward Ginger. He did a double take and then looked at Dr. Cavanaugh who simply stared him down. "That'll be all," he said in clipped tones.

"Yes, sir," the man said, leaving the office and pulling the door closed behind him.

"Forgive the fare, if you will. It's not gourmet, and not even slightly elevated. But it is fresh, and it will fill your stomach," Dr. Cavanaugh said, taking the plastic wrap off his sandwich and chips, while motioning with his head for her to do the same.

"I'm sure it's fine, Dr. Cavanaugh," she said. "Thank you. I appreciate your kindness and your consideration." Ginger took the plastic wrap off her sandwich and lifted one half of the sandwich to her nose, sniffing it.

She looked up to find Dr. Cavanaugh smiling at her. "I give you my word, it's not laced with anything. As long as you give no reason, you will not be sedated again."

Ginger smiled hesitantly at him and took a small bite of the sandwich. "I'm sorry. I meant no offense."

"Of course not. It's not in your nature to be offensive. That is easy enough to see, even to those who do not know you well."

They sat eating together, and eventually, Dr. Cavanaugh began speaking again.

"I'm not sure how to address this with you, Ginger. I understand the situation you find yourself in is very frightening and different from any you expected to find yourself in. I can understand the fear and unease that comes from waking up in a place you don't know, with people you don't know."

"Tied to a bed and drugged when you asked questions."

"And that," Dr. Cavanaugh conceded. "As I said, I am sorry about that. I will speak to Mitchell about your treatment."

"I don't think he'll care. I rejected his advances and I'm afraid he took it personally," Ginger said.

"He's not exactly the caliber of male that a lady like yourself would be drawn to. He's not familiar with the finer, delicate things in life, is he?" Dr. Cavanaugh asked.

"No, not exactly," Ginger answered.

Dr. Cavanaugh smiled at her for a moment before getting back to his point. "Anyway, my point is, I know your life seems out of your control at the moment, and I'm sure this new bit of knowledge won't help that situation. But, there has been a change that I'm not sure you're aware of."

"What change?" she asked. That was not what she thought he'd say.

"Your eyes, dear. They're so sensitive because there's been a change. Apparently, they took on characteristics of the alien who abused you."

"Abused me?" Ginger asked.

"Yes. Isn't lying to a female in order to gain access to her most private favors and trusts abuse?" Dr. Cavanaugh asked.

"Yes, I suppose it is," she answered. "And my eyes?" she asked.

"Are no longer green. They've changed greatly."

"Are they blue? They look like that sometimes," she said, playing stupid.

"No, Ginger. They are not blue. Your eyes are quite… inhuman," he said, seeming hesitant to use the word.

"Inhuman?" Ginger asked, her brows rising above the rim of the dark glasses she still wore.

"Would you like to see?" Dr. Cavanaugh asked, rising from his seat.

"No," Ginger said. "Just tell me."

He paused halfway to the wall of cabinets again and turned to face her. "Ginger, my dear, your eyes are yellow."

"Yellow?" she echoed, pretending to be shocked.

"Yes, yellow. And as sensitive as blue and green eyes are to the sun and bright lights in general, I can only guess how much more sensitive yellow eyes are."

"Yellow eyes," she said, sitting back in her chair.

The door flew open and Mitchell stomped into the office. "Why the hell is she not tied up?" he yelled.

Ginger stood quickly, using the doctor's desk to steady herself as she turned to face Mitchell. He was obviously angry, and she didn't want her back to him. But Dr. Cavanaugh surprised her. He turned to Mitchell, then calmly walked across the room to place himself between her and Mitchell.

"There seems to be some misunderstanding here," Dr. Cavanaugh said, his voice measured and steady.

"Yeah, the one that has her untied and in this office eating lunch that she hasn't earned!" Mitchell said.

"No, not that one. The one that you think gives you the right to storm into my office and begin to yell at my guest, and myself especially, about what you think can and can't be done."

Mitchell's eyes narrowed and he pulled his attention away from Ginger, focusing on Dr. Cavanaugh.

"Yes, that's right. Remember your place, young man. This is my group. My operation and my organization. If you don't approve of the way I run it, feel free to leave it and establish your own."

"You don't understand. She's combative and a liar!" Mitchell said, his voice still raised.

"She is not in the least combative. She simply doesn't respond to your dominating, physical mannerisms. And I do not blame her in the least."

"You don't know her! I tried for weeks to get on her good side. And the first chance she gets she runs off and fucks a goddamn alien. Her own mother is outraged. Why do you think she's here now?" Mitchell yelled.

"Apologize!" Dr. Cavanaugh yelled, his voice louder and more demanding than Mitchell's had been.

"What?" Mitchell asked, actually taking a step back.

"Now! Apologize to her now!" Dr. Cavanaugh demanded, striding toward Mitchell.

Mitchell backed up another couple of steps, but right before the doctor reached him, he finally stammered, "I'm sorry," a couple of times.

"You will address her respectfully. You will not blame her for choices she was not responsible for making. You will make it a point to learn and remember that these people have been manipulated and taken advantage of. They are victims. And we are their saving grace."

"But this one is valuable. We need to take full advantage…" Mitchell said.

"Out!" Dr. Cavanaugh bellowed. "Get out of my office! Miss Ginger Buchanan is under my personal protection! She is not to be accosted or attacked by you or those you dictate to. Am I clear?" he demanded.

"Dr. Cavanaugh, you don't understand what it takes to make this place run properly. I have to…"

"I don't give a damn what you've convinced yourself you need to do. I ran this operation before you, and I will be here running this operation after you. Stick to your lane, young man, or I'll remove you from my highway. Am I clear?" Dr. Cavanaugh asked, very calmly.

"Yes, sir," Mitchell snapped, shooting Ginger a hateful glare before turning and leaving the office.

192

Dr. Cavanaugh walked over to his office door and slammed it shut. He took a moment to compose himself, then turned to face Ginger with a smile on his face. "Now, then. I'm sorry for that most offensive interruption. Where were we now?"

Ginger stood quietly watching Dr. Cavanaugh. Yes, he'd protected her, but he was clearly more unstable than she'd originally thought. Not only was he obviously very involved with this movement, the Purists if she wasn't mistaken, he was its leader, and all others answered to him. He was certainly not stupid by any means. She'd have to tread lightly. If he found out it was she who'd begun to manipulate him, it could mean the end for her for betraying his impression of her.

"Ginger?" he asked again, waiting pleasantly for her to respond, still wearing his smile.

"Hmm? Oh, my eyes. You said my eyes are yellow," she said, her voice low and controlled.

"They are. But, a good pair of glasses, like those I've given you, will help with the sensitivity."

"Are they hideous?" she asked, knowing they were in fact, quite beautiful. They weren't what she was accustomed to, but they were almost just like Kron's, and Kron had gorgeous eyes.

"No," he said thoughtfully. "Not hideous, just, not usual. They will take some getting used to, but I have hope that when the alien who groomed you for mating, and betrayed you in doing so, is caught and killed, your eye color may return to your natural color. If it doesn't, a good pair of dark glasses obviously does the trick."

Ginger's heart thundered at the thought of Kron being hunted and killed. She couldn't allow that to happen. Her mission had in that very instant changed from trying to free herself, to making sure that they never harmed Kron.

"Wouldn't it be wonderful if your eyes did indeed return to their beautiful green?" Dr. Cavanaugh asked.

Ginger nodded as he walked toward her. "Here, Ginger. Have a seat, let us finish our meal, I hope it will be the first of many."

193

Ginger nodded again as she moved to take her seat once more.

"It's tuna, you know," Dr. Cavanaugh said, holding up half of his sandwich to show her. "Brain food," he said with a grin. "All the omega 3 oils."

"Ah," she said nodding. "Yes, I do remember hearing that."

"Well, eat up, then. And when you're done, I'll show you where you'll be sleeping."

Ginger's gaze shot up to Dr. Cavanaugh, who was busy rearranging the potato chips on his plate in the order of size, biggest to smallest and had no idea she was looking at him. Oh holy hell, if this man thought she was sleeping with him, she might just take her chances fighting Mitchell. At least he had one mood — he hated everything. This man was all over the damn place and completely unpredictable. That made him more dangerous than Mitchell any day of the week.

Chapter 20

Huddled over a workbench in the antiquated IT offices of Base 28, Buchanan and Zhuxi watched as Kron used every trick he knew to try to gain access to the communicator. There were several other personnel standing around them watching as well.

After a fourth failed attempt, Kron snarled and jumped to his feet. "There has got to be a way to access this damned thing!"

"Elisha could have done it," one of them said.

Kron turned to look at the man.

"He could have, I mean she, could have," the man said. "She loved playing old video games from before the first invasion. And she wrote code, too. Programs to link our ancient computers to the ones with the civilizations we were working with when Washington couldn't manage to get us a reliable one."

"No one else here retains the knowledge Elisha has?" Kron asked.

Zhuxi shrugged. "She was over-qualified when she was here. She was not hired because of those skills, just happened to have them as well as speaking multiple languages. We haven't needed anyone with that skill set before her, or since she left."

"The programs she wrote are operating without problems. We're good to go," Buchanan agreed.

"Until now. We need her now," Kron grumbled, reaching for his own personal communicator, not the one issued by Base 28.

He powered it up and a female voice spoke at once. "Greetings Elite Warrior Kron Val Kere."

"Greetings, Missy. I must speak with Ba Re' Non Tol, right away, please."

"He is in a training mission at the moment, Elite Warrior Kron. May I take a message?"

"A message?" Kron asked.

"Yes. Through Sirena Vivian I have learned it is much warmer and welcoming to offer to take a message, than issue a directive to initiate a return com," Missy explained.

"Where is Elisha Non Tol? She is who I actually am in need of," Kron said.

"She is no longer aboard Command Warship 1. She is currently on board the United Consortium Defense Space Station."

"Without Ba Re'?" Kron asked.

"Yes," Missy said.

"I need to speak with Elisha now!" Kron shouted.

"Rudeness will not be responded to in a positive light, Elite Warrior Kron."

"My rudeness is the least of concerns. My female is missing! Elisha may be able to help us trace those who took her! I need Elisha now!"

"Please standby," Missy said.

"Who is Missy?" Buchanan asked.

"Ship's computer. Artificial Intelligence," Kron answered.

"She sounds human!" Zhuxi exclaimed.

"She learns from our Sirena, who is human," Kron grumbled.

The line made a sound that let Kron know someone was back on the line, even if it was just Missy. "Hurry up! My female is in danger!" Kron shouted.

"I am aware. And I'll need more information than that," a deep growly voice rumbled in a language that sounded like snarls and growls to all in the room but Kron.

"Sire!" Kron said in Cruestaci, "I am Elite Warrior Kron Val Kere. They have taken my female! We believe that Elisha Non Tol could help us track them through the electronics we've located," Kron said.

"Who has taken her?" Zha Quin asked.

"We believe it is a group known here as the Purists. We have a device in our possession that may have been used to contact them to ask them to come for her. There is no one here that is able to access the information inside it. It shut down after the last time we tried."

"Surely there is someone on that base that can offer some assistance," Zha Quin said, while he motioned at Vennie to contact Bart.

"No. This is a remote base. We do not have updated equipment or personnel used to process that equipment. If it was similar to our own, I could have hacked through it with no problem, but it seems to be a combination of ancient earth technology, combined with pieces from several different worlds."

"It would seem they were protecting against having anyone being able to access their databases," Quin said.

"I agree," Kron answered.

"Hold, I've got Bart on vidcom," Quin said.

Quin was gone for a moment, during which Zhuxi and Buchanan looked questioningly at him.

"That male is Sire Zha Quin Tha Tel Mo' Kok," Kron said to them, switching back to English.

They simply nodded. He was a frightening male.

Then, Quin was back. "Kron!" he nearly shouted, his voice demanding an immediate answer.

"Yes, Sire!" Kron responded.

"Bart will have Elisha reach out to your base immediately. Be ready for the incoming vidcom," Quin said.

"Thank you, Sire. Thank you," Kron said.

"Kron?" Quin said, his voice becoming low and deadly.

"Yes, Sire,"

"I have had enough of this planet and its people. The more we attempt to accommodate, the more we are provoked into being the agressor. If they do not return your female, we will be forced to simply take her back and they will behave as though we were at fault."

"I will keep the Cruestaci out of it. They will not know that you are aware," Kron said. "They will assume that I have acted alone. I assume all responsibility for my actions."

197

"Just get your female back. Try to use control. But if you have no choice, use any means necessary. Get her on a transport and return to Command Warship 1."

"Yes, Sire. But…"

"But, what?" Quin barked out.

"I have no transport other than Kol's that is equipped to make the journey to Command Warship 1, and I don't wish to leave Kol without it. He may need it. And I'm here to support Kol in his mission as Consul to Earth Base 28. I cannot just leave him unsupported."

Kron waited while Quin was grumbling under his breath, and ordering someone in the background to get a conference room ready for him. Then he turned his attention back to Kron. "I'm sending an unidentified transport for you. Should it be detected during travel, it will not be identified as Cruestaci. Get your female on it and get back here. I'll handle Kol," Quin said.

"Yes, Sire. Thank you, Sire."

"End com!" Quin shouted, and the line went dead.

Buchanan and Zhuxi both looked at Kron with surprise on their faces.

"What was that all about?" Buchanan asked.

"He is supportive of anything I must do to bring Ginger back to us," Kron said. He didn't tell them he'd been ordered to return to Command Warship 1 with her the moment he had her in his arms again.

Then the main communicator for the base began chirping. Zhuxi walked over and pressed the button to accept the vidcom.

"Patroon Zhuxi!" Elisha exclaimed happily.

"Elisha! We have missed your presence today more than most," Zhuxi said.

"What's wrong? Chairman Bartholomew got a request from Commander Zha Quin Tha for me to contact my home base immediately. From the look on Bartholomew's face, I'm pretty sure it wasn't a request, and more of a demand," Elisha said.

"Elisha!" Kron said, stepping into view and taking over the vidcom. "I need you to help me reverse engineer this!" he said, holding up the communicator he'd love to crush to the floor he was so frustrated.

"Kron, hi. Okay, what's the problem?" Elisha asked.

"It is a combination of technologies. I am told you are versed in many. Please, it must be done expeditiously."

"Okay, we can try," Elisha said.

"There is no try! They have my female! We must succeed!" Kron shouted.

"Who?" Elisha asked, realizing the gravity of the situation. "Who took her?"

"The Purists," Kron answered.

"Oh, Kron. I'm so sorry. Bring it closer so I can see it. Let's get started," Elisha said.

Buchanan and Zhuxi stood back quietly watching Kron and Elisha work for almost an hour. Once they had the communicator just about functional, it shut down again, locking them out.

"Fuck!" Kron screamed.

"Wait, what flashed across the screen right before it shut down this time?" she asked.

"A design. A fingerprint," Kron said, then his head popped up and he looked at Elisha on the vidcom. "A fingerprint! I need only force the person who it belongs to to press her finger against it!"

"No! It may let whoever is monitoring it — and if it's the Purists that have your mate, they're monitoring it no doubt — know that it has been compromised if they can access the screen without you comming them, and see that it's not her using it. If they know it's been compromised, they will shut it down and it will not be of use to us. We need to go another route," Elisha said.

"Tell me what to do," Kron said.

She thought about it for a moment, then nodded to herself. "Stomp on it. Hard enough to break it, but not destroy it," Elisha said confidently.

"What?!" Kron asked.

"Trust me," Elisha said. "It will send them the signal that the communicator has been broken. Then you take the chip from it,

199

and place it in a different communicator. Take whatever information you want from it."

"I need a tracker. Will it take me to where its network is being monitored?" Kron asked.

"Possibly. I hope it will," Elisha said. "If I'm right and it works, I'll put together a quick little program to help you."

"You hope it will?" Kron asked.

"Yes, hope is a good thing. Break it," Elisha said.

Kron dropped the communicator hard enough onto the floor to let it register a shock, then he brought his boot down on it. It fizzled, then seemed to go silent and dark. "Done," Kron said, scooping up the pieces and laying them on the table.

Elisha walked him through placing the chip into another com, while she was typing away as quickly as possible. "Okay. I've been typing up a quick tracking program. I just piggybacked it on the one already running on the mainframe of the system there at Base 28. Once you've got the new communicator powered up, you place it on the station near the mainframe. I'll need a little time to go through its software. Then, hopefully, it should begin to trace its origin without further prompting. You'll use your Cruestaci communicator to view the homing signal that this one is expected to output. Just give me a little time to finish what I'm doing."

"Will they not know their software has been compromised?" Kron asked.

"I'm planning to do my best to hide the tracking program in its original code," Elisha said.

"Elisha will be successful," Zhuxi said. "She is gifted."

"Thank you, Patroon Zhuxi," Elisha said as she typed furiously on her keyboard.

"You are very welcome," he said. Then his expression changed and he looked at her suspiciously. "How are you downloading your programming to the system here?" Zhuxi asked. "We change the passwords regularly."

Elisha stopped typing and looked sheepishly at Zhuxi. "I'm not downloading anything. I'm working directly in the system. I might have a few secret back doors still in it."

"I don't give a damn what she has as long as she finds Ginger!" Buchanan said.

"Ginger! Oh, no! It's Ginger?!" Elisha said. "I'm so sorry, Viceroy Buchanan. And Kron, your mate... I hope you find her. I'm saying extra prayers for protection and guidance. We'll have a nice visit when you come back with her. I know in my heart you'll find her."

"You will know if I don't. I will not be back. My female is my world, without her, there is no point," Kron said.

Just then another tone sounded letting them know another communication was attempting to connect with Base 28.

Zhuxi walked over to the main com network and pressed a button, which split the screen in half. One half of the terminal screen was Elisha, the other half... Ba Re'.

"Kron, what have you found so far?" Ba Re' asked in English, clearly having been updated on the situation by Zha Quin.

"Nothing of much consequence. Elisha is walking me through reconfiguring the communication device we've recovered, and she's in our database now writing a program that will support the tracking abilities we will need to locate my female," Kron answered.

Ba Re's expression changed, and it was clear he was not himself. "She will help you succeed, I have no doubt," he said very calmly.

"Thank you for the compliment, Ba Re'," Elisha said, having heard his words, though she was unable to see him.

"They are not empty words," Ba Re' answered, his tone sounding defensive.

"I know," Elisha responded.

"When do you attack? Do I have time to arrive and support you?" Ba Re' asked, refocusing his attention and emotion from his wayward Ehlealah to his friend and the problem at hand.

"As soon as Elisha manages to get us coordinates," Kron said.

Ba Re' did a quick calculation in his head. "There is no way for me to arrive in time. But I will be there immediately thereafter if my assistance is needed. I will go to Quin now and advise that I wish to support you. I am in need of a battle," Ba Re' grumbled.

"You're in need of an attitude adjustment," Elisha mumbled under her breath.

"What did you say, Ehlealah?" Ba Re' asked, genuinely not having heard her.

"Nothing. Not a damn thing," she said, still typing.

"I appreciate your desire to assist me, but I believe Quin has other plans," Kron said, not feeling comfortable with repeating his earlier conversation with Quin to Ba Re' without express permission. "You should speak with him before you make any plans to leave Command Warship 1."

"I will," Ba Re' answered. "But, in the meantime, please bring me up to date that I might be prepared. Even if he refuses my request to join you, I will be prepared to help run the mission."

"It is not a mission sanctioned by the Cruestaci, or the Consortium," Kron said.

"It's not?" Ba Re' asked.

"It is not. I am going to get my female back. I will do whatever is necessary. The Cruestaci cannot be connected to my actions in the event there is nothing left of the facility or those in it when I am finished," Kron said.

"Who's going with you? Who will support you?" Ba Re' asked.

"I am," Buchanan said.

"Buchanan," Ba Re' said, acknowledging the male for the first time. It was not a time for pleasantries. He'd not acknowledged Buchanan or Zhuxi, and both understood.

"Ba Re'," Buchanan answered.

"Thank you for supporting Kron in our absence," Ba Re' said.

Buchanan shook his head. "I'm going for my daughter. I would support Kron regardless, but this is personal to me as well. Kron is mated to my daughter."

Ba Re's face registered surprise before he schooled his features and took on the usually unshakable expression he always wore.

"I have it!" Elisha exclaimed.

Ba Re' smiled proudly.

Kron's heart beat a little faster.

Buchanan sent up a little prayer that whatever Elisha and Kron were doing would lead them to Ginger before the assholes that had her had a chance to do irreversible damage to her in any way.

"I had no doubt," Zhuxi said.

"Tell me what to do," Kron said.

"Give me one minute," Elisha said distractedly as her eyes were glued to the computer terminal she was working at, and her fingers flew across the keys. "And, that should be it," she said. "Put your communicator on the station beside the one we just made."

"The one I was issued from Base 28?" Kron asked, walking toward the station to place his communicator beside the one he and Elisha had just reconfigured.

"No, your Cruestaci communicator," Elisha said.

Kron paused, but then reached into his pocket and placed it on the station beside the one he hoped would lead him to Ginger.

"It is good that I was part of this conference call so that I could give permission for Kron's communicator to be used as..." Ba Re' said, hesitating when he realized he had no clue what Elisha was up to.

"It will allow him to have support that he obviously wouldn't have otherwise," Elisha said.

"I don't understand," Kron said.

"I'm tying the new program, and the tracking software into your communicator. Missy will help guide you," Elisha said.

"You should request permission for that, Elisha," Kron said, knowing very well the security measures that had to be adhered to.

"I gave permission. I will be monitoring the mission personally. Can you tie it to my personal devices in my office?" Ba Re' asked Elisha.

Elisha paused when she realized Ba Re' was granting her permission for something she'd already done anyway. This was so far out of his realm of possibilities she was actually shocked. He was all black and white, rules etc., by the book. "I can," she said.

"I will be with you as you search for your female," Ba Re' said.

"If I'm compromised, I will destroy my communicator to protect the Cruestaci. None will know of your involvement," Kron said.

"There it is," Elisha said.

Kron, Buchanan, and Zhuxi turned their attention to the station both the reconfigured communicator and Kron's communicator sat on. Kron picked up first his communicator, and swiped the screen. He tapped a few times on the screen and smiled. He raised his eyes to Elisha's on the large terminal. "Thank you, Elisha. I will never forget this."

"It works?" Buchanan asked.

"It does. Their communicator is a homing beacon. Mine is tracking their homing signal. We're going to get Ginger. Ba Re', please tell Quin to send whatever transport he had in mind. It will not be long before we'll be ready to return to Command Warship 1," Kron said.

"I will. And I'm going to log on to shadow you as soon as Elisha ties my office into your device."

"If I fail, this was all done by me. Do not take responsibility for any of this. It was me," Kron said.

"You will not fail, Kron. You forget who you are, and what you are. You are one of our most skilled warriors. You will not fail," Ba Re' said confidently. "Consider the transport on the way. I'm going to Quin immediately."

Kron gave a single nod of affirmation.

"If you need me, Kron. Just let me know. I'll be paying close attention in case you do," Elisha said.

"You had nothing to do with this," Kron said. "Thank you, Elisha. I will owe you a debt I cannot repay."

Elisha smiled brightly. "No you won't. I just want to be godmother when you two have your first baby."

Kron smiled at her, then turned and left the IT department with Buchanan right behind him.

"Goodbye, Elisha. And thank you," Zhuxi said, as he disconnected the vidcom.

Chapter 21

Zhuxi turned and rushed from the IT department to catch up with Kron and Buchanan. He finally caught them as they hurried across the docking bay of the base toward Buchanan's transport. "Wait!" he called out.

Buchanan turned to look at him, but Kron was focused, in a hurry to get to Ginger.

"You cannot just show up!" Zhuxi exclaimed.

"We're not. We're just getting as close as we can, then we'll wait for nightfall," Buchanan said.

"Why not wait for the transport that is coming from Commander Zha Quin Tha Tel Mo' Kok? Surely he is not sending just a ride home," Zhuxi said.

"Why, what do you feel?" Kron demanded, turning to face his friend.

"I feel only what those around me feel. I can only read those in my company. Sometimes I can pick up a ghost of a feeling from those they love, though not always. But your commander is a very intelligent male. If he's sending a transport, he's sending assistance. It's what I would do," Zhuxi said.

"Ba re' said he would come if able," Kron said.

"And I'm sure he will if he's able. If not, I still believe your commander will send someone," Zhuxi said.

"He expressly said to let Missy know when we were ready," Kron said.

"I believe he is, as the humans like to say, covering his ass," Zhuxi said with a grin.

Kron's communicator pinged and he grabbed it from his pocket quickly. He read the message and looked at Zhuxi. "You're right. It's from Ba Re'. He says the transport is on the way, and if at all possible, we should wait to attempt retrieval unless we believe the circumstances warrant an immediate attack. What that means to me is that he's advising me to wait until backup gets here, unless absolutely necessary."

"Then you'll wait here," Zhuxi said.

"No. We're going," Kron said.

"What will you do?" Zhuxi asked.

"Recon," Buchanan said.

"Yes," Kron said. "We're going to see how close we can get, track the facility so that we are at least aware of where it's located. Then we'll see," Kron said. As Kron turned to get in the transport, Zhuxi spoke to him again.

"Listen to your commander, my friend. He is trying to help you. He's trying to guide you through your emotional need to get to your female now no matter the outcome. You need to free her, yes, but you need to be alive to live your life with her as well. Await the transport. Be assured that all three of you, and whoever is on that transport will leave that facility alive," Zhuxi said.

"I hear what you are saying," Kron said. Then he looked at Buchanan. "Are you ready or not. I tire of doing nothing."

"I'm ready," Buchanan said, sliding into the pilot's seat. "Let Kol know, huh?" Buchanan said, looking toward Zhuxi. "Update him."

"I will. Think with your head, Buchanan. Not your heart," Zhuxi responded.

~~~

Ba Re' was sitting in his private office, watching a map of the region of Earth that Base 28 was located in. He was particularly interested in the movement of a particular dot located on that map. "What are you doing?" Ba Re' said aloud to his empty office as he watched the dot that represented Kron's communicator and its movement from its home base to wherever it was headed.

"Lieutenant Commander Ba Re' Non Tol, Sire Zha Quin Tha requests your presence in conference room one, please," Missy's voice said pleasantly, as though it was an invitation and not an order to be followed at once.

Ba Re' shook his head. There was nothing on this ship that Quin didn't know about in some form or fashion. As he left his office and strode down the corridor, he had no doubt that he was about to have his ass chewed out because his Ehlealah, albeit estranged at the moment, added unsanctioned programming to Missy's mainframe. But it didn't matter, he'd have asked Elisha to do it even if they'd asked him before they'd begun. In fact, he'd already spoken the words that he'd given permission just to take responsibility from hers and Kron's shoulders. Kron was one of theirs, in a situation no male ever wanted to find themselves in. Ba Re' would do whatever he could to support him, and there was no question of him supporting his Ehlealah.

He paused outside conference room one and took a deep breath in preparation of whatever Quin threw at him today — figuratively, of course. He'd had no doubt Quin would find out what they'd done, but he was surprised he'd learned of it so quickly. Ba Re' straightened his spine, puffed his chest out, raised his chin and stepped in front of the sensor, causing the doors to open. "I was told to report for a meeting, Sire," Ba Re' said, his eyes staring straight ahead at the wall behind Zha Quin, and Rokai ahl, and Gaishon. Ba Re' steeled his expression so they would not realize he was not prepared to find them with Zha Quin. He'd expected to bear the brunt of Quin's anger in private, not with an audience present.

"Let's get right to it, shall we?" Quin asked.

"Of course, Sire," Ba Re' answered, realizing this was Quin in an official capacity, not his childhood friend.

"Kron is on Earth without suitable support, as Kol watches over his own family," Quin said.

"I understand there have been threats made against Kol and Ada Jane," Ba Re' said.

"Their property has been trespassed on, and images left that imply a threat, though none has been voiced specifically.

208

Patroon Zhuxi's people have volunteered to help protect Kol's family. They are secure for the time being, but I put nothing past this uncivilized planet and those who inhabit it."

"Ceresian males are quite deadly. I trust Kol's family is safe at this point," Ba Re' said.

"At the moment. We will, however, be stepping up and doing what is necessary to take care of our own." Then Quin launched into his planned speech. "I've promised a transport to bring Kron and his female home once she is retrieved. What I did not say is that on that transport I am sending a small assembly of our warriors to assist both Kron and Kol. You will be leading them."

Ba Re's brows raised slightly, but he locked them back down so no emotion showed on his face.

"Do you have any questions?" Zha Quin asked.

"What are my limitations?" Ba Re' asked.

"This is an unsanctioned mission. We are not asking permission to protect our own. We are simply doing it," Quin said. "If you can remain undetected, it would, of course, be better for all involved. If not, be as expedient as possible. We do not want to be accused of being unduly cruel. Deadly force only when called for protection of yourselves, or those we consider ours."

"Understood. Are we to wear our video transmitters?"

"I will leave it to you. Even if you do, they may not be functioning properly," Quin said with a tilt of his head.

"Understood," Ba Re' said.

"Can I talk now?" Rokai ahl asked excitedly.

"Rokai..." Quin grumbled his name as a warning.

"Gaishon is going with you, and you're taking my ship. I've been tinkering on it in my spare time. It should make the trip in half the time a standard transport would. Plus Gaishon knows the routes to stick to, to avoid detection," Rokai said with a wink.

"Gaishon is going with you. He has piloted the ship many times, and has traveled in the same corridors as Rokai. Please assemble the team you wish to accompany you," Quin said.

"Rokai," Ba Re' said without hesitation.

"I knew we were friends," Rokai said teasingly to Ba Re'.

"I simply see the value in your skill," Ba Re' said.

"I wanted to go. Quin said I have to stay here and lead the Elite Warriors since both Kol and Kron are on Earth. He's no fun at all," Rokai said.

"Rokai! This is an official meeting!" Quin snapped.

"With me and you and Gaishon, and my friend Ba Re'. Who's going to care what I say?" Rokai asked.

"I want Jhan, and as many of the Elite Warriors as I'm allowed to take. I'll also allow Jhan to choose several warriors to accompany us," Ba Re' said.

"Submit their names in five minutes time," Quin said.

"Five minutes?" Ba Re' exclaimed.

"Yes. You're leaving in ten. We need you there as soon as possible," Quin answered.

"Yes, Sire. May I be dismissed, Sire?" Ba Re' asked urgently.

"Go," Quin said.

"Gaishon, come with me!" Ba Re' said as he turned and ran from the conference room with Gaishon on his heels.

"They are going to have so much fun! And here I sit being all regal and commanding. No one would know if I went along. I'd wear a helmet and everything!" Rokai grumbled.

"Rokai, everyone would know you were there," Quin said.

"No, they wouldn't!" Rokai said defensively.

"You'd take off the damned helmet, then announce your presence so that you could add to your legend! Then when you got back here, you'd make sure everyone knew you took part so your name would be added to the escapades."

Rokai grinned. "Yes, I probably would. People love my stories about my escapades."

"There will be no escapades! This is an unsanctioned mission, intentionally avoiding all the proper channels required to visit a protected planet! Bart will have my head if he finds out. That is why you are not going!" Quin shouted.

"Fine. But I have to check one more thing on the ship before Gaishon takes off," Rokai said, getting to his feet all too smugly.

"No. No, you do not. You will remain here with me. Once they are clear of Command Warship 1, you may go about your normal day to day duties."

Rokai glared at his brother. He leaned back against the wall with his arms crossed over his chest. "I don't like you very much."

"Good, then you don't mind that I don't like you very much," Quin answered, knowing that both were particularly fond of the other now that they'd reunited.

Four minutes later the door opened and Ba Re' stood there with Gaishon, Jhan, four of the Elite Warriors from the original team that Kol had trained and commanded, and one male that Quin was surprised to see with them.

"Warrior Va'roush. I am surprised to see you among those willing to accept this mission," Quin said.

Warrior Va'roush did not allow his eyes to drift toward his Sire and Commander. He simply stared straight ahead. "Elite Specialist Jhan Re' Non Tol requested my assistance and a female has been stolen and is most likely being abused. I am going," he growled. Then he met Quin's eyes. "If allowed."

Quin knew Va'roush was personally challenging him, daring him to say he couldn't go. He also knew that Va'roush was one of their deadliest operatives. He held the position of Warrior simply because he'd been busted down in rank so many times there was nothing left to take away from him except for his affiliation with the Cruestaci military. And frankly, Quin was not willing to give up his unique skill set.

"Do all of you understand this is not an overnight mission for most?" Quin asked.

"Yes, Sire," they all answered.

"We have two males that require additional support. You will do what is necessary to provide what they need, and make sure that your presence is not detected. If it is, you will ensure that none know you are Cruestaci if at all possible. No one but Consul Kol Ra Don Tol and those in this room will know you are there. Once your job is done, you will return to us."

"We understand, Sire," they all answered.

211

"Then go safely. We hope for your speedy return," Quin said.

As they filed out, headed to the docking bay to depart for Earth, Warrior Va'roush paused and looked back at Zha Quin. "Thank you, Sire."

"Do not make me regret this, Va'roush," Quin said.

Va'roush flashed a lopsided smile. "I'll do my best." The dark green and black male turned and left the conference room, the sound of his footfalls letting Quin know he was hurrying to catch up with the team he'd been assigned to. Rokai got up from the chair he'd retaken, and acted as though he was just going to leave the conference room.

"Sit!" Zha Quin barked.

"Oh, come on! You're even letting Va'roush go! What have I done that Va'roush hasn't?" Rokai ahl asked.

"Not much!" Quin answered. "Except for being a pirating thief."

"He wiped out an entire community of homesteaders!" Rokai objected.

"That's never been proven. Besides, they were slavers, and you know it."

"My point is, there is some question. And there has been question over and over again about his self-control. And you're letting him go!"

"Rokai, have you ever seen any proof that he's stepped over his boundaries, and grossly at that?" Quin asked, leaning toward Rokai ahl.

"No," Rokai said begrudgingly.

"Because he knows how to slip in and slip out. He does not make his exploits public knowledge."

"Then why has he been on lock down?" Rokai snapped.

"Because he has a self-control problem," Quin answered, getting to his feet and preparing to leave the conference room.

"Am I free? Are we leaving here?" Rokai asked excitedly.

"You are," Quin answered.

"Finally!" Rokai exclaimed, running from the room.

"They took off thirty seconds ago," Quin called after him.

"You did that on purpose!" Rokai yelled back as he rushed toward the docking area, hoping Quin was wrong. He really wanted to be a part of this mission.

~~~

Ba Re' sat across from the males they'd chosen to accompany them on this mission to help Kron get his female back, and Kol protect his family. They were each well trained, highly skilled, intelligent males who were capable of slipping in, doing what needed to be done and slipping right back out. He trusted all of them — except Va'roush.

He looked at the male, sitting with them yet a little off to the side. He was a big male, even by Cruestaci standards. His coloring was a combination of dark green, and black. Both his size and his coloring were evidence of the fact that he was not pure Cruestaci. He had high, protruding brows, and his horns were just a small suggestion compared to most Cruestaci males. His mother was born Cruestaci, his father had been the slaver that kidnapped her from her family as a young girl. Va'roush was a product of that union. He and his mother were treated as chattel until their rescue some ten years after his birth. He'd never been shown much warmth, or love. His mother had made sure he was fed, and warm, and other than that barely interacted with him at all.

Va'roush had no idea this was not normal for mothers and sons. Until they were found and brought back to Cruestace. It didn't take him long to figure out his mother could not stand to look on him, so he'd been taken in by his grandmother. She'd done the best she could by him, but his formative years were far behind him. He was quiet, a loner, mistrusting of everyone, and scarred soul deep that his own mother wouldn't even see him. She, and the male that had fathered him, were all he'd ever known. And now he was alone, with people he didn't know, people he didn't understand, that didn't understand him.

213

As he grew, his natural skills clearly outshone those of most of the Cruestaci he went to school with. Eventually, when he got old enough, the military came calling. He refused them, until it was explained the military could be an avenue with which to avenge the treatment he and his mother had survived. Va'roush had agreed immediately to join them, and never looked back.

He should have been a General by now. Would have been a General by now, had he not constantly ignored orders, and pushed the boundaries of what was acceptable on most missions he was a part of. There was a part of him, a part he tried to keep buried down deep inside, that was wild, untrainable, and deadly beyond understanding. That was the part of him that no one ever saw. That was the part of him that he struggled at all times to contain. That was the part that thirsted for revenge, and no matter how much it got, it wanted more.

Ba Re' sat watching Va'roush, considering his allegiance to Jhan. When he'd told Jhan what was happening, and that he'd be allowed to choose two males to accompany their group, he'd said he only needed one — Va'roush. Ba Re' didn't trust Va'roush, but he trusted Jhan implicitly. If Jhan trusted Va'roush, it was enough for him. He'd set aside his uneasiness, and trusted in Jhan's knowledge of the male.

As that thought crossed his mind, Va'roush turned his attention to Ba Re', his eyes staring into Ba Re's expressionlessly.

Ba Re' stared back unflinchingly. He did not fear the male, he just didn't trust him.

"I will not kill you, Warrior," Va'roush rumbled in his naturally, guttural voice.

"And I will not kill you," Ba Re' answered. "And I'm Lieutenant Commander."

"Are we not all warriors, regardless of the pretty words they assign us? Each of us just trying to survive for another day," Va'roush said tiredly as he continued to look directly into Ba Re's gaze.

Ba Re' thought about it. Va'roush was right. It was all he could do to get through each day now since Elisha had left

Command Warship 1. And most days he didn't really give a damn if he made it through the day or not.

"You are more correct than I care to admit," Ba Re' conceded.

Va'roush stared at Ba Re' for a moment longer before breaking out into a wide smile. "Then we understand each other."

Chapter 22

Kron sat in the passenger seat, a communicator in each hand. He repeatedly looked back and forth between the two. His Cruestaci communicator provided a map of the area they flew across and a small moving dot on that map represented the transport they rode in. The other communicator displayed a screen that looked like an ancient compass of sorts. There was a red flashing signal on that screen, and Kron did his best to direct Buchanan in which direction to turn to keep that flashing signal at the top center of the screen. It was in effect leading them to the originating signal of the network it was on.

"Are we going in, or really waiting for backup?" Buchanan asked. "Because honestly, I don't know if I can wait."

"Same," Kron answered, his eyes still glued to both communicators. "I crave nothing more than rushing in and blasting everyone alive except Ginger. But, if we go in alone, we don't know what we're up against. If we fail, which is entirely possible if we are greatly outnumbered, they may cause Ginger more harm than she would have normally endured. And, while not directly ordered to wait, I was directed to remain undetected if possible, and it was implied I should wait for backup."

"Fuckers," Buchanan said, shaking his head.

"I do not even care which side you are referring to. I want my female now!"

"I wish I knew of a place that would expose her damn mother to all she's having to endure," Buchanan said.

"There are such places. One has to leave Earth to get there, but they do exist," Kron said. "Know this, Buchanan. If Ginger is lost, after I destroy all who harmed her, I'm focusing on the female who caused her to be in this situation. There is nothing that will stop me."

"If that happens, Kron, you'll have to get in line. I'll kill the bitch I married myself if Ginger is lost."

Kron glanced up from the communicators to look at Buchanan. Buchanan stared straight ahead, looking out over the landscape as they followed the homing beacon Elisha had created for them, steady and composed as he usually was though Kron knew he was in as much turmoil as he was. One of the communicators beeped and Kron looked back down at it. "Four degrees Northeast."

Buchanan expertly guided the transport on the heading Kron had instructed.

They flew for another seven or eight minutes before Kron spoke again. "Missy says we should skirt the area directly North if we wish to avoid detection. We are about to enter a region that is protected by ground to air radar."

"Tell me where to go," Buchanan said, slowing his progress.

"Let's give it a wide berth, half a mile at least from the perimeter at all times. Mark its boundaries, then find a place to set down. Once on the ground, perhaps we will be able to get a better idea of what we're up against. Hopefully we'll find we're able to wait for the transport. I don't want to risk Ginger at all if it can be avoided. It's the only reason I'm able to display any control at all," Kron said.

"Agreed," Buchanan said.

Forty-five minutes later, having completed their first reconnaissance of the facility they believed Ginger was in, they found a quiet place, far away from all civilization to set down the transport. They'd not been able to get close enough to see the facility itself without giving away their presence, but Missy had managed to provide them with an electronic 3D view of the land it sat on, and the buildings on that land. They studied the image and they did their best to patiently wait for the backup they believed was on that transport. They uploaded the information they'd gathered to the link Missy kept constantly active so that Be Re' and whoever was on the transport would be aware of all they'd learned. Then they settled in as the sun went down, to wait and watch the skies for the transport Zha Quin promised was on the way.

217

~~~

Kol had just tucked in Kreed and Kolby when his communicator began beeping. It was not the communicator he carried for Earth Base 28 and his role there, it was the one that kept him connected to his own people — to Zha Quin and Command Warship 1. He reached for the communicator, expecting to find Kron's com there, waiting to be answered, but instead found a pending com from Quin.

Kol swiped the screen and smiled as Quin's face filled the screen. "Quin! I am very happy to see you! How are you? How is Vivi?"

Quin didn't smile. He leaned forward and stared into the Vid screen. "Prepare to return to Command Warship 1 at once," he snarled.

Kol's eyebrows rose. "What?" he asked, completely confused knowing he had approximately two years left on this planet.

"You heard me!" Quin barked out.

"Yes, I did. But I have two years left on this commission. I cannot simply vacate my position, and Ada Jane and the boys will need some time to consider such a drastic life change."

"I will address the sudden vacancy of your position. Prepare your family, return them to Command Warship 1 without hesitation," Quin said, somewhat calmer.

"It will take time, Sire," Kol said, recognizing that this was not a friendly call to chat and catch up. "It cannot be accomplished in a matter of hours."

"Start the process, assess all that will be affected, and report back with an anticipated exit date," Zha Quin ordered.

"I will begin the process."

"Good," Quin said, finally sitting back in his chair.

"May I ask, Sire, what has occurred to cause this sudden need to vacate, to leave behind all we've established here?" Kol asked.

"I tire of the planet and her people, Kol. They are ruthless, unfeeling, uncaring, and at times uncivilized. They provoke us, and when we respond, we are accused of being the aggressor. It is best if we simply cut our losses and return to our own focuses. This is a business we have no need of involvement in. I have ordered Kron to retrieve his female by any means necessary and return to us aboard the transport I'm sending. I expect you and yours to be on it as well."

"Quin, it's not that simple," Kol said, feeling that Quin had calmed enough to be addressed as a friend, instead of a pissed off commander.

"It is!" Quin snapped. "I'm removing my people from an unstable environment that has repeatedly, as Vivi says, bitten us in the ass!"

Kol didn't answer right away. Then he asked quietly, "What does Vivi think of leaving our positions on her home planet?"

Quin's eye twitched. "I have not discussed it with my Sirena yet. But it matters not, I must do what is best for my people. I cannot protect my people properly in that environment, and we are simply targets waiting for another complaint to be filed the next time we move to protect our own, which is happening as we speak. We may not be able to save the next male accused of crimes on this planet. It was questionable if we'd be able to save you!"

"As we speak?" Kol asked. "You mean Kron?"

"And your own family. Did you or did you not plan to update us on the threats you've received?" Quin asked.

"I did, at some point. Once it became apparent there was an actual threat, and confrontation was eminent," Kol replied.

"Was that going to be before or after your family had been physically harmed through the ignorance of those threatening you?" Quin demanded.

"No one is harming my family!" Kol snarled.

219

"No, they are not. Pack what is necessary and return to our fold."

"We do not even have a definite threat. It could be no more than few well placed visual markers to intimidate us into leaving. This is my Ehlealah's property. We are not planning to leave. She waited long to have it back in her control. She works it, and wanders it joyously each and every day. Her roots are here. Our younglings have never known any other life. As I said, Quin, it is not that simple," Kol explained, doing his best to plead his case without directly refusing an order.

"I do not like my people being in an atmosphere ripe with opportunity for sabotage and targeting. Especially an atmosphere which provokes us, then condemns us for reacting," Quin said, though it was much less passionately than the beginning of the conversation.

"We are not alone," Kol said. "We are proactively prepared against any attack. While I am on alert myself, I feel the situation is well controlled and addressed, Quin. We are not going blindly about our day. If attacked, or pursued even, we are prepared to defend ourselves, and provide proof that we are not the aggressors."

"And Kron?" Quin asked.

"That's another situation altogether," Kol said. "But if Ada Jane, or Vivi was missing, even here on their home planet, what would be your response? I know well what my own would be."

"Anyone who opposed my actions to find her would be destroyed. They'd be lucky if I didn't destroy the damn planet on my way out once I finally had her in my arms again," Quin growled.

"My instinct would be the same. But I've learned that not all on this planet wish us to leave. There are families here, just like those on Cruestace and many other worlds we've had contact with. They want what we want — a life with those we love, free to pursue whatever it is that makes us happy. It means something to them to be part of a community, to be able to help their brothers and neighbors when needed, to be able to see their children grow up with the same values they had. They want

220

us here to help stabilize their world. They do not want to be left on their own again. They fear another invasion, and see us as the force preventing that. Not all are Purists. Not all wish to force us from the planet and curse our very existence. Do not write off the planet as a whole, Quin. Do not forget that Ada Jane and Vivi both had their origins on Earth. I cannot help but feel in my soul that the lessons and values our women learned in their youth, the very same values that make them who they are today, are the same values that run through the core of those still here trying to rebuild their world," Kol said.

Quin simply watched Kol for a moment before slowly shaking his head. "I never thought I'd see it."

"What?" Kol asked, confused.

"You have gone from warrior to politician and dignitary. My father suggested once that you would make an exemplary dignitary, and I laughed at him. I was wrong."

Kol smiled. "I'm still me. I've just learned to see more than my side of things. Give Earth a chance, Quin. It has much to offer."

"Perhaps you're right. I will reconsider my instinct to remove all representatives of Cruestace from Earth at the moment. I do not feel that it is prudent for Kron and his female to remain there, however."

"Agreed. Especially depending on how things go when he finally locates her, it may be necessary to get them off planet quickly. It may be best to have them removed from all attention from Earth until whatever fallout occurs has died down," Kol said. "I've enjoyed having him here, and I certainly will miss his presence, but his safety and that of his Ehlealah are foremost in my considerations."

"Agreed. You will not be without Cruestaci backup for long," Quin said.

"What do you mean?"

"You will understand soon. I expect to be updated. I expect to be apprised of any and all changes in your situation," Quin said. "The moment the threat becomes literal, I will take further steps," Quin said.

"Of course, but for now, all is controlled," Kol said.

"Very well. Prepare yourself, Kol. I've advised them if at all necessary to keep the Cruestaci people away from whatever is done to find and free Kron's female. But if necessary, I fully expect a blowout."

"If necessary it will be what it must be. We will explain it and justify it as necessary. There will always be those who disagree, and as long as all they do is disagree, it's not a problem," Kol answered.

"I will speak with you soon," Quin said.

"Rest easy, Quin. I am monitoring the situation as well," Kol promised.

Quin ended the call and sat back in his chair thinking about the fact that after a conversation with Kol, his ideas on how Earth was to be best handled had changed. Then he thought of his father's words — A foolish male is one who refuses to change his opinions despite the evidence easily seen all around him. All situations change by the moment, and must be constantly reassessed. A smart male will adjust his opinions and choices as the situation changes instead of stubbornly maintaining ideology that no longer applies to a situation that has since changed.

"Commander?" Missy's voice said softly, filling the small conference room he sat in alone.

"Yes, Missy," Quin answered.

"Sirena Vivian would like to know if you will be on duty all night," Missy said.

"Tell her I'm on my way," Quin said, smiling as he thought about Vivian whose belly was already beginning to swell.

"Yes, Commander," Missy answered.

~~~

Kol silenced his communicator and set it on the counter top in the kitchen. He sighed as he realized he was the only Cruestaci Consul, the only Cruestaci representative to a planet that might

222

not be very happy with his home planet and people in the next few days. It would take a monumental effort to spin whatever Kron was forced to do to locate Ginger and free her from the Purists into an acceptable scenario. There may very well be lives lost, and even those who weren't Purists would take the news personally.

"Kol?" a soft voice said from behind him.

He turned and found Ada Jane standing in the doorway between the kitchen and the dining room, quietly watching him.

"Ehlealah," he said, smiling at her and holding out a hand for her to come to him.

Ada pushed off the door jamb where she leaned and walked toward her mate. She went willingly into his arms and closed her eyes in complete peace and satisfaction when he held her close, kissing her head.

"How long have you been standing there?" he asked.

"Long enough," she replied.

"We will not be leaving our home," Kol assured her, kissing her forehead again.

"Yet," she said.

"It is not a concern at this time," Kol said. "We are home, and I will do all I can for us to remain here."

"I'm not blind, Kol. I know there are things to consider. If our kids, or ourselves aren't safe, it's not worth the risk. And I see the boys daily, growing, getting stronger, getting smarter. I worry that I won't be able to keep up one day. Is it really fair to keep them on Earth where they may not be able to rise to their highest potential because they don't have others like themselves around to drive them to be better, to be more? And I see you go off to work, and worry each time that you do. This is such a volatile landscape now. You can be speaking to someone who smiles pleasantly at you while you're speaking, but curses you to the depths of hell when you walk away, simply because of who you love."

"All of that is true, Ada Jane. But none of it is reason for us to get on my transport and go home right this moment. It is all reason for consideration if things continue to escalate, and I

223

would actually like for Kreed and Kolby to be able to live part of their childhood among my people. But it doesn't have to be at this moment — they are still so small. Right now, what we need is to be here, home, where we all feel safe for the most part, and we all know we belong, for now," Kol said.

"I'm not so sure I feel safe anymore," Ada Jane confided.

"I know, my love. I'm working on it. Know that I will always do whatever is safest for you and our sons. I will be sure to make our home secure again. Just give me a little time. I have to wait for their next move."

Ada Jane nodded. "I know you will always keep us safe."

"I will make you a promise. Their next move, will be their last move," Kol said.

Ada Jane raised her face to look at the male she loved with her whole heart and soul. "I know it will be. I have faith in you."

"And that is what makes me strong," he said.

"I kinda think you were strong before me," she teased.

Kol shrugged. "Maybe a little."

"A little?" she asked doubtfully.

"Okay, a lot. I knew you were out there somewhere and would need me one day."

"Always," she said, pulling his head down to kiss him.

"Are they sleeping?" Kol asked.

"Yes, I checked on them before I followed the sound of your voice into the kitchen," Ada Jane answered. "Billy and Bob are asleep on their bed, too."

"Then I think I'll spend a little time reminding my Ehlealah of just how much I desire her, and just how strong she makes me," Kol said, running his hands down Ada Jane's sides to her hips.

"Mmm, she must be a lucky female," she teased.

Kol swatted the curve of her ass. "You are that lucky female!"

"Don't I know it!" she said, taking him by the hand and leading him toward their bedroom.

Chapter 23

Ginger woke from the sun streaming in through the window. Her body was stiff and sore from a night of remaining on alert and ready to spring from the bed at any moment if the need should arise. Her mind was foggy and unfocused from days of no rest and constant stress. The drugs she'd been sedated with when she'd been kidnapped from her home, and on arrival in whatever fresh hell she was in, were surely out of her system by now, but no doubt played a part in her inability to focus.

She turned from her left side to lie on her right and screeched out a short scream. There, sitting quietly, almost perfectly still in a straight backed chair beside her bed was Dr. Cavanaugh.

"Good morning, dear," he said.

Ginger pressed her hand to her chest, her breath coming in fast, uneven pants as she tried to control the adrenalin that flooded her system at finding a male sitting beside her bed while she slept. "What are you doing here?" she asked, a little more irritation seeping into her tone than was wise when dealing with Dr. Cavanaugh.

"I live here," he said simply, his head tilting slightly to the right as he regarded her. "I suppose I did startle you. My apologies. I only meant to watch over you as you slept."

"Why?" she asked, her breathing beginning to even out.

He watched her silently for a few uncomfortable moments longer before finally answering as he looked off toward the wall unseeingly. "I don't sleep that much anymore, my mind is too busy. It's filled with all the things it wishes it could achieve — vengeance, justice, and perhaps from time to time even a bit of regret."

Ginger listened to the man who had been her protector of late, as well as her biggest threat. She had no clue of how to respond. "I'm sorry," she finally settled on.

Dr. Cavanaugh's eyes wandered back to her. "Thank you," he said.

"You're welcome," Ginger answered.

Dr. Cavanaugh stood from the chair he was sitting in and picked it up by its back to move it back against the wall. It was then that Ginger noticed that it was the same chair she'd used to wedge beneath the doorknob to presumably give herself a little more security. She'd at least hoped that if someone tried to enter the room, the chair would have prevented them from entering long enough for her to prepare, or at the very least made enough noise that she would have awakened immediately, and the person trying to enter would have been frightened away. Obviously, neither happened.

As Dr. Cavanaugh placed the chair against the wall beside her bed, he spoke to her conversationally. "Have you ever considered how vulnerable people are when sleeping. Their own partners, trusted and beloved spouses, could easily slip an ice pick into their ear or up their nose to pierce the brain. Or quietly and without too much effort slice through the carotid artery causing the person sleeping to bleed out in a matter of minutes. People are so frail, yet they continue to close their eyes each and every night with a companion at their side. I just don't understand the trust put blindly into others."

"It is frightening," Ginger said.

"I am guessing that is the reason you placed the chair beneath the doorknob keeping me from a room within my own home," he said.

"I... it... I meant no offense. I just don't feel safe, and I couldn't hold my eyes open any longer," Ginger said.

"I gave you my word I would watch over you," Dr. Cavanaugh said.

"I know," she said, looking down at her hands where her fingers twined and untwined, giving him the impression that she was nervous. "It's just that Mitchell is still here. And the looks he

227

gives me frighten me. I never know who is loyal to him and who is not. I didn't mean to offend you, simply protect myself from Mitchell."

"Ah, I see. Well, first, a chair beneath a doorknob isn't going to protect anyone from Mitchell." Dr. Cavanaugh paused until she looked up at him and nodded. "Second, I told you I would look after you, and I will. Trust in that," he said.

"I will try. I'm struggling to feel at home here. I'm just still off balance," she said. "But I am trying to relax and follow your advice."

"Good girl," Dr. Cavanaugh said.

"Thank you, Dr. Cavanaugh," Ginger said.

"Breakfast will be served in half an hour. Are you able to shower and dress in time?" he asked.

"I only have the clothes I'm wearing, but I can certainly shower," Ginger answered.

"I'll have clothes left on your bed while you shower. I'll be waiting for you," he said. "Be sure to wear your glasses."

"Of course," she answered.

Dr. Cavanaugh walked over to the door, opened it with ease as it was no longer locked, stepped through the door and turned to face Ginger, before performing a little abbreviated bow, flashing his gaze toward the chair that had been blocking the door, then looking at her again before pulling the door closed and presumably walking away.

Ginger blew out the breath she'd been holding and shook her head slowly. "Crap on a cracker," she whispered very quietly to herself. Dr. Cavanaugh being completely unbalanced, not even on the edge of insanity but full blown living the life, was not new news to her. Instead what had her on edge was how he managed to get inside the bedroom he'd deemed as hers without her hearing him remove the chair from beneath the doorknob, that should have kept him out. He should not have been able to get inside the bedroom without her at least hearing him knock the chair about when he came in. She glanced around the room, looking for any other entry point and didn't see a single place that could be hiding another way in. He had to have come in through the door.

"Do not make me wait for breakfast, Ms. Buchanan. I do so detest cold eggs," his voice called from outside the closed door.

"I'll be on time!" she called out, surprised that he still stood outside her door. She threw back the covers and hurriedly got out of bed, going straight into the bathroom and starting the shower. As the water sprayed from the shower head, she turned to look at herself in the mirror. She focused on her eyes, now so like Kron's. Ginger reached out and touched their reflection in the mirror. It was a practice she'd picked up in the last few days. "Please hurry," she whispered, hoping against hope that Kron could hear her, or at the very least feel her. "I need you."

~~~

As the sun rose in the distance, Kron sat on a large rock and watched the sky brightening as the sun rose higher and higher. He wondered what Ginger was doing, and sent up prayers to all the deities he'd ever heard of that she was unhurt and finding a way to blend in, rather than calling attention to herself. He held a small, tin cup of coffee in his hand as he watched the sky turn from indigo, to deep purple, then eventually a pale yellow on its way to what would be a beautiful blue. He was aware that Buchanan had awakened and joined him, but he made no mention of it, preferring to allow the man who had become his family to announce his presence at will.

"You get any rest?" Buchanan asked from behind him.

"No," Kron answered, sipping his coffee. It was nothing fancy, black and bitter, but it was coffee. And since being on Earth, he'd become addicted to the caffeine. Maybe not physically, but he enjoyed the early morning ritual of sips of the brew as he mentally planned his day and prepared for all that day would entail.

"I got a little. Decided I wouldn't be doing anybody any good if I was so tired I just fell over," Buchanan said.

229

Kron gave him strained smile.

"Should have tried to sleep," Buchanan said.

"I'm fine. Sleep will come when my mate is safe at my side, and not before," Kron said.

"That could be days!" Buchanan exclaimed. "You'll be a zombie by then you'll be so tired."

"I've been awake longer while on mission. It is not that much of a hardship." He tossed the rest of his coffee to the ground in front of him. "I will tell you what is a hardship. Standing here doing nothing at all while Ginger is facing alone all that I should be defending her from."

"Agreed," Buchanan said, as he watched Kron begin to gather weapons and additional gear. "What are you doing?

"Preparing to take a closer look. If all seems calm, I will wait. If there are indications that she is suffering while we wait, I'm going in," Kron answered, stashing blasters and disintegraters in his pockets along with knives and small handheld explosives.

"Hiking in?" Buchanan asked, hurrying to get his pistol.

"Yes," Kron answered.

"Wouldn't happen to have any more of that coffee would you?" Buchanan asked.

"There is another pack of MREs in your transport. It most likely has a coffee pack as well. I'm going ahead, catch up after your coffee."

"Naw, I'm going with you. Something to look forward to when we get back," Buchanan said.

Kron didn't respond as he used the toe of his boot to dig out a small crevice beside the rock he'd been sitting on, then drop the communicators into that small space and cover them with dirt. When Kron was done he turned and found Buchanan watching him curiously. "Better to face whatever it is alone, than risk technology they shouldn't have falling into their hands. It would implicate the Cruestaci if I am compromised."

Buchanan nodded, then the men set out toward the small mountain range they could see in the distance. The ridge closest to them separated them from the next smaller ridge, which concealed the facility they planned to target within its valley. Kron broke into a jog, with Buchanan right behind him.

There was only one thought in Kron's mind — not the searing heat as the day grew hotter by the minute, or the blinding sun, or the terrain or the wildlife they surprised as they ran by, it was Ginger. His only thought was Ginger, and her beautiful yellow eyes as she smiled up at him for the first time after they'd finalized their bond. "I'm coming, Ginger," he whispered.

~~~

When Ginger got out of the shower, she was surprised to find a pair of teal colored slacks, and a matching cream and teal blouse with floral print. Also on the bed was a clean pair of panties, a bra, a belt and a pair of espadrilles, in the same cream color as found on the floral blouse. Shaking her head at the fact that this outfit would perfectly fit into her mother's wardrobe instead of her own, she began to get dressed. To her surprise the clothes had already been sprayed with a heavy, sweet perfume, and they fit her. The shoes were a little big, but the clothing fit her relatively well. As she turned to leave her room, she noticed a hairbrush and hair accessories lying on the chair Dr. Cavanaugh had occupied earlier. Obviously he wanted her well groomed. She grabbed the brush and ran it through her hair quickly before using one of the hair clips to gather the front of her hair and clasp it at the crown of her head. Then she slid her dark sunglasses into place and left her bedroom to meet Dr. Cavanaugh for breakfast.

As she entered the dining room of Dr. Cavanaugh's home, he stood to welcome her.

"You look lovely, my dear," he said, smiling brightly as he stepped behind her to scoot her chair in for her as she sat.

"Thank you," she responded, as he took his seat.

"I knew those clothes would match your personality perfectly. And I'm very pleased I guessed the right sizes. I hope you don't mind my spritzing a bit of my preferred perfume on them prior to wear."

"No, it's fine," she lied, the scent beginning to give her a headache.

"As I said, it is my favorite scent."

"I'll remember it," Ginger said.

"Excellent. A proper lady is always fully dressed, prepared at all times for whatever task the day may bring. Her appearance put together and polished, to convey her ability to smoothly transition as needed. Not to mention, it is important that she always look her best for her man and do the extra little things that please him. She should complement him in every way. Is that not as you were brought up?" he asked.

Ginger considered telling him he was out of his fucking mind, and that was how she was brought up, but decided it might not be in her best interests at the moment. Instead she smiled demurely, falling back on her days of finishing school and cotillion that her mother had insisted she attend and excel in for guidance. "It is indeed exactly what I was taught," she answered, reaching for her coffee cup and holding her pinkie finger out exaggeratedly as she sipped. It took her a moment to realize she was sipping tea, not coffee.

"Tea," she said.

"Yes. Ladies drink tea, men drink coffee," the doctor explained.

"Of course. Thank you for thinking so far ahead for me."

"You're welcome, my dear," he said, gesturing to her plate. "I hope you enjoy your breakfast. As with lunch yesterday, it's not exactly what I'd like to offer you, but it's fresh and it will fill your belly. I've ordered more suitable fare, but it will be several days until it is available."

"Thank you, Dr. Cavanaugh. This is just fine. Please don't go to any trouble on my account," Ginger said.

"It's no trouble, and quite a pleasure to be able to provide for a female who's appreciative."

They ate in silence for a while, Dr. Cavanaugh clearly lost in his thoughts until he decided to share them with her. "You know, I just can't figure out why your mother would think you need to be deprogrammed. You are well-behaved, pleasant to be around, reasonable, and clearly intelligent. What is it that I'm missing?" he asked, setting down his fork and knife and sitting back in his chair to look at her as though evaluating her all over again.

Ginger thought about her answer. She could either tell him that she'd fallen in love with Kron against her mother's wishes, and her mother was a controlling, angry, intolerable speciest bitch, or she could tell him that she was faking everything about herself at the moment to keep herself alive until her alien mate could find her, kill him, and get her the hell away from this godforsaken place as soon as possible. Neither was conducive to her health and continued sanity.

"I think that my mother is somewhat over reactive. My father works at a base, and has several people from other worlds who work with him. I imagine that my mother must have gotten it into her head that I was going to marry one of them and run away with them. She must have panicked and contacted your organization. All I know for sure is that I woke up tied to a cot, and being hit by Mitchell."

"Let us not forget your new eye color, Miss Buchanan," Dr. Cavanaugh said. "I'm sure that contributed to your mother calling for our assistance." He looked at her condescendingly, with a sharp tone in his voice as he spoke.

"Of course. There was a moment of indiscretion, when I realized too late that I'd been taken advantage of," Ginger said, doing her best not to clench her teeth.

"It is my opinion that your mother is a very concerned lady, doing all she can to save her only daughter," Dr. Cavanaugh said.

"I would be hard pressed to disagree with you. I am fortunate," Ginger said. In her mind, she screamed Kron's name in frustration, almost willing to bear being tied to the cot she woke up on rather than have to play this demented part for a clearly unstable male who also happened to be the leader of this faction of speciest assholes. Then, somewhere in the back of her psyche she heard a voice that soothed her soul with just a few words. A voice that was so welcome and needed that it brought tears to her eyes. "I'm coming, Ginger." As she realized it was Kron's voice, she sat up and looked around herself, trying to determine if she actually heard him, or if it was her imagination.

Ginger closed her eyes and smiled to herself, reaching for the sound of his voice again. It didn't matter if it was her imagination. All that mattered was that he calmed her, and somewhere in the depths of her heart and soul, she knew without a doubt that at some point, he'd find her.

Chapter 24

It was late afternoon, when after a day of lying undetected
in the dirt beneath tree limbs, and dead leaves, Kron and
Buchanan finally decided to move back toward their transport.
They'd determined that at least there was no evidence of torture
that they could detect. As they lay perfectly still for hours,
waiting for any activity at all in the compound below their
vantage point, they'd seen several groups of people, both male
and female, escorted into the center of the compound and
allowed to walk about and interact.

Kron had searched their faces desperately for Ginger, but
she'd not been one of them. He'd looked toward Buchanan who
was lying beside him, and shook his head."She is not here."

"She may be. Maybe she's just not outside with the rest,"
Buchanan said, shaking his head. "But, we're going to find her. I
know we're going to find her."

"I will not stop until we do," Kron said, looking down at the
compound they quietly watched. "And Mitchell. I will find him,
too."

"You just worry about getting Ginger to safety once we find
her, I'll take care of that little fuck," Buchanan said.

"Make it painful," Kron said.

Buchanan nodded.

A few minutes later, devastated at not getting even a
glimpse of Ginger to confirm that she was safe and well, they
quietly began to withdraw, then once clear of any chance of
detection, stood and began to make their way back to the
location they'd left their transport when they'd first arrived. As
they descended the last ridge separating them from their
transport, about midway down the ridge, Kron realized they

were not alone, and held out his hand to prevent Buchanan from going any further.

Buchanan stopped walking and followed Kron's gaze to the movement through the trees and overgrowth further down the ridge. He sensed nothing. He shrugged and shook his head.

Kron knew he sensed movement, and it headed up the ridge toward their location. Kron gestured toward the cover of trees to their right and Buchanan — trusting Kron's judgment — smoothly moved into the small grove.

Kron very slowly moved to the left, then knelt bringing himself closer to the ground and harder to see from a distance as he crouched behind some undergrowth there.

Kron closed his eyes, focusing on the sounds of the group of what he assumed were Purists, as they moved toward Buchanan and himself.

The slight sounds of their footfalls were familiar yet barely detectable. Then Kron realized why it sounded familiar — all stepped in time, as one. His people were trained to do that as it kept them consciously light footed, if overheard gave the impression that only one approached, and the sound of their progress was almost non-existent. A corner of Kron's mouth lifted in smile. These were his people. He signaled to Buchanan to stay hidden, then raised his face to the sky, sending out a whistling sound that could easily be mistaken for a bird or insect even here on Earth.

The footfalls he'd been listening to stopped, then Kron's call was answered with another.

Kron grinned, then stood to his full height, stepping out from behind the brush he knelt behind and gestured for Buchanan to join him. They set a path toward the males who were already once again moving toward them. Five or six minutes later a familiar face came into view. Kron quickened his last few steps to get to him before embracing him. "Ba Re'!" Kron said, as relief flooded his body.

"Kron! Do you often disregard direct orders?" Ba Re' teased, holding out the communicators Kron had left hidden in the dirt beside the rock he'd sat on.

Kron accepted the communicators. "I was not sure I would not be forced to move into the compound without further hesitation. I knew without a doubt we would have been outnumbered. I didn't want these, especially my communicator, to fall into their hands. I also knew that if a transport was indeed on the way, it would track me through mine, and it would be found."

Ba Re' nodded his understanding.

"Glad you're here," Buchanan said to Ba Re'.

"As am I," Ba Re' said, embracing Buchanan.

"Buchanan, you know Ba Re', this is his brother Elite Specialist Jhan Re' Non Tol."

As Buchanan greeted Jhan, Kron realized that of the seven males standing before him, one was a complete surprise to him. "Va'roush," Kron said, his surprise at Va'roush being among his support team evident.

"Kron," Va'roush said guardedly. He was accustomed to certain warriors questioning his presence on mission, but the fact that he thought Kron questioned him was not expected. Kron was one who always gave him the benefit of the doubt and fought valiantly beside him in the past.

Kron grinned and strode toward Va'roush to embrace him. "You have no idea how happy I am that you're here!"

Va'roush's face became a mask of confusion and as he waited for Kron to stop embracing him, he made no move to return the gesture. He didn't like to be touched — it was unnatural to him.

"You are?" Va'roush asked.

"Yes! I have no doubt now that all will be as it needs to be," Kron said, patting Va'roush on the back heartily as he turned to the rest of the males there. "My brothers!" he said. Then as he called them by name, each lifted their right arm to strike across their chests in a show of loyalty. Kron returned the gesture. "Buchanan, these are members of my Elite Warrior team. They are each skilled in warfare and battle. All possess unique abilities and strengths. We will be successful in finding and freeing my mate."

"Gentlemen," Buchanan said, "welcome to Earth. I regret it's not under more favorable circumstances. May I be clear here? I don't give a damn what you do, or how you do it. Just find my daughter."

"This is Viceroy Buchanan of Earth Base 28. He is my mate's father," Kron explained.

"Do not fear, Viceroy, we will free your daughter and put everything to rights," one of them said. "None will even know we are here and she will be free and safe again."

Va'roush looked at the male who'd spoken. He raised an eyebrow. "Some may require annihilation. I'm here for that specialty."

"Thank God," Buchanan said, feeling for the first time that they'd actually be successful in getting Ginger out of the compound they'd located. He'd wondered if just he and Kron were enough to safely gain her freedom.

"God will have nothing to do with it, not yours or anyone elses. In fact, it might be best if you forget for a while that you have one," Va'roush said.

Buchanan looked at Kron who grinned at him. "I think I like him."

"Why?" Va'roush asked suspiciously.

"It is a good thing, Va'roush," Ba Re' explained quickly before turning his attention to Kron. "You are moving away from your objective."

"Yes. We moved in close enough to observe the compound as best we could from a distance. We were prepared to proceed if necessary, but we witnessed no evidence of immediate mistreatment of those held captive there. We decided to wait just a little longer to give the transport Quin promised time to arrive. We were concerned that if we were detected before we located Ginger, they may harm her."

"Do you have visual confirmation that she is there?" Ba Re asked.

"No. We do not have visual confirmation, but we've located the facility. It's a compound comprised of buildings that look to have not always been the facility it is now. There is a small home on it, which looks completely out of place. Two of the other buildings seem to be of the same style and build as the home. The majority are completely different, military in nature, hastily built, possibly temporary buildings. They're made of metal sheeting, while the home and its immediate surrounding buildings seem to be permanent, made of wood and were at one time painted to match one another."

"The house is still painted, but the surrounding buildings have faded considerably," Buchanan said. "That indicates to me that someone of importance is living, or at least using the home regularly and making an attempt to keep it in good condition. We saw a group of people that seemed to be given exercise time in the center of the buildings in what is a kind of open yard. Ginger wasn't among them, but they were watched and overseen by three armed men."

"Are they all females? Those who seemed to be captives?" Va'roush asked.

"No, actually they're not. There were two males among them," Kron said.

"That's strange," Ba Re' said. "You'd think they'd have fought back."

"Ginger was drugged. Perhaps they were, and still are as well," Kron said.

Ba Re' nodded.

"You think your mate is here, though?" Jhan asked.

"I do," Kron said. "The communicator we used as a homing device led us here. The mainframe it was running on is located here. But at the very least, if Ginger's not here, someone inside that compound knows where she is. If not, I'm sure there's information in that compound which will lead us to any other facilities they may have and we can work our way through them until we find her. I believe this is not a temporary location. Additional buildings were added to those already existing. It was set up to be a long term base."

"Let's wait for dark. We'll move in once they all are on low alert, sleeping, resting. Just another night in their mundane world," one of the Elite warriors said.

239

"Better yet, let's go in in the morning. Most attack at night, let's attack in the morning. Surprise attack, no one lives," Va'roush growled.

"Time of attack agreed; killing them all, not a good idea. We require some alive to tell us where their other locations are in the event Kron's female is not here. In addition, we are ordered to slip in and out if we can," Ba Re' said.

"We are also ordered to do whatever is necessary," Va'roush reminded Ba Re'.

"We need some to question, to speak to and find out why they took Kron's mate, and why the others are kept here," Va'roush said. "It will only take me a few moments and I will have all the answers. I only need one of them."

"I know why they took her," Buchanan said. "Her mother drugged her and called them to come get her."

"I'm sorry, what?" Jhan asked.

"Ginger, my daughter, mated Kron. My wife considered it an embarrassment and extreme insult to her and her family, so she drugged her, and contacted the Purist movement to come get her and reprogram her way of thinking. We believe that each of the people we saw here under guard are or were mated to people alien to Earth, and have been forcibly separated from them," Buchanan said.

Va'roush seemed visibly shaken as Buchanan began to explain the details leading up to Ginger's own mother turning her over to the group referred to as the Purists. By the time he was done, Va'roush had managed to regain control of his emotions, but he was obviously angry. "It is a sad thing for any individual to realize their own mother does not value them. Any such female should be erased from the face of the planet on which she lives."

"Agreed. I'm prosecuting her to the fullest extent of the law personally. It does not matter that she was once my wife, and is my daughter's mother. She has given up all rights to claim either for another moment in time. She will pay the legal price for her actions," Buchanan said.

240

"If you wish for a greater price to be paid, I offer my services," Va'roush rumbled. "There is no greater sin than a mother, who sacrifices her child for her own selfishness."

Buchanan looked at the big, intimidating male. Though he was larger than the others gathered here today, he still seemed more lithe than most of them, and his features were different, more harsh than those he'd come to know as the Cruestaci. His behavior also made it clear, this was personal to him. It was not just supporting his brothers-in-arms.

"I will keep that in mind. But at this time, if we could just get my daughter, Kron's mate, away from those who are holding her, I'll figure out all the rest later," Buchanan said.

"At first light," Ba Re' said.

"No, not first light. Give them a little time to relax and take for granted their day is just like any other," Va'roush said. "Allow them to go about their morning routines uninterrupted. Then when they have taken it for granted that this will be just another day, we attack."

"Zha Quin said slip in and slip out," Jhan reminded. "Not to be the one to ruin your fun, but… he did say it, and he is our Commander."

"Slipping in is a form of attack. I like to see how many I can kill before they realize they've been compromised," Va'roush said with a sinister smile.

Jhan smiled and nodded. "I do have a personal best," he said.

"I stopped counting," Va'roush grinned, "it became tedious."

"Then we have a plan," Ba Re' said.

All agreed. Then Ba Re' spoke again. "Gaishon stays with the ship in the event we need to call it in for a fast pickup instead of hiking out."

"It is outrageous that these people are not allowed to be with their mates," one of the warriors said. "I just don't understand the concern. If someone has found their one, their Ehlealah, why is it not celebrated? Why is there concern over their appearance, or their origin? Surely it is their heart that matters, not what they look like."

"I understand it," Va'roush said, taking his time to look around at each warrior, daring them to say otherwise. "Sometimes it is not only a stranger who will judge your appearance."

"Unfortunately, you are correct, Va'roush," Kron said.

"Come, let's return to the ship, rest, eat, prepare and plan for morning," Ba Re' said.

"I cannot rest," Kron said.

"Understandable, but you can eat. You must be strong and ready to fight in the morning," Jhan said. "Try to calm, Kron. Your female will be in your arms tomorrow."

Kron nodded, then gestured for Buchanan to precede him as they resumed their trek down the final ridge toward the transports.

A short time later they were close enough to see the ship Ba Re' and his team had arrived on. He recognized the ship as Rokai's. "Now I understand why Gaishon is your pilot, rather than one of the Elite team. But I am curious as to how you managed to take possession of Rokai's ship without him accompanying you," Kron said.

"Quin wouldn't let Rokai off Command Warship 1" Ba Re' said with a grin.

"Completely understandable. I'm more than sure he wasn't happy about it," Kron said, looking at Rokai's ship as they got closer to it.

"No, he was not. But, when it became clear that his ship was needed, Rokai didn't argue the issue. He knew that Gaishon knows the routes we were taking, and that he has more than a little experience piloting the ship. In addition, it is not registered as a Cruestaci vessel. It is registered as a merchant vessel."

"I understand," Kron said. "I'm just shocked you were able to make the trip so quickly using merchant trade routes."

"We used pirating routes," Jhan said. "It was important that we were undetected."

Kron turned to look at Jhan, his surprise evident.

"We knew that if we were seen by others who frequent those routes, they'd assume Rokai was at it again. And the routes are admittedly shorter to traverse, but Rokai has been tinkering with the ship in his spare time, as he puts it," Ba Re' said. "He promised it would get us here in half the time. And he was right."

"Amazing," Kron commented.

"It is. He is much more gifted than most would believe, and he is happy to have all underestimate him," Ba Re' said. "Just don't tell him I said that."

Kron smiled. "I won't."

Chapter 25

The next morning, at 9:15 A.M. Earth time, nine males with a common focus, spread out across the top of the ridge protecting the Purist compound from easy accessibility, and began their descent undetected. Some were working as teams, while a few were going in separately, but all were moving forward at the same time. Some would begin their search for Ginger on the Northern side of the compound, and yet others would start on the Southern side, the Eastern side, and the Western side. They would move silently, taking out any of the Purists they might happen on in order to prevent anyone knowing of their presence for as long as possible. They needed time to search for Ginger through quite possibly the entire compound if that's what it took, before they found her.

Quietly they moved through the compound, each focused on what they needed to do. It was inevitable that most of the Purists would not survive, unless they surrendered. It was expected that most would not. It had been decided that ultimately each male would make the decision of each life he came across. If that person compromised their mission, they would have to be put down. If they were undetected and the person had no idea the warrior was there, it would be left to that warrior to decide whether or not that person needed to die.

It was not a problem for most of them. They knew the members of this organization were responsible for holding the mate of a Cruestaci warrior within their fold, for breeding and spreading prejudice of anyone who was not fully human, and for the separation of many more human citizens from their alien mates. For the rescue party as a whole, removing any Purists' personnel they came across was not only not a problem, it was a pleasure.

Kron had slipped into a state of mind that left him sharp, clear-minded, lethal. This was a familiar behavior and his brothers-in-arms fully expected it each time they were out on mission, regardless of the mission. He was one of the best among the best. But, he was even more focused this time. He was ruthless, deadly, not caring who he had to go through to find Ginger. The blade like appendages that extruded from his fingers and just above his elbow while in battle had extended and their tips were glistening in the sunlight. The sun even glinted off the razor sharp tip of the blade above his elbow through the tear it made in his plain black shirt. They'd all worn simple black clothing, deciding not to don their Cruestaci uniforms. In the effort to remain anonymous, they even wore plain black battle helmets with darkened face shields, earpieces and microphones to stay in communication. Except for Va'roush. Before the mission it became clear there were only enough helmets for the Cruestaci, which meant Buchanan didn't have a communication device nor a covering for his face. Va'roush took his helmet off without hesitation and handed it to Buchanan. "It is important you are disguised. I am not known on this planet, you are. Wear this."

"I'll be fine," Buchanan said, trying to hand it back.

"Yes, you will. Put it on," Va'roush growled. The man was looking for his missing daughter and he wanted to argue about a helmet. Va'roush considered just lifting a hand and knocking him in the back of the head, but Buchanan seemed to think better of it and mumbled a thanks before Va'roush had time to act on it.

Gaishon handed Va'roush a pair of earpieces that worked much the same way those installed in the helmets did. "Here, these will keep you apprised of all that happens and allow you to communicate."

"I don't need them," Va'roush said, not holding out his hand to take them.

"Take them, Va'roush," Ba Re' said calmly.

Va'roush looked toward Ba Re', then Jhan, and reluctantly held out his hand to accept the earpieces.

"Now put them in your ears," Ba Re' ordered.

Va'roush smiled slowly as he stared at Ba Re', his sarcasm clearly seen in his expression as he put both earpieces into his ears. "Yes, General."

Ba Re' looked at Jhan and shook his head.

Jhan only offered a shrug as though he didn't understand the problem.

"I am not yet a General," Ba Re' snapped.

"Ah, but you will be," Va'roush said, smiling at Ba Re' teasingly. "Such a pretty title, for such a brave Warrior."

"Va'roush!" Ba Re' warned.

"Is always going to push the limit," Jhan said loudly, "but after all others have evacuated, he will be the warrior there to pull you out. Always. Every time."

Ba Re' held his tongue, then gave a single nod before ignoring both Jhan and Va'roush and turning his attention back to discussing the mission at hand.

In addition to the helmets/earpieces, they all wore long sleeve shirts and gloves as well so no evidence of their skin color or prints of any type would be left behind. They were all acutely aware that they were going in as an unsanctioned team.

~~~

Once the mission was underway and they approached the outer limits of the compound, other than an odd grunt, or the beginnings of a shout that was quickly extinguished followed by the warrior's voice advising that all was secure in whatever area he was in, there was no indication that their presence had been detected by those they'd not yet encountered and silenced.

Then they began to enter and search the buildings in the compound. Reports were filtering through the earpieces as they moved from room to room. It was then that it became apparent that the Cruestaci warriors infiltrating the Purist compound wouldn't be a secret much longer. Blaster and disintegrater shots were being fired and were clearly heard even without the helmets. Shouts and threats could be heard, and then the alarm sounded. Sirens, reminiscent of World War II air raid sirens filled the air with their deafening sound. All nine males went on the offensive, knowing they'd been detected.

Then Va'roush's voice filled each of their earpieces. "I've found the human mates. I'm in the large metal building near the Southern end of the compound. I do not see the target female, but there are more than I can safely move out of the vicinity. I need assistance. In the meantime I will kill all who try to enter. Repeat, I need assistance to move the captive mates."

"Coming your way," Kron responded, eager to get there and see if Ginger was indeed among them. He was hopeful that Va'roush simply didn't recognize her among the others. Kron was silently moving through the building he'd been assigned - the original home itself. There was absolutely no sound there at all, and he honestly thought it was empty, its occupant most likely warned by the siren to evacuate to wherever their safe place was on the compound. He quickly checked each of the other rooms in the house, looked in closets and under beds. Entering a bedroom that was obviously decorated for a female, he took off his helmet to get a better look without having to peer through the darkened face shield. He inhaled, hoping to pick up the scent of his mate, and instead found nothing but the disgustingly sweet, cloying perfume permeating the room. Finding no one there, he changed direction and went back toward the door he'd originally entered through. After replacing his helmet, he went around the back of the house using the rear of the building as cover while he moved toward the building Va'roush had said he was in, hoping against hope that Ginger was there.

Buchanan was armed with a blaster Kron had given him. He begrudgingly had to admit it was much more efficient and easier to handle than his favored shotgun. He wasn't scouting the compound looking for Purists and trying to neutralize any he found. He was focused on one thing — finding his daughter. He'd decided to leave the control of the situation in general to the Cruestaci, while he found Ginger. Having finished searching what

247

he thought might be the security center of the compound, he went back to the room with the monitors. He tinkered with the security tapes for a few moments, thinking maybe he could find Ginger on them, but it was quickly clear the tapes had been compromised by the Purists once it was confirmed they were under attack.

Leaving that building, he went to the next — the home that seemed to have originally been on the property. First he checked the entire exterior, then he cautiously went in the back door, holding his blaster at the ready. But he found no one in the room. Buchanan began a methodical search of each room, every single place someone may be hiding, not stopping until he was certain Ginger wasn't there. The last room he entered was a bedroom, small, but prettily decorated with lots of laces and floral patterns. He did his standard search of beneath and inside things, then assured that the home was empty, he took a moment to really look around. He examined the antique perfume bottles and other items sitting on top of the dresser and noted the sunglasses that looked out of place. He glanced over at the bed and realized that it had been hastily gotten out of. The comforter and blankets on the bed had been half dragged off the bed and were actually trailing the floor.

Then he walked back into the small bathroom that was attached to the bedroom. There was nothing out of the ordinary there, but on a whim he lifted the lid to the hamper, glancing in quickly before letting the lid fall closed. He took two steps away from it before he froze in his tracks. His head cocked just a bit to the side before he turned around and practically lunged at the half-full hamper. He tore his helmet off and reached in, snatching up the item that had caught his attention. He lifted the satiny garment from where it just barely peeked out from beneath a towel that lay atop it. He gripped the satin nightgown in his hand. Then he held his helmet close to his mouth and spoke, knowing his voice would carry through the microphone of the helmet. "Kron, she's here. I've found her night gown in the house. She's here somewhere."

248

~~~

Kron was helping Va'roush deal with the captive mates he'd found. He'd rushed into the barn and done a quick cursory glance at the group of them, only to confirm that Ginger wasn't among them. He'd schooled his disappointment, and begun to reassure those who weren't quite convinced the big, gruff, obviously dangerous male stomping through their midst and growling the entire time was a good thing.

It wasn't long before Ba Re' finished up the search of his area and joined them in the barn. "What do we have here?" he asked, coming to a stop near Kron.

"Eleven humans, all are mated to aliens. Brought here and held against their will," Kron said.

"Do any of you know how we can locate your mates?" Ba Re' asked.

"Yes!" one girl said anxiously.

"Yeah, I do," a man said.

"Me, too," another said.

Some of them were too drugged to even be able to tell the warriors their names.

"Alright. We're going to get you to safety, then you can reach out to your mates. If you're not sure how to find them, we'll do what we can to help try to track them down. We'll get you medical care, and try to figure out how to get you home," Ba Re' answered.

"No, not home. Home is what got most of us here," one of the men said.

"Then we'll find you somewhere safe, where you won't be returned to this place or any like it," Ba Re' said.

Two of the girls started crying with relief.

"Thank you," the man answered. "Thank you," he repeated, obviously choked up.

Kron, Ba Re', and Va'roush paused as they listened to Buchanan's voice as it carried through their helmets. "Kron, she's here. I've found her night gown in the house. She's here somewhere."

Kron froze in place, then turned to look through the darkened face shield of his helmet at Va'roush and Ba Re'.

"Go," Va'roush said. "Find your female."

"I'm calling in the ship. We'll get these people on it, then secure the rest of the compound," Ba Re' said.

Kron didn't hesitate, he turned and ran from the barn as quickly as he could. He didn't even take the safety precautions he should have, he simply ran, faster than he'd ever run in his life. He stopped just outside the house, and spoke aloud so Buchanan would know he was entering the home and not fire on him. "Entering the home."

Kron pulled open the door and stepped inside the house. Almost silently he moved toward the bedrooms, just as Buchanan stepped into view, grasping a light blue satin fabric in his fist.

"This is Ginger's. I'd recognize it anywhere," Buchanan said.

Kron reached his hand out toward Buchanan, who handed him the nightgown. Kron took off his helmet with one hand and lifted the soft gown to his nose, inhaling his mate's scent. He closed his eyes as a soothing calm suffused him. "It is hers. Where did you find it?"

"One of the bedrooms. I'll show you," Buchanan said.

Kron followed Buchanan to one of the bedrooms he'd given a quick cursory search, but not actually torn it apart looking for evidence Ginger had been there. "I missed it," Kron admitted.

"Doesn't matter. I didn't," Buchanan said.

Kron nodded, then looked around the room as though seeing it for the first time. He was more suspect and critical of all he saw now that he knew beyond the shadow of a doubt that Ginger had been here. "Where is she?" he whispered aloud, looking around the room. Slowly he walked out of the room, examining every inch of the walls and floors.

~~~

Standing in the secret space inside the wall of the living room, Ginger remained absolutely still as the blade Dr. Cavanaugh held pressed against her throat stung just enough to remind her that he could cut through her jugular with little to no effort. She had no doubt he'd kill her if she tested him. All it would take was a small stroke of his right hand — and the scalpel he held against her skin would move through her flesh like a hot knife through butter.

"If you make a single noise, alert them in any way, I'll kill you. Do you understand?" he hissed at her ear as he held her from behind. She shivered with revulsion at the feel of the warmth from his breath as it caressed her ear and fluttered her hair about.

Ginger's heart pounded and raced in her chest as she stood with Dr. Cavanaugh, held securely in his grasp, one of his hands was slapped across her mouth and pressing so hard it was difficult to get a deep breath since his fingers partially blocked her nostrils, too, while his other hand held the scalpel against her throat.

He'd rushed into her bedroom, grabbed her up all the while threatening her life, and forced her inside the secret space in her bedroom. He'd shoved her through the small cramped space toward its opposite end, which extended down the hallway, then turned toward the living room. She'd been afraid, thinking he'd finally crossed that line between sanity and insanity permanently. Then she'd realized what the problem was, what it was that had driven him to behave so erratically, so desperately. Kron was here! She'd seen him through strategically placed openings that allowed whoever was on the inside of the wall to spy on those in the rooms of the house. The moment Dr. Cavanaugh had grabbed her from her room, opened a hidden panel in her wall, and shoved her through it, she'd realized how he'd gotten into her bedroom the previous morning without disturbing the chair she'd had leveraged beneath the doorknob.

251

He had secret spaces built inside most of the walls. But it wasn't until she'd seen Kron that she realized why she was being pulled into it with him.

"I knew he'd come for you. I knew it. The moment I heard my men speaking of your eyes, and then saw them for myself, I knew which male you'd bedded. I knew it was only a matter of time before he'd track you here. I befriended you, kept you close to me so that he'd have to go through me when he arrived, and planned to wait as long as it took. Surely you didn't truly think someone like you mattered to someone like me?" he scoffed in a whisper. "Doesn't matter. Turns out it wasn't a long wait after all. And I was right. My nemesis has come to collect his due."

Ginger shook her head as much as she dared, trying to indicate that Kron wasn't her mate. She didn't want him targeted.

"Oh, come now. Do you think I'm an idiot? Just how many aliens with yellow skin and eyes do you think there are?" he snapped. "I knew you were his. One look at you said that much."

Ginger's first thought was 'his entire race, apparently has yellow eyes and skin', but she couldn't speak it aloud because Dr. Cavanaugh still held his hand over her mouth and the scalpel to her neck.

"Now, the question becomes, shall I struggle to keep you quiet and contained, while I plot to kill him, or should I simply dispatch you now so that I don't have to be distracted?"

Ginger started shaking her head and mumbled through the hand he kept pressed tightly to her mouth. She was denying all association with Kron, doing her best to make sure both she and Kron survived this.

"Stop it!" Dr. Cavanaugh demanded. "Not another sound!" he insisted, pressing the tip of the scalpel against her skin enough so that a trickle of blood ran down her neck.

Ginger stopped struggling, or making any sound at all. They stood silently for the better part of ten minutes as there was no sound in the house. Then Ginger listened as footsteps once again drew near, and her heart swelled as she saw her father through the wall, searching the house for her. They'd tracked her location somehow, now all they had to do was find her.

"I will kill them if they find us before I'm prepared to deal with them," Cavanaugh whispered in her ear.

Or not find her, Ginger thought, depending on if she wanted them alive or not.

A soft sob escaped Ginger as she realized she'd have to sacrifice her life for theirs. If she did nothing, Cavanaugh could possibly surprise them and then kill them. She knew Kron could most likely survive any battle with Cavanaugh. She'd never seen him in battle, but was pretty sure he had skills humans had no idea of. Her father was able to take care of himself as well under normal circumstances. But these weren't normal circumstances. The problem was, she would no doubt be used in leverage against them. They'd be forced to submit or watch her die. There was no way she'd allow her life to be used against either of them. If she made herself known, at least Kron and her dad would know the hiding place was there and wouldn't be surprised or attacked without warning. They wouldn't willingly lay down their weapons and allow fate to take its course. They'd fight. And while she might not survive, her mate and her father certainly would.

"Shut. Up," Dr. Cavanaugh practically growled in her ear as she sobbed.

Ginger gathered her courage, and all in one motion lifted her hands and pressed them against the hand Dr. Cavanaugh held the scalpel in and kicked against the wall in front of her.

Dr. Cavanaugh struggled with Ginger, actually pulling the scalpel away from her neck out of fear he'd kill her while he still needed her. He'd been intimidating her, using fear to control her rather than actually inflicting damage. If everything went to shit, he'd need her alive and well in order to get out of this damn compound. Threat of harm to her, if all else failed, was what he planned to rely on to get both males to submit and follow his demands, then get himself and Ginger to a transport after they were both dead. He was confident the rest of those searching his compound wouldn't want her dead either... But, there was nothing about his plan that said she had to be conscious.

He reached into his suit pocket and took out the syringe. "I don't need you awake for this part, you filthy, trashy little bitch," he spat at her as he jabbed the needle into her breast.

Ginger screamed beneath his hand and flung out her legs kicking the wall again as she sought to evade whatever he was injecting her with.

Chapter 26

The muffled sound of banging, and a scream had Buchanan and Kron running back to the hallway connecting the bedrooms with the front of the house.

Buchanan stood at the exact point the hallway met the living room, his weapon drawn and held out in front of him as he slowly turned in a circle and tried to determine where he'd heard the scream and the thudding noise from. It sounded like someone was kicking or hitting a wall. Kron began to walk up and down the hallway, running his hands along the sheetrock, his eyes closed as he concentrated, trying to determine the location of the noises they'd heard.

Ginger's eyes grew heavy quickly, but she did her best to fight the effects of the sedative she'd been given. She had no idea if it would kill her, or just knock her out, but she knew she had to warn the men she loved regardless.

Since the scalpel was gone from her throat, and she'd already been injected with whatever medication was in the syringe, she had nothing to loose. All threats against her had already been removed or used on her. She opened her mouth, still covered with Dr. Cavanaugh's hand, and bit down as hard as she could, doing her best to take a nice sized chunk out of his palm.

Dr. Cavanaugh was stunned by the fact that Ginger had bitten down on his hand. But when she began to shake her head back and forth while she bit down even harder, he realized she wasn't going to stop until the flesh gripped between her teeth was torn from his palm.

"Let go!" he ordered, panicking, punching the opposite side of her head with his other hand.

The harder she bit, the harder he hit her, and it didn't take long until the commotion matched with Cavanaugh's shrill screams brought both Kron and Buchanan to exactly the point in the wall in which they were concealed.

Ginger was fading fast, but her teeth were locked on Cavanaugh's flesh and she refused to let go. As she started to slide to the floor, she realized her feet were against the wall, and she began to kick again, as much as she could with her waning strength against it.

Dr. Cavanaugh screamed again when her teeth broke through the flesh she'd taken hold of, then cursed her as her teeth finally tore through his palm. Ginger spat the chuck of flesh at him, smiling as his blood ran down her chin, staining her lower face and neck.

"Fucking bitch!" he shrieked, drawing back with his good hand and striking her across the face as hard as he could.

Ginger was now collapsed on the floor at his feet and could fight no more.

But she didn't need to. She'd been found.

Cavanaugh could hear someone on the other side of the wall, trying to break through it. Somewhere inside his warped mind, he knew he should be trying to get her to her feet and hold her as a shield in front of his own body, but the pain radiating from his hand had him raging more than he usually did when angered. Instead, he kicked her unconscious body as outrage filled him at the sight of the sinew showing through the wound she'd put on his hand. "I'll kill you!" he screeched, kicking her again before falling on his ass beside her, and cradling his injured hand as he whimpered.

The sheetrock above Dr. Cavanaugh's head shattered and came apart, raining down on him and Ginger, as a yellow hand punched through it.

Dr. Cavanaugh shrieked again, turned to his knees and his one good hand to try to hurriedly crawl away. But another punch through the sheetrock had him partially exposed and frozen where he was as he looked up to see the face of the person who was tearing apart his home. His expression turned to terror when a very familiar, very pissed off alien reached through the sheetrock and yanked him through what little remained of the

256

wall, throwing him flat onto his back on the living room floor. "Kill him!" Kron snarled as he turned back to the wall to find Ginger.

Buchanan stepped forward, aiming his blaster at Cavanaugh's head.

Dr. Cavanaugh was terrified. This was not at all the way this was supposed to play out. The stupid Buchanan bitch was supposed to be his ticket out of here, as well as his way to control the males now facing him, but she'd made him so angry he'd lost control and drugged her, which made it hard to force her to even stand in front of him, much less walk or run with him to whatever transportation he could find to escape on.

Buchanan looked at Cavanaugh with disgust and kept his blaster trained on Cavanaugh. "I hope you rot in hell, you sonofabitch," he said.

"Wait!" Kron shouted. "Don't kill him yet!"

"He needs to die!" Buchanan said, his voice calm and deadly.

Kron had already checked her and wasn't able to find a wound that would account for the blood staining her face and chest. He'd confirmed that Ginger had a pulse as well, so he picked her up off the floor and cradled her unconscious body against his chest. "What did you do to her?" he demanded on a growl, walking toward where Buchanan held Cavanaugh at the opposite end of his blaster.

"Nothing! It's what she did to me!" he said, holding his bleeding palm up.

Kron handed Ginger to Buchanan, who took her from him and started trying to wake her. "Darlin'? Wake up, Ginger. Wake up for Daddy," Buchanan encouraged.

Kron strode toward Dr. Cavanaugh, not stopping until he pressed his face up against Dr. Cavanaugh's forehead, his fangs dripping with saliva, his skin armored with its natural defensive scaling, his serrated claws fully extended as he regarded the man. "I warned you. I told you if you didn't stay away, if you didn't disappear, I'd be back," Kron said around his now too large fangs.

"You warned about Ada Jane, and she's not here!" the simpering doctor said as he cradled his profusely bleeding, aching hand.

"But I am, and the female you were stupid enough to take is mine. You will tell me what you did to her, or I'll make you beg for death," Kron said.

"Where's she injured?" Buchanan asked, his voice filled with worry, still trying to determine where she was wounded.

"She's not wounded, I am!" Dr. Cavanaugh shouted.

"I can't find a wound!" Buchanan said, tearing the blouse Ginger was wearing and searching for anything that would cause the blood loss. But there was nothing. "I don't see anything but a tiny nick," Buchanan said, his hands pressing against Ginger's neck and face where the blood had stained her skin and was still sticky and wet.

"She's breathing, but she's not waking up, Kron. What did he do to her?" Buchanan asked.

Kron had turned to look at Buchanan, but now turned back to focus on Dr. Cavanaugh, knowing this man would tell them what they wanted to know or he'd die a slow and painful death.

"You will tell me what you did to my mate. You will tell me how to revive her," Kron snarled, his razor-like claws piercing Cavanaugh's flesh where he gripped the man's shoulders.

"I didn't do anything that wasn't deserved," Cavanaugh burst out on a scream.

Ginger shifted slightly in Buchanan's arms. "She's moving!" Buchanan exclaimed.

Kron turned from Cavanaugh and rushed over to where Buchanan still held Ginger in his arms.

"Ginger! Leerah! Wake for me," Kron begged. But Ginger simply settled back into her father's arms, completely unaware that Kron was speaking to her or that her father held her.

Kron was suffused with rage as he turned to stalk back over to Cavanaugh, but he was gone. When Ginger's movements had distracted both Kron and Buchanan, Cavanaugh had taken the opportunity to slip out of the still open front door.

"Cavanaugh!" Kron growled, starting toward the door.

"Sonofabitch!" Buchanan shouted.

But before Kron could get out of the door, Cavanaugh was pushed back through it and into the house, his head at a strange angle as a dark green and black hand wrapped in his hair kept his chin up and pointed at the ceiling.

"The other mates are processed. I decided I might be of use here," Va'roush said. "I wasn't very helpful there anyway. I'm not much for soothing those who need it, I'm more the kill anyone I don't recognize and figure out if I should have later on. Good thing I came when I did, look what I found trying to get away," Va'roush said just as jovially as if he was laughing with friends. "And lucky for me, I don't recognize him. That means I get to kill him, yes?"

"Don't let him kill me! I... I have the information you need," Cavanaugh begged.

Kron's chest heaved as he tried to control his emotions. "Look at my mate," he growled, turning toward Buchanan.

Buchanan walked over and carefully laid Ginger in Kron's arms. Kron lifted his arms slightly to show her to Va'roush.

Va'roush looked at the female Kron now held in his arms. She was covered in blood, and unconscious. "Is she dead?" Va'roush asked.

"No, but she's not waking up," Buchanan said.

"What did you do?" Kron snarled, his eyes focused on Cavanaugh.

"Until you set me free, I'll never tell," Cavanaugh answered defiantly.

"You will never be free," Kron growled stalking toward Cavanaugh, stopping just out of reach in case he tried to lunge toward Ginger again. "The only question is how quickly, or slowly you die. If you wish to suffer, continue to defy me."

Cavanaugh hated Kron. He hated all aliens, but he hated Kron more than most. He was responsible for injuring his hands and ending Cavanaugh's surgical career. He lost all patience and presence of mind when Kron threatened him again. "I knew she was yours," he spat. "I knew it, and I used her stupidity to gain her trust. She lived in my house, submitting to my whims, as I turned her against you, simply because I could. You think you're in control? Not hardly. And unless you release me, she will die, and it will be on you! There is nothing you can do short of releasing me, to make me cooperate!" Cavanaugh shouted maniacally, truly believing he could regain control of the situation.

"Hah, ahahahahah," Va'roush barked out a robust laugh. "I'll take that challenge," he said as he grinned, forcing Cavanaugh's head to turn so he could make eye contact with him.

"He's mine," Kron growled.

Va'roush met Kron's glare and hesitated before he gave him a single nod. "To finish," he said. "But until then, he's mine to question. You need answers for your female, yes?"

"Yes," Kron growled in response, looking down at Ginger in his arms as he cradled her closer.

"Allow me," Va'roush said. Then he looked at Buchanan. "Human, turn away or be complicit."

Buchanan didn't turn away, in fact, he stepped closer.

Va'roush returned his attention to the man he held within his grip. "Do you know why most fear me?" he asked conversationally. "I'm sure you do not, we are not even acquainted. I will share the reason anyway. It is because my father's people are a vicious race. They even turn on each other if one has something the other wants badly enough. They are very animalistic, they respond to their basest tendencies. There is not usually right or wrong in their minds, in their hearts. There is only need, and want. They feel a need, they react, take whatever it is they want, or need. They walk away from whatever it is they have no feeling for, unless of course someone else wants it, then they'll hold it forever, or very methodically kill it. But, if they despise something, whatever it is they despise is destroyed beyond all recognition. They do whatever it is they feel the need to do — impulsively. Luckily for you, my mother's people are more controlled," he said. Then Va'roush grinned coldly. "Unluckily for you, I've learned to ignore that more controlled side of me at will."

"She's not dead! I didn't kill her! You can't hurt me!" Cavanaugh shouted, clearly terrified of the alien holding him in his grasp. "You can't kill me!"

"I can do whatever I wish to do!" Va'roush roared. "Did I not just explain that?"

"Tell me how to wake her!" Kron bellowed at the same time Va'roush roared right at Cavanaugh's ear.

"She's sleeping, you idiot!" Cavanaugh shouted, his nerves and self-control completely shot. "Can you not see that she's sleeping?!"

"She's unconscious! She's bruised — her face, her head, she's covered in blood, she cannot be awakened. She is not simply sleeping! What did you do?" Kron shouted, demanding an answer.

"What did I do? I did nothing! She did it! The stupid bitch bit me! This whole thing is her own fault!" Cavanaugh screamed. "If the idiot female had simply done as she was told, we'd be on a transport this very instant, and you'd be lying dead at my feet!"

Va'roush lifted a hand and slapped Cavanaugh hard enough from behind that his head jerked forward, leaving a handful of hair in Va'roush's hand. Va'roush shook the strands of hair from his hand, then grabbed Cavanaugh's head quickly gripping another handful of hair to keep Cavanaugh steady.

Then Va'roush looked at Kron. "Her head and face are bruised?" he asked.

"He struck her," Kron snarled.

"She bit me! Did you not hear me?" Cavanaugh yelled. "I did nothing wrong! I saved this female! I brought her from the barn they're all kept in. I brought her into my home, protected her and gave her shelter, while I waited for you to come for her, and this is what she did to me," Cavanaugh said, holding up his bleeding hand to show Kron, and the monster that held him still in his grasp. "And she wouldn't let go! No matter how many times I hit her, she wouldn't let go!"

"So you not only held her hostage, threatened her male, and forced her to your home for what is I'm sure nefarious reason, you beat her, and when she dared to fight back, you did this to her? Do you think she deserves this?" Va'roush bellowed.

"She bit me! Tore the flesh from my hand!" Cavanaugh screeched defensively.

Va'roush only thought about it for a split second, then he snarled. "Tell me, if I bite you, will you try to beat me, as well?" he asked. Va'roush didn't hesitate. He opened his mouth and sank his many shark-like teeth into the skin on the side of Cavanaugh's head. He took just a bit of the skin in front of the ear, part of the ear itself, and part of the scalp just above the ear, scraping against the skull there when he did. He spit it on the floor and grinned as he smiled at Cavanaugh while the man shrieked non-stop. Then he raised his arm and punched Cavanaugh on the other side of the head repeatedly until he was in danger of passing out. "What is wrong? Why are you not beating me? Surely that is how you respond to being bitten, or is it only how you respond to females weaker than you? Answer me! I've delivered a much worse bite," Va'roush said. "I wish to see you beat a male, a strong male who is capable of ripping your head off your shoulders!"

Cavanaugh was screaming and shrieking. The pitch of his screams was so shrill that Kron, Va'roush, and Buchanan all winced.

"Stop shrieking! Or I'll bite off the other side, too, just to be sure you understand what a real bite is like! Go ahead! Keep screaming like a wounded female! Keep it up!" Va'roush promised. "It just angers me more."

Cavanaugh continued shrieking, his arms flailing in the general direction of his bleeding head.

"How does it feel to be the receiver of physical violence. How does it feel when one much stronger, and I'm willing to bet, less sane than you are, decides to exert his superiority over you?" Va'roush shouted.

When Cavanaugh didn't answer and just continued to shriek and sob, Va'roush shrugged and looked at Kron. "He's not answering. I'll bite him again."

Cavanaugh's eyes rolled back in his head and almost immediately his body became limp, held up off the floor only by Va'roush's grip on his head and hair.

"Thank the gods! He was becoming irritating," Va'roush grumbled, releasing his hold on the man to let him fall to the floor.

"I need him awake!" Kron yelled. "I need to know exactly what he drugged her with, and how much he's given her!"

Va'roush looked at Kron for a moment, then shrugged again before leaning over the unconscious man. He grabbed him up and began shaking him. Eventually Cavanaugh's eyes opened and he began to rouse, sobbing and crying, working up to a scream when his eyes focused on Va'roush once more.

"What did you drug her with?" Va'roush demanded, shouting right in Cavanaugh's face. "How much did you give her?" he shouted.

Buchanan walked back over to the torn apart wall, which had hidden Cavanaugh and Ginger from sight when they'd first searched the house. He stepped inside the space and poked around, until something caught his eye. "A syringe!" he exclaimed, picking it up and bringing it to show Kron. "Nobody uses these damn things anymore unless they're in the field! They're ancient!"

Kron took the syringe from Buchanan to get a better look. "Unless they are trying to inflict pain," he said, holding the syringe up to the light, trying to see if there was any trace anywhere in the syringe that would give an indication of how full it was before the drug was injected into Ginger. "I can't tell," Kron said. "Whatever it was is clear, and there's only a minute drop or two inside. I can't tell how much was in it, and I'm not sure what it was."

Buchanan took it from him and held it up to the light himself. "I can't either," Buchanan said. "But we can have it tested and find out what it was. I wouldn't be surprised if it's the same thing, or close to the same thing we found left in the plastic bag I found in her mother's purse."

"It won't do us any good if she dies," Kron growled out, barely able to control his frustration and anger. "We waste time here. We need to get her to medical treatment now!"

"Go, Kron. I will finish this," Va'roush said.

Kron shifted Ginger's weight to one arm and held her close as he walked toward Cavanaugh, still held securely by Va'roush. He raised his free hand up into the air over Cavanaugh as he pointedly clacked his razor sharp claws together. He pressed the tip of one claw into the pad of his own thumb causing a thin line of blood to follow the curve of his claw and then his finger, then to run down over his hand and wrist. When he reached Cavanaugh, he raised his hand above his head, the claws angled down in just the right way to slice into whatever he plunged them into. He brought his hand down slowly, his bladed claws piercing the skin of Cavanaugh's face as he dragged them down to his chest. "Consider yourself lucky that her survival means more to me than your demise, else I'd be staying to finish you personally."

And that was all it took. Cavanaugh realized Kron was leaving him with the black and green monster who'd bitten his ear off, and he started rambling, believing he could manipulate Kron more easily than the one who held him.

"She's just sedated. I didn't want her dead, I needed her alive so I could escape if need be, but she bit me! And she wouldn't stop biting me!" Cavanaugh said through terrified tears. "I just sedated her! She got a little more than usual, but it's not going to kill her! I need her to make my getaway!" he screamed, beginning to completely lose his grip on reality. "I cannot get away safely if she's not alive! She is not dying!" Cavanaugh's eyes were wide with pain and fear as he stared intently at Kron with his head still held at an unnatural angle. "She'll wake up," he whimpered.

"When? What did you drug her with?" Kron demanded.

But Cavanaugh didn't respond, instead he pressed his lips together defiantly. "If I tell you everything, you'll kill me. Don't leave me here with him! Don't let him kill me, and I'll care for her until she wakes. She will wake!"

264

"Do you believe him?" Buchanan asked, not sure what scenario was the best one.

"Her heart is beating regularly, it is not weak or faltering. I believe he would have used her to get himself to freedom," Kron said.

"I'm not lying to you. My life is in the balance," Cavanaugh shouted. He was beginning to shake uncontrollably, most likely going into shock due to the blood loss and the terror he was experiencing at the hands of those he feared most — aliens. "I'm going into shock. I could die if I don't get treatment," he whined. "I need medical treatment, too, so I can care for her while she's sleeping!"

"I'm taking my mate back to the ship. I will have her assessed there. I do not trust him to even look at her. I can't base her welfare on anything he says," Kron said.

"I'm coming with you," Buchanan said, leaning over and grabbing up both his and Kron's helmets.

"The ship is on the Southern end of the compound. It is secure," Va'roush advised.

Kron nodded, then he was moving toward the open door of the house as Cavanaugh began to scream in protest.

"What about this one?" Va'roush called after Kron as Kron rushed through the front door. "I gave you right of kill!"

"The welfare of my mate is more important. Do what you will," Kron said. "Just be sure he does not walk away."

"Do we need him?" Va'roush asked.

Buchanan paused and looked back at the scary as hell green and black alien. "We may. We have others in custody, but he was apparently their ring leader," Buchanan answered honestly. "And I have yet to locate Mitchell," Buchanan said. "Care to tell me where Mitchell is?" Buchanan asked Cavanaugh.

"Yes! I will!" Cavanaugh sobbed. "He's gone to stalk the blue one, Ada Jane's mate and their family! There, you see? I helped. Don't let him kill me!" Cavanaugh begged.

"You're a traitor to your own people, to your own agenda. As much as I think none of you are worth the air you breathe, a complete lack of integrity, even in your fucked up group of

265

terrorists, just really pisses me off. At least have the backbone to stand behind what you profess to believe in rather than selling them out to save your own skin," Buchanan said.

"They seem to change loyalties often," Va'roush said.

"As Kron said, do what you will," Buchanan said.

"I'll catch up," Va'roush said smiling sinisterly, then slammed the door that separated him where he stood inside the house from Kron who moved steadily away and Buchanan who'd paused just outside the door to answer Va'roush's questions.

He focused on Cavanaugh. "Looks like we'll get to play after all," Va'roush said with a rumble in his voice, which almost sounded like a rough purr. "I do so like to play. I don't get to do it often enough. They think me uncontrollable. Can you believe that? Me!" he said, releasing his grip on Cavanaugh's head and cracking unusually long and multiply jointed knuckles.

"No," Cavanaugh begged.

"Oh, yes," Va'roush said. "You should have faced Kron before I arrived. He's still got mercy buried somewhere inside him. I wasn't even born with it."

Chapter 27

Kron broke into a jog with Ginger held close against his chest and Buchanan caught up quickly, jogging along beside him with both their helmets in his hands.

Then the screaming started from the house they'd just left, causing Buchanan to glance at Kron.

"You don't hear a single thing," Kron said without looking Buchanan's way. He knew they answered to different authorities, and while Quin wouldn't give a damn, Buchanan's superiors might. If it ever came to light they were there during the attack, this was not something Buchanan needed to reveal.

"No, I do not hear a single thing, and I've never met or spoken to Warrior Va'roush either," Buchanan answered, as he kept pace until they reached the South side of the compound.

As they approached the ship, there were two Cruestaci warriors escorting the three Purists who'd surrendered away from the ship.

Kron moved quickly past them, looking them in the eye with a snarl as he moved quickly up the ramp to the warrior about halfway up who was guarding the entrance.

Buchanan at least had the presence of mind to turn his face away from the three Purists so they wouldn't see his face.

As Kron approached the guard standing on the ramp, the male began giving him updates. "We are ready to leave as soon as the last of our team returns. They are making a final sweep of the buildings, making sure we didn't miss anyone."

"Move aside, I need medical treatment for my female," Kron ordered.

"Of course," the male answered as he moved aside, though he still followed and continued to update Kron. "The three Purists that surrendered are being escorted back to the barn we found the captives in. They'll be cuffed, and strapped to the beds, just as they'd done to the captives."

"Are all the rest dead?" Buchanan asked, since Kron was ignoring the guard. "How many are there?"

"Far as I know, about fifteen," the warrior answered. "If we received aggressive resistance, they were terminated. We did not have time to deal with such behavior. This is not a war, it's a rescue mission."

"Va'roush should be along momentarily. He was not far behind me," Kron said. "Who else is still out?"

"Jhan and Ba Re'. I will let the others know about Va'roush. He has removed his ear piece. We were going to send a warrior for him," the warrior answered.

"I don't think it will be necessary," Kron answered.

The warrior inclined his head, his eyes only briefly touching on the female Kron carried before he returned to his post. The pity he felt could be seen in his demeanor. Each Cruestaci warrior knew how precious a mate was. To have her stolen from you and tortured was unthinkable.

"She will be well, Kron," the male said before he went back to stand watch on the ramp.

Kron burst onto the main deck of the ship with Ginger in his arms, calling out to Gaishon before he even saw him. "Gaishon! I need medical care for my mate! And contact Kol, let him know Purists are targeting him as we speak!"

"I've already contacted Kol, they are safe after they repelled an attempt to trespass on his land early this morning," Gaishon said as he rose from his pilot's seat and walked toward Kron, his eyes on Kron's mate. "Our medical abilities are limited, Kron. This isn't an official transport," Gaishon said. "We do not have a medical bay."

"Do you have Missy onboard?" Kron asked.

"We do. Rokai added her database to this ship," Gaishon confirmed. He looked at the unconscious woman in Kron's arms again, took in the distraught state both Kron and Buchanan were in, then decided to show them to the hidden room that only he and Rokai knew of. Rokai would be angry, but so be it. "Here,

268

come with me," he said. He strode through the seated section of the ship, where any who were transported aboard the ship would sit on the seats and benches installed solely for that purpose. Then he passed through the small galley he and Rokai had prepared more meals than he cared to remember in, while hiding away from those who wanted to take their heads. As he left the galley and it appeared he was walking toward the engine room, he stopped and pressed his hands to the metal wall of the small corridor connecting the different parts of the ship. The wall slid back, revealing a secret room. "The bed is clean, and Missy can read her vitals from in here. If she needs oxygen or sedation, the room can be sealed off and whatever is needed can be provided to this room through the ventilation system. If she requires either, I suggest you secure her, then leave the room unless you wish to breathe in whatever it is Missy gives her."

"What about ingestible or injectable medications or procedures?" Kron asked.

"We have only first aid supplies. Stitches, antidotes for poisons, things of that nature and as I said, oxygen and sedation. We are able to stabilize until we get to a healer," Gaishon explained.

"What is this room?" Kron asked, walking past Gaishon.

"Saferoom. Hidden away just in case we were ever boarded unwillingly. If ventilation of the rest of the ship is cut off altogether, this room remains a survivable habitat."

"It's tiny," Kron said absentmindedly as he approached the small bed and gently laid Ginger out on it as Buchanan moved out of the way to give him and Gaishon room to walk around each other.

"It's all we needed," Gaishon said as he squeezed past Kron and waved his hand across the wall. A virtual keyboard was displayed at once, and Gaishon began typing on it. A section of the wall slid away much like the first had, displaying a small, clear display for the information Missy would provide to scroll across. "Missy?" Gaishon asked.

"Yes, Warrior Gaishon," Missy answered.

"Elite Warrior Kron is aboard with his mate. He needs medical intervention," Gaishon said.

"We are limited in medical functionality," Missy replied. "But I will do what I can to stabilize the injured parties until they reach a medical facility."

"This display is actually the same as in the medical clinic aboard Command Warship 1. Results from the scans and monitors will come up on the clear panel as they do there. Rokai put it in. Missy will also provide information to the healer on duty on Command Warship 1."

"Thank you, Gaishon," Kron said.

"Thank Rokai. He's the one that made these improvements. It was originally just a hidden room with ventilation independent of the rest of the ship. He's been expanding and improving the ship while he's assigned to Command Warship 1," Gaishon said.

"I will thank him the moment I see him," Kron said.

"I'll be keeping your female in my thoughts, Kron," Gaishon said. "Gods willing she recovers." Then he was gone, headed back to pilot them out of the Purists' compound.

"Missy," Kron said, knowing Missy would recognize his voice and likely even knew he was onboard before Gaishon told her. "Please scan my mate. I know she's been drugged, I fear she's been given too much and it will harm her," Kron said.

"Hello, Elite Warrior Kron. I will do my best to assist you," Missy replied. There were a few moments of silence during which Missy was scanning Ginger's vital signs, and readouts began scrolling across the clear pane of glass. Kron could read them, but Buchanan could not since the information was in Cruestaci. He looked worriedly at Buchanan, and they held each other's gaze until Missy once again started speaking.

"Her heart rate is somewhat weakened, though not alarmingly so. Her respiration is slow but sufficient. Her blood pressure is lower than normal, but it is not at a dangerously low level. We are unable to test her blood for illicit substances, but we do have certain antidotes onboard that counteract most poisons. The problem with them is that they can themselves be deadly if poisons are not the reason for her condition. Has she been poisoned, Elite Warrior Kron?" Missy asked.

"We believe she is sedated, not poisoned," Kron answered.

"One moment," Missy said. The room was silent for several minutes, then Missy was back. "Elite Warrior Kron, it is the opinion of the Master Healer, that as long as your female maintains her current levels of vitality we not administer the poison antidotes. If she should begin to worsen, we will revisit the option. Is that acceptable?"

Kron looked from Ginger, where he reached out and took her hand in his, to Buchanan. Buchanan nodded. Kron nodded back. "Yes, Missy. That is acceptable."

"Very good. The scans I've been able to complete have been forwarded to the medical unit aboard Command Warship 1. If our Master Healer sees anything that warrants noting, he will contact you through me. I will continue to monitor her heart rate, blood pressure, and respiration. You and the male with you are experiencing high stress levels and high blood pressure. Should I send your scans to Master Healer as well?"

"No, that won't be necessary," Kron answered.

"Are there any other injuries that should be addressed?" Missy asked.

"You'll need to ask Gaishon if there were any injuries to our warriors," Kron answered.

"I will, and I will alert you should anything change with your mate, Elite Warrior Kron," Missy said.

"Thank you, Missy," Kron said and took a seat on the edge of the bed, looking down at Ginger as though his gaze was keeping her there and alive.

"So we wait," Buchanan said.

"It's all we can do," Kron answered.

Buchanan took a seat on the foot of the bed and thought about all that had transpired in the last few days. Ginger was no longer in their hands, and was presumably safe now, but there could be others in the same situation they'd found her in. "We didn't get them all," Buchanan said. "Mitchell is still out there, and who knows how many followers and supporters he has?"

"He will be found. They will all be dealt with, of that I have no doubt," Kron said. "But for now, we found Ginger, and the other mates who'd been subjected to them. And Cavanaugh is no more," Kron answered.

"True, but I have no doubt this is far from the end of the Purists. I'm afraid this will just convince them to fight harder. They may even go public and play the victim card. There are a lot of unhappy, disillusioned humans on the planet just looking for someone to blame for their misfortune. They could easily get behind the Purist movement," Buchanan said.

"Unfortunately, it is not uncommon for just that very thing to occur in societies that have experienced upheaval. Not only when those from other worlds try to intervene, but even when their own kind present options for healing that make those easily led feel threatened."

"How do we prepare for their next move?" Buchanan asked.

"We can't. We make sure we are safe, make sure those we love are safe, fortify our defenses, and more importantly our offenses, then we wait. That's all that can be done."

"I hate waiting," Buchanan said.

"As do I. But it is often the smartest thing to do," Kron said.

"I just hope that he's dead. If Mitchell is dead, at least it's one less zealot we'll have to deal with," Buchanan said.

"If he's not, and he's decided to make Kol his target, he is not long for this world. He will be pursued and he will be eliminated," Kron said.

Buchanan nodded. "Yes he will. If I have to do it myself, alone, this damn organization will be exposed and face the consequences of their actions," Buchanan said.

"If there are any left to face the consequences," Kron said, gently stroking Ginger's freckled cheek, "I want them all dead."

"It will be left to me. You need to get my daughter off this planet and away from all this prejudice. We're going to end up in another war, a civil war this time. Fighting amongst ourselves for ridiculous reasons. And if the Purists win, they'll have those helping us maintain our freedom removed from our world, leaving us wide open for another invasion. I don't want Ginger here if any of that happens," Buchanan said.

"Nor do I. But I've promised to help secure Kol's home as well," Kron said, thinking over all he'd committed to.

"I'll help Kol, he's my friend, too. Besides, you've been ordered home," Buchanan said.

Kron gave a reluctant nod. "Once Ginger wakes, if she is even willing to remain at my side, perhaps I could delay my return for a few days only, just to be sure that all who threaten Kol have been eliminated before we return to my home as my Sire has ordered."

"It won't be necessary, Kron. I'm here to see to it, and Zhuxi's people are in place. You saw them. You know what they are capable of," Buchanan said. "You can't be everywhere, protect everyone and take care of my daughter at the same time. If you do that, or try to do that, something will always go wrong. You can't be everywhere at once. You have to decide which is more important. Joining the security that is already protecting Kol and his family, or taking Ginger home with you. She is going to want to be at your side. Protect her, bond with her again, make sure that you are never separated and she is never threatened again."

~~~

Jhan and Ba re' finished the final sweep of the Purists' compound, ensuring that no one was left behind to identity them, and no other captives had been overlooked. Once they were sure they'd missed nothing and no one, they turned their path to the Southern edge of the compound where they knew Gaishon was waiting. Ba Re's steps paused. "The transport Kron and Buchanan arrived in, it will have to be moved as well. It is evidence he and Kron were here."

"I can go for it," Jhan offered.

273

"No, you go back and let them know I'll follow in Buchanan's transport. We will land outside the airspace of Base 28, then Buchanan can take the transport onto the base himself."

"Are you sure?" Jhan asked. "I can come with you."

"There is no need for concern. There is no one left here to offer a threat. It's a matter of a quick hike to the transport, then I'll meet you near the base. Tell Gaishon, when you are in the base's vicinity, not to cross into its airspace. As soon as I arrive, I'll board the ship, leaving Buchanan to take his own transport back onto the base," Ba Re' said.

"Why don't we just have Buchanan fly it back now?" Jhan asked.

"He's with his daughter. He will not wish to leave her until he knows she will be well. It is but a minor inconvenience. I don't mind the extra bit of effort. When you land, do not allow anyone off the ship. Have Gaishon begin searching for the mates of the captives who know how to reach them now. We will repatriate them privately. If we turn them over to the base, we are as much as saying, 'Yes, it was us who attacked and killed the Purists,'" Ba Re' said.

"I will see to it. I will expect your arrival soon," Jhan said.

Ba Re' smiled at Jhan and slapped him on the shoulder before he turned and set out at a jog in the opposite direction.

Jhan resumed his route through the now deserted compound toward the south where Gaishon waited with the ship and all others from the rescue team. Halfway there, Va'roush fell into step behind him. His hands and clothes were covered in blood, but he seemed completely calm and at ease.

"Are you well?" Jhan asked without breaking stride or turning to look at the male.

"Very well," Va'roush answered. "It is always a good day when an abuser of innocents is brought to justice."

Jhan smiled to himself. The male disturbed some warriors that he knew, but not Jhan. He and Va'roush had learned to depend on one another many years earlier as they struggled to survive what was basically a suicide mission. In fact, the only reason Jhan was alive today was because Va'roush had refused to leave him behind. Jhan had learned then that he could trust the male in any situation and Va'roush would never let him down. They'd spent many missions since, hidden away waiting for their target to arrive or to see if they'd be needed, all the while getting to know one another better. Because Jhan didn't judge him, or mistrust him simply because of his lineage or the extremes he went to in order to deliver his own brand of justice, eventually Va'roush had trusted him with the story of his past, and Jhan found that in addition to the trusts they shared, he actually liked Va'roush. It was simply a matter of understanding what made the male tick. His mother had been abused so badly by his father, that she couldn't even love her own child. Granted her abuser was the child's father, but he was still her child, and who his father was wasn't his fault, though Va'roush carried the guilt as though it was.

"I suppose that would make it a good day," Jhan said. He glanced over his shoulder to see Va'roush keeping pace with him with a bright, blood covered smile on his face. All the male really wanted was to be loved. But he'd been taught his whole life he wasn't worthy of love. His grandmother had tried, but by the time she'd actually met him, he was already almost eleven years old. Va'roush was respectful to her, but he never really opened up to her. He was afraid she'd see in him what his mother did. So he kept his head down, his mouth closed and was thankful that at least no one beat him or starved him or his mother anymore. Va'roush simply couldn't contain himself when people, especially women or children, were being abused. He had to rectify it. And to Va'roush, that meant destroying the abuser in any way he could.

"The ship's up ahead..." Jhan said.

"I see it," Va'roush answered.

There were no longer any guards outside it. They'd all apparently boarded and were waiting for the last of them to return to the ship.

As they hurried toward it, the ramp extended for them. They ran up the ramp as it closed behind them right at their heels. Jhan went straight to Gaishon in the pilot's seat. "Take off.

275

Ba Re' is hiking out. He'll be taking the transport Buchanan and Kron left, back to Base 28. He said we are not to enter their airspace, land somewhere just outside it and he'll meet us there. No one gets off until he arrives. I'll speak to the captives and we can contact as many of their mates as possible in the meantime."

Gaishon had already heard their conversation via the earpieces they wore and simply inclined his head and began powering up to lift the ship into the air at Jhan's confirmation.

Chapter 28

Ba Re' moved quickly, yet silently back toward the place they'd first spied Buchanan's transport. It was necessary that they return the transport to Base 28. Once the attack on the Purists' compound was discovered, anyone or anything nearby that could tie Base 28 to the area, would also link the Cruestaci to the attack since Kol was Consul of that base. They'd all worn helmets to conceal their faces, except for Va'roush, and he didn't look Cruestaci. There were a lot of aliens in the multi-verse who had varying colors across their skins, mere suggestions of horns and facial features that the Cruestaci didn't have. Even if he was described, it wouldn't exactly point to Va'roush... there were too many others to consider.

Besides, Ba Re' was fairly certain it would be their word against the Purists, who clearly had an agenda, but if hard evidence was found, they could end up facing questions and even charges they didn't wish to have directed at them. They'd hoped to not have to kill so many, but once they became aware of the number of humans kept there against their will, who'd been drugged and beaten into submission, and the level of resistance they encountered from the Purists, there had been no other way to safely extract Kron's woman, and all those held with her.

He was not the least bit concerned about the captives they'd found revealing who'd rescued them. They'd been warned. And they were so glad to be rescued, Ba Re' had no doubt they'd never speak of the details of that rescue. They didn't wish to cause trouble for those who'd given them back their freedom. They had no desire to return to their families, and only wanted to be reunited with their mates.

His mind at ease after thinking through all that occurred on mission, Ba Re' topped the last ridge and looked down to where they'd originally landed beside Buchanan's transport. He

277

couldn't see it from here, but had no doubt it was still there. He paused to remove his helmet and wipe his brow. He looked up at the blinding yellow sun beating down on him, squinting before he pulled his gaze from the sky. "This is a hot, miserable place," Ba Re' mumbled. Tucking his helmet under his arm, he started his final descent down the last ridge, anxious to get to the transport and meet his people outside the airspace of Base 28 so they could make their last stop. Kol's home was their final scheduled stop before returning to Command Warship 1, to be sure all was as secure as possible and bring them home if Ba Re' could talk him into it. That stop was as important as rescuing Kron's female and bringing Kron back home. Quin had tasked him personally with trying to convince Kol to return with them.

Ba Re' sighed at thinking of trying to convince Kol to return home. He knew it would require convincing Ada Jane as well, and Ada Jane had wanted to come home so badly that she'd left Kol behind when she'd decided to take measures to get herself back to Earth. "Go to Earth, free Kron's woman, bring all my people back, I tire of this planet!" Ba Re' mumbled to himself in a growled imitation of Quin's orders. "And get in and out without anyone knowing you're there," he added sarcastically.

He'd made it halfway down the side of the ridge and was finally able to see the transport. Then he stood where he was, hidden by the surrounding trees and undergrowth and watched the transport for a short time before deciding that it was exactly as they'd left it. No one had happened upon it. Since the transport was unaccosted, and Ba Re' was so far out from the compound, he was unconcerned about being observed as he casually made his way the rest of the way down the ridge.

Once on level ground, he simply walked right up to the transport and waved his hand over the sensor on the door. The pilot's door lifted, granting access and he got in, then put his helmet on the seat beside him. He accessed the controls and powered up the transport, sitting back and relaxing in his seat while he waited for the whirring engines to send an electronic message to the controls to tell him it was ready for operation. As

278

Be Re' waited, he flipped a few switches here and there, checking the readouts on the control panel.

Then a piercing sensation had him snarling and slapping a hand to the place where his shoulder and neck came together and knocking a now empty syringe to the floor of the transport. The next thing he knew he was slipping sideways out of the seat, and falling face down on the floor between the seats. Ba Re' was grabbed from behind and roughly turned over. It was only then he was able to see his assailant.

"Fucking aliens," Mitchell snarled. "Always think you're so much better than everybody else. You're not much better today are you?" Then Mitchell pulled his fist back and punched Ba Re' in the face repeatedly until between the drug he'd been given and the blows to his face, he finally lost consciousness. The drug he'd injected Ba Re' with caused temporary muscular paralysis, preventing Ba Re' from being able to fight back or protect himself in any way.

Mitchell kicked Ba Re' out of the way, then opened the door to allow his four fellow Purists to join him. After they were safely inside with him, he tossed Ba Re's helmet out of the transport and slammed the door.

"That was way too easy," one of the them said.

"Only because they think they're so fucking great and everyone else is stupid," Mitchell said. "Tie his ass up. No way to tell how long 'til the drugs wear off. And lean him against the wall, make sure he's breathing from time to time. I need him to stay alive."

"And what do we do if they wear off faster than we expect?" one of the men asked with attitude.

"We drug him again!" Mitchell snapped. "When we get to the New Hampshire location, we straight jacket his ass, chain him up in a cell, drug him regularly if necessary and begin the next stage of our plan. Things have changed."

The four men with him looked at him, completely clueless to what he inferred.

Mitchell shook his head. "Cavanaugh is gone, I'm in charge now. And we have a brand new bargaining chip."

The men looked even more confused.

"One of theirs! We have one of theirs now!" Mitchell yelled frustratedly. "Gotta surround myself with more intelligence," he mumbled.

~~~

Gaishon skirted the airspace of Earth Base 28, looking for a suitable place to land and wait for Ba Re' to join them. He and Jhan had already made contact with three of the alien mates of the humans they'd rescued from the Purist compound. One of them, a female, on learning that her mate was alive and waiting for her to come to him, was already on the way to meet them outside Base 28. She was traveling in her personal transport and had been advised to remain undetected.

Gaishon located a suitable place to land, and brought the ship to the ground. All remained on the ship, as Gaishon accessed the cloaking mechanism that Rokai had installed, which would make them invisible to the naked eye. It was the same camouflage used by the Cruestaci ships when on foreign planets and lands. It helped keep their ships undetectable.

It was just over an hour when they detected a transport in their vicinity, circling the base they'd settled a suitable distance from. A quick confirmation allowed Gaishon to confirm that the ship belonged to the female alien, who true to her word, had come at once to be reunited with her mate.

Gaishon and Jhan watched as the female circled the public airspace just outside the perimeter of the base.

"Scan the ship for occupants," Jhan said.

Gaishon typed in a few commands on the control panel and a fresh screen popped up. They considered the information on that screen before Gaishon spoke. "Only one aboard. Same identifiers as the female we contacted concerning her mate."

"Fine. Contact the female," Jhan said.

Gaishon disengaged the cloaking mechanism and reached out to the female, advising her of their location.

It took no more than a few minutes for her to adjust her route, and return to their location. As she landed, the male who was her mate, paced anxiously, watching everything going on in the main cabin of Rokai's ship as they awaited the arrival of his mate.

Almost as soon as the female's transport landed, she was on the ground, rushing toward the much larger ship sitting quietly in the dry, sandy red clay of the dirt characteristic of this region of Texas. She wasted no time, her need to reach her mate and insure he was safe outweighing all security measures she may have taken otherwise.

"Lower the ramp," Jhan said. "Four warriors position yourself along the ramp. Keep watch as her mate approaches her." Then he turned to the male who'd stopped pacing and was simply standing perfectly still, watching the female he adored more than life itself standing in plain view of the windshield of Rokai's ship, wearing the same look on her face that her mate wore on his.

Gaishon lowered the ramp and the four warriors headed down it, stopping at points halfway down and just before ground level with their weapons drawn. Then the male was allowed to descend the ramp. He paused before he left the ship, looking back at those assembled there. "I don't know how to thank you," he said. He walked back to them and held out his hand to them. Each male standing there shook his hand and wished him well. "If I may make a suggestion," Jhan said.

"Of course," the male answered.

"Trust no one except your mate. Not even your own blood. Your family especially can believe they know what's best for you when you've been so blinded that you cannot see it for yourself. Our families can often be as detrimental to our survival as they are at other times necessary to our survival. Especially if they don't understand any changes we've embarked on. Your mate will always have your best interests first and foremost in their consciousness," Jhan said.

The male nodded. "I understand that now. Thank you. Without you, I have no idea what would have happened to me."

Jhan inclined his head. "We were never here. You likely have not even been listed as missing — it is assumed your family knew where you were for the most part. But if it ever comes to light, you were awakened by unknown individuals who took you to an equally unknown location and reunited you with your mate."

"That's exactly what happened," the male said grinning, then turned and headed toward the exit of the ship and the ramp beyond that would take him to his mate.

They watched as the male hurried down the ramp as best he could, then rushed toward the female who was already sobbing and moving toward him with open arms. Their embrace and kisses had all who watched smiling. Except Va'roush. Va'roush watched with a jaded, completely impatient attitude.

"Come now, Va'roush. Do you not feel anything watching life mates being reunited?" Jhan asked.

"Yes, I do. I feel nauseated. I believed we were coming here to free a female — which we have done — and assist Kol with threats made against his family. Why are we personally involved in..." he waved his hand toward the couple fifty feet away still easily visible as they spoke to one another non-stop, embraced repeatedly, and exuded immeasurable happiness, "this!" he finally said.

"It is heartwarming to be able to do more than simply fight. It gives us all hope," one of the warriors said.

Va'roush scowled and looked toward the male. "It weakens those involved! Now instead of being focused on survival, focused on justice, focused on vengeance, they are focused on one another. Anyone who seizes either of them, has the complete cooperation of the other. It's a weakness," Va'roush spat, crossing his arms and watching the couple who'd begun to look back toward Rokai's ship as they talked, obviously moving their attention to the ship and those on it. "And now they want even more from us," he grumbled.

They approached the ship and spoke with one of the warriors still guarding the ramp. Gaishon listened via the controls he manned, all communications that filtered through all helmets having to go through him. "They are offering to take the other humans from our hands and return them to their mates," Gaishon explained.

Jhan and Gaishon shared a look. "It would certainly make our situation a lot easier," Jhan said.

"And shorten our time on this planet," Gaishon said. "I'd like nothing better than to finish up and get to Kol's so that we address that issue, then head home."

"I will speak with the female," Jhan said, securing the face shield over his helmet and striding toward the exit of the ship. "Try to hail Ba Re'."

"Working on it," Gaishon replied.

Chapter 29

"We have been here long enough to disembark by now," Kron said, checking Ginger's pulse and temperature by placing his hands on her throat then her face for the hundredth time since getting her onto the ship, despite the fact that Missy was monitoring those base vital statistics for him. "What is taking so long?!"

"Probably waiting for Ba Re'. Once Ba Re' gets here with my transport, we'll go to the base, then the others will to go to Kol's. Once we're assured Ginger's alright and can make the trip back to your home, we'll meet up with them before they leave, get you both back on this ship and away from here."

Kron took a deep breath and huffed it out impatiently. "We are wasting more time. I just need to make sure she's alright."

"We both do," Buchanan said, doing his level best to maintain a small amount of reason. He got up and walked over to the hidden opening they'd entered the room through. "I'll find out what's happening," he said, as a small space of the wall slid open.

A short time later he was back.

"We're transferring the human mates," Buchanan said.

"To who?" Kron asked.

"I don't know who she is," Buchanan said.

"Stay with Ginger," Kron said, going to check himself, worried that if the other humans went to the wrong mediary, they'd just end up having to be rescued again. He made his way to the front of the ship, wondering who they'd decided to hand off the other humans to. He'd been on this planet long enough to be familiar with it at least, and couldn't imagine who they'd found to trust the humans to after less than one night here. Kron came to a stop behind Gaishon's seat and looked out the windshield. He saw a female standing there — a very impressive female. She was tall and statuesque. Muscular, but not overly so, she still looked feminine. Her hair was a silver, but with darker tones swirling through the thick mass that was pulled back tightly at the back of her head in a severe pony-tail. She wore a uniform, and often reached out to touch the arm of one of the males that had been held captive with Ginger as she passed him moving up and down the ramp of her own ship. "Is she his mate?" Kron asked.

"Yes. They've volunteered to take the rest of the humans onto her ship and return them to their mates," Gaishon said.

"She's wearing the uniform of the offices of the Immigration and Earth Boundary Enforcement Agency," Kron said. "She should have access to all records and locations of the aliens assigned to Earth and approved to be here."

"Maybe that's why she's offered to take the rest of them. Help get them back to their mates quicker, and we can just be done with it," Gaishon said.

"Also means she can figure out this ship is not supposed to be here," Kron said.

"We just gave her back her mate. I honestly don't think she cares," Gaishon said, watching the female stop to kiss her mate once more.

"True," Kron answered. He looked around and didn't see Ba Re' nor the transport he was bringing back. "How long until Ba Re' is here so we can get Ginger onto the base?" Kron asked.

"I'm trying to contact him now. I'll let you know as soon as I speak to him," Gaishon answered.

"I'm going back to sit with Ginger," Kron said.

Gaishon nodded and kept trying to hail the transport Ba Re' was on.

Kron went back to the safe room Ginger was in and took a seat beside Buchanan at the foot of the small bunk Ginger lay on. He took her hand in his again and looked down at the woman he loved more than life. "I feel responsible," he admitted quietly.

"How are you responsible for this? I'm the one that did nothing about her psycho mother," Buchanan said.

"If I'd refused to claim her, if I'd refused to bond with her when she insisted we mate, none of this would have happened. She's like this because we bonded. Her mother sent her to the Purists because we bonded. She was drugged and abused because we bonded. She ran from me because she was angry because of the circumstances in which we bonded. My mate is lying here unconscious because we bonded. All that happens as a result of this situation is because we bonded. I am to blame," Kron insisted.

"No. Not at all. Her mother, the sick fucks she was in league with, the whole fucked up political climate of the world we live in is to blame. No one should be persecuted because of who they love. This is not your fault, Kron. If you recall I asked you to take her as your mate. I knew you cared for her, and her, you. And while I've never been to your world, or even the Warship you call home, I knew without the shadow of a doubt it was a better place for her than anywhere on Earth at the moment," Buchanan said. "Don't blame yourself, don't second guess yourself. You belong with Ginger, and Ginger belongs with you. Her anger should have been directed at me, not you. None of this is because you two bonded. You're just caught in the crossfire."

"I believe that if I'd controlled myself, there would have been a better time. All of this could have been avoided," Kron said. "She may choose to leave me in her past."

"She won't," Buchanan said.

The door to their hidden room swooshed open and Jhan stood there.

Kron stood, preparing to gather Ginger in his arms and depart the ship. "What is the plan? Are you circling back for us or shall we meet you at Kol's after your business there is done?"

"Ba Re's not answering," Jhan answered.

Kron had lifted Ginger and was holding her against his chest. His head snapped in Jhan's direction, his eyes narrowing. "Explain that," Kron said.

"We've been transferring all who were held captive to the female's ship that came for her mate. The entire time Gaishon has been attempting to hail Ba Re'. We've had no response at all."

286

"Have you traced his position?" Kron asked.

"Via the transmitter he wore in his helmet. He does not respond, but it shows he's still in the same location."

"Perhaps there's a problem with the transport. We'll go back there," Kron said.

"A problem with both the transmitter in his helmet, and the transport?" Jhan asked. "Not likely. That's why I'm standing here. We're going back. If you want your female sheltered in Earth Base 28, go now. Otherwise, prepare to wait for treatment for your female. We're going back for Ba Re', you should prepare for conflict there as well."

"I'll..." Kron started, stepping toward Jhan, planning to say, 'I'll come with you.' But he didn't finish the statement. He had Ginger to care for, her condition was still in question. He couldn't possibly do both.

Jhan watched Kron struggling with himself, trying to figure out a way to both go with his fellow warriors to determine that Ba Re' was well and safe, and to stay with his female to determine that she was well and safe. He couldn't do both. "Secure your female," Jhan finally said. "She needs you, and I am not alone. We are more than prepared to do whatever needs to be done."

Kron was clearly torn, and stood stock still while he fought out an instinct to do both things that were calling to him. Finally, he snuggled Ginger closer to his chest and looked at Ba Re'. "How will we rejoin you?" Kron asked.

"Regardless of what lies ahead, the last stop is Kol. We will have him contact you before we depart from his home so that we can make arrangements for you to join us," Jhan said.

"Very well," Kron said uneasily, still warring with himself and what he needed to do most.

A bad feeling in the pit of his stomach, and growing impatient by the second, Jhan remained where he was, his gaze moving from Kron, to Ginger and Buchanan. "You need to go now. We have no more time to spend here."

Kron nodded and adjusted Ginger in his arms before striding toward Jhan with Buchanan following right behind.

"I regret that we are unable to get you closer to the base. It is several miles from here," Jhan said.

"We'll be fine. I got my communicator. We can contact the base for a ride once you're out of sight," Buchanan said.

Remembering that he did indeed have his as well, Kron nodded. "I do as well. Go, find Ba Re', please let me know he is well. Come back for me if he is not."

~~~

Kron, holding Ginger, and Buchanan walking beside them, moved safely away from the ship, and watched from a distance as it lifted into the air and away from them and their view. Only then did Buchanan take out his communicator and reach out to Zhuxi.

"Buchanan!" Zhuxi exclaimed almost immediately on answering his com. "I have been worried with no word from you. Kol is as well! Is everyone safe? Did you find Ginger?"

"Send someone to pick us up. We're about two miles from the Eastern perimeter of the base. We've got Ginger with us but she's unconscious. We need to get her to medical," Buchanan said.

"I am coming," Zhuxi said and ended the com.

Kron held Ginger against his chest as he reached for his Cruestaci communicator. He powered it up and glanced at the screen. "I can't get our mainframe from here. I was using the one in your transport to access it before," he grumbled.

"You trying to reach Kol?" Buchanan asked.

"Yes. I wanted to let him know all that has happened, and that Ba Re' is missing," Kron answered.

"He might be just fine," Buchanan said.

"He might not be."

"Use your base issued communicator," Buchanan said.

"And if someone is able to discern from the records that I contacted him?"

"You contact him all the time. We all do," Buchanan said. "They can't record conversations without government permission, and even then they have to notify the Consul of the base that it is possible any verbal communications to and from the base might be recorded. Kol's Consul. Nobody's told him a damn thing, or he'd have said so. Besides, we're close to base, and you just went for a run."

Kron thought about it and realized he was being overly cautious. As he held Ginger with one hand he gave Buchanan his Cruestaci communicator and pulled his base issued one from his pocket.

"You find her?" Kol answered at once.

"Yes. She is unconscious. We are only a short distance from the base waiting on Zhuxi to come for us. She will be under medical care soon," Kron answered.

"Is she breathing?" Kol asked.

"Yes, and her heart rate is good as well according to Missy."

"Missy?" Kol asked.

"A team has arrived. They will be in touch soon, but there is a problem," Kron said.

"What problem?" Kol asked, going on alert.

"Ba Re' is not responding. He remained behind to bring the base's transport back to the base. He is not answering and it is unlikely both the transmitter in his helmet and the transport he was to come back to the base in have failed. Jhan has returned to the last place we know he was to search for him. Buchanan and I are moving toward the base to stabilize my mate," Kron said, realizing they'd all been separated whether intentionally, or coincidentally. "And you are home protecting your family," Kron added.

Kol was quiet for a few seconds before he finally answered. "Divide and conquer," he said simply.

"Whether planned, or conveniently occurring, yes," Kron said.

"Who's on the team?"

289

"Ba Re', Jhan, four warriors of our Elite Team 1, Va'roush, and Gaishon is piloting," Kron said.

"Gaishon?!" Kol exclaimed.

"It's Rokai's ship. Unsanctioned. There is no evidence that any Cruestaci are here other than you and myself."

Buchanan nudged Kron's arm as they walked toward the base, and indicated with the lift of his chin the transport approaching them.

Kron nodded.

"What are their orders?" Kol asked.

"Last time I spoke with our Sire he demanded that all his people return to his fold right away. He tires of the vulnerability this planet and our presence here places us in, with our inability to respond defensively."

"I spoke with him as well. I am not leaving here yet. There is much more to consider before that happens," Kol said.

"Zhuxi's approaching now," Kron said, watching the transport just ahead of them as it began to lower for them to board it.

"Take care of Ginger. I will contact Jhan," Kol said.

"They won't answer. They're on a closed network," Kron said.

"Damnit!" Kol cursed.

"It's not worth letting others know they are here. They are to remain undetected if at all possible. If it becomes apparent that cannot happen, then we'll do whatever is necessary to carry out our mission and get home safely," Kron said.

"How are we supposed to be efficient under these circumstances?" Kol asked irritatedly.

"In any way that we can," Kron answered.

"I don't like it. Not at all. It is not like Ba Re' to go silent while on mission. Va'roush... that would be normal, Ba Re', not at all normal," Kol said.

"I know. I wait anxiously to hear as well. How am I to care for my female and stand with my brothers at the same time?" Kron snarled.

"You can't. But no one will protect your mate as you do. Your brothers have each other. Let me know the moment you hear that Ba Re' is safe, and how Ginger fares as well," Kol answered.

"I will. Be safe, Kol, we are far too exposed here," Kron said.

"And you," Kol answered.

~~~

"Where did you find this transport?" Buchanan asked as he got in the transport and quickly moved to the opposite side so Kron, still holding Ginger, could get in right behind him.

Zhuxi grinned. "In maintenance. It is from before the time that travel logs were kept. Besides, it is scheduled for demolition and is no longer tracked in any manner. I thought it clever to pull it from demolition and use it to come for you."

"Very clever," Kron said.

Zhuxi didn't look over his shoulder, he simply saw to the business of returning them to base. "How is she?" he asked.

"They drugged her. We have no idea with what, and she's not waking. But, her vitals are steady if a bit slow," Buchanan said.

"We will be but a minute and she will be receiving medical care," Zhuxi promised. "We've identified the residue in the plastic bag you found in your wife's purse. If it is the same drug, it should not damage her long term, as long as she was not given too much," Zhuxi said.

Kron held Ginger close and stroked her skin with his fingertips. She didn't respond at all. "She's not even reacting to my touch," he said, giving up getting a reaction from her and cradling her head against his chest as he rested his cheek against her. He closed his eyes as he struggled against the frustration boiling inside him. He needed to be here beside Ginger, but he also needed to be with those searching for Ba Re', and with Kol as well as he protected his own family.

"Easy, Kron. You are only one male. You must have faith in those you call brothers," Zhuxi said.

"I do," Kron objected, irritated that Zhuxi had read his private thoughts.

"Then behave as though you do," Zhuxi answered. "Ah, look. The base. Your female will soon awaken."

Chapter 30

As the old, rusted transport they rode on began its descent to Base 28, Kron's focus became Ginger once again. He was finally able to push away his anxiety and concern over all else he was unable to control or be a part of, and focus on the woman who'd become his future. She needed him, all of him, his entire focus and to give her any less would be completely unacceptable.

On landing, the transport didn't come to a stop as anticipated. Instead, it taxied around the buildings until it finally stopped behind what could only be described as a scrap heap. Zhuxi killed the engine and engaged the emergency brake. "There is another like it, and I believe the parts and pieces make up three more as well," Zhuxi said. Part of his job at the base was to oversee inventory, and address the disposal of all scrap materials.

"Maybe it would serve us well to keep the two still functioning transports, and a few spare parts, and just get rid of the mountain of scrap metal and unusable pieces. It could be five disassembled transports just as easily as three," Buchanan said.

"My thoughts exactly," Zhuxi said.

Kron didn't wait for either male to accompany him. He simply got out of the transport and started for the back entrance of the main building with Ginger still in his arms. The moment he entered the building he began running, and didn't stop until he reached the medical unit.

The medic on duty looked up when Kron entered the suite. "What happened?" he asked, standing to receive the injured woman.

"She was drugged," Kron answered, walking past the medic and laying Ginger on the nearest bed. "She needs medical attention at once."

"What drug was she given?" the medic asked, pressing his stethoscope against her chest and listening for a heartbeat.

"We don't know," Kron answered.

The medic froze, his movements just stopping as he looked at Kron.

"What?" Kron asked.

"How am I supposed to treat that?" he asked. "If you don't know what she was drugged with, how am I supposed to counteract it?"

"I don't know! You're the damn medic. Figure something out!" Kron shouted.

Buchanan rushed into the room with Zhuxi right behind him. "What's wrong?" he asked, going to stand beside Ginger's bed.

"I can't treat her for an overdose if I don't know what drug she took!" the medic said.

"She didn't overdose! She was kidnapped, and drugged!" Kron shouted.

"Jimmy, we found this when we found her. Can you run some tests on this to figure out what it is?" Buchanan asked, handing the syringe they'd found with Ginger to the medic.

"Yeah, I can," he answered, throwing a shaded look at Kron.

"At least it's something," Kron snapped.

"They do not have the level of technology we are accustomed to," Zhuxi said, standing behind Buchanan. "We are lucky we were even assigned a medic after our doctor was reassigned."

"I expected medical care for Ginger. I never even considered what type of care was available here," Kron answered.

"We'll run the residue through the computer analyzer and see if we can identify it," Jimmy said. "Once I get that started, I'll draw some blood so we can measure the amount of it in her system. It'll give us an idea of what we're up against."

"How long will that take?" Buchanan asked.

"Fifteen, twenty minutes," Jimmy answered.

"Perhaps it will match the residue you tested for me earlier," Zhuxi said.

Jimmy looked up at Zhuxi, then over at Buchanan. "She's your daughter?" he asked.

"Yes, she is, Jimmy. She's my daughter."

Jimmy nodded. "I'm doing my best. Maybe call a doctor to be sure and get her treated fully. I've only got basic nursing training, and not a lot at that."

Kron took his communicator out and swiped his hand across the screen.

"Elite Warrior Kron, I can see from your location that you have not started your return trip yet," Missy said.

"I have not. I need to speak to the Master Healer," Kron said.

"Hold please," Missy responded.

A few unbearable moments later and the Master Healer was looking at Kron on the small screen of his communicator. "Elite Warrior Kron," the Master Healer greeted.

"Master Healer. Thank you for answering my com. I need help with my mate."

"She has been moved from the ship she was on and I was no longer able to monitor her," the Master Healer answered.

"Yes, sir. She is now in the medical unit of Earth Base 28. Their capabilities are quite primitive and there is not a doctor or healer on duty. Can you please speak with the medic we have here. He is trained in battle injuries, treatments that would most likely be performed in the field while on mission," Kron said.

The Healer gave a single nod of agreement.

Kron handed his communicator to Jimmy. "This is our Master Healer. Perhaps he can advise you."

Jimmy took the communicator from Kron and looked down at the screen. A very scary, horned male looked back at him. "Hello, sir," Jimmy said.

"Greetings. Please tell me the status of our patient," the Healer asked.

"She's stable. I've attached monitors for her blood pressure, and heart. I'm in the process of running an analysis of the residue in the syringe that was brought in with her."

"Put the female on oxygen as well. Her respiratory rate was low while we monitored her. It will insure she is breathing properly until the results of the tests are known."

"Yes, sir," Jimmy answered, temporarily abandoning the syringe to place an oxygen mask on Ginger. He also attached an oxygen sensor to her finger to measure oxygen saturation rates.

"Is she stable on all monitors?" the Healer asked.

Jimmy took a moment to look at each monitor before answering. "Yes, sir, she is."

"Very good. Now, have we identified the residue in the syringe?" the Healer asked.

"No, sir. Not yet," Jimmy responded.

"Let's get that addressed now. We cannot proceed until we know what her body is processing," the Healer instructed.

"Working on it now," Jimmy answered, setting the communicator beside the machine he was preparing to run the residue through.

"She's going to be fine, Kron. Has to be. I won't accept any less," Buchanan said.

"I fear what I will do if she is not," Kron said, doing his damnedest to hold on to control.

"Elite Warrior Kron," the healer's voice said from the communicator Jimmy had near his work station. "She has survived for hours as far as we know without any further deterioration. That is encouraging. Do not assume the worst. We need information to be able to proceed, but I do believe we have time. All is not lost."

Kron gave a nod and did feel a bit of relief. Then realized the healer couldn't see him. "Thank you, Master Healer," he said aloud.

~~~

Gaishon landed the ship in the same area he had when they'd first arrived in search of Kron. It was clear that Buchanan's transport was no longer here, but they were still picking up a signal from Ba Re's transmitter from this general location — a search was required. It took less than five minutes to locate Ba Re's helmet with the transmitter still intact. Then immediately afterward they located multiple sets of bootprints, and the marks left by the transport itself when it lifted in the air and departed.

Jhan stood looking at the tracks in the dirt, the helmet he now held in his hands, and his mind raced. He had no doubt — Ba Re' had been taken. "Fan out! Search every single millimeter of this ground. Ba Re' has been taken. They've surely left some indicator of their identity, we need only find it." They searched for hours and found no more than a group of bootprints which seemed to be where several males had lain in wait. There was not a single other indication that any being had recently wandered into the area except for the tracks and marks from their own ship and their movements that morning and the day prior.

Absolutely certain they'd done all they could at the moment, Jhan did the one thing he didn't want to do. He ordered everyone back onboard the ship where Gaishon waited, and contacted Quin. Jhan stood at attention alone, facing the vidcom screen, waiting for Quin's vidcom to come online and complete the connection. He'd had the warriors assigned to assist him, wait out of view. He alone was taking responsibility for the fact that his brother was missing.

~~~

Quin was speaking to Bart, explaining his desire to withdraw Kol from his position on Earth. So far it had been an easy, relaxed conversation.

"I understand, Quin. I do. But to withdraw Kol without warning in the middle of his term as Consul, without a valid reason, would only indicate to those who do not trust you, to those who expect you to be undependable, who accuse your people of being volatile, that they were correct."

"Correct about what? That I refuse to allow my people or myself to be taken advantage of. I refuse to leave ourselves exposed to their prejudice and ridicule when we react in a defensive manner to provocations that anyone would react to? The civilization is primitive at best, self-serving, and now they are organizing into prejudicial groups to sabotage others of their own kind at every turn simply because they associate with any being not native to their planet. It matters not what opportunities we offer them, or what beneficial changes we've made in their world. They cannot see the opportunities before them because they are so caught up in blaming all but themselves for the situations they find themselves in. And once they push those offering a better way of life, to the point that we completely withdraw, they call us volatile and undependable. We are in a no win situation here. They are terrorists on their own soil, attacking both their own people and other peoples who have taken a stance to maintain the freedom of the world they live in. They are without intelligence. They don't deserve to survive, yet we're locked into dragging them in the next step of their lives while they fight us and accuse us of wishing to commandeer their planet with every move we make for their betterment! And why? Because we look different, have different customs and ways of handling conflict? It is a war on the verge of occurring. I'm removing all my people from Earth immediately."

"Have you forgotten that your own Ehlealah, your Sirena, is human and from this very planet?" Bart asked.

"No, I have not! But the planet she remembers, the people she remembers are far from those we are exposing ourselves to now. It is not worth the risk, Bart. If a conflict arises, as we respond to defend ourselves, or even defend another group of humans, we will be blamed for attacking any others not in the group we are defending. There is no way through this but to leave them to their own demise," Quin said. "If they push us, we will react. And when we react I would not be surprised if we are brought up on charges again — just as Kol was for defending his Ehlealah who was under immediate threat of death. I cannot allow our people to be placed in that position again. We will not be used as pawns in their political games of control. Let them kill one another — they're good at it, we will not be held responsible for defending ourselves and those important to us," Quin explained.

"What of Ada Jane? Does she want to leave? She and Kol have children they are raising on the land she grew up on. She is very attached to the land and all around it," Bart asked, doing his best to convince Quin to postpone removing the influence of the Cruestaci from Earth.

"I have spoken to Kol. He's asked for more time. I have not decided if that is for the best or not. But I do know if I issue a directive he will not hesitate to obey. His Ehlealah will have no choice but to return to our people with him."

Bart opened his mouth to reply, but Quin turned his head away from the vidcom screen and snapped at whoever was trying to get his attention.

"Did I not make it clear I was in conference?" Quin asked someone off the vidcom, his irritation high.

Bart heard a voice reply that Jhan needed to speak with him immediately, their situation had possibly become one of life or death.

"Give me one moment, Bart?" Quin asked, already leaning forward in preparation of speaking to Jhan once his image was switched to the vidcom screen.

"Of course," Bart said, curious now about where Jhan was and what made Jhan's situation so dangerous.

Quin waited until Bart's image was replaced with Jhan's on the main viewing screen of the vidcom in his private conference room. Jhan was standing before the vidcom screen on Rokai's ship, his image alone visible, his hands clasped behind his back, appearing completely in control, but his face gave him away.

There was a tic in his left eye that kept repeatedly tugging it down, and his lips were pressed together in almost a grimace. Quin had known Jhan since childhood, and this was the tell he, Ba Re', and Kol had come to recognize as the indication that Jhan was preparing to hurt someone. They'd pushed him too far when this expression graced his face.

"Jhan? What has happened?" Quin asked.

"Sire, I take full responsibility, and request that I may be allowed to rectify the situation personally. I will bear the full weight of all repercussions," Jhan said.

"Has the girl been killed?" Quin asked, knowing that if Jhan addressed him as Sire, rather than Quin, this was an official com, not one between lifelong friends.

"No, Sire. She has been rescued and returned to the base with Kron. I believe she is undergoing medical evaluation and/or treatment at this time," Jhan said.

"Excellent. Is there a problem with security at Kol's residence?" Quin asked.

"We have not reported to Kol's residence as of yet, Sire."

"Then what is the problem you are attempting to accept responsibility for? What is it you wish to rectify?" Quin asked, his own expression conveying his confusion.

Jhan seemed to fortify his stance, lifted his chin just a touch higher and looked Quin right in the face. "Ba Re' has been taken, Sire. We do not know by whom, though I believe it to be surviving members of the Purist movement. We believed the situation was completely controlled and successful. We were obviously mistaken, resulting in Ba Re' being taken by them. I'm requesting permission to do whatever is necessary to retrieve him — alive — and I'm prepared to accept any consequences after I am successful."

"Taken? How has he been taken?" Quin asked, slamming his hand down on the armrest of his chair. "Explain to me how Ba Re', a soon to be appointed General in our military can be taken by a group that is little more than a home grown domestic terrorist organization?" he bellowed.

300

"We efficiently and expediently located Kron's female and liberated not only her, but eleven other humans who were being held against their will. They'd been drugged and beaten into submission. Their only crime, in the eyes of those who held them, was to be the mate of an alien being unfortunate enough to be assigned to Earth. Once their mating was complete, it appears they were targeted by the movement and in most cases turned over by their own families, then drugged and beaten into submission. We had three members of the Purists surrender without further issue. All others were killed due to extreme resistance. After our final sweep of the compound as we prepared to return Elite Warrior Kron, his Ehlealah, and Viceroy Buchanan, to their home base for medical assistance, Ba Re' advised that he would return to a small transport assigned to Buchanan at the base. He stated that it was but a small inconvenience he did not mind as it would allow Viceroy Buchanan to spend more time with his daughter, who is Kron's Ehlealah, aboard our ship. I agreed and left Ba Re' to do just that. It was the last time I saw him. We've returned to the location the transport was last known to be. It's gone. Ba Re' is gone. His helmet was left behind, thrown haphazardly to the ground, and there are multiple bootprints around the area. It is all an indication, to me at least, that he's been taken. May I have permission to locate and return him to his rightful place on Command Warship 1?"

"What have you done, Quin?" Bart asked, having heard the entire explanation since Quin's slamming his hands on his chair forced the vidcom he'd paused with Bart to become live at the same time Jhan was speaking to Quin.

Quin's eyes flicked to Bart's briefly before he reached out and muted Bart's vidcom. Then he got up and strode closer to the vidcom projector. He stared into Jhan's eyes while his mind turned over possibility after possibility. In his mind he ticked off different actions and the reactions they'd cause. Jhan waited patiently. He knew this was where Quin excelled. His risk analysis, his strategy and battle plans were practically unequaled. One had to but allow him a moment to think things through and he'd present the best plan of action, even during the heat of battle. If all else failed, he'd personally lead an attack and blast whatever resistance they encountered out of existence. But the last thing Quin would ever do was leave a warrior behind. He stared at Jhan, who stood quietly, waiting for his response, but he didn't see Jhan — he was weighing his options. Finally, deciding on a plan, he spoke.

"Go to Kol's residence. Explain what has happened. He is familiar with the planet and its inner workings. If at all possible, I want to avoid an all out war. It is possible he will have connections we can access to find these people and where they may have taken Ba Re'. Start there. I'll contact you once I've spoken with Chairman Bartholomew in depth. But do not lose heart. We will not be leaving Ba Re' behind regardless of what must be done to retrieve him."

It was obvious Jhan was disappointed. He wanted to go in with no limitations at all and destroy everything in his path until he'd found his brother, but he was being forced to address diplomacy first. Quin recognized this.

"Jhan?" he said, reverting to his friend's first name, taking the conversation down to a more personal level as opposed to an official one. "We are not leaving Ba Re' behind. I must simply cover all bases first."

Jhan nodded.

"There are four of us who will watch our grandchildren's children play at our feet when we are too old to do anything else. Ba Re' is one of those four. We will bring your brother home, Jhan. Trust me, and be patient. Go to Kol, and I will contact you there," Quin said.

Jhan nodded again. "Thank you, Quin."

302

Chapter 31

Quin stood firm, watching Jhan as he ended the vidcom, then he adopted a completely different expression of disinterested arrogance as he returned to his seat and unmuted Bart's vidcom.

"Really? You're going to mute me, after I overhear you've got a retrieval team on Earth, and one of your people is missing? Presumably taken by members of the Purists? And it's a high ranking member of your military?" Bart near-shouted.

Quin looked at Bart, wearing the cool, unaffected demeanor that had gotten him labeled as cold so very long ago. "Chairman Bartholomew, I must ask you to refrain from further comment, and demand your silence on the issue. This is a matter of Cruestaci military intelligence, which frankly, does not concern you."

"Does not concern me?! You've got a team capable of starting a war on a planet you do not have permission to be on! At this particular point in time, nothing concerns me more!"

"I beg to differ, Chairman. If there was an unsanctioned team on any planet for any reason, and that team had been sent to retrieve the mate of one of the warriors assigned temporarily to that planet, who'd been taken by a domestic terrorist group, I feel certain it would create unrest among that planet's people were they to find out the security of that planet was so lax that said team was able to land there under the radar. Further, the fact that kidnapping people at random was such a possibility, it would undermine their security at an even deeper level. One might even assume it would shake the very foundations of trust that planet's citizens may have in its governing body to protect them and keep them safe. Vast changes would be afoot I'm sure."

Bart's eyes narrowed. "Are you blackmailing me, Quin?"

Quin raised a single eyebrow and stared down his surprisingly very Romanesque nose at Bart. "I would never do such a thing. I do however think that were it me in a governing position of said planet, I'd be collecting every bit of information I could find to pass along to the leaders of the hypothetical retrieval team so they could find their missing member and leave the ungrateful rock of dirt floating unaccosted with its people intact before they feel the need to begin destroying all they come across at random until their team member is returned."

"And now you're threatening me!" Bart exclaimed.

"I would never threaten a governing official, nor a family member. You are both," Quin said.

"I bet Rokai would beg to differ! And why the hell is there an unsanctioned team on Earth, Quin? Explain to me why you felt the need to send a team, with two of your most lethal warriors to Earth without going through proper channels! Do you have any idea what this could cause?"

"There is no unsanctioned team on Earth. But hypothetically for the sake of argument, if there were, it would have to be a matter of defending one of our own to warrant such a team. And might I remind you that any female who is claimed by a Cruestaci warrior, immediately receives Cruestaci citizenship. If a female who'd been claimed by a Cruestaci warrior suddenly found herself in the grip of a domestic terrorist group, that would be grounds for sending an unsanctioned team in. And furthermore, it would be grounds and reason enough to begin withdrawing the Cruestaci people who were there with approval of multiple governing agencies, burdened with the task of attempting to reorganize and contribute to their thankless society!" Quin said, ending on a shout as his words got progressively louder. "None of this would have been necessary, hypothetically, if anyone else had bothered to subdue, disband and eliminate all members of and indication of said domestic terrorist group!"

Bart clenched his jaws. He was angry, and he felt betrayed. He'd expected Quin's complete trust when dealing with Earth and the red tape surrounding any association with Earth. Bart had stuck his neck out, even put his career on the line when defending Kol when Kol was accused of unnecessarily killing the former Consul of Base 28. Bart shook his head in disbelief. Quin had betrayed the trust they'd built. He'd completely circumvented the process of having a team, any team at all allowed on Earth. And even worse, he'd not come to Bart for help when the situation first arose, which is what most likely lead to the situation they were now faced with. "If you'd come to me to begin with, this entire thing could have been avoided."

"No! Had you been consulted, you'd have regulated us to the point of sending a formal greeting asking if they'd be so kind as to release her! Hypothetically," Quin said.

"There are ways to do things, Quin…" Bart said.

"And they're being done," Quin said, his tone brooking no argument.

"Hypothetically," Bart said.

"Exactly," Quin answered.

"You've broken whatever trust we'd managed to build, Commander Tel Mo' Kok. Professionally, it's unfortunate. Personally, it's not something that can always be overcome."

Quin was surprised at Bart's comment, but before he could formulate a response, Bart spoke again.

"I will consult the intel we have on the Purist movement. Any pertinent information will be forwarded to you personally. I will hold you accountable for any unexplainable occurrence. And that is not hypothetical."

The com ended without hesitation, leaving Quin unable to reply at all. He snarled, glaring at the empty conference room around himself, then pressed a button on his chair.

"Yes, Sire!" Vennie answered at once.

"Com Kol's residence immediately," Quin demanded.

"Yes, Sire. Standby please," Vennie said.

~~~

Kron stood beside the bed Ginger lay on, holding her hand, smoothing her hair and whispering over and over again that it would be okay. They were waiting for identification of the chemical residue from the inside of the syringe they'd found with Ginger.

Buchanan went back and forth from comforting Ginger, and comforting Kron.

"We've got it!" the medic shouted. He grabbed the printout coming off the printer and started reading. "It's a gamma-amniotic glycine and propofal blend," he said. "It doesn't appear to be anything readily available on the market," he added. Then he moved to the laboratory computer and started typing. After a few minutes he shook his head. "There's nothing similar here. It's got to be an unregulated drug."

"What does that mean?" Kron asked.

"It means there is no known medication of its equal available on the market. Somebody somewhere created this drug illegally. It's either available on the black market as a 'designer' drug," Jimmy said, raising his fingers to make imaginary quote marks in the air, "or it's specifically created for or by whoever injected her with it."

"I wonder if the pills she was given were the same thing," Buchanan said, looking at Kron.

"They were, sir. There is a slightly different makeup to the liquid in the syringe, but basically, it's the same blend," Jimmy explained.

Kron's chest rumbled irritatedly. "How do we counteract what we know is in her system right now?"

"I've done a quick search on the two drugs. I believe we could create a blend that could wake her. The only hesitation I have is if this drug was not regulated when it was manufactured, it could contain any number of impurities that could react with the antidote we try to administer and create more problems than we are dealing with now," the Master Healer said.

"What do you suggest?" Buchanan asked.

"We wait. Her blood levels do not indicate excessive levels capable of causing death or permanent disability. It is my opinion that we keep her monitored at all times until she either wakes, or begins to diminish. If her vitals begin to diminish, then we use the blended antidote. It would be worth the risk at that time," the Master Healer said.

"Agreed," Kron said.

"Agreed," Buchanan said.

"I'll send the formula for the antidote blend I believe would be most beneficial to her, and we'll have it ready if we need it. Will you be able to obtain the drugs listed in the formula I'm sending?" the Master Healer asked.

"If they're fully regulated we should be able to, if we don't already have them here," the medic said. "We had a doctor assigned here not too long ago, and he had a pretty impressive inventory."

"Excellent," the Master Healer said.

Kron leaned over Ginger again, kissing her lips before brushing his thumb lightly over the bruises on the side of her face and over her cheekbone from Cavanaugh striking her. They'd cleaned her up, especially the blood still staining her face and clothes from biting Cavanaugh, and put her in one of Kron's shirts after they'd gotten her stabilized and the monitors in place. Once the blood was washed away, the bruises on her face were much more evident. It broke Kron's heart that she'd had to endure such abuse while he ran aimlessly around the country searching for her. He took a deep breath and let it out on a slow, even sigh. "Never again," he whispered, then pressed his lips very lightly to the bruising on her face. Then he settled into the chair beside her bed and rested his head against her arm. His hand gently stroked her wrist and hand as he just waited. He needed her to wake up, and that's the only thing that mattered to him at this particular moment. Kron took a deep breath as he threaded his fingers through hers. Who was he kidding, he wondered. It was the only thing that mattered ever. Without Ginger, there was nothing that would ever be able to anchor him to reality again.

Buchanan watched as the medic took the formula the Cruestaci's Master Healer forwarded to him, so he could begin to make the compound that was supposed to intercede on Ginger's behalf should the worst happen. He'd been grateful for many things in his life, but never had he been more grateful than for the presence of the Cruestaci people in his life and on this planet. He cast a glance over his shoulder at Kron and smiled to himself. Kron was snoring softly with his head on Ginger's upper arm. Kron had been in a constant state of stress and unrest since he and Ginger mated, unable to sleep at all, and he more than deserved the few minutes of sleep he was able to grab at her side.

Buchanan knew Kron blamed all that had occurred on the fact that he and Ginger had bonded. He selflessly believed that if he'd denied himself, convinced Ginger that her life would be better without him, none of what they were going through would have occurred. But Buchanan knew Kron was wrong. Ginger would never be happy with anyone but Kron. Ginger was a sweet girl, but she'd always been headstrong, independent, adventurous. In all areas of her life she pushed the envelope, except when dealing with her mother. And that's where they'd all failed her. They'd believed her mother would never betray her own daughter — but they'd been wrong. This entire situation was the fault of himself, and everyday assumptions anyone would have made. He believed his wife, though growing steadily more extreme, would never put their daughter at risk, and everyone else assumed Ginger was safe with her own mother because she'd always been safe with her before. But the woman her mother was now, was not the woman she'd always been. And that's why Ginger was lying in a hospital bed in the medical unit at Base 28 with her mate sleeping at her side. It was most certainly not because Kron had bonded with her, claimed her as his. That was the one saving grace of the entire situation.

Buchanan watched as Kron lifted an arm during his sleep and draped it over Ginger's hips, pulling her closer to him as he tucked his hand beneath her other side. Yes, Ginger belonged with this male. He'd had no doubt that Kron would never, ever allow her to be harmed or threatened in any way again.

~~~

Kron rested his head against Ginger, her scent and her nearness lulling him into a state of relaxation he'd not been able to even consider since she'd left the base in anger at both himself and her father. The warmth of her body called to him as he yawned and adjusted his forehead where it pressed against her. And the next thing he knew, he was walking beside her down the corridor of Command Warship 1. He held her hand snugly in his and smiled at her when she turned her face to him and grinned. "I love you. I love this!" she said, looking around the corridor and gesturing with her free hand at the walls and floors they passed and walked. "I cannot believe the life I'm living!"

"Are you happy, Leerah?" he asked, watching her happily walk beside him.

"I am!" she exclaimed.

Then suddenly he was standing in a field of lush, pearlescent white grasses. The grasses were thigh-high and blew gently in the breeze, giving the impression they were some great waving ocean. Kron heard laughter to his right and looked in that direction to find Ginger standing among the swaying grasses with three tiny shraler kits doing their best to keep up with her. "You spoil them!" he called out.

"But I love them so! I have to!" she answered laughingly.

"And what will you do when they are each two-hundred pounds?" he asked.

"Love them more?" she asked, shrugging and smiling at him. "Kron?" she asked.

Kron's expression changed. There was something unusual about the tone of her voice when she called his name. Something wasn't right, but he couldn't quite put his finger on the problem.

"Kron?" she said again, but this time her voice was fainter, raspy, tired.

"What's wrong?" he asked in his dream.

"Kron?" she asked again, this time her voice was weak and cracked as she tried to speak.

His dream, he thought. Of course, this was a dream. That's how they'd been on Command Warship 1, and now found themselves in the white fields of Cruestace. It was a dream.

"Kron?" Ginger's voice called again. He looked around, but the field was gone, and Ginger was nowhere to be found. Forcing himself to wake, he lifted his head and looked around the darkened medical unit.

Ginger lifted her hand and placed it on his arm where it still covered her hips.

Kron quickly gave her his undivided attention, turning his head and focusing on her, his eyes glazed and swollen from too little sleep. "Ginger," he rushed out.

She smiled weakly at him. "You finally heard me. I've been calling and calling you. You must have really been deeply asleep," she said. Her voice sounded weak, and very tired, just like it did in the dream he'd had, but she was smiling at him so beautifully.

"I haven't slept much," he said. "How do you feel? Are you well? I'll call the medic, they must have left us to rest after they finished with the formula the Master Healer sent. Do you need anything? I will get you anything you need, Leerah!" Kron rushed out, unable to decide on just one question at a time.

Ginger smiled at him again. "I don't need anything."

"How do you feel? Do you hurt anywhere? Do you need medicine?" he asked.

She shook her head. "No. I just need you to know that I'm sorry. I was such a fool."

Kron shook his head. "You were not a fool. I was. Everything you survived was my fault for bonding with you. I should never have bonded you without proper timing, thinking it through and planning for all circumstances. I take full responsibility. Please forgive me, Ginger," Kron asked, the pain he felt easily read in his eyes.

311

"That's nonsense, Kron. It's me that caused it all. I ran off so full of anger, refusing to speak to you or my father. I'm so sorry. I never, ever meant to make you question our bond. I know you're my mate, and I want to be your mate. I hope you still see me that way. I was just so angry I behaved rashly. Please forgive me."

"There is nothing to forgive. I should have moved more slowly with you. I knew you were already dealing with your mother trying to plan your future. I can understand why you felt your father and I were doing the same. I am sorry we didn't handle it differently."

"I didn't give you a chance to move slowly. I knew I wanted you, and I pushed the issue. I've always been that way. Once I know I want something, I rush ahead and don't consider anything else. Then, afterward, I should have given you a chance to explain. I should have listened to you both. Then, maybe none of this would have happened. But none of it is because of our bond."

Kron held her hand in his, loving the feel of her fingers clasping his. "I fear that had you gone home without myself or your father at any time, the outcome might have been the same, simply because you loved me. You can't blame yourself," Kron said, reaching up and stroking her cheek with his thumb. "Your mother would not have accepted me," he said sadly, "she never will."

"After what she's done, it doesn't matter. I thought that eventually she'd come to find a way to be at peace with our bond. But, now, I don't even want to be around her. How could I ever trust our children with her? I don't even want to look at her."

Kron smiled at her. "Our children?" he asked.

"Our children," she confirmed.

"So, you still love me? You still want to be at my side?" he asked.

"More than ever. I love you, Kron," Ginger said. "Thank you for not giving up on me."

"Never!" Kron promised. "I will love you forever and I will never give up."

Ginger smiled at Kron. "Good. We'll have each other forever and ever."

"Longer," Kron said, and leaned forward to kiss her forehead.

Ginger's eyes fell closed and she sighed. "I'm so tired," she said.

"Then sleep, my Ginger. Sleep. I will contact your father and let him know you've awakened so that he can be here the next time you wake."

"Okay," she answered, not even opening her eyes.

Kron let go of her in order to use his communicator to contact Buchanan and the moment the weight of his arm lifted off her body she opened her eyes and looked at him. The unease was easily read in her eyes.

"Do not fear. I am never leaving and you will never be in danger again. I give you my vow," he said.

Ginger offered him a shaky smile and slowly closed her eyes again.

Kron sent Buchanan a text telling him that Ginger had awakened briefly and that he should come sit with her if he wanted to be there when she next awoke. Then he threaded his fingers with hers again, and laid his other arm over her waist. "Sleep well, my Leerah. I am watching over you."

Chapter 32

The next time Ginger's eyes opened she struggled to focus on two men standing at the foot of her bed. Their voices were hushed as they argued in whispers. She knew right away one was Kron, then she blinked a few times before she realized the other was her father. She lay there quietly as they spoke to each other, listening to their words without them realizing she was awake.

"There was no one there," Kron said. "Kol said they think it was recently deserted. As recently as hours before they arrived. But there was no trace of Ba Re'."

Buchanan shook his head. "He can't have just disappeared. They have him, I know they do."

Kron took a deep breath and forced it out in irritation. He shoved his hands into his hair and growled frustratedly.

"Kron?" Ginger asked, her voice cracking from not being used.

Kron and Buchanan both turned to her at once. "Ginger," Kron said, moving quickly to stand beside her.

"Ginger! How do you feel, sweetheart?" Buchanan asked, going to the other side of her bed and smiling down at her.

"I'm weak, but better," Ginger said, smiling at her dad.

Kron stood beside her bed, holding her hand in his as she and her father spoke for the first time since she'd gone missing. Finally, she turned and looked at him.

"Hi," she said.

"Hi," he returned, smiling down at her.

"What's going on?" she asked, holding tightly to his hand.

"You are awake, we are very pleased," he said.

"No. Not that. Why are you arguing?" she asked.

Kron and Buchanan looked at each other then down at Ginger.

"We are not arguing, my Leerah," Kron said.

"Then why are you whispering to each other like that? It sounds like you're hissing. And who's missing?" she asked.

Kron didn't want to lie to her, not about anything, but he didn't want to upset her either. "Ba Re' is missing, but we will find him."

"That's the one that Elisha is mated to, right?" she asked. "Why was he here? I thought he went back with Elisha."

"He did," Kron said, sharing another look with Buchanan.

"Tell me," Ginger urged.

Kron looked down at her again. "Ba Re' came here to lead a team to help me locate and free you. After we found you and the mission was successful, Ba Re' was to return your father's transport to the base. He never made it. We believe that he was alone and the same people that had you, have taken him."

"He was taken because he came to help me," she said, struggling to try to sit up.

"He was taken because he came to help me," Kron countered. "This is not your fault. We will find him. We will free him, and we will destroy all those responsible," Kron said.

"I'm so sorry," Ginger said.

"It is not your fault. You were not responsible," her father hurried to assure her.

Ginger lay there, her mind rushing with thoughts and flashes of all she'd recently been through. And no matter what they said, she felt guilty, responsible for Ba Re's disappearance. She thought about the rest of those who were being held by the Purists. "What about the other people that were being held?"

"They're free, most likely already reunited with their mates," Kron assured her.

"Dr. Cavanaugh?" she asked.

"Dead," Buchanan said, vehemently.

"Mitchell?" she asked.

"We don't know. He wasn't there," Buchanan answered.

"Then he's the one that has your friend," Ginger said. "He's the one you need to find."

"That is what we believe," Kron said.

"You have to find him, Kron. I'm fine, and I'll be here when you get back, but you have to go after him," Ginger said.

"I cannot protect you if I am searching for him. And I cannot search for him if I'm protecting you," he said, his inner struggles making themselves known.

"I will be fine. Go after him," Ginger insisted.

The door to the room opened and Zhuxi stepped in. "Kron, you are needed in the meeting room right away."

"I'm staying with Ginger, she's just awoken," Kron said.

"There is a com waiting for you. Your Sire, Chairman Bartholomew, Kol, and your team are awaiting your presence," Zhuxi said.

Kron looked over his shoulder toward Ginger torn between his sworn position with the Cruestaci, and his newfound vows to Ginger.

"Go. I'm right here. I'll be here when you get back," Ginger said.

"I don't want to leave you here for even a moment," Kron said.

"Maybe they've found Ba Re'," Ginger urged. "You should go speak to them. I'll be right here."

Kron hesitated, before finally sighing and nodding. "Very well. But I will return as quickly as possible."

"I'll stay right here with her, Kron," Buchanan promised.

~~~

Kron stepped into the meeting room and found himself face to face — as much as one could be via a vidcom meeting — with Sire Zha Quin Tha Tel Mo' Kok, Chairman Bartholomew, Jhan with his team of warriors standing respectfully several feet behind him, and Kol via his handheld communicator. Kron immediately took his place front and center of the vidcom station, then came to attention.

"My apologies for making you wait," Kron said.

"How is Ginger?" Kol asked.

"She has just awakened, and is much improved," Kron answered.

"Good" Quin said, "get her to Kol's home, get on the transport I sent, and bring her home."

"But, Sire, Ba Re' is still missing," Kron said.

"I'm well aware that Ba Re' is still there," Quin snapped.

"Kron, all unsanctioned Cruestaci Warriors must leave the planet. It's become apparent that if they don't leave soon, I won't be able to hide the fact that they're here any longer," Bart said. "I've got more than a dozen bodies in Utah, three survivors suffering from heat exhaustion and being restrained in a deserted barn for three days before they were found, who claim aliens with black helmets and uniforms killed their friends and left them to die after kidnapping just as many humans that were in their care. If this keeps up, I won't be able to keep it under wraps. I do not want to deal with that situation, so all must go."

"But, I'm sanctioned. I can be here. I can stay and find him!" Kron objected.

"Thirty minutes ago the survivors gave an official description of one of the faces of their attackers. Your face was clearly described by all three. You were at the scene of the massacre as they're calling it. You were seen carrying an unconscious female up the ramp to a waiting ship. At this time, it's best if you leave the planet. The only Cruestaci Warrior staying on Earth is Kol. We feel that if he left, it would be suspicious, basically a silent admission of guilt, as he holds an official position," Bart said. "Everyone else is leaving. Everyone!"

"Return to the ship, Elite Warrior Kron. We need you back here to help with responsibilities on Command Warship 1," Quin said. It was obvious his temper was being held in check with quite a bit of effort. "Bring your female home, and assume your duties here. Now!"

Kron didn't want to accept the order Quin had just given him. He couldn't conceive of leaving any warrior behind, much less Ba Re'. His gaze wandered to the portion of the vidcom screen Jhan was on. He looked Jhan in the eye, and then, he

317

detected small movement of Jhan's head. Jhan just barely gave him a slight inclination of his head as he looked him in the eye. Jhan was telling him to go home.

"If I may be of help here..." Kron said, still not quite convinced.

"You may be of help by resuming your position here," Quin said. "Rokai is now in charge of the Elite Teams. While he is excelling, he could use your assistance without a doubt."

"I will do all I can to find Ba Re' through standard channels," Kol said, looking intently at Kron. "But it is imperative that you, and the team sent to assist in finding your female, return to Command Warship 1, or at the very least, leave Earth's atmosphere. Do you understand, Elite Warrior Kron?"

Kron swallowed, straightened his stance and came to attention. He was being given a direct order by not only his Elite Commander, but also by his Sire. "Yes, I understand." He'd fucked up. He'd let his face be seen and now he could be placed at the scene where so many Purists had been killed. They were trying to protect him, and the Cruestaci, by removing him from the planet all together.

"Good. Then I'll expect you here shortly, where you and your female will board the transport and return to Command Warship 1 with the retrieval team, without further delay," Kol said.

"Yes, sir," Kron agreed begrudgingly, slamming his arm over his chest in a show of loyalty.

~~~

Kron went back to Ginger's room in the medical unit. He walked into her room, still feeling completely unbalanced and though he understood them, not at all at ease with the orders he'd received.

Ginger was reclining on pillows placed behind her back to support her while she sipped on a cup of broth and listened to

318

her father tell her how she was found. She glanced up when Kron walked in and set down her cup the moment she saw him. "What's wrong?" she asked.

"Are you my mate by your own will?" he asked.

"Yes, of course I am," she answered.

"Could you be happy with me away from here?" he asked.

"I will be happy with you anywhere," she said. "What's happened, Kron? Why are you asking me these things?"

"I need to be sure," he said. "I've been ordered to return to Command Warship 1. Immediately," Kron said.

Ginger sat up a little straighter, concern showing in her expression. "But..." she started, not sure what to ask first. She had so many questions about not only herself, but her family, Ba Re', Mitchell, there was so much left unfinished.

"I've been told to bring you back with me. I want you with me, I need you with me, but I will not force you. We have not had the time afforded to newly mated couples to solidify our bond. I do not wish to rush you to make a decision in any way, but if I go, I am not sure I will be allowed back," Kron said.

"It doesn't matter how quickly we became mated. All that matters is that you're mine, and I'm yours. I'm going with you," Ginger said, pushing the tray away from her and beginning to pull back her covers to get out of the bed.

"Are you sure?" Kron asked hopefully.

"Of course I'm coming with you. My life is where you are," she said.

"But, your plan for your life. The animals you wish to care for," he said.

"Are you trying to dissuade me?" she asked, giving him a half smile.

"No, I am not. I simply thought we'd have more time. Time to figure out all the things we both want and how to make them all fit. But now..."

"Now we don't. Plans change. You have animals up there, right?" she asked.

"Many creatures," Kron said.

319

"I can take care of them. And even if I don't, you'll be there. We'll be together. It'll be fine. We'll work it out," Ginger said.

Kron went to her side and pulled her into his arms. "I love you, Ginger. I promise you will be happy."

"I know that. And so will you."

"I have the transport ready to take you to Kol's home," Zhuxi said from the doorway.

Kron turned and looked toward him. "I will miss you, my friend," Kron said.

"You will see me again," Zhuxi assured him.

"Daddy," Ginger said.

"You'll see me again, too, darlin'. But I think this is for the best. Whatever's happening, whatever will happen, you'll be safer up there than down here. Go be a wife to your mate, be happy and I'll see you soon. Until then, we can visit on vidcom!" Buchanan said enthusiastically. He saw the hesitation in her eyes, she would be leaving the planet and her family behind. "I honestly just want you gone from here, Ginger. All hell's going to break loose before it finally gets better. I may have to be responsible for things that might come to light. I don't want to have to worry about you in the middle of it while we're trying to battle all we have to to find Ba Re'. This is a good thing, Commander Tel Mo' Kok, demanding Kron return and bring you home. It gets you both out of harm's way."

"I know. And I really meant what I said, I'm going where Kron goes, but, I won't be here with you anymore..." Ginger said. "And Momma..."

"Momma has made her bed. She's in custody. But you need to remember she was willing to risk your well being. And if we released her, and she saw you right now, she'd just turn you over to them again. She's not good for you right now. You have to understand that," Buchanan said.

Ginger nodded. "I know," she whispered. "But I'll miss you. I won't be able to see you whenever I want to."

"Not for a while, but I'll come visit as soon as I can, or you can come for a visit once all this crap has been ironed out," Buchanan said.

"Kron," Zhuxi said.

Kron turned to look at Zhuxi.

"I've already packed all your belongings. The transport is holding at Kol's for your arrival," Zhuxi said.

"We must go, Ginger. We are all they wait for," Kron said.

Ginger hugged her father once more, and kissed his cheek. "I'll miss you," she said, with tears in her eyes.

"It's just like if you moved out of state. We'll vidcom everyday," Buchanan said, hugging his daughter.

Ginger nodded, then pulled away from her father and turned to Kron. "Okay. I'm ready," she said, moving to put her feet on the floor.

Kron reached out and steadied her, placing an arm around her waist and holding her hand with his other hand. "Are you well enough to walk?" he asked.

"Probably not, but I'm not letting that stop me," she said, smiling nervously at him.

"Kron," Buchanan said, "take care of my girl."

"I will die for her," Kron vowed.

"No! Nobody's dying! We're taking care of each other!" Ginger insisted.

"We will be well, and the moment I can bring her back for a visit, I will," Kron promised.

"Not soon, I have a feeling this is about to get ugly," Buchanan said.

Kron nodded.

"Come, I'll be escorting you to Kol's," Zhuxi said, stepping back out of the way so they could walk out of the door.

~~~

Kol watched Ada Jane packing all the clothing and toys she could cram into as few bags as possible. "I am sorry for this turn of events, Ada Jane."

321

She glanced up at Kol who was standing in the doorway. "It's alright. It keeps us safe and frees you up to help search for Ba Re'. I understand."

"I do not wish to see you leave. I do not wish for you to leave your home behind," he said.

"Kol," Ada said, straightening up and looking at him. "It was only a matter of time before this decision would have to be made anyway. The boys need to go back."

"It should have been in our own time frame," Kol said.

"Things don't always work out the way we want them," she said, swiping at a tear and going back to packing.

"I can help you," Kol said.

"That's not necessary. I'll get it. You have other things to attend to," Ada said.

Kol nodded. "It will not be for very long."

"We'll be fine until you're back, Kol. Stop feeling so guilty. You're doing the right thing, we all are."

"But you look so unhappy," Kol said, watching his mate try to be strong despite the occasional tear she wiped irritatedly from her face.

"I am unhappy. But I won't always be, and I know this is unavoidable. As I said, I understand."

"Thank you, for understanding," Kol said.

"You don't have to thank me. If you were missing, or even me, I would want every one of your friends to do everything in their power to find us. You can't help find Ba Re' if we're not safe so you don't have to worry about us, too. And if what you think is going to happen, happens, the best place for us is up there."

Kol nodded again, and looked around the room. Part of him was dying inside knowing he'd have to give up his mate for even a little while.

"I'm almost done here, then I'll get Billy and Bob ready to go," Ada Jane said.

"I'll get their food, and their beds together. Is there much else to finish packing?" Kol asked.

"No, that's it," Ada Jane said. "There is nothing else to take with us."

Kol smiled sadly at her, then turned and left the bedroom on his way to pack up their dogs.

Chapter 33

Zhuxi landed the transport on Kol's property, just feet from the ship that would be taking the retrieval team, and Ginger and Kron back to Command Warship 1. "We are here," Zhuxi said, as he watched two males turn their attention his way.

"Yes, we are," Kron answered, looking toward the ship before he turned toward Zhuxi. "I just can't believe they are forcing me home before we've found Ba Re'."

"I have found that things are not always as they seem, Kron. Do not assume for one moment that your people, or our people, are giving up on Ba Re'. It is simply in your best interests to leave this world for a while," Zhuxi said.

"I will try to remember that," Kron answered.

"Take care my friend. I am always at your disposal," Zhuxi said, bowing his head.

"And I'm at yours. I hope to see you soon, Zhuxi," Kron said.

"You will see me sooner than you think," Zhuxi promised. Then he turned to smile at Ginger. "Do not allow your male to get himself in trouble, Ginger Val Kere."

Ginger grinned when she heard her name with Kron's last name. "I won't."

"Be happy, Ginger. It is all your father wishes for you," Zhuxi said.

"I will, and tell him I'll see him soon," Ginger said.

"I will give him your message," Zhuxi answered.

Jhan walked down the ramp and looked in the direction of Zhuxi's transport.

Kron saw him and unstrapped himself. "We should be going. They've already waited too long for us." He opened the door and tossed down his duffel that contained all his clothing and boots. Then he jumped from the transport to the ground rather than bothering to open the mobile stairs that would unfold from just beneath the door.

Ginger followed him to the door, then leaned toward him, allowing him to take her into his arms and place her on the ground.

"Until we meet again," Kron said, striking his arm over his chest as he gave Zhuxi a slight bow.

"Until we meet again," Zhuxi repeated to him, striking his own arm over his chest.

Kron and Ginger moved back away from the transport as it began to lift into the air, then turned back in the direction of the base. Kron watched until he couldn't see it anymore then began to lead Ginger toward the larger ship waiting for them. It was clear she was still a little unsteady on her feet, but was trying to be strong. "I will carry you," he said, pausing to gather her in his arms.

"You will not," she said. "You think I want your friends to see me weak and incapable the first time they see me?" she asked. "Just give me a second, and let me lean on you, I'll be fine."

Kron smiled. "They have met you, Leerah," Kron said.

Ginger looked up at him with surprise in her expression.

"This is the team that came to help me retrieve you," he explained. "They will be pleased to see you conscious at all."

Ginger nodded. "Okay, then."

Kron lifted her into his arms and carried her the rest of the way to the ship, and up the ramp where Jhan waited for him. "Jhan, is there news?"

"Some," Jhan answered, before changing the subject. "I see your female is much recovered. We are all pleased to see this."

"Thank you," Ginger said, smiling at Jhan. "Thank you for coming after me, for helping get me back to Kron."

Jhan smiled as she looked at him, but it was clear the smile was only for her benefit because the rest of his expression did not reflect his smile. "I feel I am looking into Kron's eyes," he said. "You are most welcome..." he paused, not remembering her name.

"Ginger," she said.

"Ginger Val Kere," Jhan said.

Ginger smiled brightly. "I just love that," she said, looking up at Kron.

"What?" Kron asked.

"The way my name sounds with yours," she answered.

"Elite Warrior Kron Val Kere x Buchanan," another male said from inside the ship.

Kron turned to him. "Va'roush."

"You made us wait long enough," Va'roush said.

Kron shook his head at Va'roush's bluntness. "I'm aware. It couldn't be helped. We left as soon as we received the directive from Sire Tel Mo' Kok."

"Hmpf," he grumbled, looking down his nose at Kron and Ginger. Then he got to the point. "It is good to see you both here alive and well. Welcome, female, to our world."

Kron chuckled as Va'roush turned and walked away from them.

"He's a little scary," she whispered to Kron.

"He is always gruff, but honest, and selfless. He was as determined to find you and avenge any injustice you suffered as I was. In fact, he is the one who ultimately ended Cavanaugh's life. Va'roush was outraged to learn of all he and his organization had done to you and others like you. It is his way. He hates to see anyone suffer under those who are stronger."

Kron walked into the ship itself and set Ginger down on her feet. Then a high pitched screech that he knew all too well caught his attention. He turned in the direction it came from and leaned over just in time to gather Kreed into his arms as he stumble-ran at him. "Kreed! Why are you here?" he asked.

"Because they are going with you," Kol said, walking up the last bit of ramp and into the ship with his arms loaded with bags of clothing.

"I thought you were staying behind," Kron said.

"Hello, Ginger," Kol said, then looked at Kron. "I am."

"There you are!" Ada Jane said, coming up the small, tight corridor from the back of the ship where the hidden room was with Kolby on her hip.

"Mamama," Kreed said, smiling at Ada Jane.

"Don't smile at me, I told you to wait," Ada said.

"You'll make sure they get there safely," Kol said, coming back from dropping the clothes in the small hidden room.

"I will. We all will," Kron said.

"The boys know you, trust you," Kol said.

"They will be watched as though they are mine, even after we arrive. Do not fear, Kol," Kron promised.

Kol nodded, clearly having trouble with the idea of being separated from his mate and sons.

"We must go, Kol," Jhan said.

Kol nodded. "Don't worry, Ba Re' will be found," Kol said.

"I have no doubt," Jhan answered, staring expressionless at Kol.

"I'll be back. Give me one second, or two," Kol said. He turned around and walked down the ramp, appearing a few moments later with two leashes in his hand, and two very large dogs prancing excitedly at his sides. He held both leashes out to Kron.

Kron took the leashes in one hand, then handed Kreed to Ada Jane so he could control both Billy and Bob. Kol looked at Kron. "I'm sending them all home with you. I don't know how long it will be until I can return, but I will return. Keep them safe, Kron, just as you did when I was kept away from them before."

"They will be happily waiting for you when you arrive," Kron promised.

"And there's always vidcom," Ginger said. "That's how I'll keep up with my father until I can be with him again," she said.

Kol nodded. "That is true." He didn't bother to explain that away from his Ehlealah, he would be miserable, and much more dangerous than he was when she was near to help him remain grounded. "Travel safe, my brothers. Protect the females and younglings with your lives," Kol said.

All of the males aboard the ship came to attention and saluted him with their hands over their chests. "Yes, Elite Commander!" they all answered, almost in unison.

"Fear not, they will be safely aboard Command Warship 1 before you have even had time to miss them," said Li'Don, one of the males who had long served under Kol before he'd gone to Earth.

Kol doubted it, but appreciated the promise anyway. He looked at Ada Jane, and stepped toward her, taking her and both sons she held on her hips in his arms. Ada Jane started crying again. "All will be well, my Ehlealah. I give you my promise."

Ada nodded. "I know. I just hate leaving you."

"I will think of you every single moment you are gone from my side," he whispered, pressing his lips to hers.

"You will think of exactly what you are doing and not be distracted by me. You will come to me safe and just as I leave you this minute!" she demanded.

Kol smiled. "As you wish, my Ada Jane. I love you, you are my life. Travel safe, Ehlealah. You and the boys will be the subject of much attention. The boys will enjoy the warriors' attention. You should not enjoy them quite as much," he said, kissing her again.

Ada Jane laughed for him so he'd feel a bit more relaxed about them leaving. "I will not enjoy anyone at all."

Kol grinned at her, kissed her once more, then he kissed each of his sons — who tried to bite him — then turned and walked down the ramp. He knew if he didn't do it now while he could, he wouldn't let them leave at all.

"Are we ready?" Gaishon asked once he finally saw Kol leaving the ship.

"Yes, let me just get Billy and Bob and the boys back into our room, and we'll be good for takeoff," Ada Jane said.

Kron looked at Ginger. "Will you be alright here for a moment?" he asked.

"Of course, go help her," Ginger said.

As Kron followed Ada Jane toward the hidden room, he heard Li'Don offer Ginger a place to sit. "Come, Ginger Val Kere, seat yourself comfortably to await your male." Kron smiled to himself. Ginger was right, he loved the way their names sounded together. He helped get Ada Jane situated, then stayed a few minutes longer to make sure she'd be okay.

Finally she looked up at him. "Kron, you don't have to babysit me. We'll be okay once we're on our way. Go see about your mate. She's never done this before and has no idea what she's headed toward. At least I know what to expect."

"Are you sure?" Kron asked.

"I am. If I need your help with these little ruffians, I'll let you know," Ada said.

"I will be waiting," Kron said.

Kron walked back up the corridor and his eyes found Ginger right away. She smiled brightly at him as he approached her and sat beside her.

"Are you okay?" Kron asked.

"I'm terrified. But excited, and happy, too," she said, laughing lightly.

"All will be well," he said. "You will have many adventures."

"I'm looking forward to them," Ginger said.

"I suggested she take the seat she is in so that she will be able to see the view clearly as we travel," Li'Don said to Kron.

Kron turned to look at him. "Thank you," Kron said, smiling. Then he looked around at the other warriors seated and talking amongst themselves as they lifted into the air and began to move forward in preparation of departing Earth.

"Where are Jhan and Va'roush?" Kron asked, looking around for them and not finding them.

"I don't know what you mean," Li'Don said.

Kron's head canted slightly to the side. "You know exactly what I mean! Jhan and Va'roush! Where are they?" he asked.

"They are right here with us. They are keeping watch over Elite Commander Kol Ra' Don Tol's family as we return home. Do you not remember seeing them?" Li'Don asked, looking directly at Kron with a straight face.

Kron looked away from the warrior, thinking over his words, then he realized what was happening. They were all making a show of returning home, even evacuating the family of the Cruestaci Consul to Earth. And the two deadliest warriors among them, had slipped off the ship and were staying behind, undetected. He looked back at the warrior. "Of course, it must be the stress of searching for, and worry over the welfare of my mate that had me confused for the moment."

The warrior smiled at him, then looked straight ahead out of the windows as Gaishon turned them toward the skies.

~~~

Kol stood in the darkness watching Rokai's ship, piloted by Gaishon, whisk his family away from him, away from Earth, and back to Command Warship 1. He knew in his heart of hearts that they'd be safer there than with him on Earth, but that didn't make the pain he felt at being separated from them any easier to bear. And it didn't help that he knew Ada Jane was devastated at having to leave her family land. She was hiding it well, but he knew firsthand how much their home meant to her.

"They will arrive safely," Jhan said, watching the ship shoot across the sky.

"They will," Kol agreed.

"Now what?" Va'roush asked.

"Now, we find Ba Re', and take out a terrorist organization. If it starts a civil war, then so be it," Kol said, turning to walk toward the tree line.

"It is just the three of us. It will be quite a task, but with just a few, we will be almost undetectable." Jhan said as both he and Va'roush followed Kol.

"We have allies," Kol said.

Va'roush and Jhan shared a look, then hurried their steps to keep up with Kol. "What allies? Who are they?" Jhan asked.

As soon as they were under cover of the trees, Kol stopped walking. "Zrakad?" he called.

The leaves rustled and a male stepped into sight with a cocky grin.

"Ceresians," Va'roush said.

330

"Are you disappointed?" Zrakad asked, looking directly at Va'roush.

Va'roush shook his head slowly. "Not in the least. Your kind are well known as respected warriors."

"And dangerous ones," Zrakad added. "As are yours."

Va'roush inclined his head.

Zrakad turned his attention to Kol. "Tell me, Consul, what has been decided so far," he said as almost a dozen other Ceresian males stepped into view.

"We find the Purists' facilities, and thereby Ba Re'," Kol answered. "Using any means necessary."

Jhan nodded his approval. "And we leave behind no evidence that we were ever there. There will be no witnesses this time."

Chapter 34

Gaishon maneuvered the ship into the perfect location to allow him access to the docking level of Command Warship 1 as he requested permission to land.

"Rogue 1 requesting permission to dock," Gaishon said.

"Permission granted, Rogue 1. Proceed to docking lane 3," a voice replied.

Gaishon watched as the doors to the docking level receded from both the top and bottom, granting him access. He proceeded without hesitation.

Ginger looked up at Kron questioningly. When he looked down at her, she whispered, "What did they say?"

"I forgot that you cannot understand them. He asked permission to land, and it was granted," Kron answered, looking up to watch as more and more of Command Warship 1 came into view as Gaishon began the process of docking the ship. His heart beat a little faster, and excitement filled him. No matter what had happened on Earth to permanently make that world a part of him, this was home. This was where he'd spent his life since pledging his loyalty to the Cruestaci, and he always got a rush of excitement when returning to the ship.

"You're happy," Ginger said, squeezing his hand where it held hers.

Kron looked at her again. "This is home to me. I always feel a rush of excitement coming home to this ship."

"Then it's my home, too," she said, leaning her head against his shoulder and watching as they emerged into a huge docking station. Ginger picked her head up and looked around. The space was filled with more small ships and transports than she could count, and there were hundreds of males working in and around the docking space. "It's so big!"

"This level is for the docking of all transports, regardless of their purpose. It takes many warriors to keep them in pristine condition, and the docking level itself in perfect working order," Kron said.

"It's like a small city in itself!" Ginger said.

"You have no idea how correct you are, Ginger Val Kere," Li'Don said.

"Prepare to be locked into place, Rogue 1," the voice coming through the control panel Gaishon sat at advised.

"Prepared," Gaishon answered.

There was a slight jerking motion as something was attached to the ship they sat in, and it made Ginger's stomach flutter nervously. Her hand gripped tighter to Kron's.

"That is to be expected. The ship is now secured in its berth. We can disembark," Kron said, standing.

A bark reminded Ginger that Kol's wife and family were waiting to disembark as well. "We should help her. She's got a lot to manage."

"Would you like me to get you settled first, then come back for them?" Kron asked.

"No, I can help," Ginger said.

"Very well," Kron said, smiling at his mate proudly. He was glad she was not the type of female to want to be catered to at all times. Her strength had been one of the things that had drawn him to her, but it had also been a contributor to their issues. Truthfully, he'd not known what to expect from her when they arrived onboard Command Warship 1. He'd known it would be okay and they could work through anything, but she'd honestly not had time to process the changes in her life before he'd whisked her away to a completely new way of life filled with things she'd never even imagined before. But she'd surprised him yet again by rising to the occasion and being more concerned about Ada Jane and her family, than herself.

Li'Don and Gaishon followed Kron and Ginger back to the hidden room Ada Jane and her kids had claimed for the trip and waited while Gaishon pressed his hand to just the right place on the wall to make the door slide hydraulically into itself, opening the room to them.

Ada Jane looked up at Gaishon. "Are we there?"

"We are," Gaishon said. "Welcome back to Command Warship 1, Ada Jane Don Tol."

"Thank you," she said, taking a deep breath and letting it out slowly. "I can't believe the trip was so fast. I was prepared for quite a bit longer trip."

"Rokai has made many improvements in his ship since you were on it last," Gaishon said proudly. "What can I help you carry?"

"Anything you wish to carry," Ada Jane said with a smile.

"I shall start with your bags," Gaishon said, stepping forward and taking two bags of clothing. Several other warriors followed suit and by the time they were done, there was nothing left to move onto Command Warship 1 except for Ada Jane, Kolby and Kreed, and the dogs.

"We're here to help, too," Ginger said.

"Thanks," Ada answered. "Could you take one of the boys?"

"Sure," Ginger said, stepping forward and holding her hands out to them to see who would allow her to carry him. Naturally, Kreed smiled at Ginger and blinked his eyes slowly as he looked up at her. Then he moved toward her so she could pick him up. "I'll take my boyfriend, here," she said, lifting Kreed into her arms and snuggling him.

Ada Jane smiled as she watched Kreed flirting with Ginger.

"I'll take Billy and Bob," Kron said.

"And I'll get Kolby," Ada said. "Thank you all so much for your help."

"We're family," Kron said. "It's what we do."

Ada smiled sadly and nodded as she led the way out of the room and eventually off the ship.

Ginger and Kron stayed behind Ada Jane so both Kreed and Billy and Bob could see that she was in front of them and not panic.

As they stepped off the ship and onto the ramp that would lead them to floor level, Ginger's steps stuttered a bit when she saw those who waited for them.

"Ada Jane! Welcome back!" a light green alien with Rastafarian braids called out as he hurried to her.

"That's Rokai ahl. He's our Sire's brother, and it was his ship that was sent to bring us back," Kron whispered quietly to her.

"You mean Elite Lieutenant Commander Rokai ahl," Rokai said haughtily as he shot a look at Kron, then grinned at him.

Kron just smiled and shook his head. "Of course," he responded, before stopping to wrangle the dogs as the rest of the group approached Zha Quin, Vivian, and Rokai ahl.

An unnaturally large, very gruff, red alien with a huge rack of horns stood at the base of the ramp with a small, very pregnant, dark haired human female at his side. "Welcome back, Ada Jane," he said in clipped, but very good English.

"Thank you, Commander," Ada Jane said.

"Please, you may call me Quin," he said graciously.

"Thank you, Quin," Ada Jane said.

"Ada Jane!" Vivian called out and wrapped her arms around Ada Jane as Ada came into reach.

"Vivi! I'm so glad to see you!" Ada said.

"Me, too! I missed you! And who is this?" Vivian asked, smiling at Kolby.

"This is Kolby, and Ginger is holding Kreed," Ada said.

"Oh, my gosh! They look so much like Kol," Vivian said, tickling Kolby then Kreed.

Vivian turned her attention to Ginger. "Hi, I'm Vivian, Quin's mate. Welcome to Command Warship 1."

"Thank you," Ginger said. "I'm Kron's mate, and I'm really excited to be here."

"Welcome female," Quin said in his grumbly voice, bowing deeply when he greeted her. "Your mate has performed admirably."

"Thank you," Ginger said proudly.

"This is my mate, Sire Zha Quin Tha Tel Mo' Kok," Vivian said proudly, wrapping her hands around Quin's arm lovingly. "I call him Quin."

"What about me?" Rokai said, waiting to be introduced.

"And this is my brother-in-law, Rokai. He's Quin's brother," Vivian added with a snicker, and he's very..." she paused looking for the right word.

"Impressive," Rokai supplied.

Kron had been a few steps behind while he wrangled the dogs, and now walked up to them. "And he's a skilled warrior despite his humbleness, and refusal to be in the spotlight," Kron added sarcastically.

Rokai laughed heartily at Kron's comment.

Ginger looked over her shoulder and smiled at Kron.

"Elite Warrior Kron, we welcome you back with many thanks for your service on Earth," Quin said.

"Thank you, Sire," Kron answered.

"What are you leading?" Quin asked.

"Puppies!" Vivian said delightedly.

"Not hardly," Ada Jane said. "Beasts," she added with a chuckle.

"Ada Jane and Kol's pets," Kron said. "And I see you've met my mate."

"We have. We are delighted for you," Quin said. He lifted his arm to gesture toward the entrance of the inner parts of the ship. "Let us move to the interior of the ship," he said.

"Ada, you and your family will be in the quarters you and Kol were in before you returned to Earth," Vivian said.

"I was hoping we would be," Ada admitted. "Thank you."

"And Kron, when we knew your mate was coming back with you, we assigned you new quarters in the same vicinity as ours. You're next door to General Lo'San and Synclare," Vivian said.

"How is Synclare?" Ada Jane asked as they all walked down the corridor as a group, "And Rosalita! If Rokai is here, I'm sure Rosie is."

"Synclare is more pregnant than me!" Vivian exclaimed. "But very happy. And Rosie is just Rosie. Nothing ever shakes her, and she keeps Rokai in line."

"She does indeed," Rokai agreed. "Now, give me a youngling!" he said, catching up with Ada Jane.

"If he wants to come to you," she said, pausing so Rokai could see if Kolby would go to him.

Kolby looked at him suspiciously, but Rokai grabbed him anyway. "Hello little Kol!" he said. "Come, I will tell you all about Uncle Rokai!"

Everyone laughed and they started walking again. It wasn't long before Rokai shrieked. "Ow! He bites, Ada Jane!"

"Yes, they both do, but Kolby more so than Kreed," Ada answered.

"You are a mean youngling," Rokai said to Kolby good naturedly. Kolby clacked his teeth at Rokai again. "And insolent, too!"

"He's like you, only you were older," Quin said.

"I did not... well, perhaps I did bite, but just a little," Rokai said. Then he held out Kolby toward Ada Jane. "Here, take your biting youngling." As soon as Ada Jane took him back not even stopping her conversation with everyone around her as she did, Rokai focused on Ginger.

"Let me try that one," he said.

Ginger raised an eyebrow and looked from him to Ada Jane, who nodded her approval. "Do you want to go play with Uncle Rokai?" she asked, looking at Rokai to be sure she got his name right.

Rokai grinned at her as he took Kreed from her. Just before he walked away he focused on her. "Your male is very highly regarded. He is a fierce warrior, and a loyal friend. You are a fortunate female."

"Thank you, Rokai," Kron said.

"Thank you, Kron. I will not forget that you assisted me when no other would. Many blessings upon your union," Rokai said. Then before either could answer he turned his attention to

Kreed and walked away bouncing Kreed in his arms and snapping at him when Kreed tried to bite him, too."

Ginger linked her hand around one of Kron's arms and looked lovingly up at him. "I'm so proud to be yours, Kron."

"I am proud that you chose me," Kron said.

The group moved toward the lower residence level where the couples' quarters were. As they got off the lift Vivian pointed to her right. "That way is General Lo'San's, and Rokai's, and your home, too, Kron and Ginger. This way," she said, indicating to her left, "is our home, and Kol and Ada Jane's."

Since everyone had something that belonged to Ada — a child or a dog — they all turned to the left. Ada Jane stopped in front of her door and lifted her hand to the scanner beside it.

"Welcome home, Ada Jane Don Tol," Missy said.

"Thank you, Missy. Could you please program the door to open when I approach since I'll usually have my hands full?"

"Yes, I can do that," Missy said. Then the doors swooshed open and Ada Jane stepped through. She stopped a few steps into the home and looked around her. It was exactly as it had been the last time she'd seen it. Kol's uniform shirt was even thrown over the back of the couch. "Feels like forever since I've been here. It's exactly the same, yet so different now," she said.

"They are, but they're better different," Vivian said.

Kolby started fidgeting to get down.

"Okay, okay," Ada said, setting him on his feet.

Kolby started checking things out, and then Kreed wanted down, too.

Rokai set him on his feet, then went to stand next to Kron.

"What about Billy and Bob?" Kron asked.

"You can just take them off the leashes and let them have the run of the place," Ada said. "They entertain the boys and vice versa."

Kron did as she asked, put the leashes on the counter in the kitchen then walked back over to Ginger and took her hand in his. "Thank you for the welcome, but I think we're going to call it a day and go find our quarters," he said.

"Come with me, I'll show you," Rokai offered.

338

As Kron turned to leave, Quin stepped in front of him. "I am pleased you've returned, Elite Warrior Kron."

"Thank you, Sire," Kron said.

"And I'm pleased to have you at his side," Quin said to Ginger.

"Thank you," Ginger said, not sure if she should call him Sire or not.

"Please make yourselves comfortable and we'll speak in depth in the morning. We have much to discuss. I'd planned to do so immediately, but Vivi informs me that you should be given time to set your affairs in order."

"Thank you, Sire," Kron said.

"Um, thank you?" Ginger said, making it sound like more of a question.

"Not affairs in order like that! He means take a minute, get used to your home, relax a bit," Vivian said with a laugh.

"Oh, good!" Ginger said.

"Once you've settled in, we'll get together and introduce you to the other women and show you around," Vivian said.

"I'd like that," Ginger answered.

"Are you coming or not?" Rokai asked impatiently from the door.

"Go, enjoy your evening," Quin said, giving a short bow again.

Kron and Ginger followed Rokai out of Ada Jane's home and to their own.

"That's Lo'San's, and this is mine," Rokai said, pointing to first one door, then the other. They were actually across the hall from each other.

"Try to relax, Kron," Rokai said, "and do not think about what's happening on Earth. It is not what you think it is anyway."

"What do you mean?" Kron asked.

"Just what I said. Just relax. You'll learn all about it tomorrow," Rokai said.

"Have they found Ba Re'?" Kron asked anxiously.

"I don't know for sure. Quin says I cannot keep a secret, but I do know that actions are in process to locate him and bring him home," Rokai said. "Can you believe it? He thinks I can't keep secret!"

"You did just tell me what is happening," Kron said.

"Because you are a part of it!" Rokai insisted.

"I see, okay. Oh, and thank you for the use of your ship. Everyone on it was very impressed with the changes you've made. You are very talented, Rokai. I don't know why you prefer to be underestimated."

Rokai grinned, then shushed Kron. "Don't tell anyone I made the changes. I prefer to be underestimated because then I always have the upper hand."

"Then you better tell Gaishon. He readily told us all about the changes you'd made. Your skills are quite surprising," Kron said.

"Because you underestimated me," Rokai shrugged.

"No, I did not. I am one that is quite aware of all you're capable of. Your skills are impressive for anyone. You are gifted."

Rokai shrugged again, it was difficult for him to accept praise. "Thank you, Kron. I simply allow people to see what it is they wish to see, rather than the truth." He thought about it for a split second, then turned his attention to Ginger. "Again, welcome Kron's female. I particularly like your eye color in combination with your hair color. You remind me of flames."

"She does have a certain fire," Kron said.

"Thank you, Rokai. I appreciate that," Ginger said.

"You are welcome. Now, I must find Gaishon and tell him to stop telling my secrets."

Rokai started to walk away, only made it a few steps, then turned back quickly and embraced Kron. "I am happy you are not missing as well. I have very few friends. I count you and Ba Re' among all three of them." Rokai patted Kron's back, then stepped back and hurried away from them once more.

Kron smiled at Ginger.

"I like him. He's very colorful — figuratively, I mean," Ginger said, "almost flamboyant."

"As do I. He is a good male, though he'd rather no one was aware of it," Kron said.

340

Ginger looked toward the door that was their home. "Shall we go in?"

Kron looked toward the door. He nodded and smiled. "We shall. Are you ready?"

"Definitely," she said.

Kron reached out and pressed his hand to the sensor. "Welcome home, Elite Warrior Kron," Missy said.

"Hello, Missy," Kron said.

"Please have your mate press her hand to the sensor pad," Missy asked.

Ginger stepped forward and looked for Kron to tell her it was okay to do so. When he urged her forward, she placed her hand on the pad. The pad lit up briefly, then the door opened.

"I have logged your information into my data banks, Ginger Val Kere. It is very good to see you again. Should you need anything at all, simply speak my name and ask," Missy said.

"Thank you, Missy," Ginger called out, looking curiously at Kron.

"You are welcome," Missy answered.

"She monitored your vital signs on the ship when you were first found," Kron explained.

"She's the computer, right?" Ginger asked in hushed tones.

"I am so much more!" Missy exclaimed. "We shall be great friends."

Kron chuckled at Ginger's expression, then grasped her hand in his and together they stepped over the threshold into their new home. They looked around and then turned to look at each other. "It's perfect," Ginger said, smiling brightly.

"It is," Kron said.

Ginger let go of Kron's hand to explore their new home. "There's a kitchen!" she said. "I can cook for you!"

"Can you cook?" Kron asked.

Her brows came down. "Kind of. Enough to feed you and learn to do better," she said hopefully.

"I will look forward to it," Kron said confidently.

They walked back into the living room, then the bathroom. "It's got a regular tub," Ginger said.

"All suites that have human mates have been outfitted with an actual tub. Our Sirena loved hers so, our Sire decided they were necessary for all the human mates."

"And that's Vivian?" Ginger asked.

"Yes. Our Sire is next in line for the throne of Cruestace, and Sirena Vivian is his mate. She will rise to the throne with him."

"She's very nice," Ginger said.

"She is," Kron agreed.

They walked around the corner closest to the bathroom and found that their home had two bedrooms. "This is truly one of the better quarters. Some are only one bedroom. We have extra room for your father when he visits," Kron said.

Ginger turned from the master bedroom they were exploring. "You are wonderful," she said. "You sound like you're looking forward to his visits as much as I am."

"I am. Buchanan is my friend," Kron said truthfully.

"Can we let him know we made it here?" she asked.

"I will take care of it in the morning," Kron said.

"I love you," Ginger said, walking slowly toward Kron.

"And I you, my Leerah," he answered, watching her walk toward him.

"Do you know what I'm thinking now?" she asked.

"I hope you are thinking what I am," he said, smirking as he stared into her eyes.

"I think we need to christen each room of our new home," she said, finally reaching him and pressing her body against his while she reached up to pull his face to hers for a kiss.

"What does that mean?" he asked, pulling back to look at her before her lips actually met his.

"It means, we finish this here, and then we go and do the same in each and every room," she whispered, then licked his mouth so he'd open for her.

Kron's eyes flashed to orange, then yellow again as he lifted her and settled her across his hips with his hands beneath her bottom holding her against him, as he moved toward the bed. "I like your idea, very much!" he said.

342

"Show me how much," she said, letting go of his shoulders, pulling her own shirt off over her head and dropping it to the ground.

A rumble was the only response she got before her mate dropped her to the bed, looking down on her like a starving man at a buffet of food.

Ginger smiled at him as she kicked off her shoes, planning to be completely nude for him in a matter of seconds.

Kron did the same, toeing off his own shoes, before he crawled up her body, kissing and touching everything he could reach.

"I will never tire of touching you," he whispered as he sat back on his heels and pulled her jeans off. His eyes went heavy as he focused on the silky scrap of fabric she called panties. He pulled them off her legs and his chest rumbled again as he slipped a hand beneath each knee and lifted her legs up and back so he could more easily see the parts of her that were only for him. He leaned forward, intending to plant himself between her legs to lick and tease until he could take it no more, but she stopped him.

Ginger brought her legs down and used an arm behind herself to leverage her body into a semi sitting position despite the fact that Kron was trying to force her backwards. "No, it's my turn this time," she said, as she pressed her other hand to his chest.

Kron's brow furrowed as he looked questioningly at her.

"You lie back," she said seductively. "Let me please you."

"I..." he started to object.

"Will lie back and let me have my way because you love me," she said, biting her lower lip as her eyes looked up and down his body and her fingertips stroked her own breasts still caught snuggly in her bra.

He objected no more. Kron sat back and pulled his own shirt off, then once he was flat on his back, he unfastened his pants and lifted his hips to shove his pants around his ankles and kick them off. Lying completely naked beside his mate, Kron almost lost control when she lifted a leg and straddled him at

343

about knee level. When she leaned over and took his hardened cock in her mouth, sucking and running her tongue over his sensitive flesh while she stroked his balls at the same time, his claws shredded the sheets on their bed in his effort to allow her to have her way instead of flipping her over and taking her so hard and fast she'd beg him to stop.

But then, as he watched her, she allowed his cock to fall slowly out of her mouth, and shimmied up his body until she was holding herself, hovering just over his hips.

Ginger reached down and grasped him in her hand, then held him steady as she pressed the crown of his cock against her wet slit. She used the weight of her body to bear down on him, and depute the tight grip her body held him in, he slid all the way inside her, not stopping until she was so full she couldn't possibly take another centimeter. Ginger took only a second or two more to adjust to him deep inside her, then she began to rock her hips while she lifted herself up off him, then slid back down. On each upstroke, she gripped him as tightly as she could, on the down stroke, she pushed against his reentry.

After a few minutes, Kron reached out and grabbed her hips, helping her keep up the pace she'd begun. He let go only once to reach up and pull her bra down, causing her breasts to pop out of the cups and spill over for him to better see. He lifted his upper body off the bed and captured one nipple in his mouth, just as she slammed her body down over his, taking him as deep as she possibly could.

Both were breathless and panting, and Kron had no choice but to simply lie back and let her have her way before he lost the tight hold he kept on his body and finished before they were both ready.

Ginger worked her hips so expertly it wasn't long before they both felt the need to chase their orgasms. She'd had her eyes closed, but opened them and looked down at him. Her eyes flashed orange, reflecting her passion and desire for him, just as his did for her. "I can't stop. I'm going to come," she said as her nipples drew up into tight little buds and tiny little chill bumps broke out all over her body just as she tipped over the edge.

"Do it," he growled.

She closed her eyes and let her head fall back on her shoulders as her hips faltered in their rhythm her pleasure was so overwhelming.

Kron felt his balls draw up tight in preparation of coming, but he couldn't let her lose the pleasure she was just shy of. He steadied her with one had as he held tightly to her hip with the other and rolled her beneath him to her back, then he angled his hips and drove into her with all he had.

"Yes, yes, yes!" Ginger screamed as her body convulsed.

Kron shouted out his own completion as his body matched hers for every ounce of ecstasy they could wring from one another. His chest heaving from the exertion, he fell on top of her, just barely holding his upper chest enough off her to keep from smothering her. After minutes of rest, her hands came up and stroked his back as her arms held him lazily against her.

"Amazing," she said.

"It is not a strong enough word," he said.

"Now what?" she asked coyly, opening her eyes and looking at her mate as he raised up enough to see her face.

"I believe we must christen each and every room in our home," he said smiling wryly at her.

"Every room?" she teased.

"Even the closets," he insisted, lowering his head to nibble at her neck.

And every room in their quarters was christened — some of them twice. Then they fell asleep wrapped in each other's arms, happy, sated and more bonded than ever before. It was the first of many nights that would end just the same way.

Epilogue

Kron walked into the commissary with Ginger's hand in his. His smile was big and bright as he greeted friends he'd not seen in a very long time.

"You are very popular," Ginger said, returning the smile of everyone that waved and greeted them from across the room.

"He is kind, everyone likes him," a female voice said from behind them.

Ginger and Kron turned around to find Vor and Li'Orani behind them.

"Li!" Kron said excitedly, pulling the female into his arms.

Ginger didn't need him to tell her that this female was his sister.

"Welcome back, brother," she said. "And who is this?" she asked.

"This is my Leerah, Ginger," Kron said proudly, presenting Ginger to them. "Ginger, this is my sister, and her mate, Vor."

"Hello," Ginger said, holding her hand out to shake Li'Orani's.

Li'Orani ignored her hand, and pulled her in for a hug. "Welcome, not only to the ship, but to our family as well."

"I am pleased to make your acquaintance," Vor said.

Ginger looked up at the large, orange male. "As am I. How is it some of you speak English so well?" she asked.

"I volunteered for Sirena Vivian's personal guard. She taught us to speak English," Vor said.

"Personal guard?" Ginger asked.

"Her position requires that she is guarded at all times. Even when she refuses," Vor said sardonically.

"Her position... oh, Lord, she's like the queen or something, isn't she?" Ginger asked.

"She is," Kron said smiling.

"I didn't bow or anything," Ginger said.

"You don't have to. She is not as concerned with her status as others are. She most likely enjoyed meeting others from her world, and was appreciative of the fact that she didn't have to stand on customary behavior at your arrival," Vor said.

"I thought you were visiting Mother," Kron said.

"I was, we were. But we've returned," Li'Orani said.

"Are you bound?" Kron asked.

"No," Vor answered grumpily.

"But, we do have permission to proceed," Li'Orani added. "Mother was quite taken with Vor."

"Congratulations," Kron said.

"Perhaps," Li'Orani said. Then her gaze traveled to a place over Kron's shoulder and she began to walk away. "Welcome back, brother. I am pleased you're here."

Kron watched as she practically floated away so graceful in her every movement, and Vor lumbered along behind her after he slapped Kron on the shoulder.

"I'm not sure if they're happy or not," Ginger said.

"I think for the most part they are. Vor will be happier once Li'Orani accepts him, but she won't do that until she is absolutely ready. She's got a lot to overcome. Just the fact that she allows him to keep her company is a good thing," Kron said.

"Come, let's get something to eat," he said.

Ginger walked along beside him, her hands looped around his arm. They garnered quite a bit of attention as they walked through the large seated dining area. "Why are they all looking at us?" Ginger asked.

"Because you are beautiful," Kron answered.

"I'm not sure that's it," she answered.

"It is, as Rokai said last night, you remind him of flames with your red and gold hair, and yellow eyes," Kron said.

Ginger smiled up at him, practically glowing under his compliment to her appearance.

As they approached the serving line, Kron introduced Ginger to all he spoke to, and she smiled until her cheeks hurt. By the time they finally got to their table, she was truly famished, and eagerly dug into everything on her plate. They were eating and laughing, and kissing from time to time when they realized they were no longer alone.

Kron looked up to find Vivian and Quin standing there beside the table. "Sire," he said, scooting his chair back to get to his feet.

"There is no reason to stand. Please, sit and enjoy the remainder of your meal," Quin said.

"Thank you, Sire," Kron said, sitting again.

"I trust you rested well your first night with us," Quin said, speaking slowly in clipped tones.

Ginger didn't answer. She was staring at the huge, fluffy, fanged Kitty standing beside Vivian.

Kron looked over at Ginger when she didn't answer Quin, and chuckled. "She is a lover of animals, Sire. I don't think she's ever seen a shraler before."

Quin raised an eyebrow. "She can have this one," he snapped.

"You are not giving away my Kitty," Vivian said. Then she bent over to put herself in Ginger's line of sight. "Hi!" Vivian said, smiling and waving at Ginger.

"Oh! Hi! I mean, your highness, er, Vivian, ma'am," Ginger said.

Vivian looked at her for a minute then laughed out loud. "Oh, that's good. I haven't had that response yet. But, Vivian or Vivi, will do just fine," Vivian laughed.

"I'm sorry, I just wasn't sure what to call you since I've found out that you're royalty," Ginger said, blushing.

"It's okay. It's no big deal. I'm just a girl like yourself that happened to find her prince, literally, out here among the stars," Vivian said.

Kitty looked at Vivian and rowred at her.

"He's hungry," Vivian told Quin.

"If he's breathing he's hungry," Quin answered.

"You're just mad because he pushed you off the bed last night," Vivian said.

Quin looked down at her, with his eyebrow raised again.

348

"What? He got cold so I let him sleep with us," Vivi said.

"He did not get cold. He's got fur," Quin answered.

Kitty got tired of waiting and walked around the table to Ginger, who couldn't help but stare at him. Ginger looked at Kron. "Will he bite?" she asked.

"No, he doesn't bite. Unless we tell him to, or he thinks you're a threat," Vivian said.

"Hold your hand out, if he likes you, he'll allow you to pet him," Quin said.

Ginger held her hand out, and Kitty sniffed her, then he put his massive head beneath her hand and rubbed his head beneath her fingers. Then he stole a piece of meat off her plate.

Ginger laughed instead of being irritated, which made Kitty take another piece of food off her plate.

"And now you have a friend for life," Vivian said.

"I love animals. I'm excited to meet all the unusual animals I'll come across."

"Allow me to get you more food," Vivian said. "I won't be but a minute."

"Oh, no, that's not necessary. We're actually finished. We were just sitting here talking and people watching," Ginger said.

"I was introducing her to those who came in for breakfast this morning," Kron explained.

"You're done, then?" Quin asked.

"Yes, Sire," Kron answered.

"Then if you will accompany me to the conference room, we have a few things to discuss," Quin said.

"Of course, Sire," Kron answered, getting up, but hesitating to step away from Ginger.

"Would you mind sitting with me while I eat?" Vivian asked Ginger.

"Of course not," Ginger said. "I'd be glad to sit with you."

"Thanks. Then after I eat, I'll take you around and show you where everything is," Vivian answered.

Kron leaned over and lifted Ginger's hand to his lips and pressed a kiss to it. "I don't know how long I'll be," he said by way of apology.

"I'll be fine. Take your time," Ginger said.

"I'll contact your father after I meet with Sire Tel Mo' Kok," Kron said.

"Thank you. Maybe I can contact him, too, later this evening," she said hopefully.

"I'll find out when we can do that. Either this evening or tomorrow for sure," Kron said.

Quin had taken a few steps away and waited for Kron to join him.

"If you need anything, just call Missy's name, and tell her who you are and what you need," Kron said.

"I'll be fine. Go ahead," she encouraged.

Quin stepped forward and kissed Vivian, then turned and walked away with Kron at his side. As they moved away, two very intimidating males stepped forward and stood near the table. Ginger looked warily at them.

"Don't mind them, they're my guard. That's Kail, and that's Asl," Vivian said. "Guys, go get breakfast or something," Vivian said to them. Then she turned her attention to Ginger. "I'll be right back," she said, turning to waddle away and get her own breakfast.

"Sirena, please, be seated. Allow us to get your breakfast. We know well what you prefer," Asl said, urging Vivian to sit down.

"But there might be something new I want," Vivian said.

"If there is anything new, I will bring it," Asl promised.

"Well, okay. But bring Kitty a plate, too," Vivian said.

"I always do," Asl said, giving her a bow.

Vivian sat down right beside Ginger and Kitty started trying to climb into a chair across the table from them.

Kail pulled out the chair a bit so Kitty could sit.

"Now, tell me all about you, Ginger," Vivian said. Then a woman with beautiful hair, silvery-gray with streaks of white framing her face walked in. "That's Synclare. She's mated to General Lo'San," Vivian explained. "Synclare! Over here! And what are you doing out of bed?"

"I cannot take lying there another minute!" Synclare shouted across the room to Vivi. "The moment Lo'San left to go meet with Quin, I got dressed and here I am."

"There are a lot of humans here," Ginger said.

"Not a lot, but some, and there will be more, I'm sure," Vivian said.

Asl walked up with two plates and placed one in front of Vivian, the other in front of Kitty. Kitty's had several huge bones on it, and a selection of foods similar to those he'd gotten for Vivian.

Vivian looked up at Asl and batted her eyes at him. "Coffee?" she asked sweetly.

"You cannot have coffee. Our Sire said you are not to have coffee at all," Asl answered.

"Your Sirena says she can," Vivian snapped.

"Sirena, please," Asl said.

She sat there for a moment, during which Synclare joined them.

"Synclare, Ginger. Ginger, Synclare," Vivian said still looking accusingly at Asl.

"Stop giving your guards a hard time," Synclare said. "You know pregnant women are not supposed to have a lot of coffee."

Vivian glared at Synclare for a minute, then turned back to Asl. "Litah?" she asked.

"Gladly," Asl answered, bowed to her once more and went to get her Litah.

"I'm Lo'San's mate," Synclare said, holding her hand out to shake Ginger's.

"I'm Kron's," Ginger said.

"Oh, he's so sweet!" Synclare said.

"Thank you. I think so," Ginger said.

"Now, tell us all about you, and how you met Kron," Vivian said.

"I will, just as soon as you tell me how to get my own Kitty," Ginger said with a glint in her eye.

"Oh, I like her!" Vivian said to Synclare who was already giggling at the idea of Quin dealing with more than one Kitty on

351

board, at least until Vivian and Quin returned to the planet for the birth and raising of their child. "And of course I will," Vivian said, "Kitty needs a friend."

~~~

Quin led the way into his personal conference room, taking his customary seat at the far side of the round table. "Have a seat, Elite Warrior Kron," Quin said, gesturing to the other seats at the table.

"Thank you, Sire," Kron said, choosing one a few seats away.

"I trust those who bruised your female's face have suffered sufficiently," Quin said.

Kron nodded. "As I saw to her welfare, Va'roush addressed the issue."

Quin huffed a laugh. "I have no doubt the male breathes no more, and suffered more than most," Quin answered.

"Indeed," Kron said on a soft snarl.

"Very well. To the subject at hand... I asked you to join me this morning as I feel there is information you are not aware of. I forced you to leave Earth abruptly, but it was unavoidable. A speedy departure was unavoidable in order to give the impression that we were abiding by the wishes of the Purists and their demands."

Kron's mouth fell open. He never once thought the Cruestaci would bow to the demands of anyone.

"I can see that you're surprised at that statement. Let me reiterate. Give the impression of abiding by their wishes, not literally."

Kron smothered a smile, knowing something was going on and Ba Re' wouldn't be long missing.

"Normally, I wouldn't take the time to bring any warrior up to date on an operation they are not part of. However, you know more about this situation than most, and I will value your input as it moves forward," Quin said.

"I will do all I can, Sire, but I don't know as much as some might," Kron said.

"Understood," Quin said. "Now, you may have noticed that Jhan and Va'roush did not return with you. As far as you are concerned, they did. They were onboard that ship with you."

"Of course, Sire. They guarded Consul Don Tol's family during our trip back," Kron said.

"Exactly," Quin said. "Now, allow me to explain. They've stayed behind and have joined forces with the Ceresian warriors already protecting Kol's home. Kol, Viceroy Buchanan, and Patroon Zhuxi are aware of the situation as well and contributing as well. We will not stop until Ba Re' is returned to us."

Kron was visibly relieved. "I cannot tell you how relieved I am. I was never more conflicted than when forced to leave Earth without Ba Re'."

Quin sat forward with a smile on his face. "Let me be clear, Elite Warrior Kron. I will not rest until Ba Re' is found. I will destroy buildings, I will crush all opposition, I will kill any who try to stop us. I may even decimate friendships I thought I could rely on, but I will do whatever it takes to find Ba Re' and return him to his rightful place among us. No one, especially not Ba Re', is being left behind."

From The Author

Thank you for purchasing this book. I hope that my stories make you smile and give you a small escape from the daily same ole/same ole. I write for me, simply for the joy of it, but if someone else also smiles as a result, even better. Your support is greatly appreciated. If you liked this story, please remember to leave a review wherever you bought it, so that more people can find my books. Each review is important, no matter how short or long it may be.

See you in the pages of the next one!

Sandra R Neeley

Other books by this author:

<u>Avaleigh's Boys series</u>

I'm Not A Dragon's Mate!, Book 1

Bane's Heart, Book 2

Kaid's Queen, Book 3

Maverik's Ashes, Book 4

Bam's Ever, Book 5

Vince's Place, Book 6

Whispers From the Bayou series

Carnage, Book 1

Destroy, Book 2

Enthrall, Book 3

Lore, Book 4

Murder, Book 5

Aubreigne, Book 6

Haven series

Haven 1: Ascend

Haven 2: Redemption

Haven 3: Transcend

Haven 4: AVOW

Riley's Pride

Riley's Pride, Book 1

Richie's Promise, Book 2

Travis's Gift, Book 3

Roman's Vow, Book 4

Lazarus's Savior, Book 5

Variant

Beginnings, Variant 1

Valor, Variant 2

Sin, Variant 3

Standalone Novels

WINGS

Short Stories and Novellas

CAT

Only Fools Walk Free

Safe On Base: A Howls Romance (loosely connected to Riley's Pride series)

Blessed Curse

Halloween Treats, An Avaleigh's Boys Novella

About The Author

My name is Sandra R Neeley. I write Paranormal, SciFi, and Fantasy Romances. Why? Because normal is highly overrated. I'm 57, I have two kids, one 35 and one 15, one grandchild, one husband and a menagerie of animals. I love to cook, and I love to read, though since I started writing I don't get as much time to read as I once did. I'm a homebody and prefer my writing/reading time to a crowd. I have had stories and fictional characters wandering around in my head for as long as I can remember. I'm a self-published author and I like it that way because I can decide what and when to write. I tend to follow my muse — the louder the voice, the greater the chance that voice's story is next.

I am by no means a formal, polished, properly structured individual and neither are my stories. But people seem to love the easy emotion and passion that flow from them. A bit of a warning though, there are some "triggers" in them that certain people should avoid. I'm a firm believer that you cannot have light without the dark. You cannot fully embrace the joy and elation that my people eventually find if you do not bear witness to their darkest hours as well. So please read the warnings supplied with each of the synopsis about my books before you buy them. I've got five series published at this time, Avaleigh's Boys - PNR, Whispers From the Bayou - Fantasy PNR, Haven - SciFi Romance, Riley's Pride - PNR, and Variant - a dark genetic manipulation romance, a couple of standalone novels, several short stories, and much, much more to come. I'm always glad to hear from my readers, so feel free to look me up and say hello.

You can find me at any of these places:

357

authorsandrarneeley@gmail.com
https://www.sneeleywrites.com
https://www.sneeleywrites.com/contact
https://www.sneeleywrites.com/blog
https://www.facebook.com/authorsandrarneeley/
https://www.facebook.com/groups/755782837922866/
https://www.amazon.com/Sandra-R-Neeley/e/B01M65OZ1J/
https://twitter.com/sneeleywrites
https://www.instagram.com/sneeleywrites/
https://www.goodreads.com/author/show/15986167.Sandra_R_Neeley
https://www.bookbub.com/authors/sandra-r-neeley

Stop by to say Hi, and sign up to be included in updates on current and future projects.

Printed in Great Britain
by Amazon

67346755R00203